THE WORLDS OF THE FEDERATION

NCC-170

STAR TREK®

THE WORLDS OF THE FEDERATION

WRITTEN AND ILLUSTRATED BY
SHANE JOHNSON
Color Art by Don Ivan Punchatz

POCKET BOOKS
New York London Toronto Sydney Tokyo

The facts and background details regarding the STAR TREK universe as presented in *The Worlds of the Federation* are solely the author's interpretation of that universe.

Another *Original* publication of POCKET BOOKS

POCKET BOOKS, a division of Simon & Schuster Inc.
1230 Avenue of the Americas, New York, NY 10020

ISBN: 0-671-66989-3

First Pocket Books trade paperback printing August 1989

10 9 8 7 6 5 4 3 2 1

Printed in the U.S.A.

ACKNOWLEDGMENTS

This author would like to express the deepest appreciation to the following people for the help and encouragement that made this book a reality:
Lawrence Aeschlimann, James Atkison, Alan and Lyrae Beckner, Bob and Kathy Burns, James Chambers, Bill Christmas, David Holt, Kathy Johnson, Shaun Johnson, Gary Kerr, Bob Klem, Mike Kott, Steve McClellan, David Merriman, Michael Okuda, Larry Oler, Barry Smith, and Rick Sternbach.

I also wish to thank the authors of the following volumes for laying the foundation upon which **The Worlds of the Federation** was built: The Star Trek Spaceflight Chronology, The Star Trek Concordance, The Making of Star Trek: The Motion Picture, The Making of Star Trek, The Star Trek Maps, the Star Trek photonovels, the Star Fleet Medical Reference Manual, and Spock's World. I wish especially to mention the efforts of Geoffrey Mandel, John Upton, Doug Drexler, Eileen Palestine, Jeff Maynard, and Anthony Fredrickson – they have contributed to the internal order of the Star Trek universe, helping to make it as real a place as any fictional existence can be. I am most pleased to carry on the continuity they have established.

Special thanks to Kevin Ryan and Dave Stern of Pocket Books for their untiring efforts on my behalf. This book would not exist had they not gone beyond the call of duty in its creation. Thanks also to Brenda Sims of Paramount — her knowledge of Star Trek is much appreciated. And gratitude, of course, to Gene Roddenberry.

The color illustrations are beautiful, Don — you've really defined the wonder of the worlds of Star Trek.

I'm going to get some sleep, now.

85

766

24

This book is dedicated to the memory of

Allen Everhart

Friend and fellow artist, he went to be with
the Lord that day in April aboard the USS Iowa

We miss you, buddy

MEMORY ALPHA HISTORICAL ARCHIVE
DATABANK EXTRACT (HARDCOPY)

SUBJECT: **THE WORLDS OF THE FEDERATION**

CONTENTS

080

59

128

PREFACE

TO THE WORLDS OF THE FEDERATION

As a governing body and a political organization, the United Federation of Planets is founded on a simple but important idea: diversity. Indeed, diversity makes up the very fabric of the Federation, which is essentially an amalgamation of different worlds, races, and cultures. Out of respect for diversity comes recognition of individual rights—the rights of all beings to self-determination, the right to choose and follow their own destiny.

Starfleet's Prime Directive is founded on this conviction and states unequivocally that no Federation personnel may interfere with the normal development of any culture. As a result of this policy, newly encountered races have quickly gained confidence in the Federation. This confidence has done much, throughout Federation history, to tear down the natural uneasiness and apprehension felt by the many alien cultures we have encountered, allowing them to join, with trust, the Federation's growing body of member worlds.

39

This volume is a concise guide to the history and culture of these worlds. Also included herein are entries on non-member worlds. All of them are notable, for their culture, animal or plant life, geological makeup, or position in space. Some of these worlds are hostile toward the Federation, resulting in the ever-present threat of interstellar conflict.

255

In a very real sense, I am a child of the United Federation of Planets. As an android, I am the product of many different technologies developed on many different worlds. I serve proudly aboard one of the finest vessels in Starfleet, the USS **Enterprise**™, allowing me to witness the galaxy's richness and diversity firsthand. This edition, whether yours by hardcopy or by computer projection, can only serve to increase awareness of that richness and reaffirm the trust and respect that binds the Federation worlds together.

714

— Lt. Commander Data
Science Officer
USS **Enterprise**, NCC-1701-D
Stardate 82965.4

INTRODUCTION

THE UNITED FEDERATION OF PLANETS
AN HISTORICAL OVERVIEW
[Excerpted from the UFP Spaceflight Chronology, Terran Revised Edition]

566

09

34

Even before the formation of the UFP, Earth [Terra] pioneered the commission of alien crew members to complement the strengths of its human crew. For all their belligerence, Tellarities proved adept engineers, and Andorians showed an uncanny knack for interstellar communication and navigation. This spaceflight cooperation brought planets ever closer, until political alliance seemed the next logical step.

The momentum to formalize the growing interdependence among planets had been building for decades as friendly worlds leaned ever more heavily on one another for vital goods and services. Finally, the most important political event in the Interstellar Age came to pass.

The United Federation of Planets was formally incorporated at the Interplanetary Conference at Babel. Founding members were Terra, Vulcan, Alpha Centauri, Tellar, and Andor, and later many other members were admitted at periodic intervals by the consent of member planets. The UFP's continuing vitality and growth stands as an eloquent testament to the wisdom of forming this alliance.

So much of what Federation citizens take for granted was decided upon and inaugurated by those visionary founding fathers. The current monetary system of Federation Credits was established then, as were the Standard Interstellar Symbols every child learns along with his ABCs. The space/time matrix of stardates was instituted as the Federation's official chronology, so that discrepancies caused by the special relativity theory [2087 on Earth would be 2092 on Alpha Centauri, etc.] could be reconciled among planets. In addition, a space census was ordered—Earth registered ten billion planetary residents, eight million solar citizens, and three hundred fifty-four interstellar colonists—and has been repeated every decade since.

Responding to the desire for interstellar exploration and the need for interstellar security, the UFP Starfleet was founded at this first Babel Conference, and the strategic placement of Starbases was outlined by Starfleet Command. These Starbases serve as the Federation's outposts throughout its defined territories. They are responsible for sector security and stellar emergency assistance, and they also serve as complete maintenance and refitting depots for starships. Starbases also coordinate galactic communication, initiate new research activity, and provide welcome shore leave for spaceweary starship crews.

The exploration of unknown sectors of space was recognized at this time as the primary goal of the new UFP and given a very high priority. Though one of the first starships launched for that purpose, the USS **Archon**, was lost in the vicinity of the Beta III star system, other pioneering ships, like the USS **Horizon**, vigorously pursued this goal.

Space medicine made great leaps forward during this harmonious mingling of alien cultures, and the field of comparative anatomy took on a whole new meaning. Valuable insights were gained into such problems as long-term sensory deprivation, radio immunization, and space stress. Equipment such as the medical scanner and bone-setting laser was designed. In addition, a clearinghouse of planetary medical societies was begun to guard against unknown epidemics like the "Pluto Plague," which mysteriously decimated all life at the Pluto Research Base [it was later found to be a mutant strain of Omega Virus clinging to a souvenir sold to a researcher by an unscrupulous Orion trader].

There were, however, some unfortunate growing pains that accompanied the founding of the UFP. The new Starfleet was quickly integrated with crews and captains from member planets. A space war-game disaster tragically highlighted the lack of standardized training for Starfleet officers. To prevent further chaos and tragedy, Starfleet Academy was chartered to provide centralized training for Fleet officers. From that point forward, all starship captains have been graduates of the Academy.

The Earth Centenary Conference was assembled in 2100 to assess the previous century of spaceflight and to offer predictions for the coming hundred years. Authorities traced the evolution of propulsion, communications, and electronics and the development of political and economic alliances among the UFP members and other worlds. Other speakers looked to the future with forecasts ranging from the prophetic to the short-sighted. Transporters were predicted, as was the impossibility of speeds faster than warp four.

As of the middle of the twenty-second century, the UFP had consolidated its position as a galactic presence. And none too soon. For there was another galactic power making its presence felt, through acts of savagery at the outer borders of the Federation. The Romulan Star Empire, once thought to be little more than a Vulcan children's fable, was thirsting for conquest.

After a brief but bloody war, the Federation finally settled into an uneasy peace with the Romulan Empire. A similar chain of events followed with the Klingon Empire, which is now one of the Federation's newest allies. Recent encounters with the mysterious Ferengi have been tense but peaceful, with the exception of a few limited military engagements.

PLANETARY CLASSIFICATION SYSTEM
(UFP STANDARD)

	Surface	Atmosphere	Description	Example
A	tenuous, may not be present	reducing: methane, etc.	radiates heat, "failed" star	Jupiter
B	tenuous, may not be present	reducing	non-radiant	Neptune
C	iron/silicate	reducing, dense	high surface temperature	Venus
D	nickel-iron/ silicate	[A-G] none; [H-N] tenuous	asteroids	Ceres
E	silicate, some metals	reducing/ oxidizing	large molten core	Janus VI
F	silicate, some metals	oxidizing	very young (less than 10^9 years)	Delta-Vega
G	silicate	oxidizing, thin	desert planet	Rigel XII
H	silicate	variable	geologically active	Gothos
I	metallic/ silicate	fluid, very dense	small, young	Excalbia
J	silicate	very tenuous: noble gases	moons	Luna
K	silicate	tenuous: some water	adaptable with pressure domes	Mars
L	silicate/water	oxidizing	geologically inactive	Psi 2000
M	silicate/water	oxidizing	geologically active	Terra
N	water entirely	oxidizing	pelagic planet	Argo

PAGE KEY
AND SYMBOLS

DATA SOURCE SYMBOLS

DATA DERIVED FROM
MEMORY ALPHA
FEDERATION HISTORY DATABANK

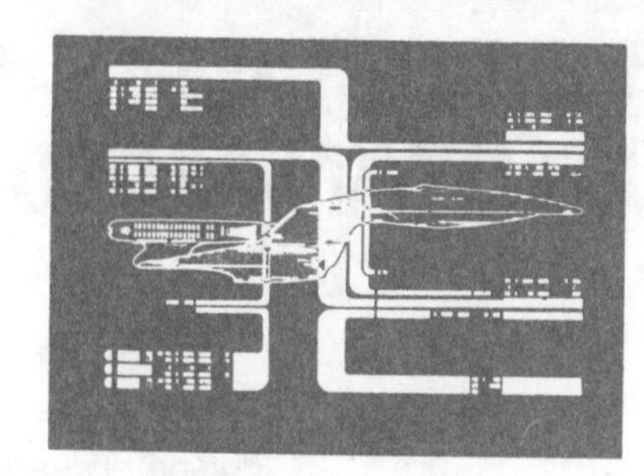

DATA DERIVED FROM
USS ENTERPRISE LIBRARY COMPUTER

FEDERATION CATALOGUE NAME

PLANETARY CLASSIFICATION

ORDER OF UFP ADMISSION (IF MEMBER)

INDIGENOUS NAME

PRIMARY (STAR)

GALACTIC COORDINATES

DATA SOURCE SYMBOL OR PLANETARY EMBLEM (IF ANY)

4 **ANDOR (M)**
FESOAN
EPSILON INDI
(25.8, 60.1, −2.4)

Epsilon Indi is the home system of the Andorian race, a humanoid-insectoid species that was the third intelligent civilization contacted by Terran explorers. Andor, the eighth of nine planets orbiting an orange dwarf star, is a large, hot, dry world with little surface water. There are, however, vast underground reserves that feed surface geysers heated by geothermal energy; oases surrounding these geysers are the centers of the planet's main population areas, since the great majority of Andor's plant life thrives where subsurface water is plentiful.

Andorians are the only species known to the Federation that displays characteristics of both mammalian and insectoid species. Like standard mammalian humanoids, the Andorians have an internal skeleton to which the body's musculature is anchored. However, they also feature a limited exoskeleton, which lends added strength and protection to the limbs and torso.

The Andorian retina is composed entirely of intensity-sensitive rods and is incapable of discerning color. Color is, however, added to Andorian vision by the dual antennae, which, in addition housing auditory receptors, feature a complex matrix of light-sensitive cones. These cones cover the entire spectrum of color visible to Terran eyes, as well as limited infrared wavelengths. Because of the correlation of four independent light-receptive organs, Andorian vision can be correctly described as "quadriscopic," resulting in superior depth perception. Andorian auditory capacities are also highly developed, allowing Andorians to hear a wider range of frequencies than is possible for most humanoid species. Because of their monodirectional antennae, the Andorian people usually listen with the head down and slightly tilted. Andorians are all ambidextrous.

The Andorian people are an admittedly violent race. By heritage, they are a race of warriors with a history of savage conquest. They place a high value upon family relationships and obligations, often placing them above public duty. Andorians will not quarrel without reason and are deceptively quiet in their relationships with others; this has, in the past, invited attack by others who quickly learned that, once unleashed, Andorian savagery and fighting ability is almost unequalled.

NOTABLE FEATURES

10

SYSTEM PROFILE

232

7

NUMBER OF MOONS (IF MORE THAN FOUR)

80° 60° 40° 20° 0° 20° 40° 60° 80°

75

CONTINENTAL SURVEY

551

24

78

MEMBER WORLDS

1 EARTH (TERRA) (M)

EARTH

SOL

[23.9, 61.8, 0.0]

Terra is the third of ten planets orbiting Sol, a yellow star of moderate size. It is extensively populated and is the home world of the human race; since all other humanoid races throughout known space have proven to be genetic variants of the Terran human race, it is theorized that Terra served as a "seed world" in an ancient life-form transplanting experiment. One hypothesis holds that an advanced race, referred to as "the Preservers," once traveled the galaxy, rescuing and transplanting primitive cultures that faced extinction. Finding the early human race to be physiologically versatile and psychologically adaptable, it is held by some that their survival was insured by spreading them among many suitable worlds.

Terra is one of the founding worlds of the UFP. It is a major cultural and scientific center, with unmatched research and learning facilities. Starfleet, the primary exploratory and defensive force of the UFP, is headquartered here, and Starfleet Academy is based in the port city of San Francisco, North America.

One of the most technologically advanced planets in the Federation, Terra produces forty-three percent of the vessels and weapons systems used throughout the UFP, with construction plants in fourteen planetary systems; Leeding Engines Ltd., a Terran-based manufacturer, has become the UFP's leading producer of warp drive systems technology.

Terra's moderate climate and diverse terrain make it a favorite shore-leave world. The Federation's fifth largest city, Lunaport, is found on Terra's only natural satellite, Luna, and is extensively populated with citizens from across the UFP. This underground city is unsurpassed for recreational facilities, transportation systems, and lodging. The UFP Aerospace Museum-Smithsonian Annex is located on the lunar surface, in the area known as the Sea of Tranquility. The site of the first manned lunar landing is preserved within its walls, maintained in zero-atmosphere for the protection of the centuries-old footprints and equipment. Also on display here is the Terran space shuttle **Joshua**, the craft that performed the first rescue of personnel marooned in trans-lunar space, and the UNSS **Icarus**, the first vessel to make contact with Alpha Centauri and the civilization located there. One recent acquisition is the transporter room of the USS **Moscow**, the site of the first transporting of a human being.

NOTE: Terra is the technical catalog name for Earth, used by non-natives.

43

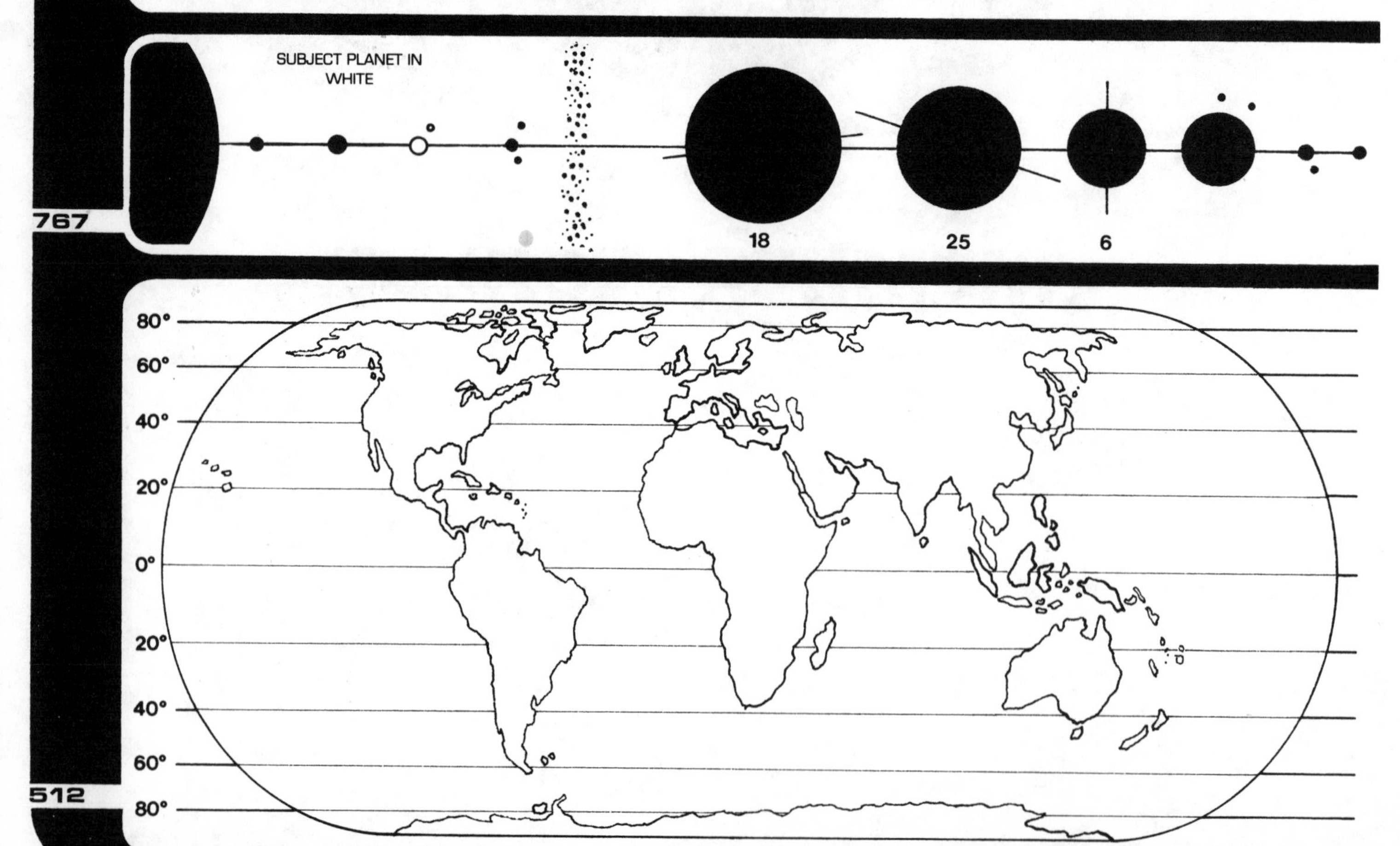

MEMORY ALPHA HISTORICAL ARCHIVE
DATABANK EXTRACT (HARDCOPY)

SUBJECT: HUMAN

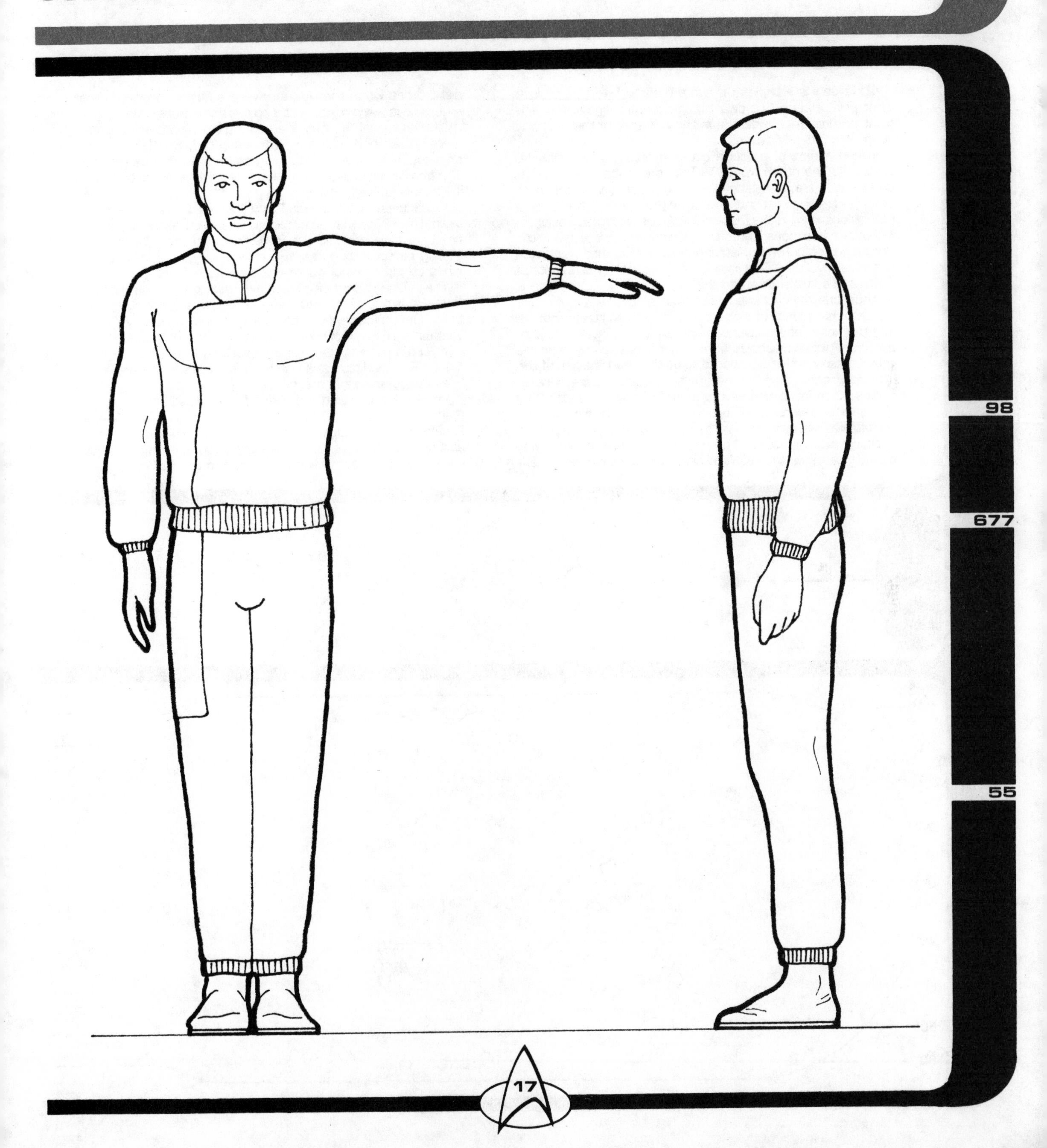

VULCAN (M)
T'KHASI
40 ERIDANI A
[19.5, 60.0, −0.6]

40 Eridani is a triple star system comprised of a brilliant giant primary and two dwarfs, one red and one white. The giant primary, 40 Eridani A, is the only star of the group to support a Class M world.

Vulcan is part of a double planet grouping that orbits 40 Eridani A. The other world, T'Khut, is a Class H planet that moves in a trojan relationship with Vulcan, in which both planets revolve around a common point. T'Khut is a monstrous sight in the Vulcan sky. A virtual lifeless cauldron, its active volcanoes and dust storms are visible from the Vulcan surface. Terran astronomers later named the trojan pair after figures in Terran mythology, and the inhabitants of T'Khasi gracefully accepted the names of Vulcan and Charis as their official Federation designations.

Vulcan is a planet of high surface gravity and temperature and the home of an advanced and extremely intelligent people. The Vulcanoid species is the second most common in the known galaxy and is considered to be the seed species of the Romulan race as well. They are an ancient, peaceful race, dedicated to logic, and have a strong sense of honor. They are socially incapable of outright lies or betrayal but will sometimes remain silent rather than express a truth that might prove injurious to others. Their devotion to logical thinking came as the result of near self-extermination in ancient times when the Vulcans were a hostile, warrior race whose lives were ruled by strong passions. Surak, the father of Vulcan logical thought, lived during the planet's last great wars. After both sides were devastated, Surak met with emissaries from both sides to establish a workable peace. The philosophy of logic eventually prevailed, and the planet of T'Khasi was finally united.

Vulcans possess the capacity for mind-touch, a limited telepathic ability that allows them to share the thoughts and emotions of others. Its use, however, requires a lowering of strong personal barriers and serves only as a last resort when other forms of communication have failed.

The Vulcan Science Academy, located in the city of ShiKahr, is one of the Federation's foremost learning institutions. Several large port cities are located across Vulcan's vast land area, which covers eighty-six percent of the planet.

Vulcan's planetary system supports a total population of 14.9 billion, and almost a fifth of those reside in the system's heavily industrialized asteroid belt.

Vulcan is a founding member of the United Federation of Planets and has contributed much to the growing body of Federation knowledge. Vulcan UFP representatives have settled many interplanetary disagreements, including those surrounding the admission of Coridan to the Federation.

457

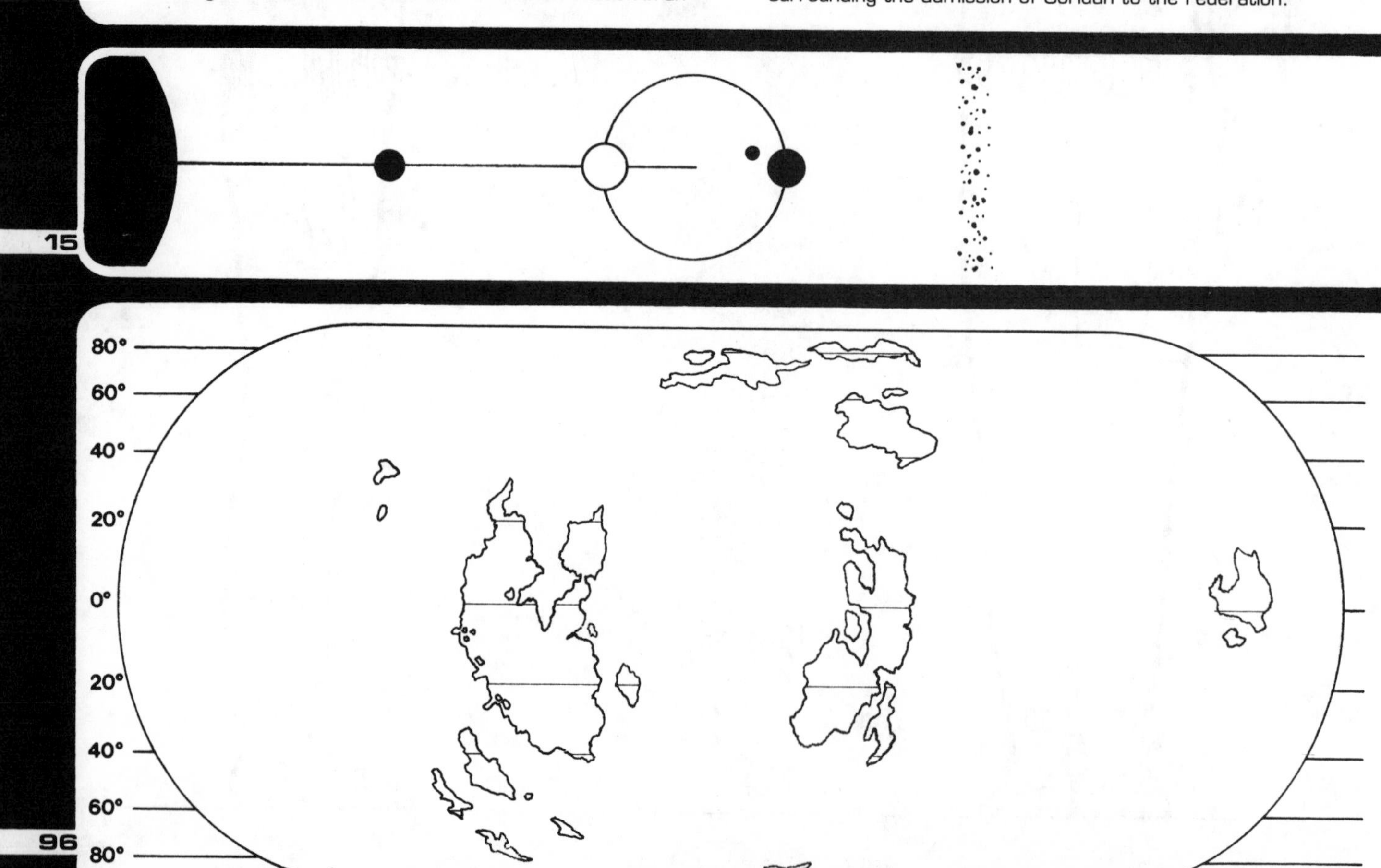

MEMORY ALPHA HISTORICAL ARCHIVE
DATABANK EXTRACT (HARDCOPY)

SUBJECT: VULCAN

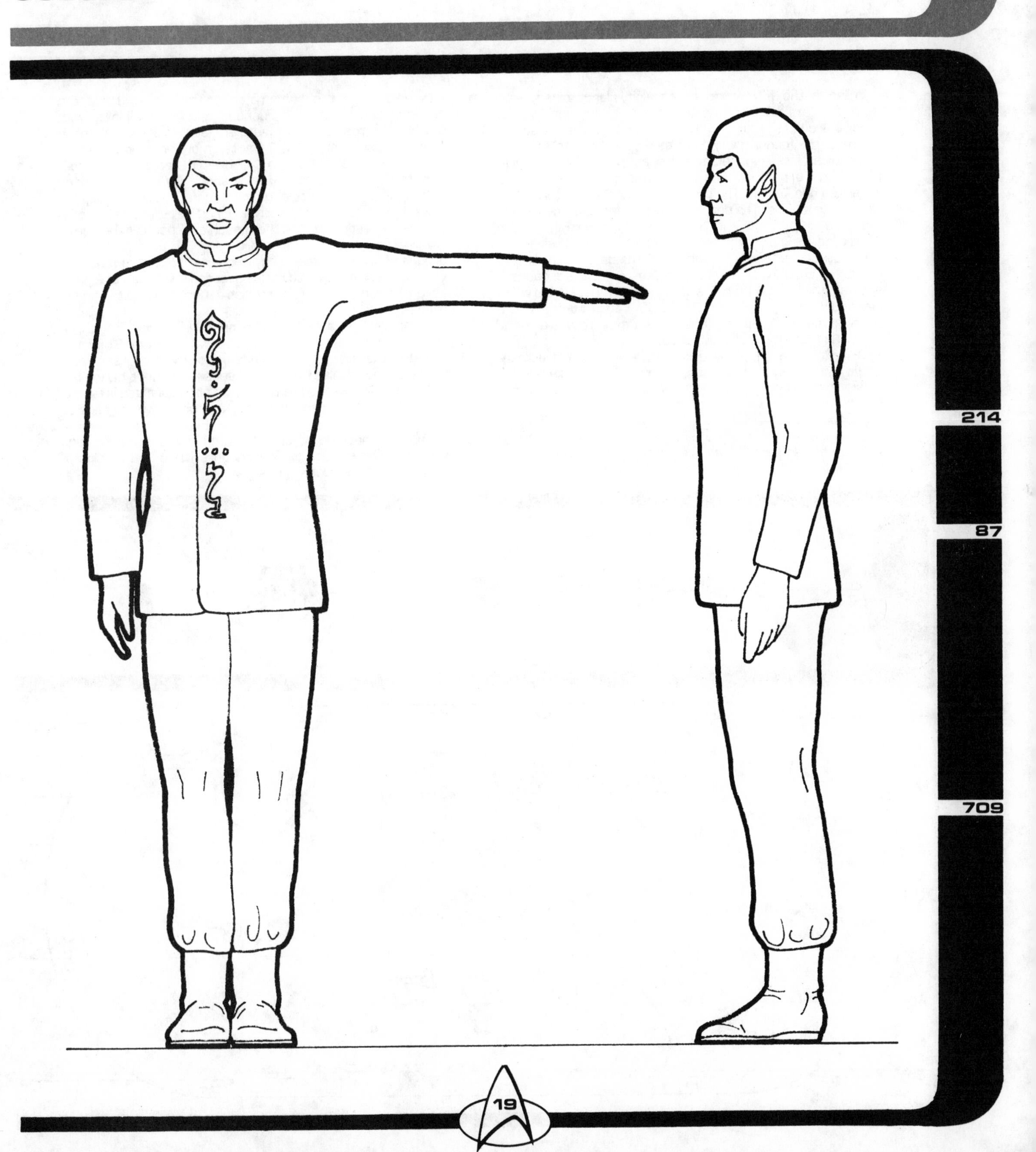

TELLAR (M)
MIRACHT
61 CYGNI
[25.0, 60.1, 2.6]

Tellar is the fifth world of an eight-planet binary star system. The planet and its two moons, Kera and Phinda, revolve around the larger of the two suns, an orange dwarf.

One of the founding worlds of the Federation, Tellar is the home of an intelligent, humanoid species of porcine derivation. Terra's contact with Tellar was the first that the Tellarites had known. The sudden alien encounter threw the planet into a panic. The people of Tellar, fearing an invasion [a fear fueled by rampant rumors of Terran evil], nearly destroyed their planetary economy by storming their financial institutions and demanding all funds stored there. Planetary chaos was averted when a worldwide broadcast showed the native people a benevolent meeting between Harland Anders, captain of the USS **Earickson**, and the Tellarite monarch, Gartov. This incident of panic was an early inspiration for the Prime Directive.

Tellarites are generally quite boisterous and argumentative, often without reason, a quality often taken for belligerency among other races. Most Tellarites enjoy argument, and debate is a primary form of entertainment among the people of the planet. Tellarite speech, regardless of language, is always very rough and guttural, while English and most of the softer tongues are difficult for Tellarites.

451

While largely humanoid, Tellarites do sport several notable variations upon the human norm. Their lower limbs are hooved, ending in a hardened, split dermal pad with dewclaws in the rear. This feature is almost unknown among biped species, making the Tellarites most uncommon in that aspect. They also have a heightened sense of balance, despite their rather rotund body shape. While their senses of hearing and smell are extremely keen, Tellarite eyesight is quite poor. Sharp-eyed at birth, young Tellarites become increasingly nearsighted as they reach adulthood at the age of twelve Terran years. Young are born live, almost always in groups of six. Life expectancy is lower than that of most advanced species. Tellarite males average a life span of eighty-seven Terran years, while females generally live to the age of ninety-three.

Tellar itself is a rather unremarkable world. Fifty-three percent of its surface is covered with water. Since the planet's axis stands at only one-point-seven degrees from orbital perpendicular, there is no seasonal change during the Tellarite year. Average temperature at the surface is eighty-three degrees Fahrenheit by day and sixty-two degrees at night.

Tellarites have an advanced aptitude for engineering, and they contribute much to Federation science in the fields of propulsion and structural design.

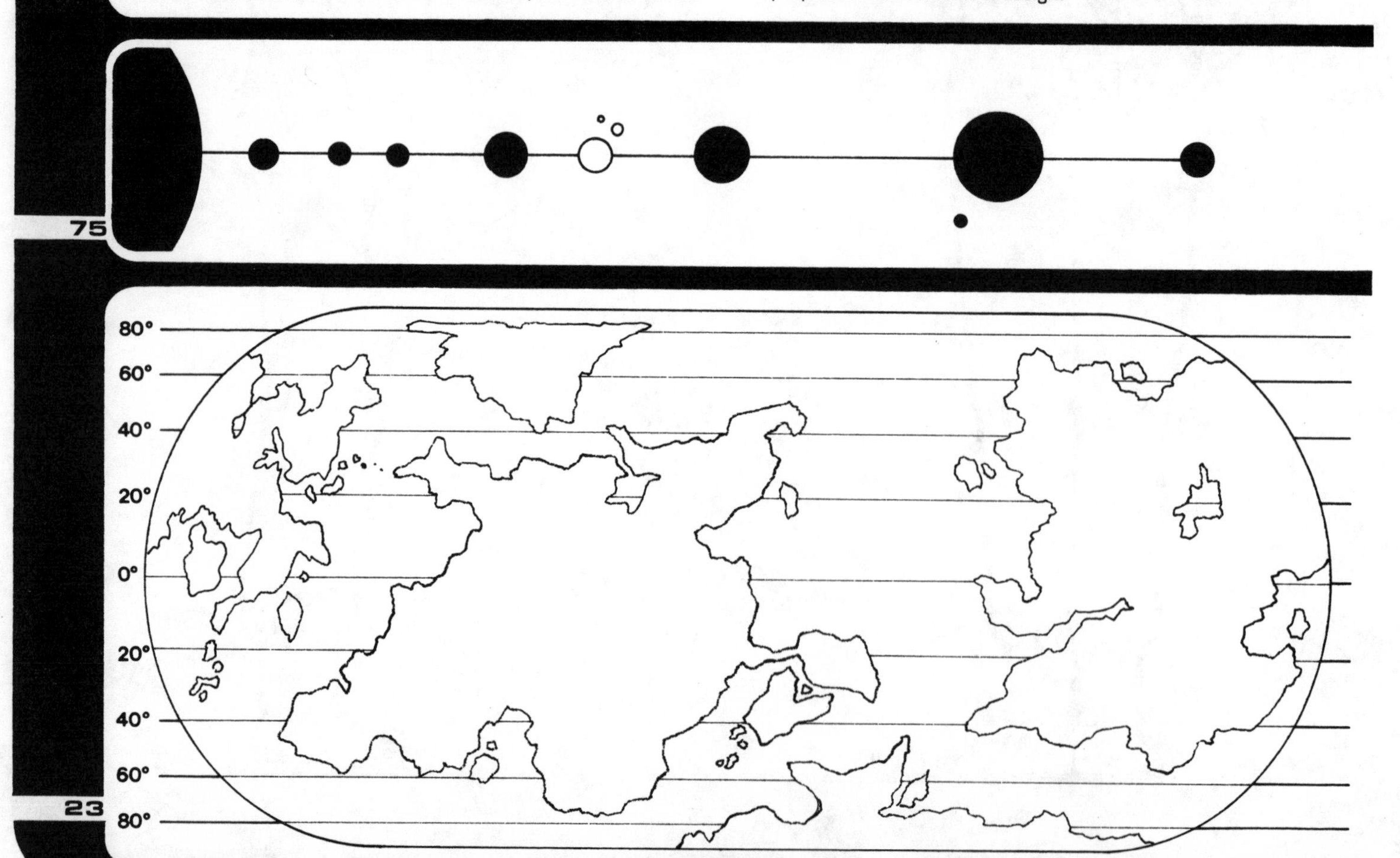

MEMORY ALPHA HISTORICAL ARCHIVE
DATABANK EXTRACT (HARDCOPY)

SUBJECT: TELLARITE

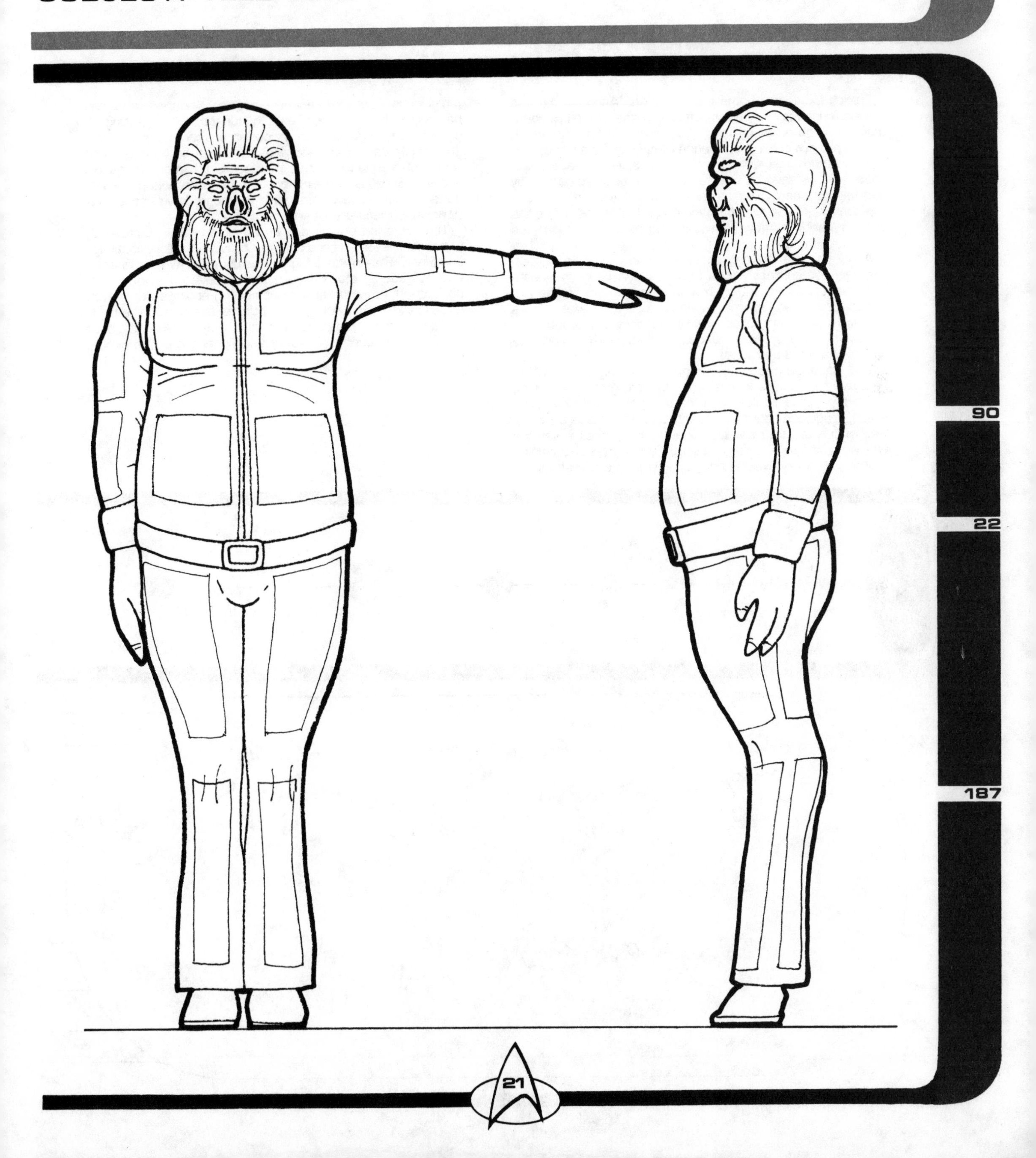

ANDOR (M)

FESOAN

EPSILON INDI

[25.8, 60.1, −2.4]

Epsilon Indi is the home system of the Andorian race, a humanoid-insectoid species that was the third intelligent civilization contacted by Terran explorers. Andor, the eighth of nine planets orbiting an orange dwarf star, is a large, hot, dry world with little surface water. There are, however, vast underground reserves that feed surface geysers heated by geothermal energy; oases surrounding these geysers are the centers of the planet's main population areas, since the great majority of Andor's plant life thrives where subsurface water is plentiful.

Andorians are the only species known to the Federation that displays characteristics of both mammalian and insectoid species. Like standard mammalian humanoids, the Andorians have an internal skeleton to which the body's musculature is anchored. However, they also feature a limited exoskeleton, which lends added strength and protection to the limbs and torso.

The Andorian retina is composed entirely of intensity-sensitive rods and is incapable of discerning color. Color is, however, added to Andorian vision by the dual antennae, which, in addition housing auditory receptors, feature a complex matrix of light-sensitive cones. These cones cover the entire spectrum of color visible to Terran eyes, as well as limited infrared wavelengths. Because of the correlation of four independent light-receptive organs, Andorian vision can be correctly described as "quadriscopic," resulting in superior depth perception. Andorian auditory capacities are also highly developed, allowing Andorians to hear a wider range of frequencies than is possible for most humanoid species. Because of their monodirectional antennae, the Andorian people usually listen with the head down and slightly tilted. Andorians are all ambidextrous.

The Andorian people are an admittedly violent race. By heritage, they are a race of warriors with a history of savage conquest. They place a high value upon family relationships and obligations, often placing them above public duty. Andorians will not quarrel without reason and are deceptively quiet in their relationships with others; this has, in the past, invited attack by others who quickly learned that, once unleashed, Andorian savagery and fighting ability is almost unequalled.

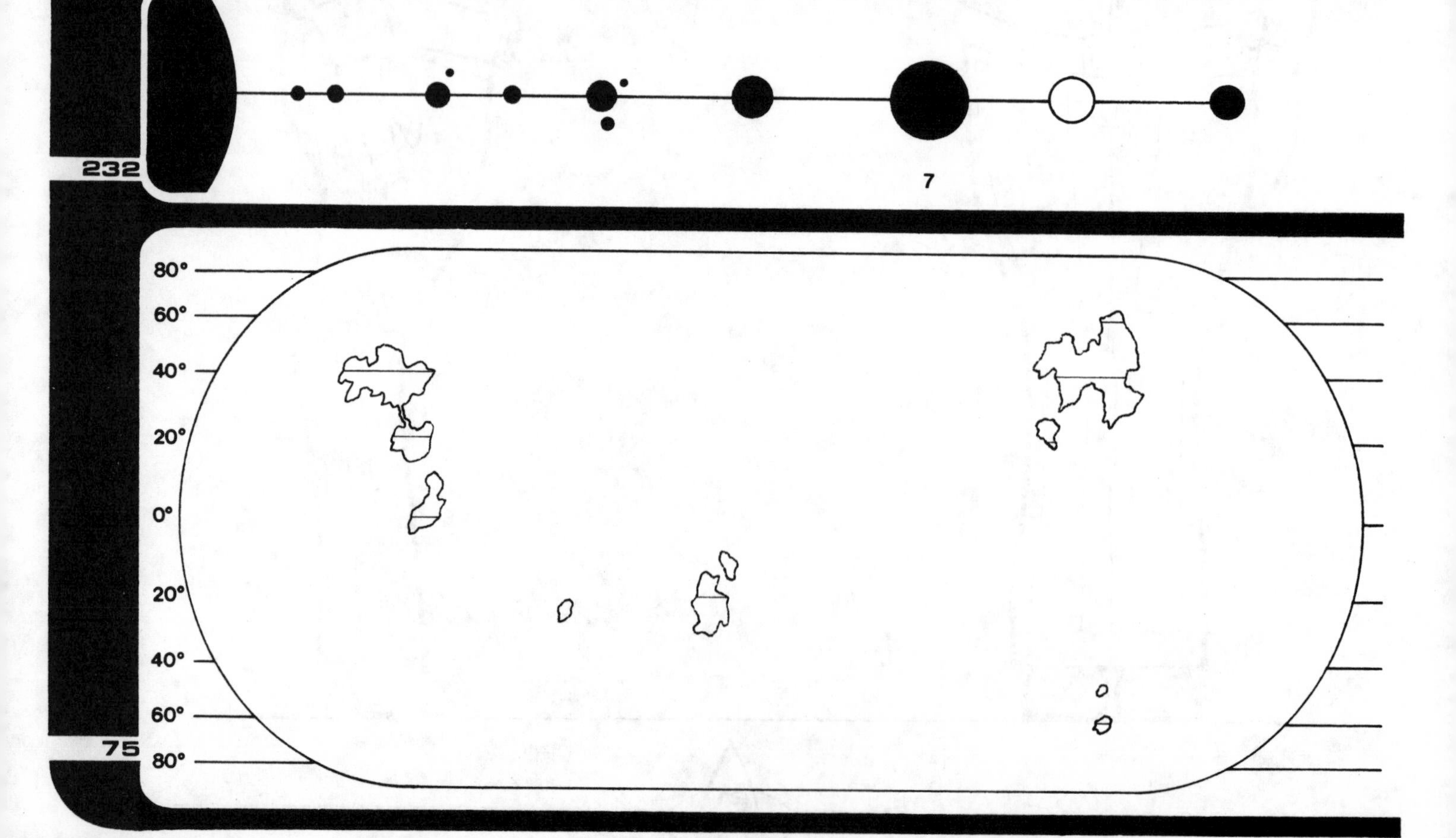

MEMORY ALPHA HISTORICAL ARCHIVE
DATABANK EXTRACT (HARDCOPY)

SUBJECT: ANDORIAN

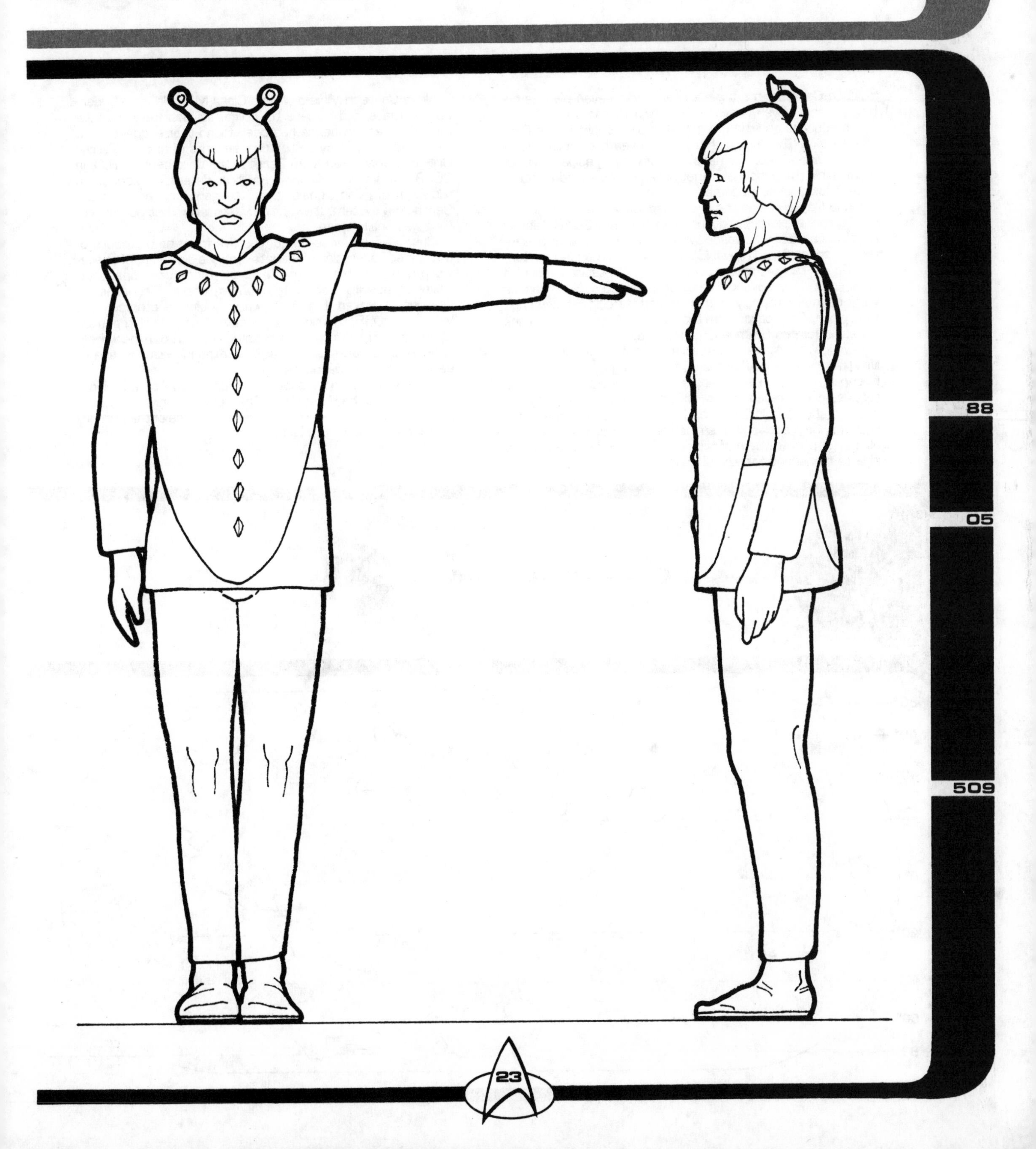

ALPHA CENTAURI VII (M)

AL RIJIL

ALPHA CENTAURI

[24.6, 62.5, −1.0]

Alpha Centauri is a triple system, with seven planets orbiting a pair of yellow stars. The third star is a red dwarf, which appears as little more than a bright light in the Centaurian sky. The fourth, fifth, and seventh planets are all Class M and support humanoid life of varying social development. Only the people of planet seven have reached a state of technological advancement.

Alpha Centauri was the first inhabited world encountered by Terran explorers. In the Terran year 2048, actual physical contact was made with representatives of a Centaurian space fleet. The UNSS **Icarus**, commanded by Captain Roger Tauber, met in space with a Centaurian vessel in orbit around the seventh planet of the system. Both parties were open and friendly, and an immediate cultural exchange took place. An excerpt from the log of Lt. Commander Frank Jocasta, **Icarus** Science Officer, reads:

"I've just spent the two most exciting days of my scientific life talking with the Alpha Centaurian physicist Zefrem Cochrane. Of course, since neither speaks the other's tongue, we've relied almost exclusively on the language of mathematics. . . Using a math I can still only barely comprehend, he's shown that space can be visualized as moving along the curved wave of time . . . if this is so, man will be able to transcend the speed of light."

Alpha Centauri VII is a classic Class M world, nearly identical in mass and climate to Terra. Its population is quite humanoid, and evidence has been found that suggests that the Centaurians may be the descendants of ancient Terran Greeks transported from Earth in the third century B.C. In 2039 the starliner **Enterprise** first detected evidence, in the form of radio signals, that intelligent life existed in the Centaurian system. It was nine years later that actual contact was finally made.

Alpha Centauri was one of the five founding members of the United Federation of Planets, and the discovery of space-warp principles by Zefrem Cochrane made deep space exploration possible for Federation explorers. Cochrane Industries delivered the first warp engine prototype, the WD-1, in 2055; this tiny unit propelled Rosy the chimpanzee at warp 1.5 during a successful controlled experiment. Federation borders were quick to expand with the use of early Centaurian warp systems.

Alpha Centauri now supports a population of 21 billion, second only to the Sol system. The Delthara University Complex, located on the northern continent, is one of the primary learning facilities of the UFP.

786

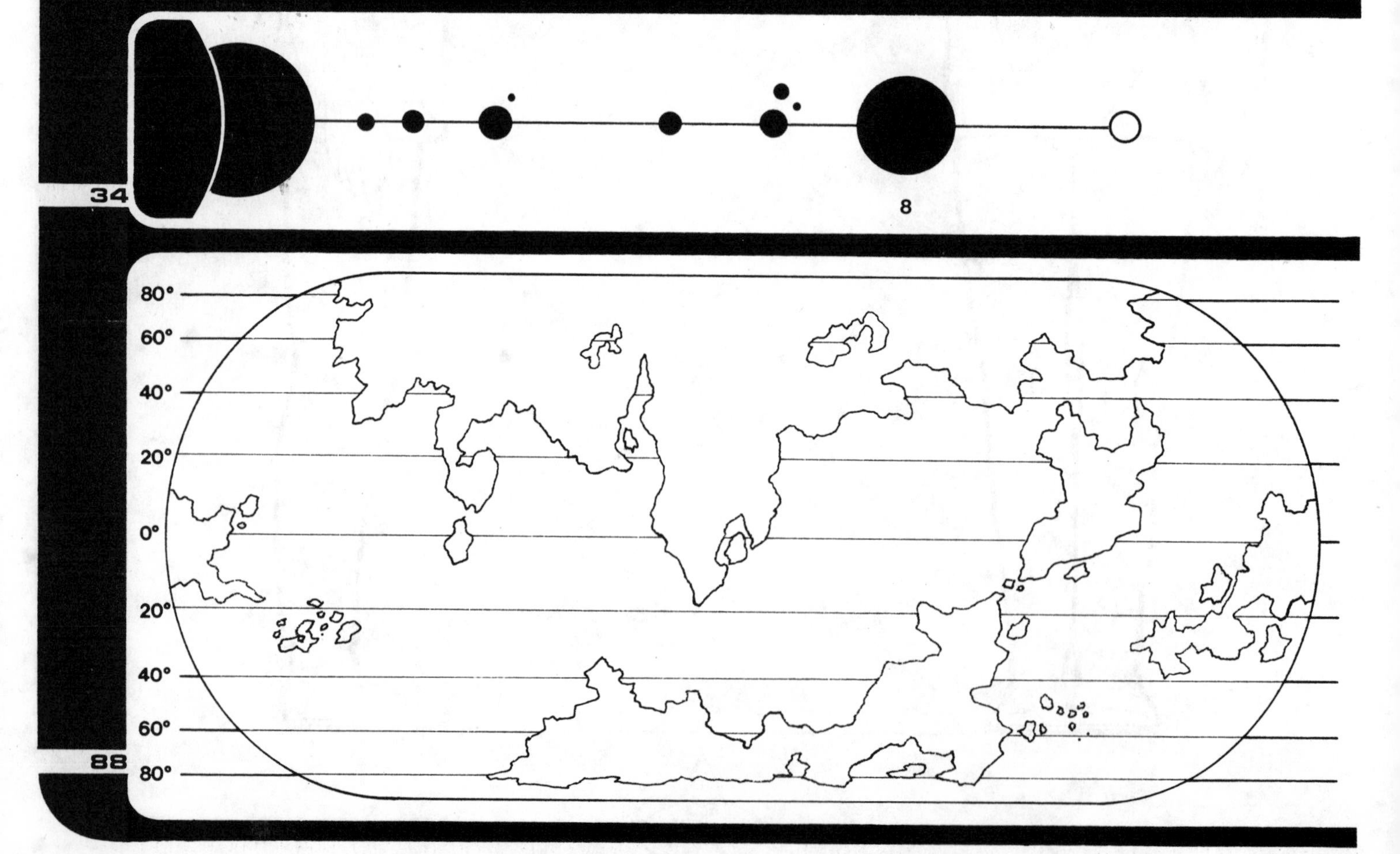

MEMORY ALPHA HISTORICAL ARCHIVE
DATABANK EXTRACT (HARDCOPY)

SUBJECT: CENTAURIAN

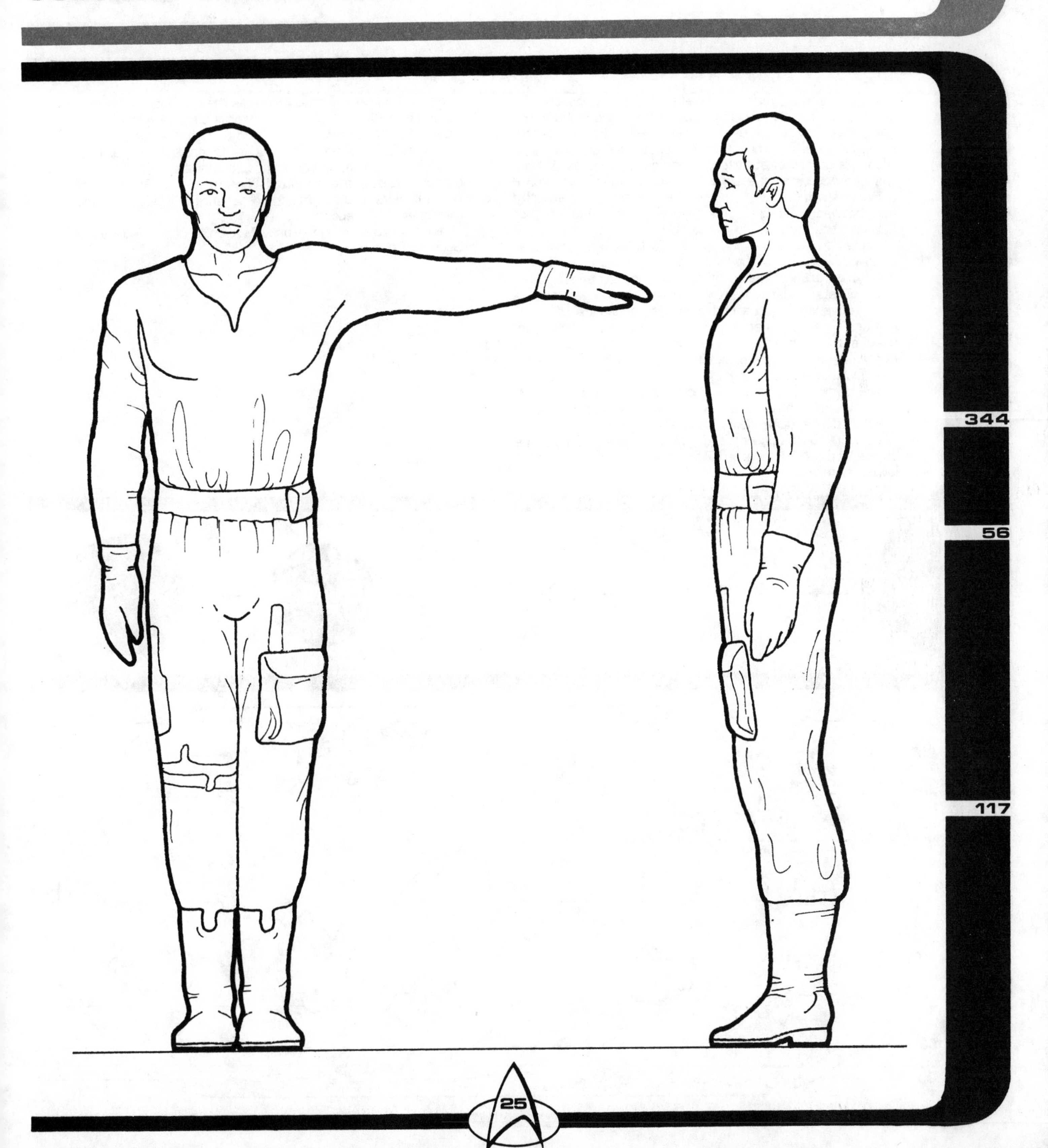

ALPHA III (L)

KERICINDAL

ALPHA

[28.5, 52.8, 19.0]

Alpha is a system of five planets orbiting a moderate-size yellow star. The two outer worlds, Alpha IV and Alpha V, are gas giants that slowly revolve around each other as they orbit Alpha. The first and second planets are uninhabitable. Alpha I is barren of atmosphere and geologically dead, while the second planet is essentially a volcanic cauldron with a poisonous atmosphere. This system features an asteroid belt between the first and second planets and another between the third and fourth worlds.

Alpha III is a Class L world, rather Earthlike but geologically inactive. Established in the twenty-second century as a Terran colony, the planet was found to have no native civilization, although later excavations revealed that an intelligent culture of an advanced nature had died out thousands of years earlier. That race had called their world Kericindal, and, despite the fact that they apparently possessed a high degree of technological capability, they never left their planet to explore space.

The dominant species found on Alpha III by the first settlers was a reptilian biped of limited intelligence. These creatures are quite docile, and they quickly develop attachments to individual persons, which makes them a prime choice as pets. They also exhibit a loyalty uncommon to most lower life forms.

Alpha III is perhaps best known as the home of the famous Statutes of Alpha III. This document is considered to be the most important statement of human rights since the Fundamental Declaration of the Martian Colonies. Its pages provided for the formation of an independent star system to be modeled loosely after Plato's **Republic**. The Statutes of Alpha III have also set major precedents in interstellar law throughout the Federation.

Alpha III is a member — one of seven — of the Federation Security Council.

214

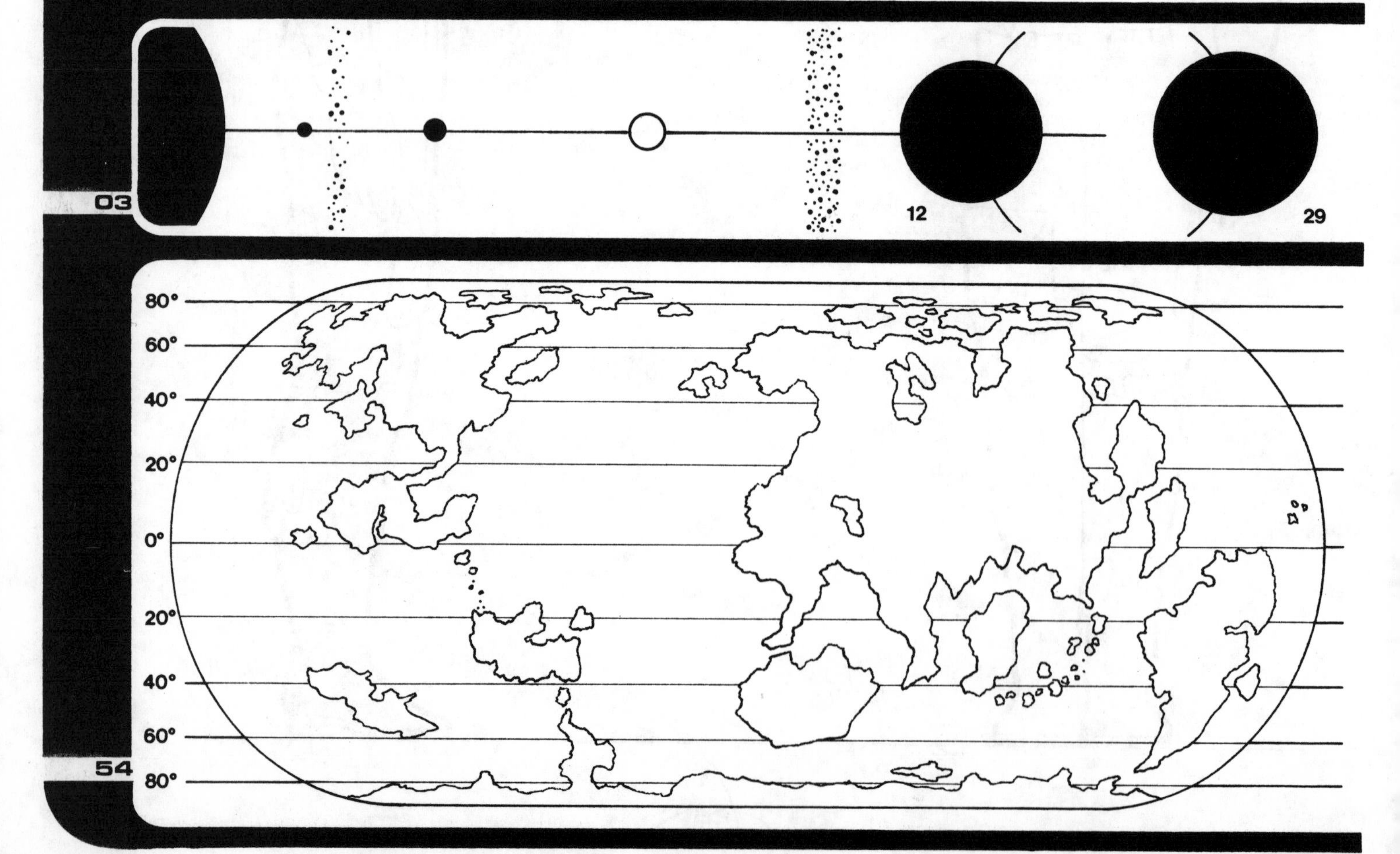

MEMORY ALPHA HISTORICAL ARCHIVE
DATABANK EXTRACT (HARDCOPY)

SUBJECT: ALPHAN REPTILIAN BIPED

65

708

HEIGHT:
.94 METERS
WEIGHT:
30 KILOS
AVERAGE LIFESPAN:
23 YEARS

144

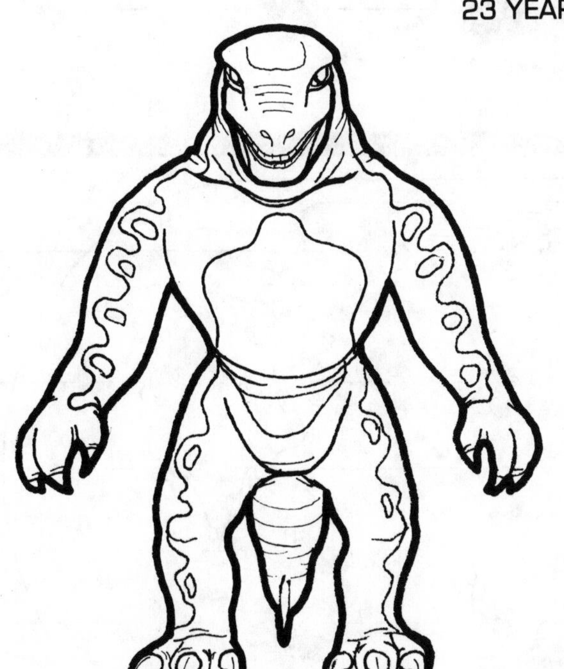

VEGA IX (M)
KESIR-TOSHARRA
VEGA
[28.2, 61.3, 6.9]

Vega is a large white star with ten planets. Vega IX is Class M and is inhabited by both a small human settlement and an advanced humanoid race. Neither group is native to the planet. The humanoid civilization, a colony of the planet Delta III, predates the Federation settlement by nearly a century. A race native to Vega IX did once exist, controlling a vast area of space once referred to as the Vegan Tyranny. That race became extinct, and their exact nature is unknown, but it has been speculated that they were cybernetic or completely mechanical in composition.

One legacy of the original Vegans is Vegan choriomeningitis, a virulent disease that causes inflammation of the brain tissues, high fever, tingling of the arms and lower back, and death within twenty-four hours if left untreated. It has been determined that the disease microorganism was synthetically created by the Vegan race. Unfortunately, its existence was not detected until the organism had been carried, by colonists, to other Federation worlds, resulting in a widespread outbreak of the disease. A vaccine was quickly developed and is now a standard part of pre-exploratory immunization programs.

Vega IX's dominant life form is a hostile, apelike creature known as the Scora. These animals are quite large, often reaching fourteen feet in height, and are strictly herbivorous. Scora possess incredible physical strength. Fortunately for the planet's civilized inhabitants, these creatures prefer to remain in the remote lowland areas surrounding the planet's many mountain ranges.

909

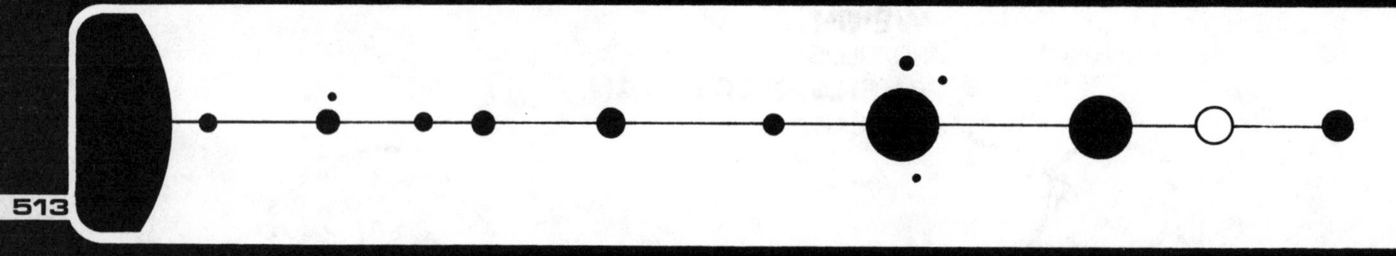

513

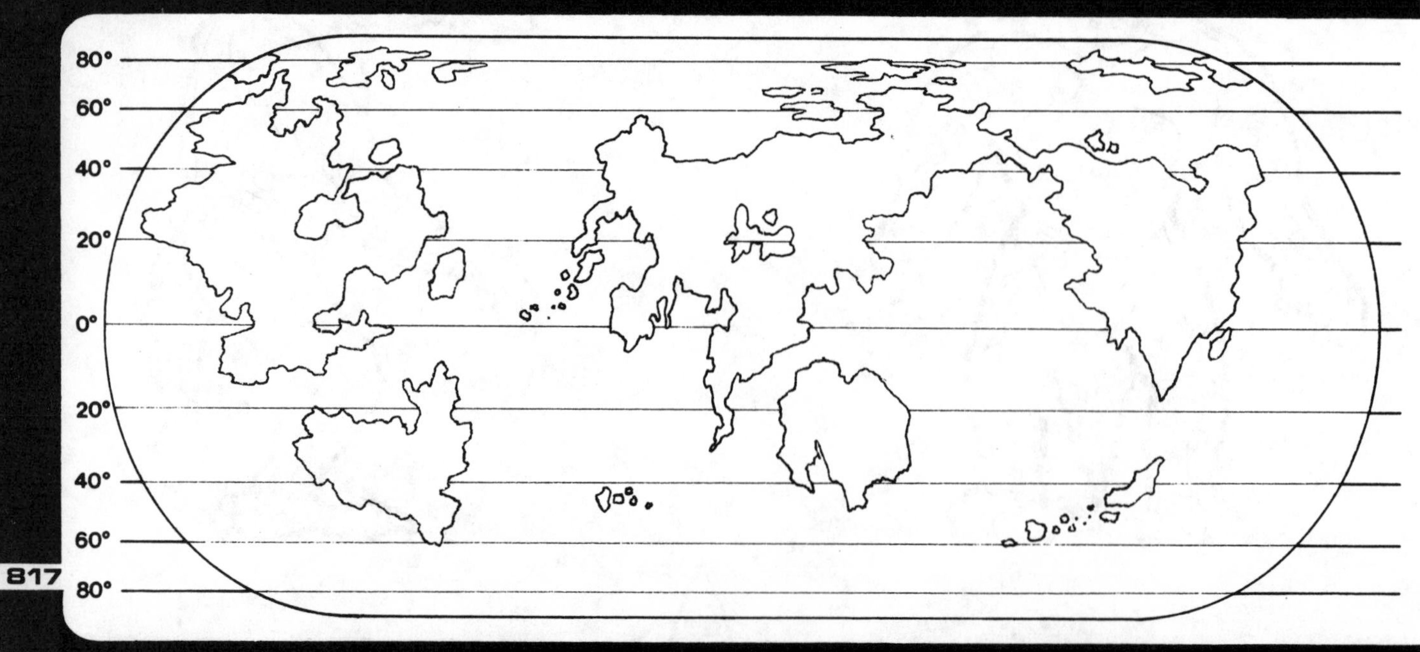

817

MEMORY ALPHA HISTORICAL ARCHIVE
DATABANK EXTRACT (HARDCOPY)

SUBJECT: VEGAN SCORA

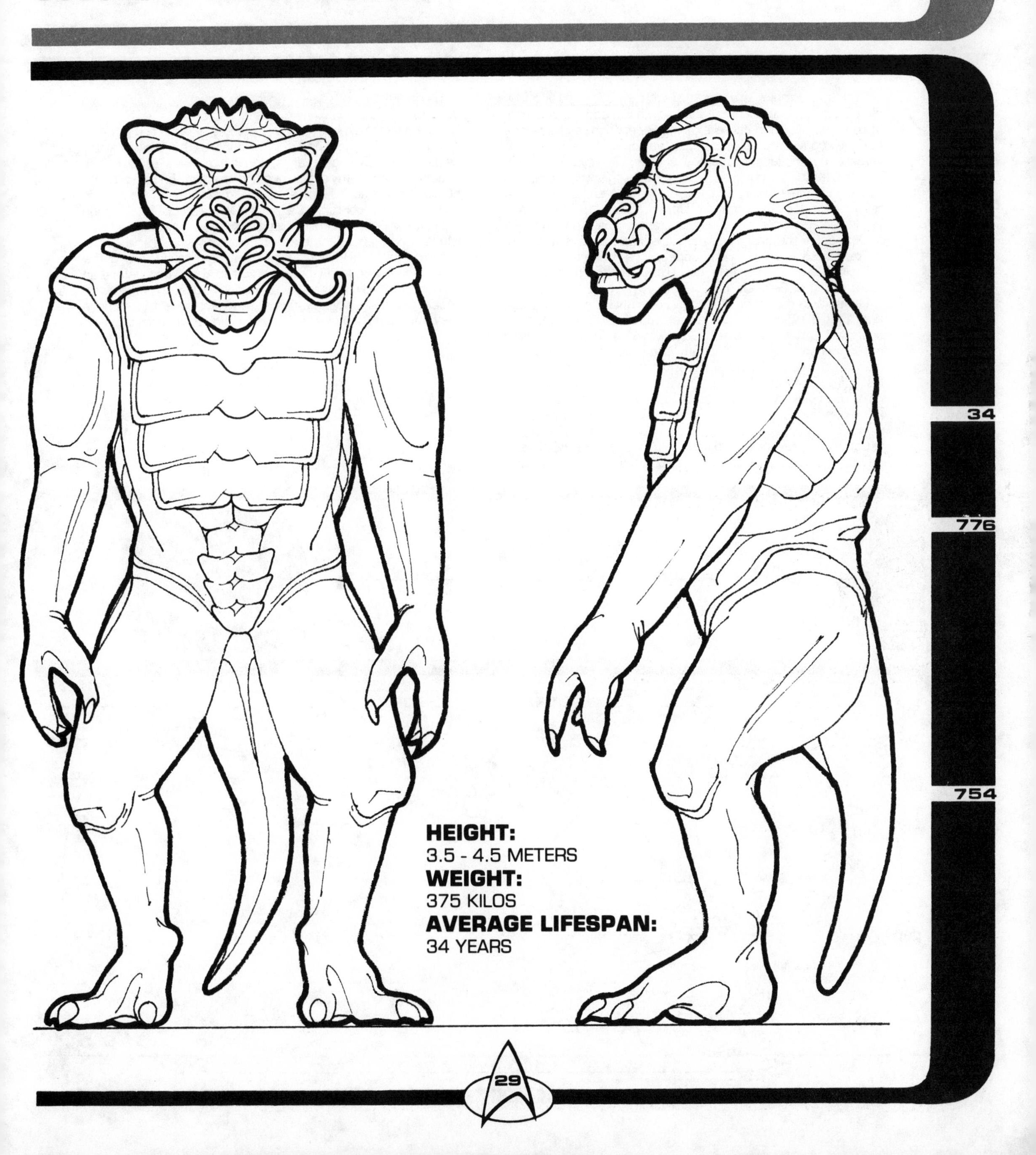

HEIGHT:
3.5 - 4.5 METERS
WEIGHT:
375 KILOS
AVERAGE LIFESPAN:
34 YEARS

DENEB II, IV, V (M)
KRETA, KIDTA, KELTA
DENEB A
[142.7, –143.4, 382.5]

Deneb is a major star system with a total population of over 29 billion inhabitants. It ranks with Sol and Rigel as one of the major cultural centers of the Federation, and its location well above the galactic plane makes it one of the most remote of all Federation members. Deneb is a system of five planets, all of which orbit a white supergiant in a binary system. Planets II, IV, and V are Class M and support intelligent life of many varieties. Deneb III is a Class N waterworld that features many non-sentient animal life forms.

Deneb II is the only planet in the system to have a native civilized culture. Humanoid in appearance, this population of 1.8 billion is on the verge of interstellar flight, with a Richter scale rating of G-minus.

Deneb IV is the home of a small Federation colony, population 17,000. Most of the planet's surface is a beautiful, unspoiled wilderness, making this world a favorite among personnel on leave. Vast oceans and smaller swampy seas dominate the planetscape. The most well-known indigenous life form is the carnivorous Denebian slime devil. This amphibious, quick-moving predator usually feeds upon Deneb IV's bountiful stock of native fish and other sea life by spearing its prey with large, forklike foreclaws. Slime devils range in size from a few inches to several feet long, and they use a form of natural radar to locate their prey. Fortunately, the slime devil does not exist in great numbers, so attacks upon humans, while not unknown, are quite rare.

Deneb V is the most heavily populated world in the system. A major Federation port, it harbors a Starfleet training center, extensive naval yards, and orbital leave facilities. The Federation Academy of Sciences, located on the Fertol continent, has produced some of the most revered scientific minds of this century. Denebians once took legal action against the Federation in a fraud case when Harcourt Fenton Mudd, an independent trader, fraudulently sold the Denebians rights to a Vulcan fuel synthesizer. Mudd, facing the death penalty under Denebian law, fled the planet before an arrest could be made. As a goodwill gesture, the local Federation authorities refunded the Denebians the moneys they had lost. As a result, the case against Mudd was dropped.

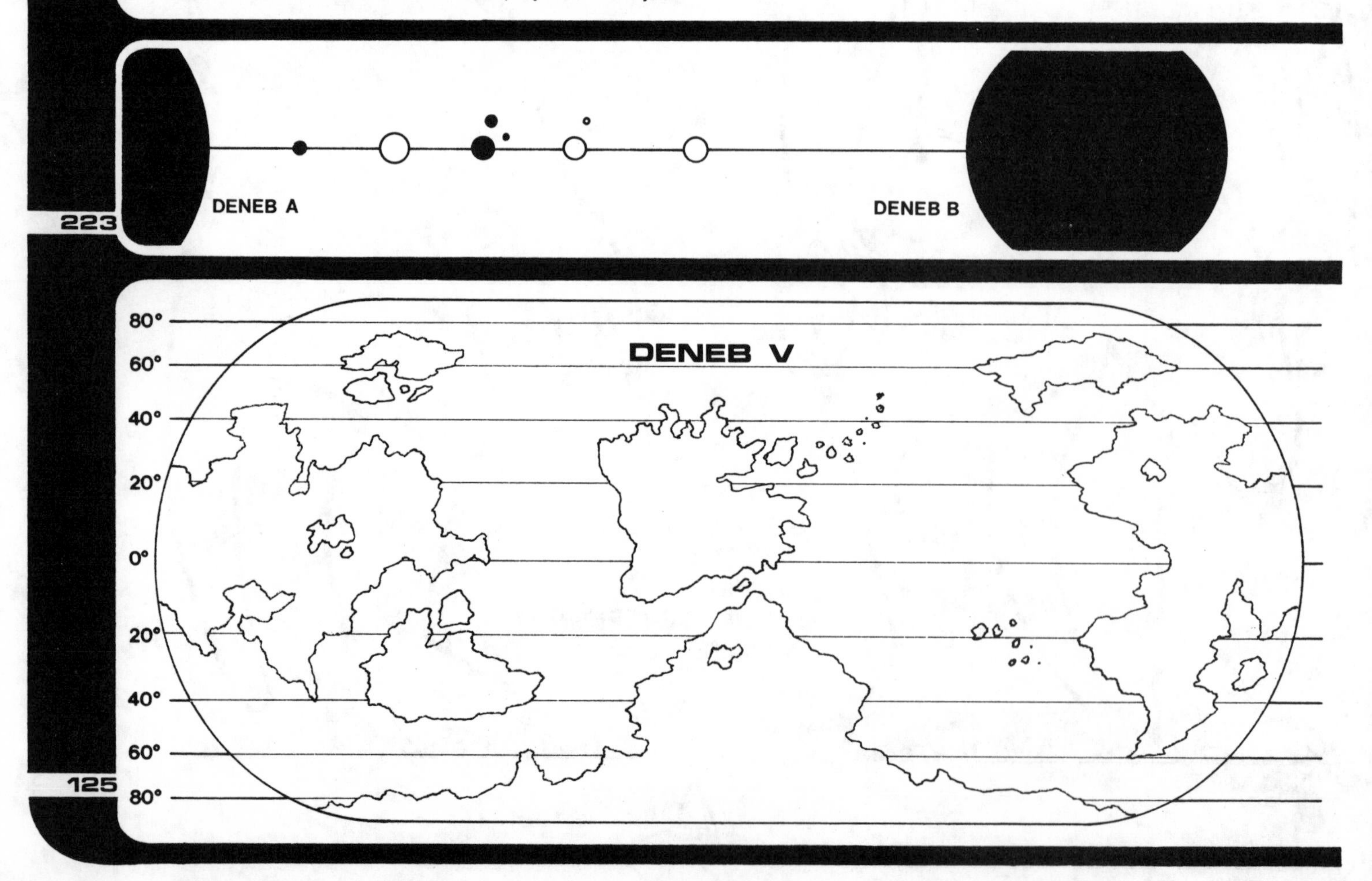

MEMORY ALPHA HISTORICAL ARCHIVE
DATABANK EXTRACT (HARDCOPY)

SUBJECT: DENEBIAN SLIME DEVIL

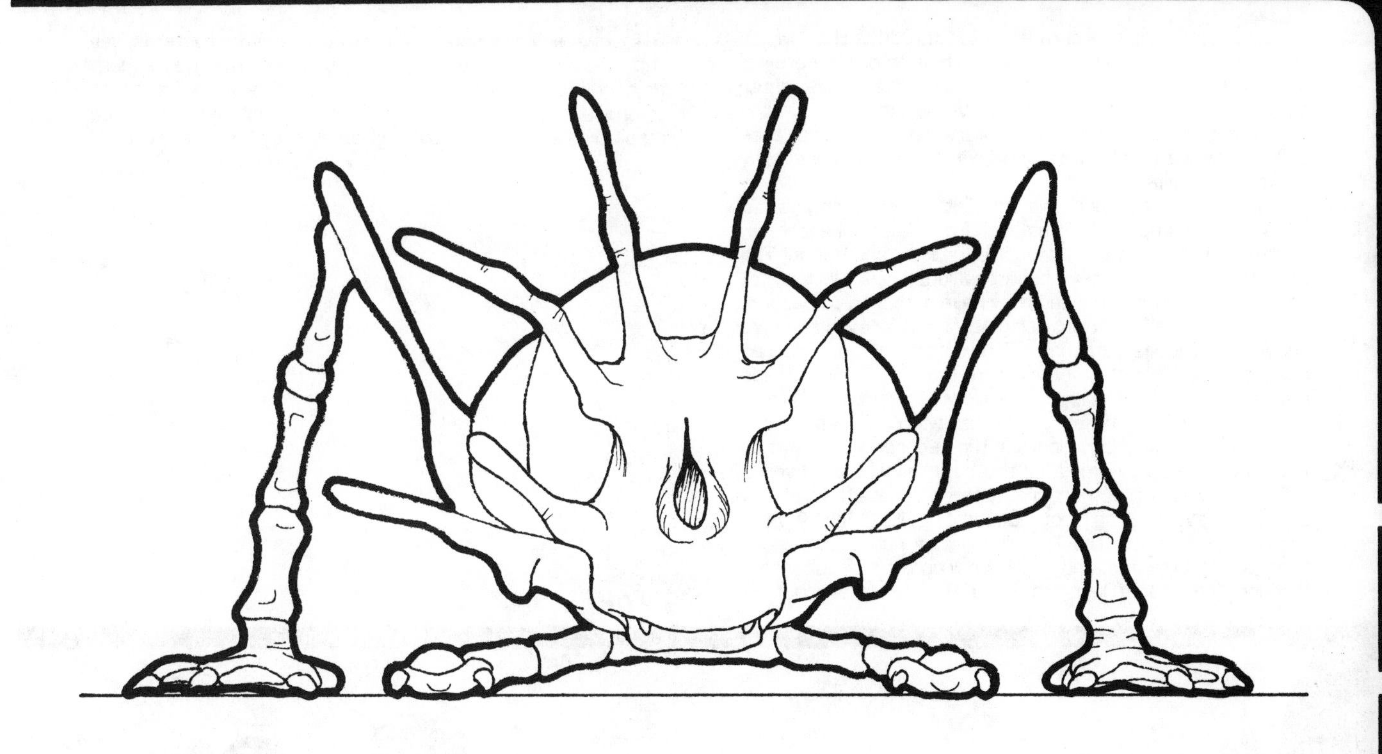

090

22

LENGTH:
0.1 - 1.2 METERS
WEIGHT:
7 - 26 KILOS
AVERAGE LIFESPAN:
17 YEARS

555

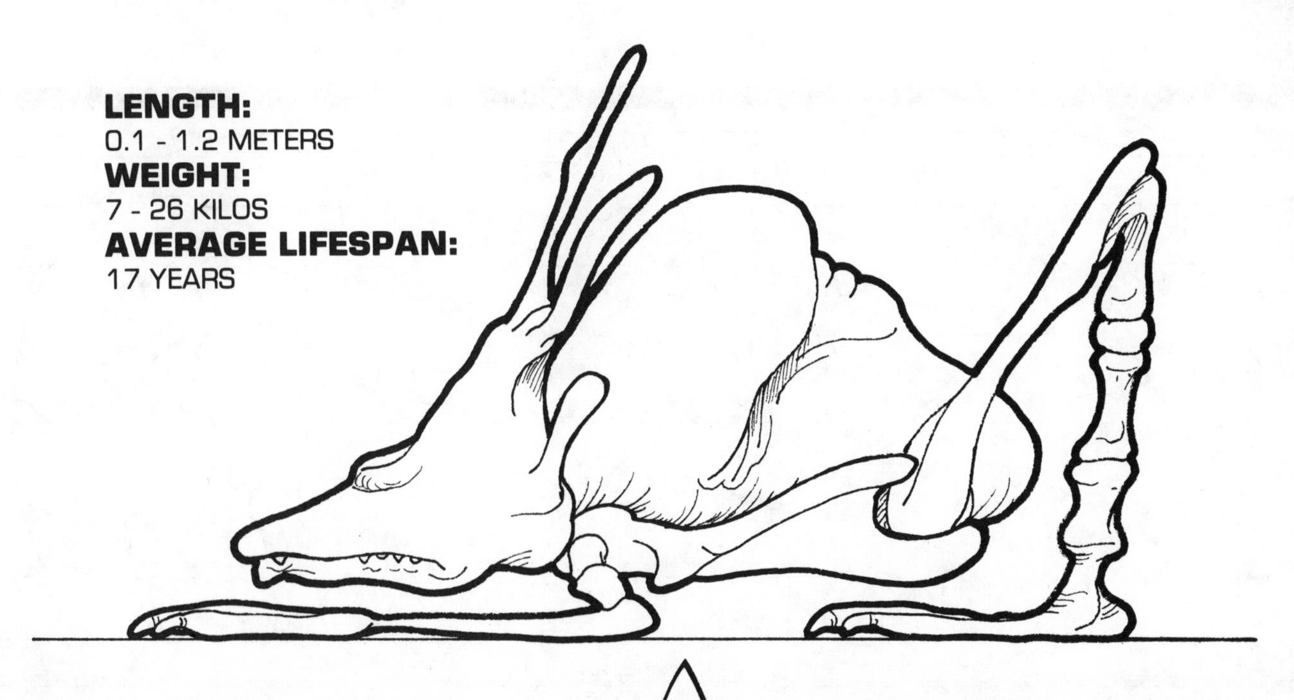

MARCOS XII (L)
NO INDIGENOUS NAME
MARCOS

[26.9, 82.8, −2.2]

Marcos (or, more accurately, Marcos XII) is the twelfth planet in a twelve-world system. It orbits an orange star of moderate size, and its orbit lies just beyond the outer perimeter of a dense asteroid belt. While the planet itself is not geologically active, its only natural satellite, Lora, contains many lively volcanoes and lava flows that constantly reshape its surface.

Marcos is not a remarkable world. It supports a humanoid population, comprised of races from many Federation planets including human, Vulcan, Centaurian, and Vegan. The colony's six million citizens have developed a viable form of anarchistic government, and they have managed to become almost totally self-sufficient using advanced farming and production techniques. Although a Federation member, Marcos has thus far resisted entry into the interstellar trade market, preferring to rely upon its own resources.

A planet of few notable life forms, Marcos does harbor one of the most curious plants in the Federation. Known as Piersol's Traveller (named for the botanist who discovered it), this treelike organism migrates freely across the planet's surface, never taking root. Supporting itself on several footlike appendages, the Traveller draws nutrients directly from ponds, streams, and other small bodies of fresh water through the use of tentacle limbs. Travellers are not intelligent in any way and have no known sensory systems, yet they seem to possess some form of instinct that takes them from one food source to the next. Travellers are not a threat to animal life forms, with the possible exception of whatever small creatures they may step on as they blindly seek food.

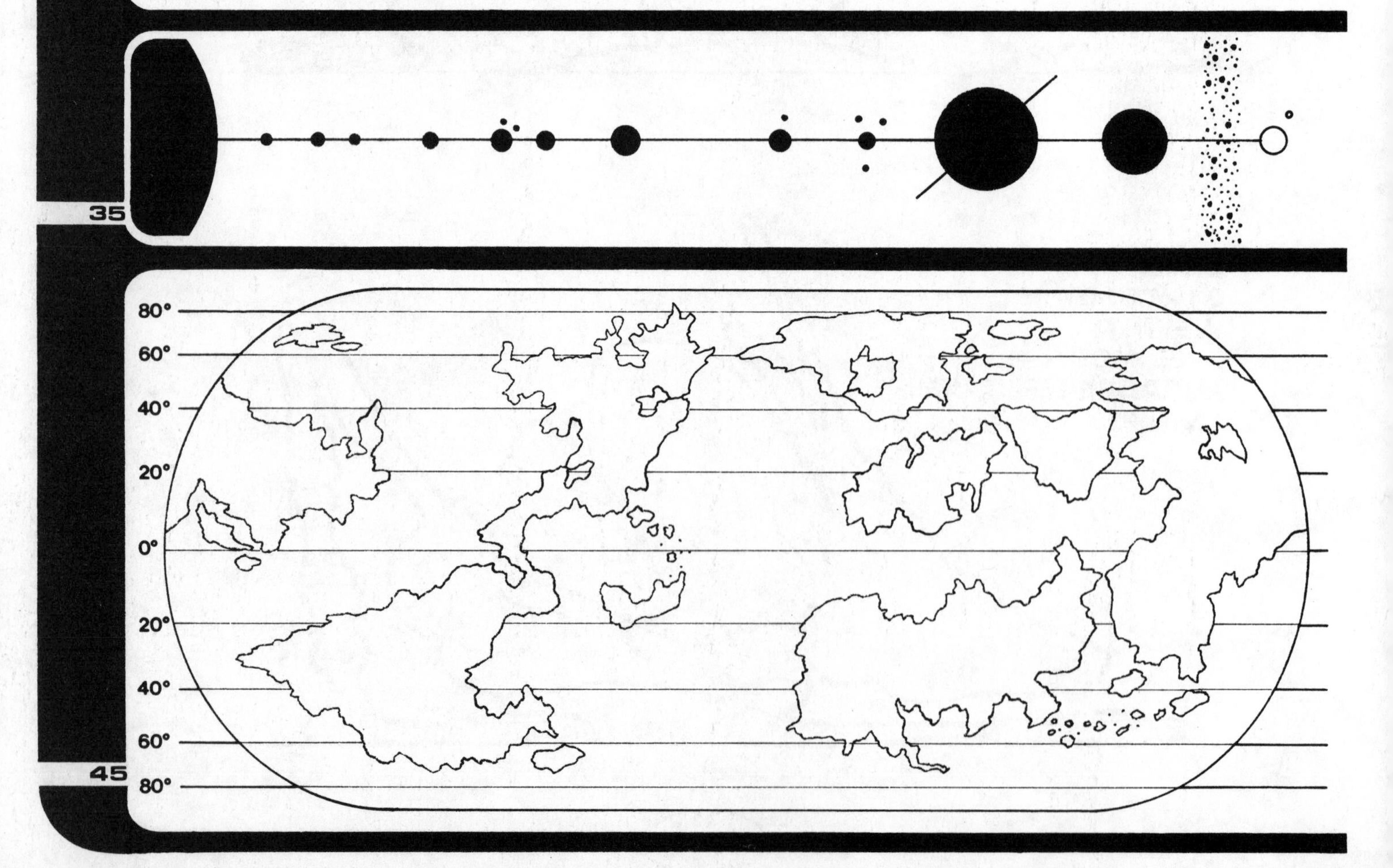

MEMORY ALPHA HISTORICAL ARCHIVE
DATABANK EXTRACT (HARDCOPY)

SUBJECT: PIERSOL'S TRAVELLER

IZAR (M)
NO INDIGENOUS NAME
EPSILON BOOTIS
[36.7, 84.7, 17.6]

A heavily populated world with extensive port facilities, Izar is the third planet of five orbiting a small orange star in a binary system. The other star in the system is a small blue dwarf.

An early Earth colony, Izar is now a totally independent world that is heavily populated, despite a reputation for having some of the most severe weather in the Federation. High winds, dust storms, and tornadoes are commonplace. As a result, much of Izar's city area exists underground, since the planet is geologically stable and earthquakes are virtually unknown there.

Starfleet's Kharicson Training Base is located there, on the continent of Pangaea. This facility is one of the major shuttlecraft flight instruction centers currently in use. New Seattle, the largest city and planetary capital, is the home of the Izar Institute of Meteorology, the Federation's most extensive weather-study center.

Izar is perhaps best known as the home of Garth, one of the most brilliant starship captains ever to serve Starfleet. His exploits are required reading at Starfleet Academy, and many cadets regard him as something of a legendary hero.

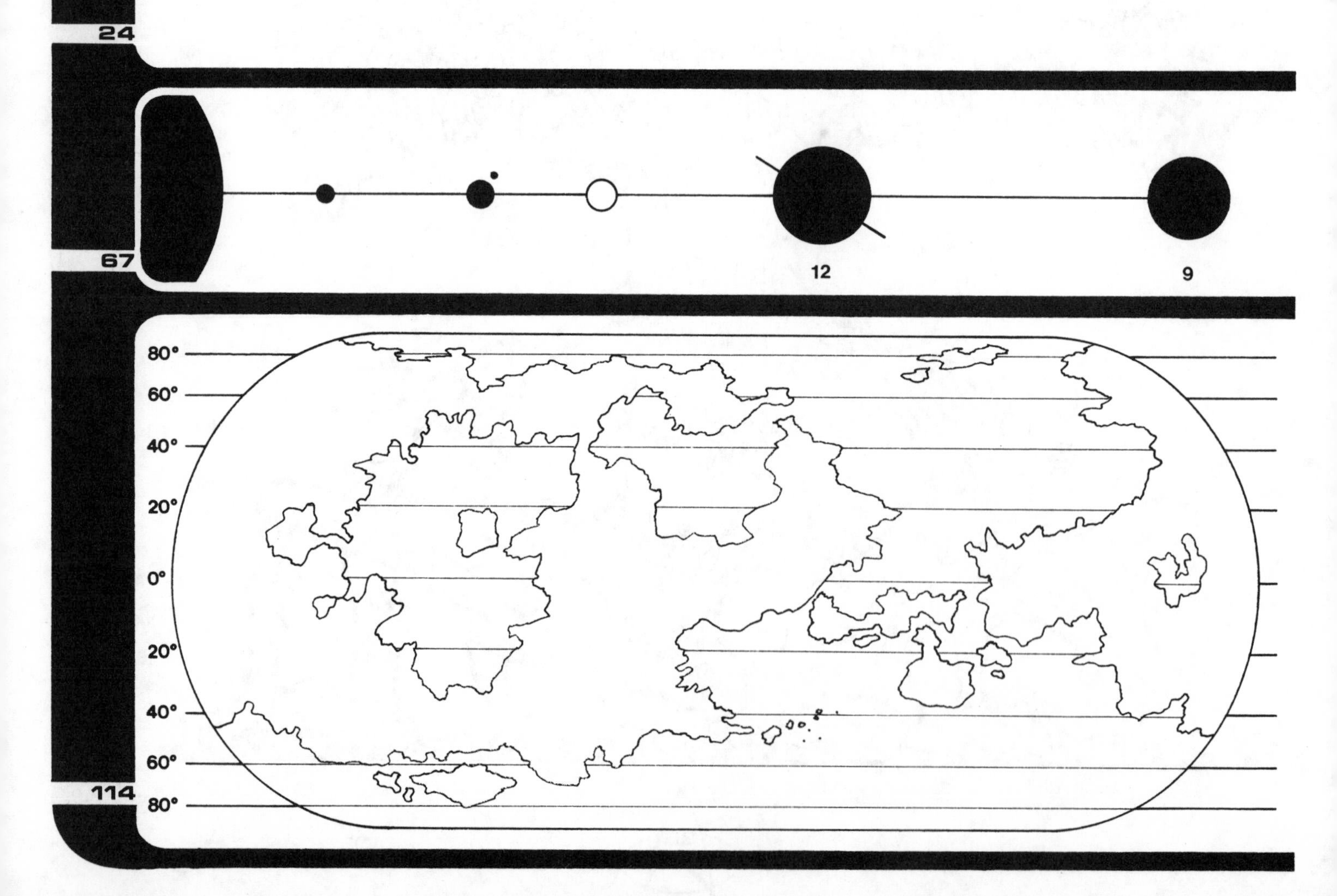

MEMORY ALPHA HISTORICAL ARCHIVE
DATABANK EXTRACT (HARDCOPY)

SUBJECT: INSTITUTE OF METEOROLOGY — BUILDING 'A'

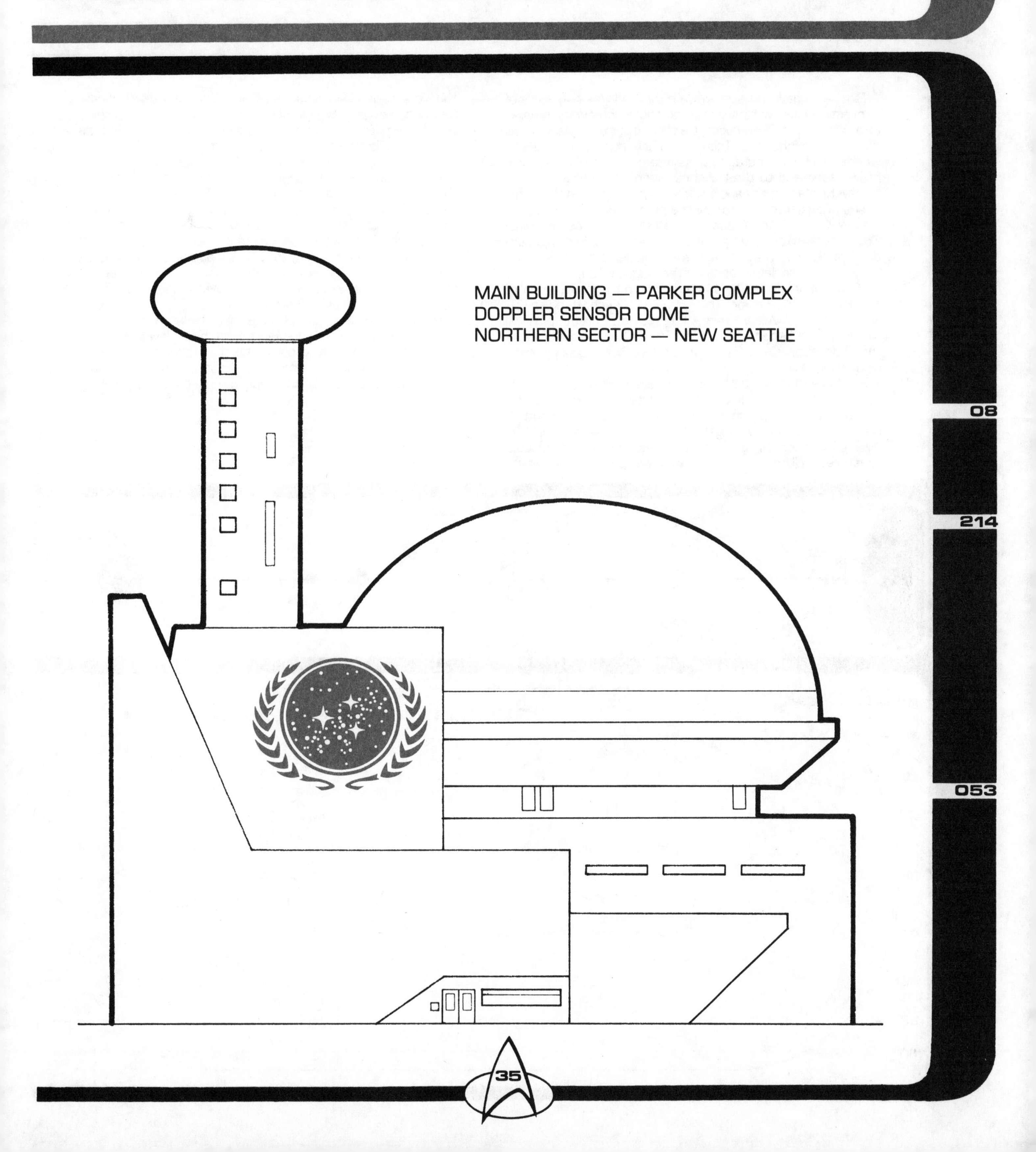

11

RIGEL II, IV-VIII (M)

NO INDIGENOUS NAMES

RIGEL

[−209.9, 7.7, −136.0]

Rigel is a quadruple star system that includes two stars of interest, a blue-white super giant and a somewhat smaller blue-white giant. They support a total of thirteen planets, six of which are inhabited. This remarkable number of Class M worlds can be attributed to the system's extensive habitable orbital zone and to the Hakel radiation belt that surrounds the system's primary and shields the planets from the lethal doses of radiation emitted by the super giant.

Rigel II and Rigel IV, sometimes referred to as the Rigel Colonies, were settled by Terran humans less than two hundred years ago. They are now major Federation worlds with a combined population of more than eight billion.

Rigel V is inhabited by a peaceful humanoid population of approximately 1.3 billion. This culture is thought to be an offshoot of the Vulcan race, due to the great physical similarities between them. Rigel V has been a member of the Federation since 2184, when the Rigel Accords were signed into law.

Rigel VI and VII are a double planet system in a trojan orbit. Rigel VI is a major trade center that coordinates much of the cargo transportation that takes place between Rigel and its sister UFP members. Rigel VII, a large Class M world, is widely inhabited by a belligerent race of Neanderthaloid creatures called the Kalar. Technologically quite primitive, the Kalar rate a D-plus on the Richter Scale of Culture, and it has become general practice to avoid Rigel VII altogether. Early attempts at contact only resulted in armed conflict, as the native Rigellian Kalar prefer solitude.

Rigel VIII, also referred to as Orion, supports a native humanoid population of aggressive, yellow-skinned warriors that number approximately 5.4 billion. After they were given the capacity for interstellar travel by early Earth explorers, Orions colonized the two planets of Rigel's blue giant secondary star and went on to form a pirate empire. Trading primarily in Orion females, they built a sizable slave trade as demand for the green-skinned, sensual, and aggressive female dancers increased. The slave trade was finally abolished by Federation intervention.

Rigel XII is a Class G desert planet. Its large deposits of raw dilithium have made it invaluable to the Federation, which operates a small mining colony on the planet's surface. A vast, fully automated, underground dilithium refining facility runs continually in order to supply the needs of the UFP.

77

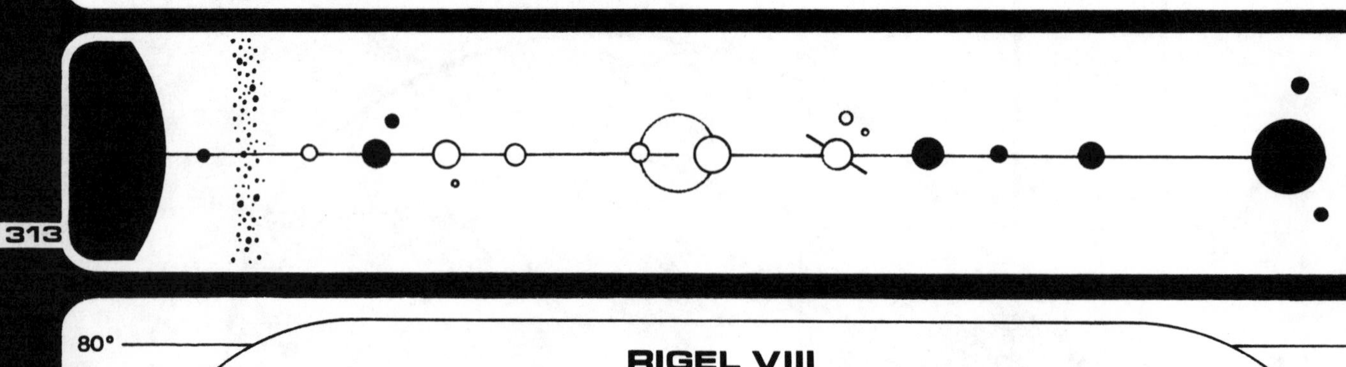

313

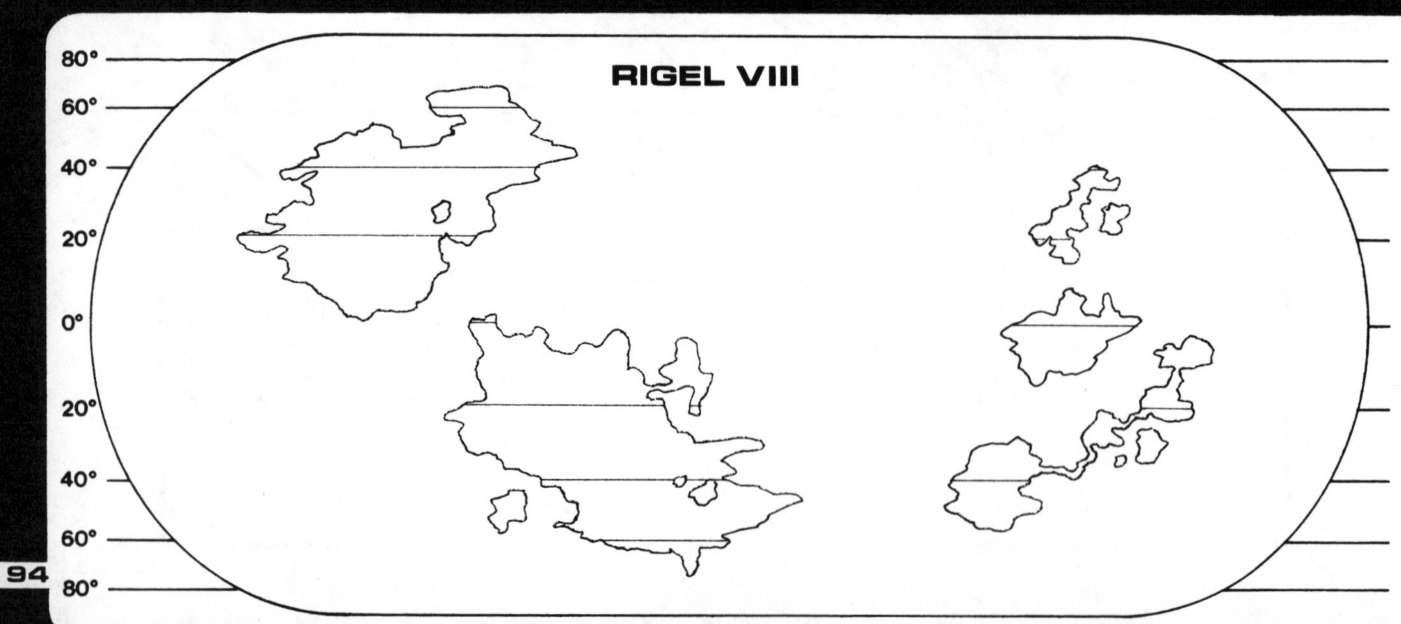

94

MEMORY ALPHA HISTORICAL ARCHIVE
DATABANK EXTRACT (HARDCOPY)

SUBJECT: RIGELLIAN KALAR

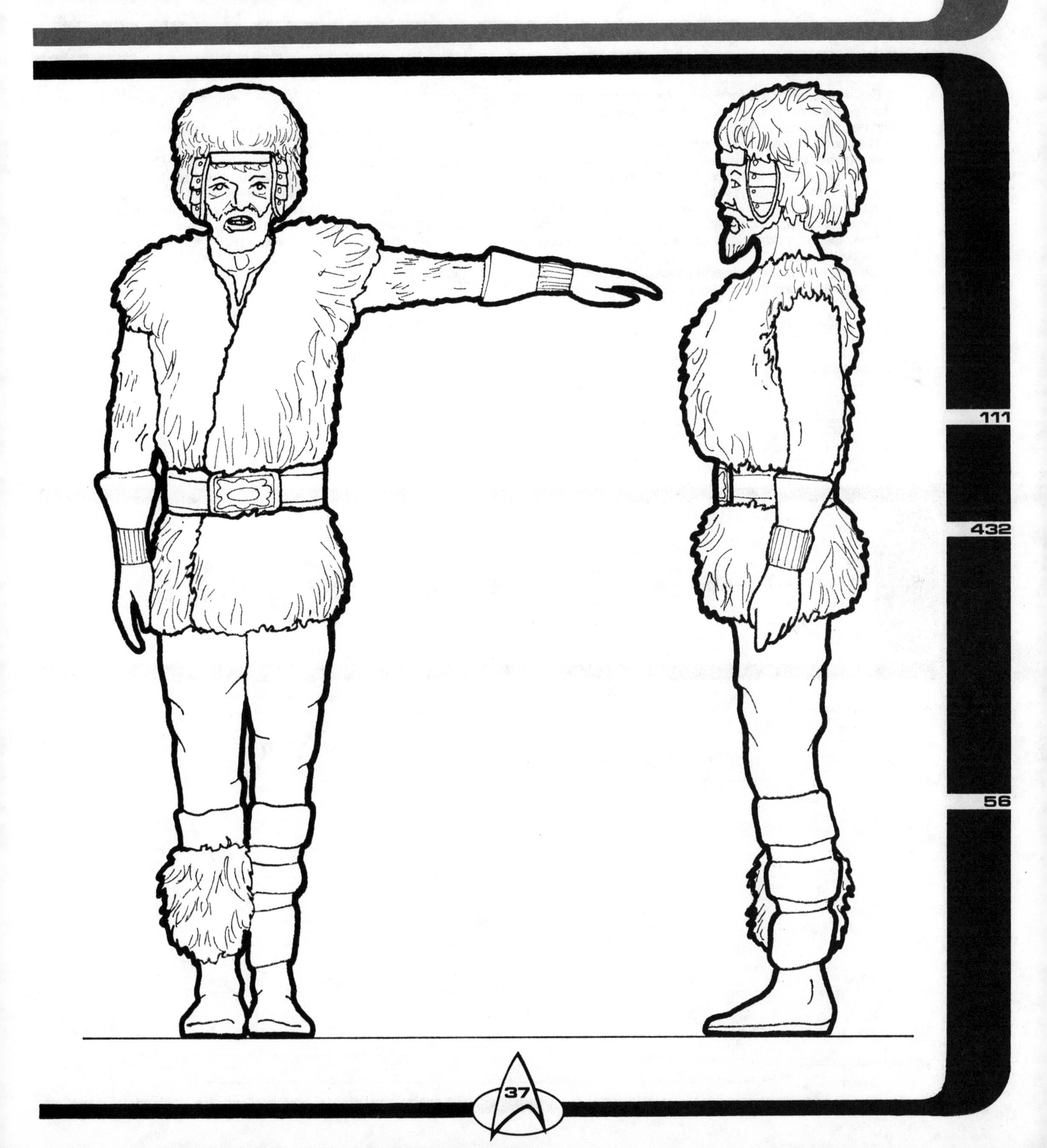

1
2

CAIT (M)

FERASA

15 LYNCIS

[41.9, −228.3, −12.6]

Cait is the second planet of twelve orbiting a moderate-sized yellow star. It is the only habitable planet in its system and has two moons, Rea and Sura.

The native Caitians are a distinctly feline race, and it is believed that they are the descendants of an ancient Kzinti colonization group. They are bipedal, with a thick orange mane, long tail, and large golden eyes that provide excellent low-light vision. The Caitian language consists of multiple soft tones, spoken with a deep, purring resonance; this style of communication makes it difficult for the Caitians to adapt to phonetic languages.

Caitians have excellent hearing, with a frequency range far beyond that heard by normal humanoids. For this reason, most Caitians who enter Starfleet specialize in communications and sonic sciences.

Unlike the Kzinti, the Caitian race is not hostile in nature. Their reputation as one of the most cooperative and intelligent members of the Federation makes Caitian crew members much sought-after throughout Starfleet.

The asteroid belt that lies between the fifth and sixth planets of the Caitian system is an abundant source of ores and valuable minerals, not the least of which is dilithium. Orbital refining platforms within the belt provide a large percentage of the dilithium crystals used in that area of Federation space.

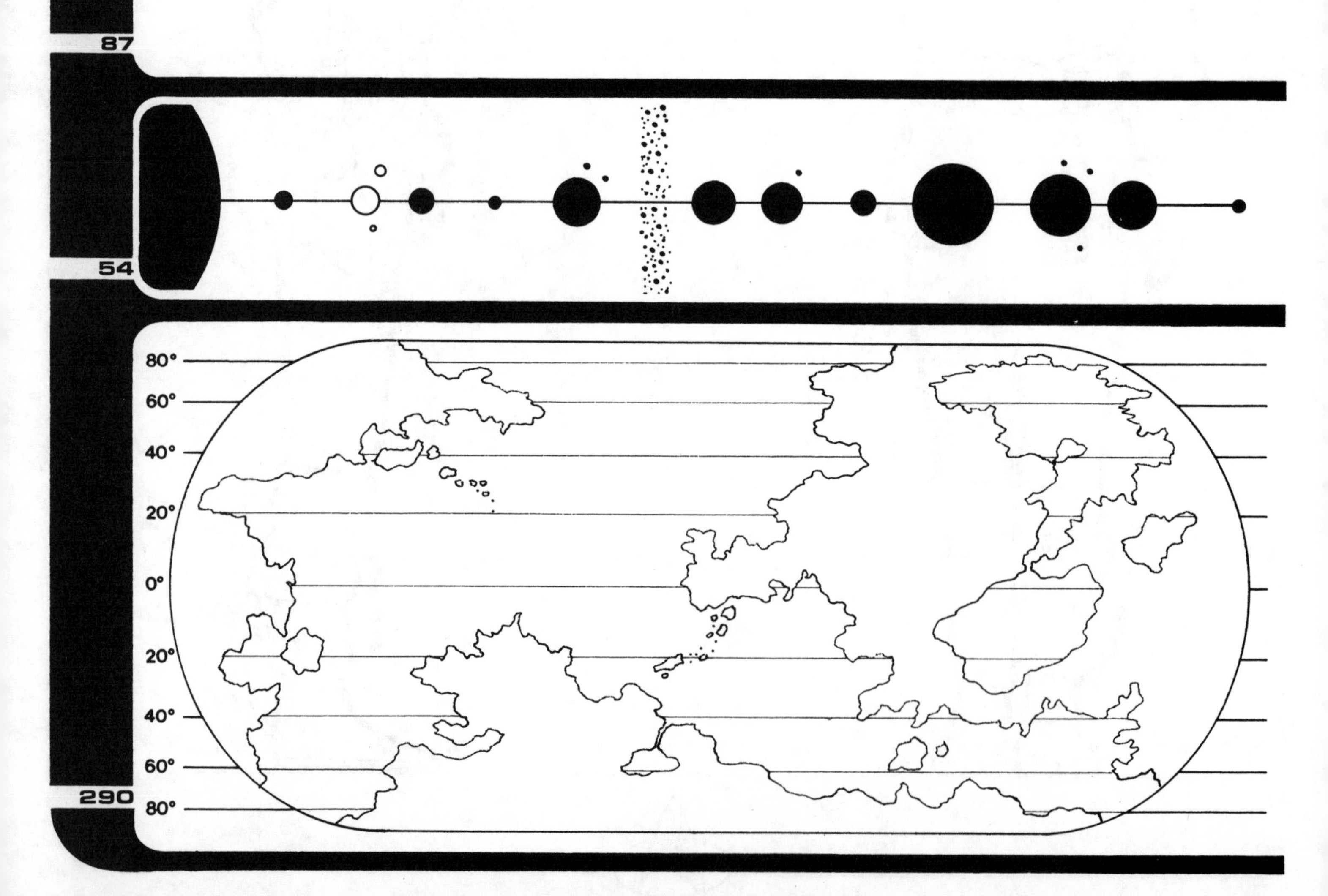

MEMORY ALPHA HISTORICAL ARCHIVE
DATABANK EXTRACT (HARDCOPY)

SUBJECT: CAITIAN

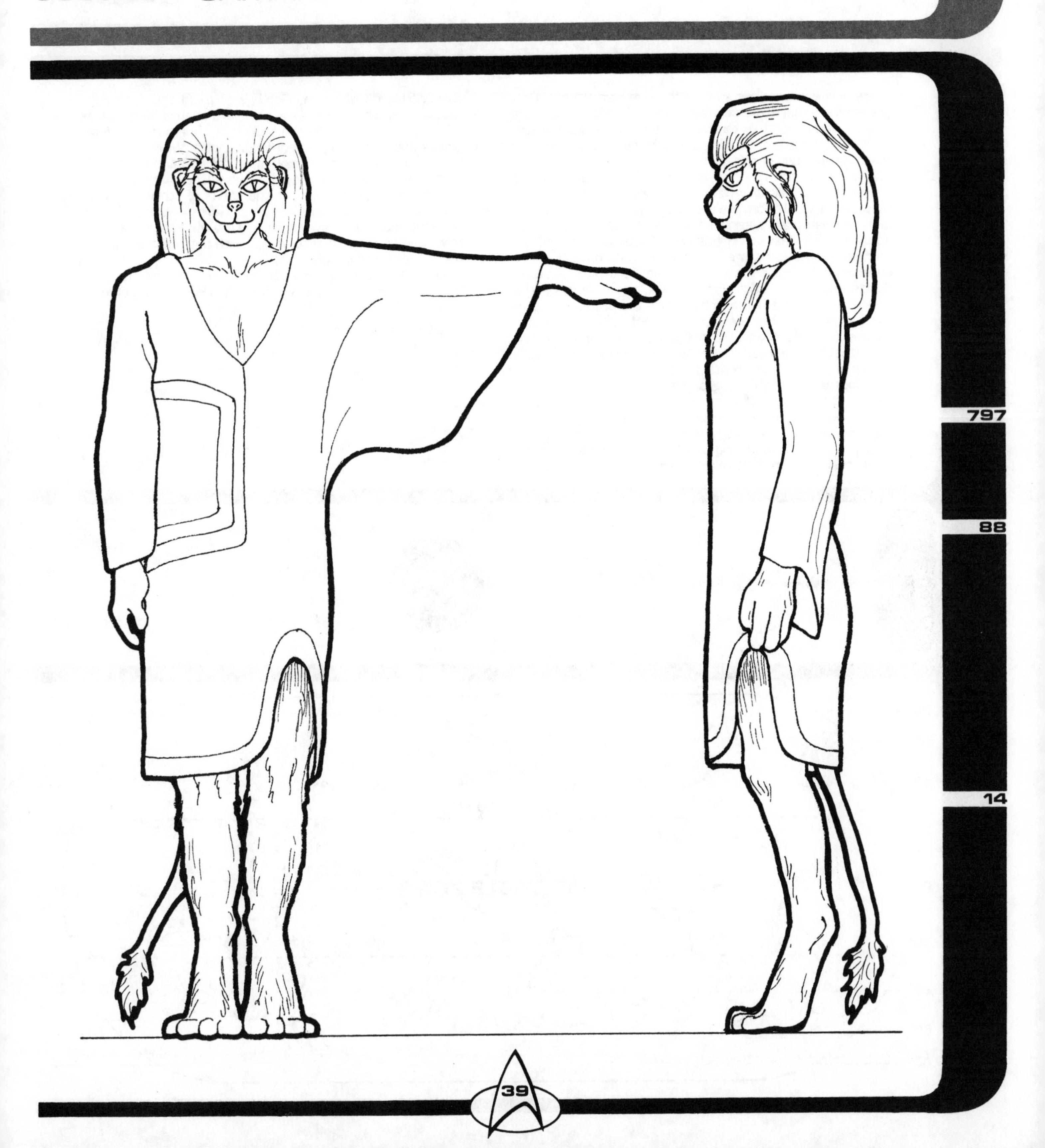

13

ANTOS IV (M)

DORAFANE

ANTOS

[18.1, −20.4, −6.1]

Antos is a yellow giant star system with five planets. Only the third and fourth are capable of supporting life. Antos III is Class K and supports a tenuous atmosphere and some surface water. Native life is limited to only the most primitive of invertebrates and simple plants.

Antos IV is the home of a race of benevolent, ancient humanoids considerably older than mankind. Although it is Class M, Antos IV's climate is lethally frigid at both the upper and lower latitudes, leaving only an equatorial band that supports life. The native inhabitants have established an extremely advanced culture in this region and have built city structures that seem to defy known Federation limits in design and construction. From space, the civilized central region shines like a belt of light around the planet, owing to the strangely luminescent properties of Antosian metals. Federation contact with the Antosians has been extremely limited, at the request of the Antosian people, and little is known about their culture, technology, or architecture.

Antos IV, while a Federation member, has limited their participation in Federation matters to contact by subspace radio. The reason for such aloofness was long a mystery until Captain Garth of Starfleet, maimed and dying, was forced to make an emergency landing there. In order to save his life, the Antosians shared with him a secret they had kept for untold thousands of years; Garth was given the Antosians' medical abilities, including the power to change his shape at will. They had perfected the technique of cellular metamorphosis and were able to rearrange their cellular structures to imitate any object or being of similar size and mass. This talent was considered by the advanced Antosians too dangerous to be allowed into the hands of other races. Indeed, the process quickly rendered Garth of Izar mad, and he remained so for several years. Only the introduction of a new drug returned him to sanity, with the resultant loss of his shape-changing ability.

Antos V is a gas giant with seventeen moons. The third moon, Sowtha, is Class L and harbors a Federation refueling depot.

99

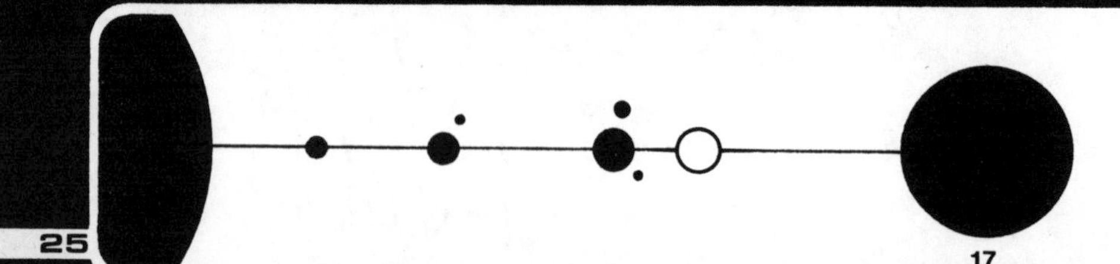

25

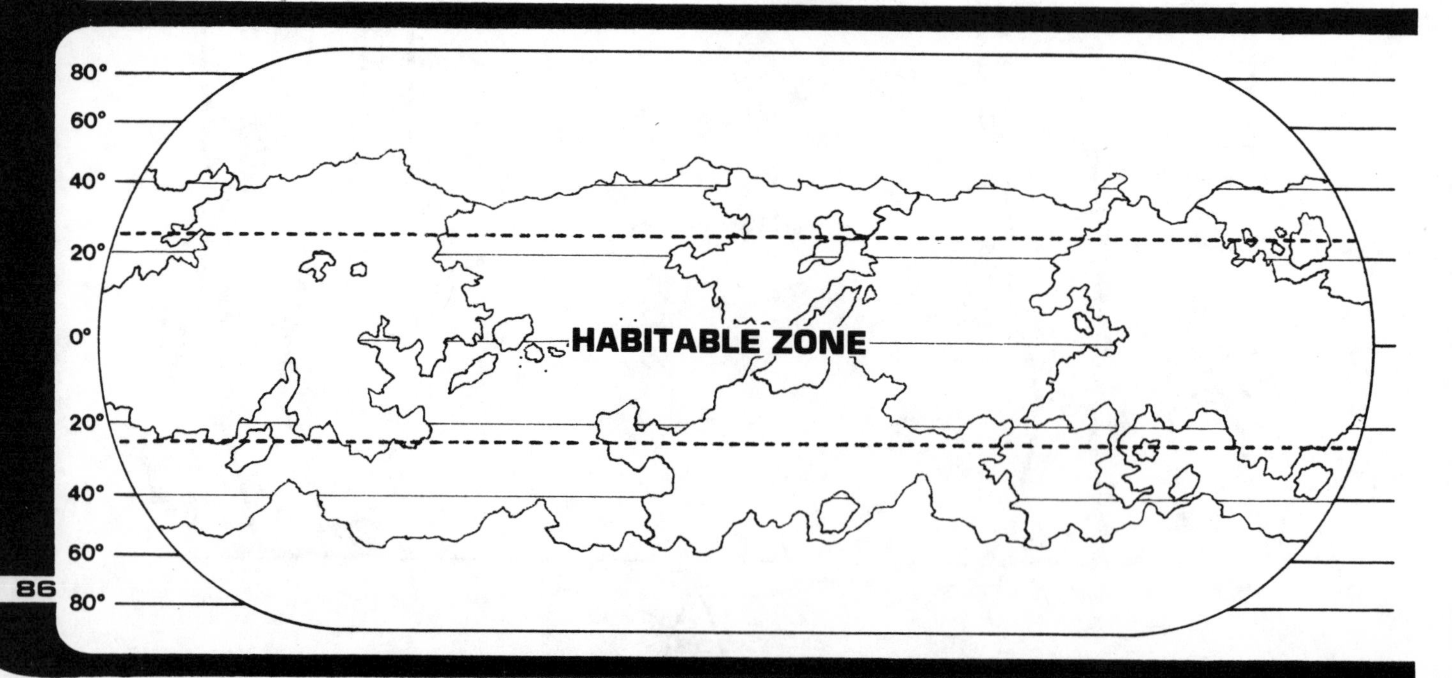

86

MEMORY ALPHA HISTORICAL ARCHIVE
DATABANK EXTRACT (HARDCOPY)

SUBJECT: ANTOSIAN

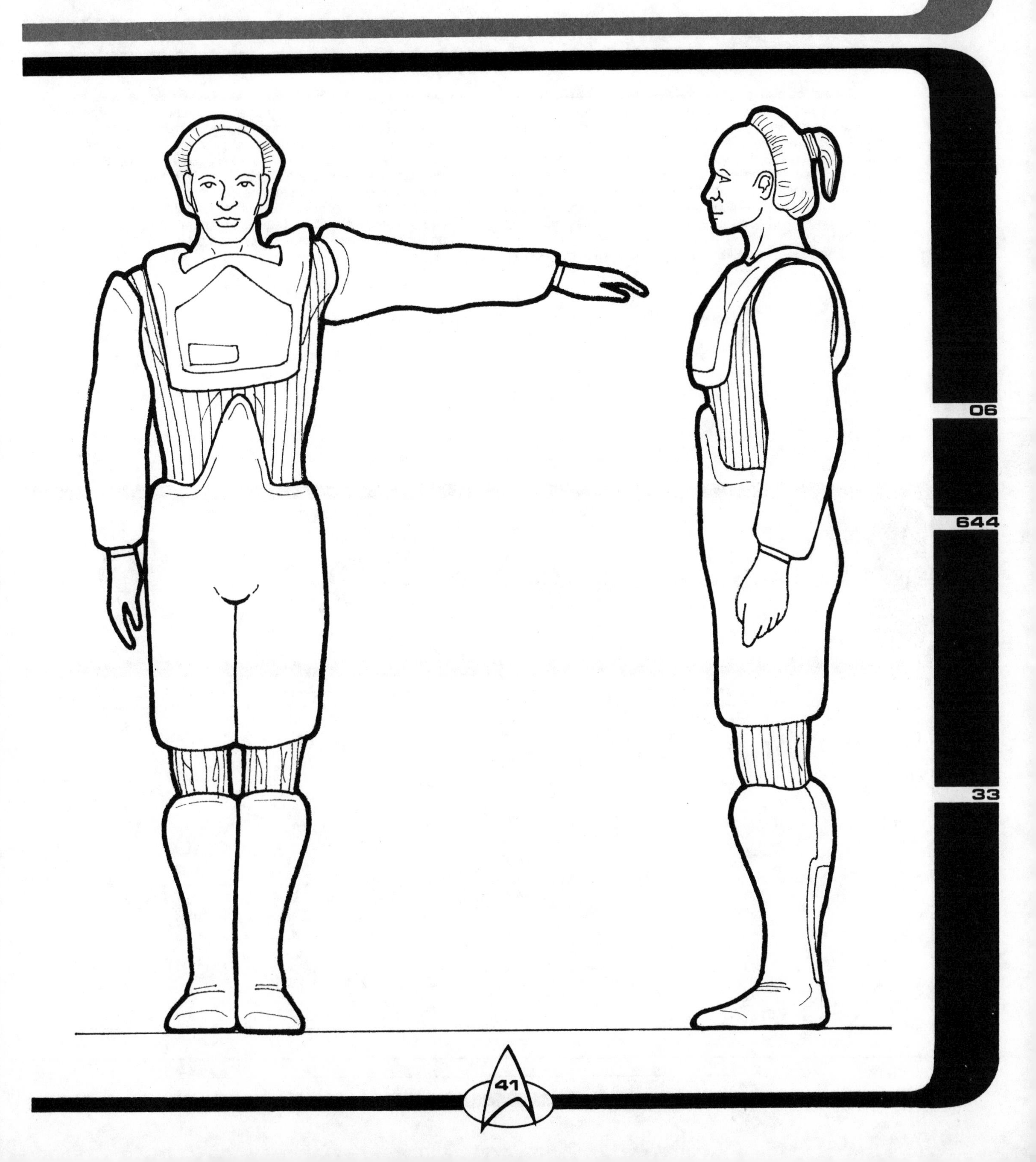

14

CATULLA (M)
CENDO-PRAE
THETA PICTORIS
[277.6, −73.7, −13.9]

Catulla is the sixth planet in the system of Theta Pictoris, a moderate-sized red-orange star with nine planets. In mass, Catulla is quite similar to Terra, and it has two moons, Milon and Milar. The planet is the home of a thriving humanoid society of about 9.5 million that has built a huge industrial network covering the planet. Long ago, a massive nuclear war all but wiped out the accumulated knowledge and culture of the planet. The Catullans have struggled for centuries to regain the level of technology and civilization they once had established.

Ambassador Tongo Sil of Catulla is a man of extraordinary vision and ability. His studies in space science and interplanetary relations have resulted in several breakthroughs in treaty negotiation, bringing peace and cooperation to several Federation planets. His efforts have brought him the Palm Leaf of Axanar Award, the Seltye Commendation, and the Nobel and Zee Magnee prizes.

Harrell Hullworks, one of the Federation's leading producers of warp spacecraft bodies, is located on the northern edge of the continent of Tesakar, with separate construction facilities above in geosynchronous orbit.

018

03

31

80°
60°
40°
20°
0°
20°
40°
60°
80°

69

MEMORY ALPHA HISTORICAL ARCHIVE
DATABANK EXTRACT (HARDCOPY)

SUBJECT: CATULLAN

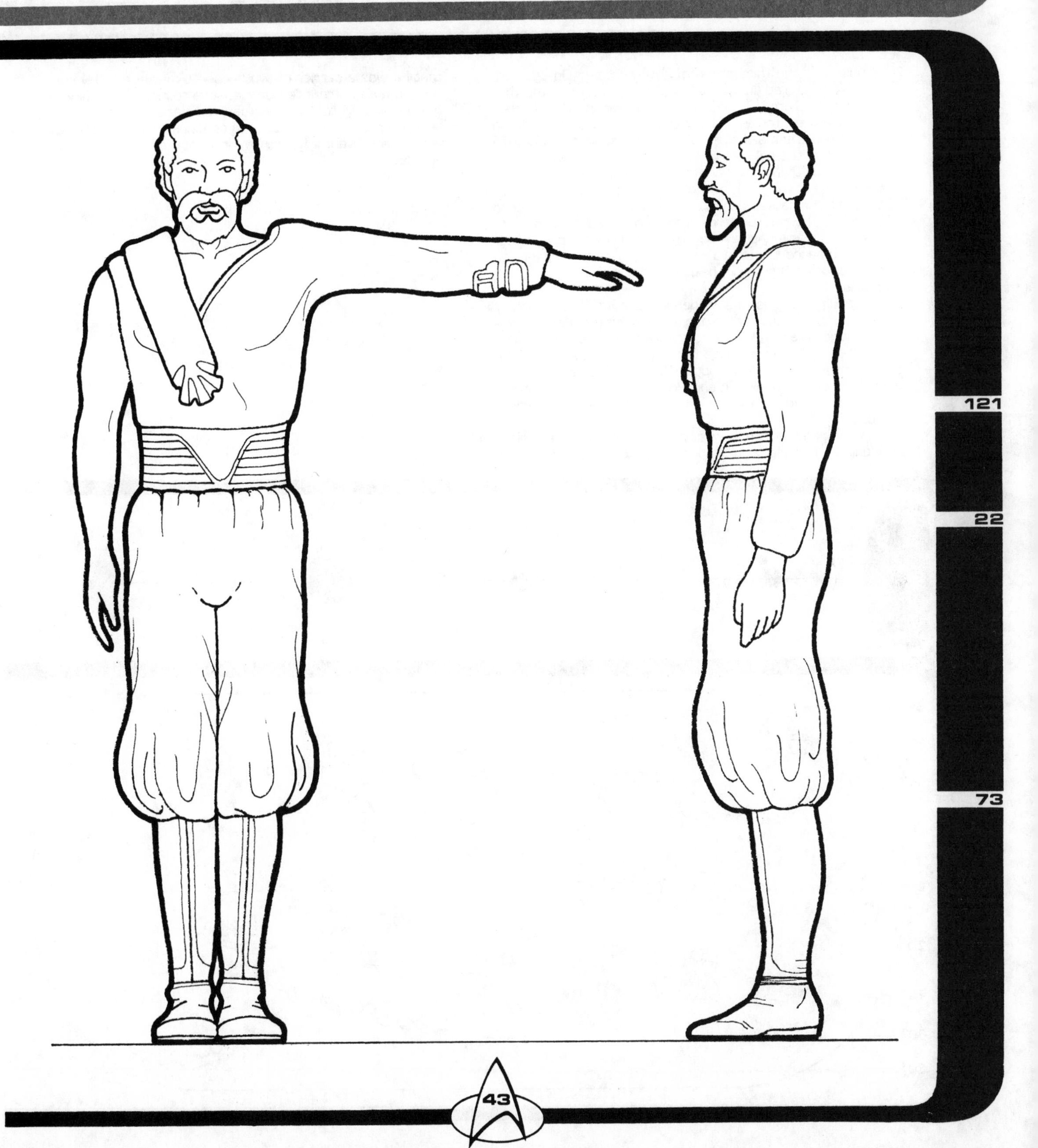

15 TIBURON (M)
SIMERAN
OMEGA FORNACIS A
[−121.9, −207.4, 236.4]

Tiburon is the third planet of seven orbiting Omega Fornacis A, a dim red dwarf in a binary star system. Somewhat larger than Terra, Tiburon has seven moons that harbor several outer colonies. The atmosphere on Tiburon is rich in oxygen and is somewhat thinner than those of most Class M worlds. It is the only habitable planet in its star system.

Tiburon is the home world of an advanced humanoid race that is one of the most distant members of the Federation. Although the natives exhibit several physiological differences from the humanoid norm, they are essentially human. Genetic analysis has revealed that the Tiburons are slightly mutated descendants of Terran humans giving credence to the world-seeding theory held in many circles.
circles.

The Simeran Sciences Academy is located in the planetary capitol city of Onakk and is one of the most prestigious communications and electronics centers in the Federation. Simeran alumni have made important contributions to the body of Federation knowledge. Several of these scholars, such as Dr. Rota Sevrin and Professor Andrew Tempest, have authored textbooks currently in use at Starfleet Academy.

A specialist in communications, Dr. Sevrin also dealt in acoustics and electronics theory before it was discovered that he was a carrier of synthococcus novae, a highly contagious but controllable disease. As a result, his travel was limited strictly to technologically advanced worlds, which severely hampered his ability to continue the research that was his life. Eventually, Dr. Sevrin went mad and committed suicide.

187

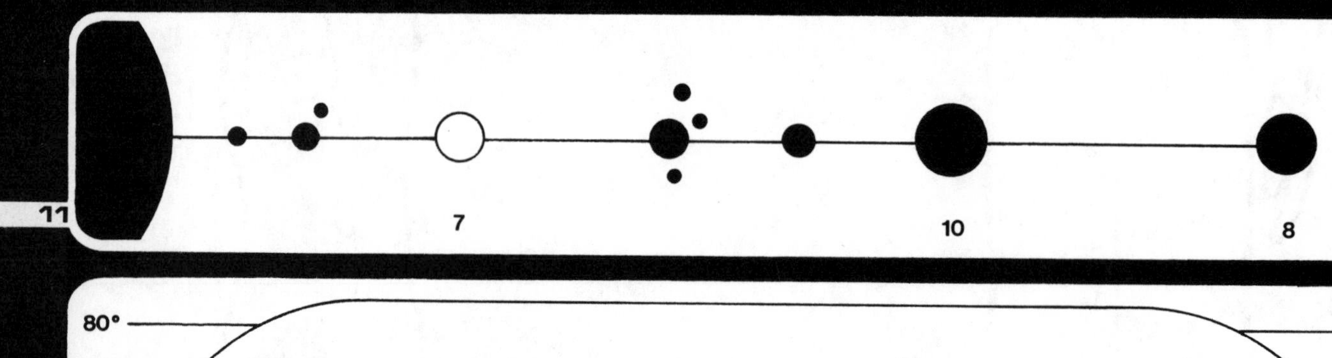

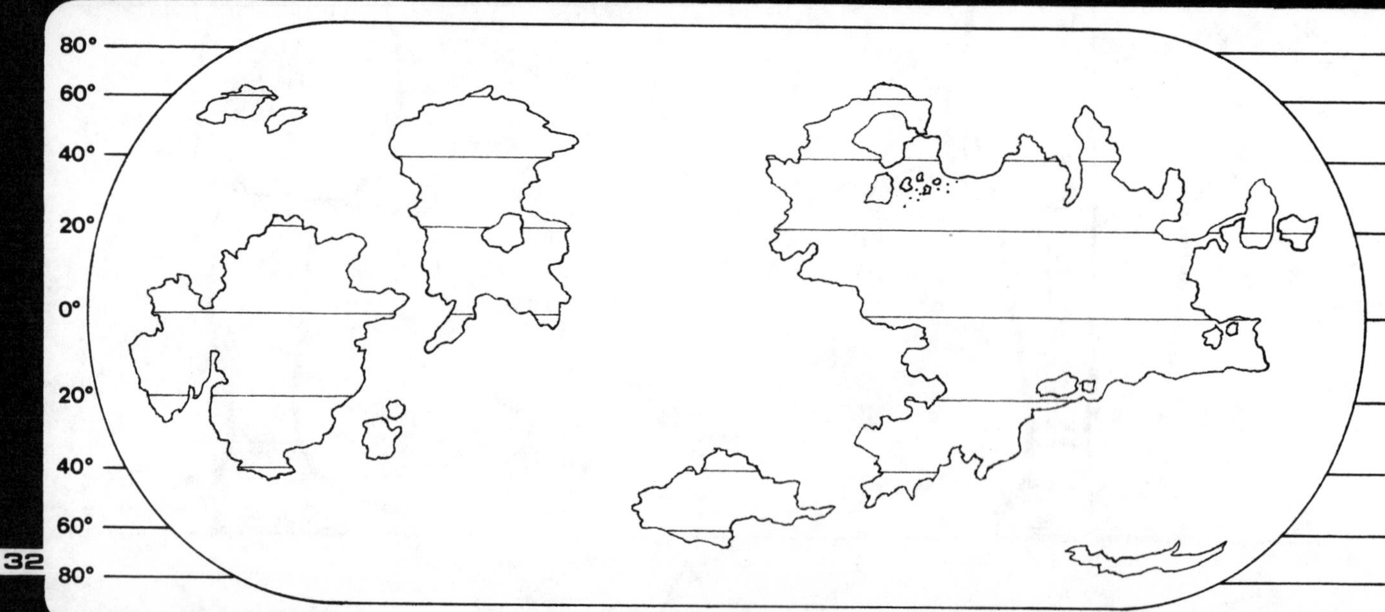

MEMORY ALPHA HISTORICAL ARCHIVE
DATABANK EXTRACT (HARDCOPY)

SUBJECT: TIBURONIAN

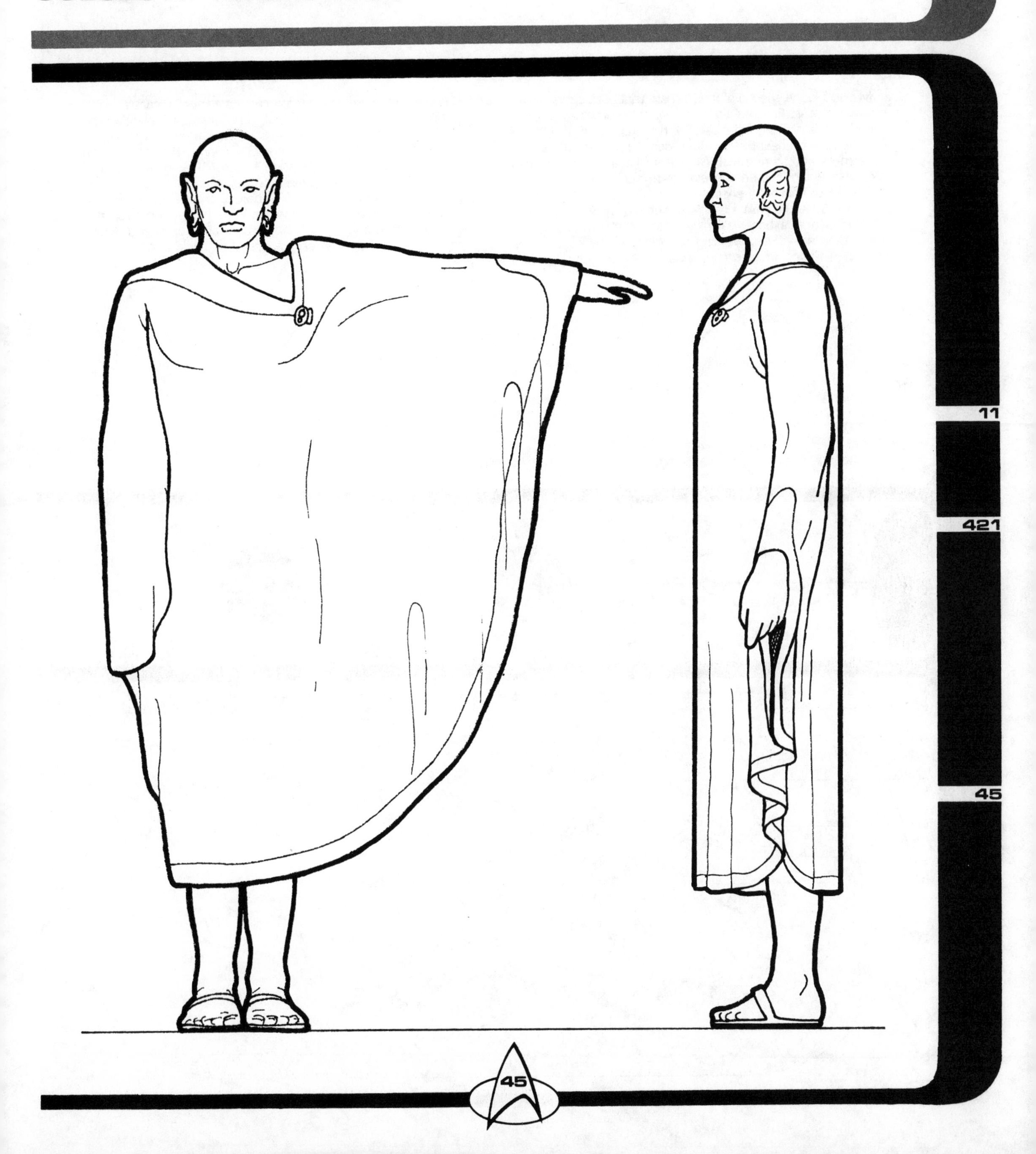

16

MERAK II (M)
NO INDIGENOUS NAME
MERAK

[11.2, 72.7, 17.1]

Merak II is the second of four planets that orbit a moderate-size white star. Established as an agricultural colony, little of the planet is actually inhabited, with a population of approximately four thousand. However, despite the small number of farmers and administrators, Merak II provides more than sixty percent of the seed grain, corn, and wheat flour consumed in its sector of space.

At one time the planet's entire crop was nearly wiped out by a mysterious botanical plague of undetermined origin. Federation scientists, working feverishly in the face of the total annihilation of all crops, isolated the plague organism and determined that properly refined zienite, a rare mineral antibacterial agent, could halt and possibly reverse the damage done. The Federation starship **Enterprise** was immediately rerouted to the planet Ardana, the only known source of zienite in Federation space. After a few days of negotiation, the **Enterprise** crew successfully delivered the necessary mineral to Merak II, halting the plague in time.

Merak II has one moon, named Watcher by the colonists. Planets three and four of the system are gas giants, which are separated by a widely dispersed asteroid belt.

59

376

80°
60°
40°
20°
0°
20°
40°
60°
80°

55

MEMORY ALPHA HISTORICAL ARCHIVE
DATABANK EXTRACT (HARDCOPY)

SUBJECT: MERAKAN

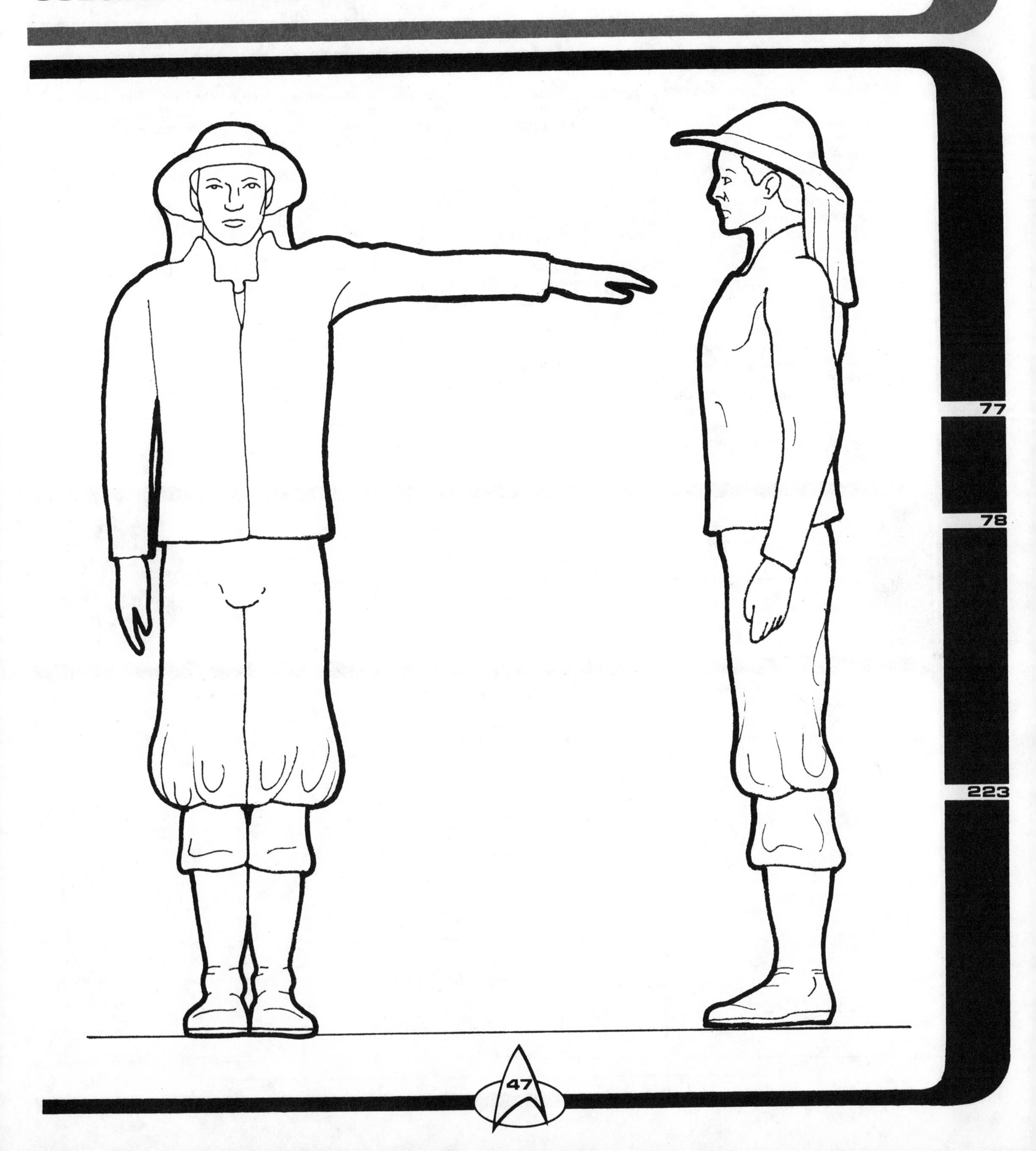

17

ALDEBARAN (M)
NO INDIGENOUS NAME
ALPHA TAURI
[10.6, 56.5, −15.1]

Aldebaran is the third planet of four in orbit around an orange giant in a binary star system. An early Federation colony, Aldebaran is a major Federation port world with extensive leave facilities.

The Alpha Tauri system also contains a red dwarf star, which orbits the orange primary at a distance of 97.5 billion kilometers. A vast trail of mineral and ice debris extends outward for millions of kilometers behind the red dwarf as it travels its circular path, somewhat like the tail of a comet, and the brightly reflective trail is a beautiful addition to the Aldebaran night sky.

The New Aberdeen Naval Yards, located on the eastern coast of Aldebaran's primary continent, is the sixth largest in the Federation and is a major producer of dreadnought and heavy cruiser-type vessels. The ship components, assembled at the ground-based facility, are ferried into orbit and fitted in a major orbital spacedock center.

A small humanoid population of approximately one million Aldebaran natives is centered around New Aberdeen, which also has a Starfleet supply center and several private shipyards. These industrial facilities provide employment for a majority of the Aldebarans.

The native animal life of Aldebaran is generally quite simple, consisting largely of invertebrate sea life. The Aldebaran shellmouth, a slow-moving mollusk that exists in great numbers in the saltwater shallows, is widely prized as a delicious menu item and is a staple of the many seashore restaurants on the planet.

33

ALPHA TAURI A

B

212

80°
60°
40°
20°
0°
20°
40°
60°
80°

22

MEMORY ALPHA HISTORICAL ARCHIVE
DATABANK EXTRACT (HARDCOPY)

SUBJECT: ALDEBARAN SHELLMOUTH

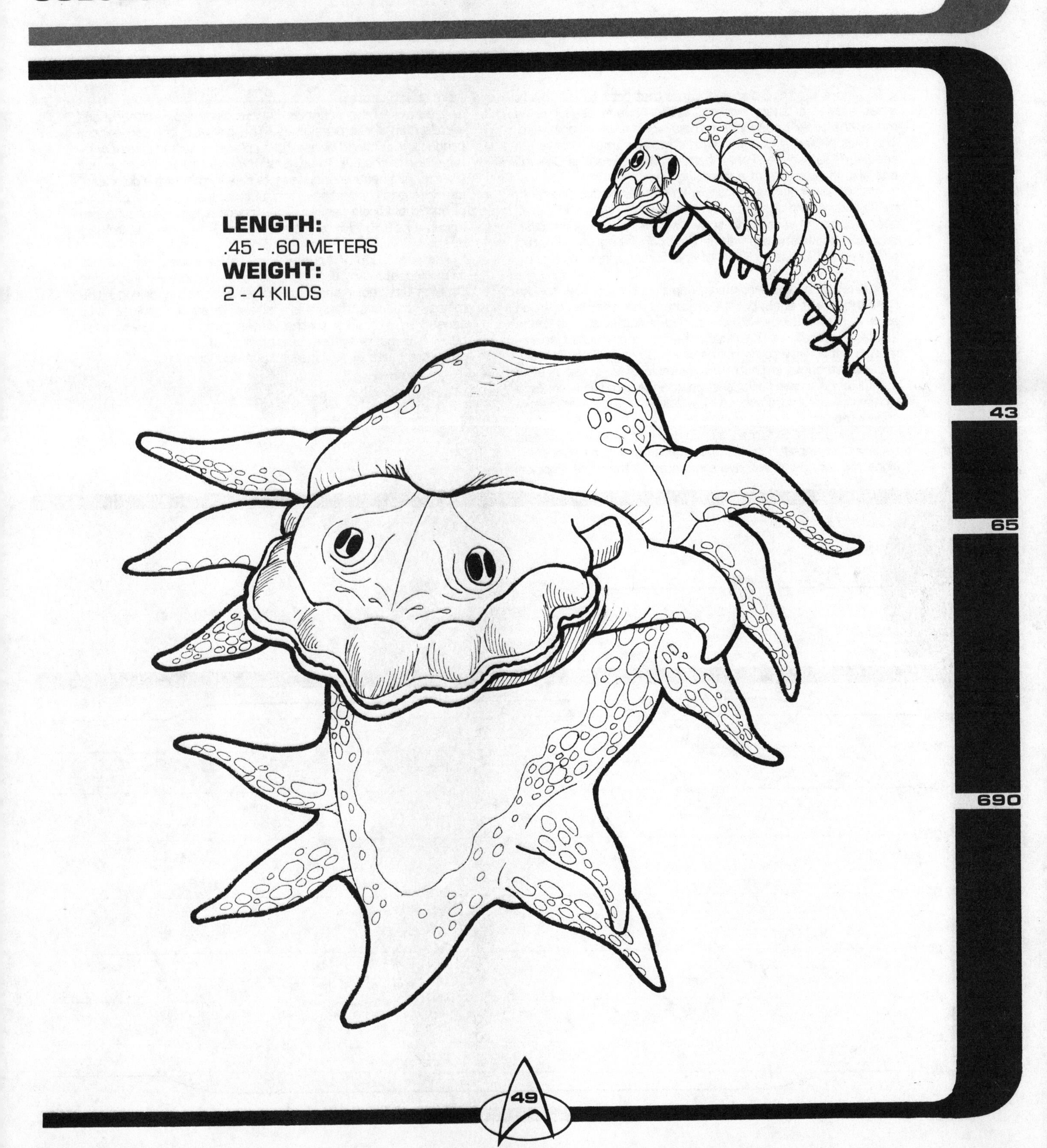

LENGTH:
.45 - .60 METERS
WEIGHT:
2 - 4 KILOS

MU LEONIS II (M)

ARDANA

MU LEONIS A

[8.5, 106.3, 9.8]

Ardana is the third planet of three that orbit Mu Leonis A, a red star in a binary system. While Ardana itself has no moon, the other two worlds in the system support one each. The first planet is Class C, with daytime temperatures exceeding 800 degrees Fahrenheit, and the second is Class D and also is incapable of supporting life.

Ardana's population, contrary to popular native tradition, most likely did not originate on the planet. Tests conducted over a period of years have shown a considerable genetic difference between the humanoid population and native primates, which carry DNA of a different amino acid complex.

The origin of the Ardanan people has been lost to the obscurity of the ages, but it is apparent that they brought an advanced technology with them. The ruling class has made its home literally in the clouds, having constructed an immense antigravity complex known as Stratos City. This airborne metropolis is the finest example of selected gravity manipulation known to Federation science, and the manner in which it accomplishes its levitation is not completely understood.

The citizens of Stratos City are devoted completely to the arts and sciences. Law-keeping forces are not necessary, since the city dwellers have eliminated all forms of violence from their culture.

Ardana is the only known source of zienite, a mineral ore with antibacterial properties. The planet's primary export product, it is mined beneath the planet's surface, usually by hand due to the ore's softness. Workers must wear proper filter masks because zienite in its raw form emits a colorless, odorless gas that attacks the judgment and control centers of humanoid brain tissues. This produces a state of extreme irritability, followed by confusion, insanity, and ultimately death.

The population of Ardana was, for centuries, divided into two classes. An upper class of intellectuals inhabiting Stratos City kept a secondary class of citizens working in the mines, unaware that their lack of mental prowess was caused by exposure to the zienite gas. At Federation request, this caste system was eliminated, and all citizens now enjoy the fruits of Ardana's export industry.

676

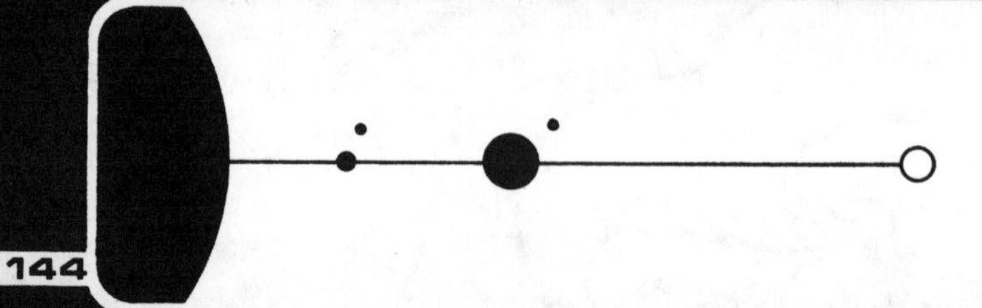

144

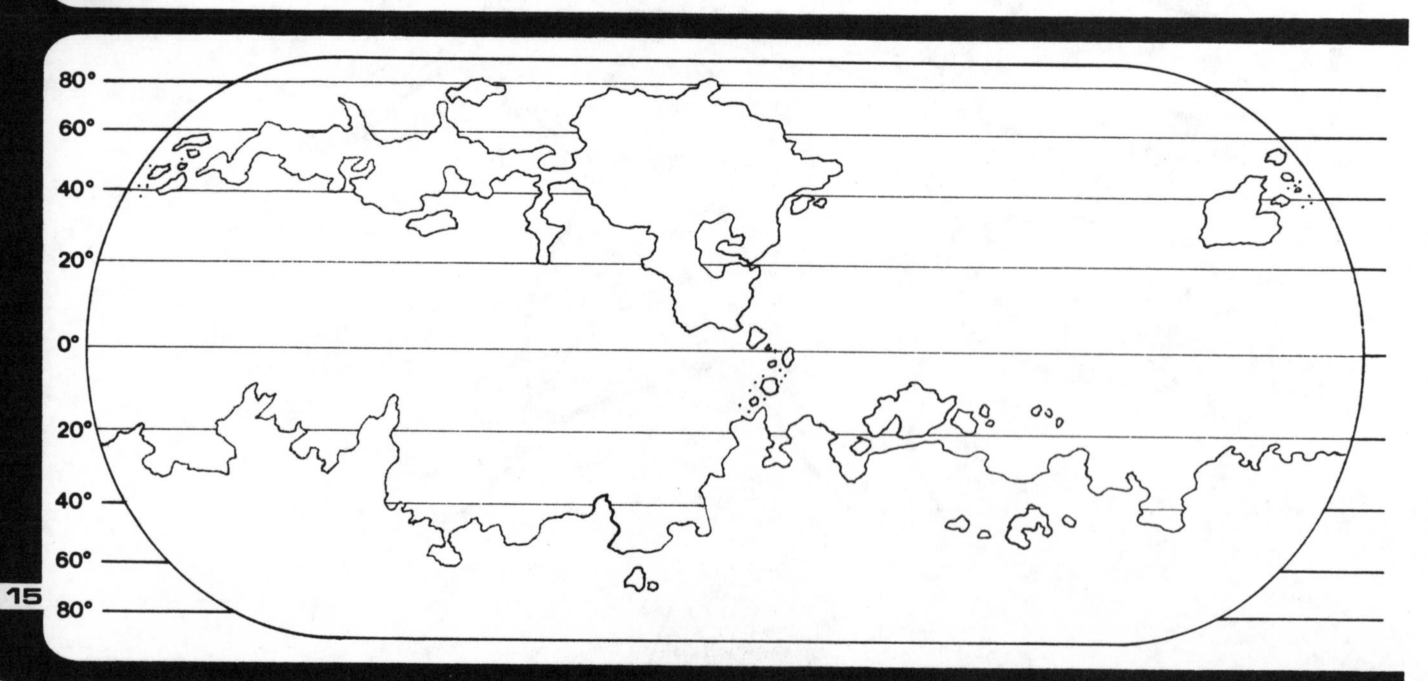

15

MEMORY ALPHA HISTORICAL ARCHIVE
DATABANK EXTRACT (HARDCOPY)

SUBJECT: ARDANAN

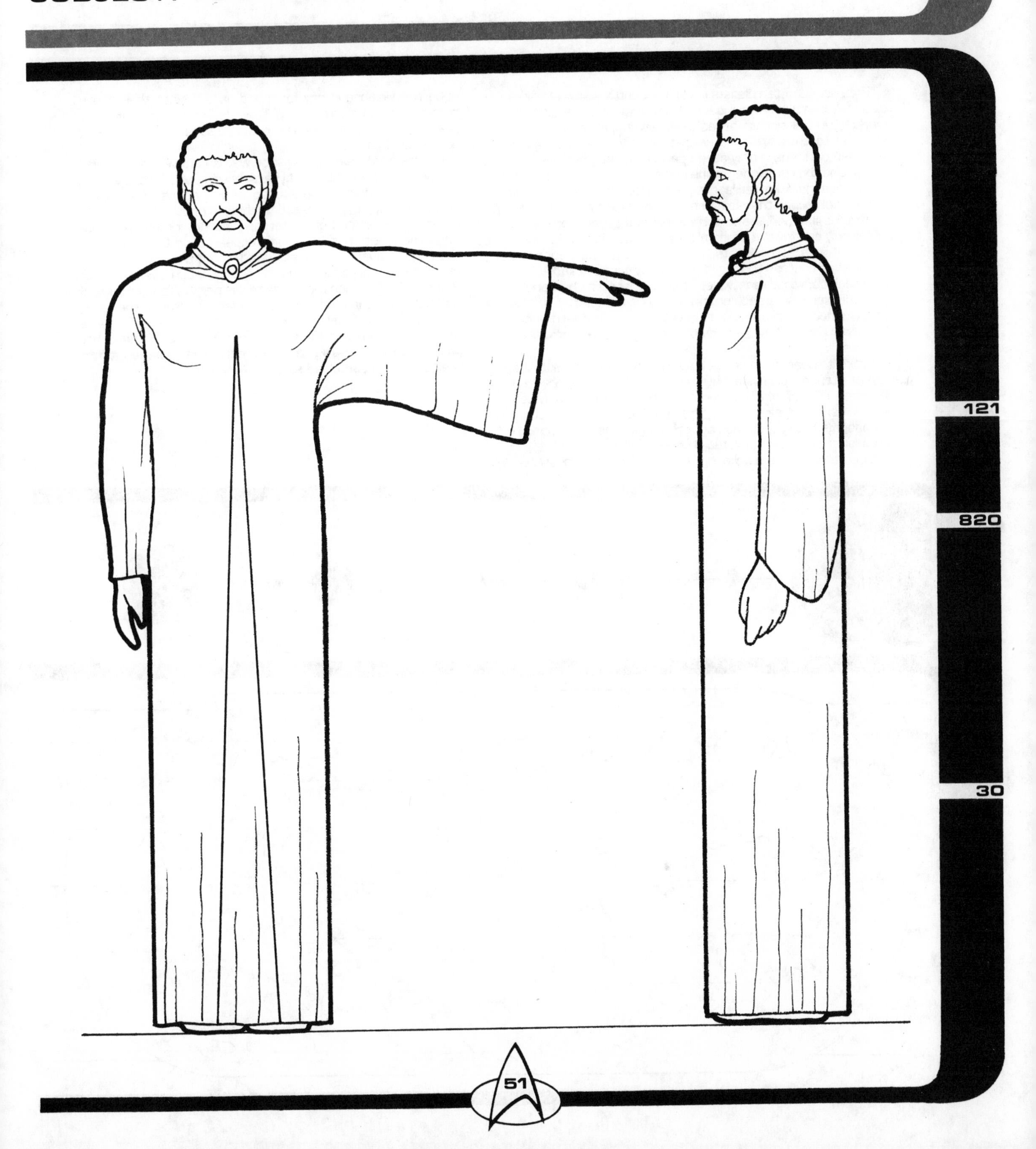

19

ARGELIUS II (M)

NELPHIA

ARGELIUS B

[−154.7, −59.2, −121.2]

The second of ten planets in orbit around a yellow star in a binary system, Argelius II is a textbook example of a Class M world. The balance of gases in its atmosphere is virtually identical to that of Terra, with strikingly similar seasonal weather patterns. Forty-seven percent of Argelius II is land mass, and the remainder of the planet's surface is divided into five oceans. Like Terra, the planet has one moon, but it is somewhat larger than Luna and has a limited atmosphere.

Argelius II is well known throughout the Federation for its hospitality and for the peaceful nature of its inhabitants. As a result, it is a favorite site for shore leave. Its hedonistic culture has spurred the creation of many vacation and entertainment centers planetwide. The Argelians are humanoid, and they are so peaceful and pleasure-loving that it has become necessary for the different planetary governments to import administrators and other ruling officials from other planets.

Unlike its peaceful present, however, Argelius II's past was one of intense worldwide military conflict that nearly resulted in the annihilation of all life fourteen hundred years ago. Much like Vulcans, Argelians struggled to adopt a new planetary philosophy, but rather than choosing logic, they developed a philosophical system devoted to pleasure.

Since their Great Awakening, the Argelians have absolutely abhorred violence in any form and have opened their doors to any and all who may wish to visit. Outworlders are embraced with open arms and are invited to take up permanent residence if they so desire.

One rather unwelcome visitor was an entity that traveled the galaxy for thousands of years, preying upon those worlds where fear could be generated in abundance. This being, known as Redjac, possessed the bodies of others in order to commit murder and other terror-inducing crimes. The non-corporeal entity had previously appeared on Earth as Jack the Ripper, a late nineteenth-century murderer whose acts of brutality terrorized the city of London, England for months. Redjac then moved on to the planet Alpha Proxima II and performed in much the same way. Eventually, the being made its way to Rigel IV, where the natives gave it the name of Beratis. Following its attack upon Argelius II, the entity was destroyed by a Federation vessel that beamed it into space in a disassembled state.

18

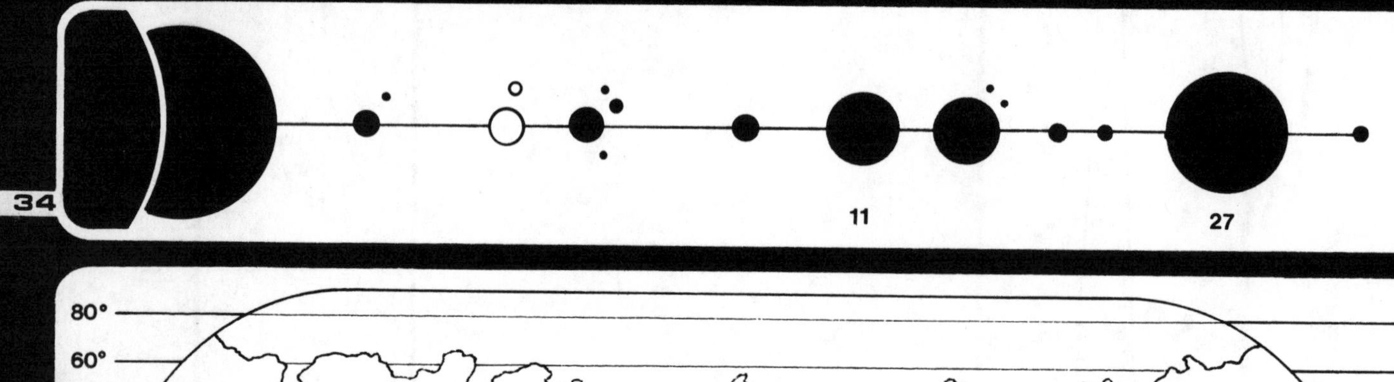

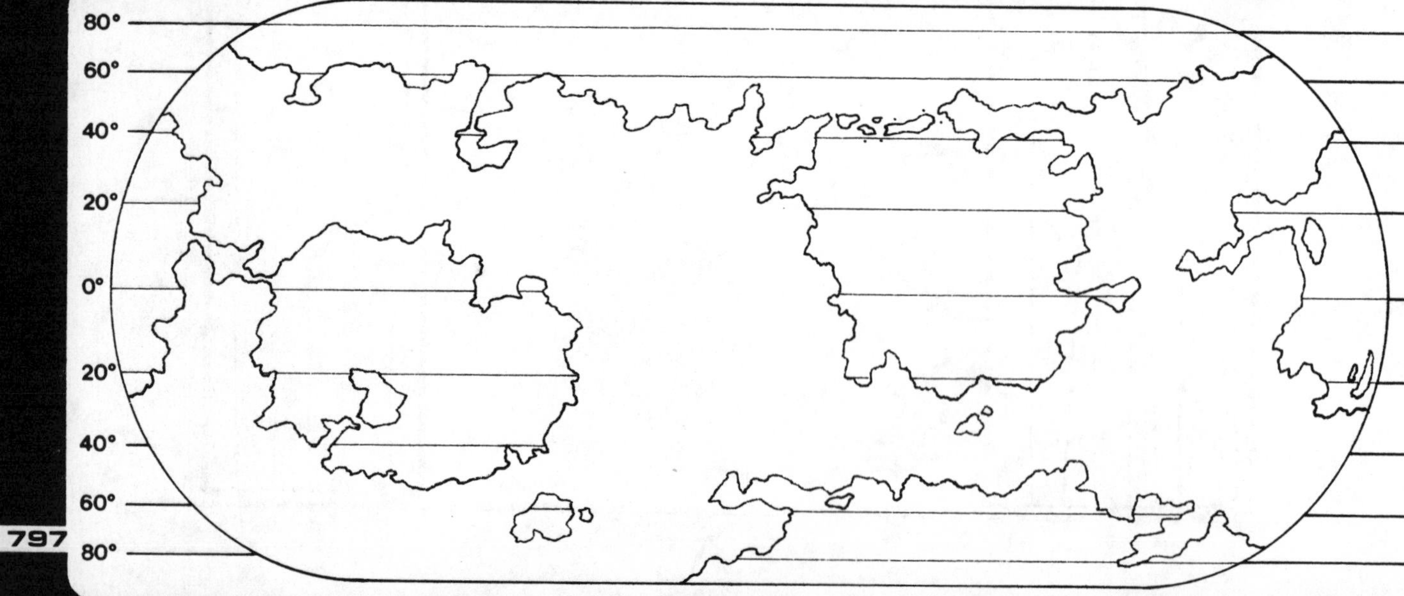

MEMORY ALPHA HISTORICAL ARCHIVE
DATABANK EXTRACT (HARDCOPY)

SUBJECT: ARGELIAN

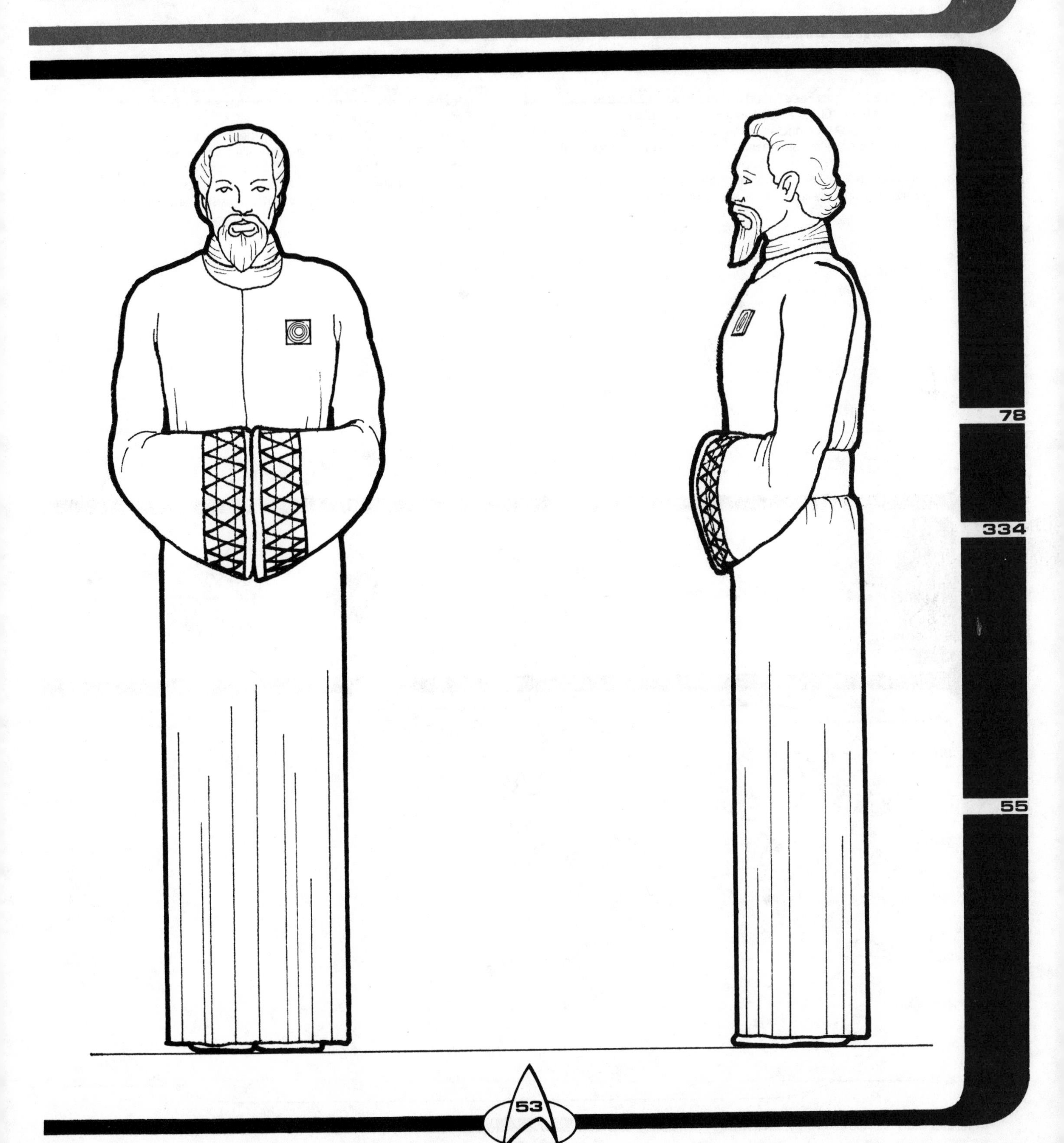

DARAN V (M)

NO INDIGENOUS NAME

DARAN

[−127.5, −139.2, −19.7]

Daran V is a Federation member world with a population of 3.7 billion. Originally an early Earth colony, Daran has a sizable Deltan population as well. More recently, Tellarite settlers have made Daran the site of a large industrial complex.

Daran V is the fifth of ten planets that orbit a moderate-size orange star. None of the other worlds in the system is capable of supporting life, although planet six has an orbiting Federation spaceport.

Daran was threatened with destruction when it was discovered that an asteroid ship called **Yonada** was on a collision course with the world. While the artificial world was still 396 days away, a method was found to redirect its course and spare the populations of both **Yonada** and Daran V.

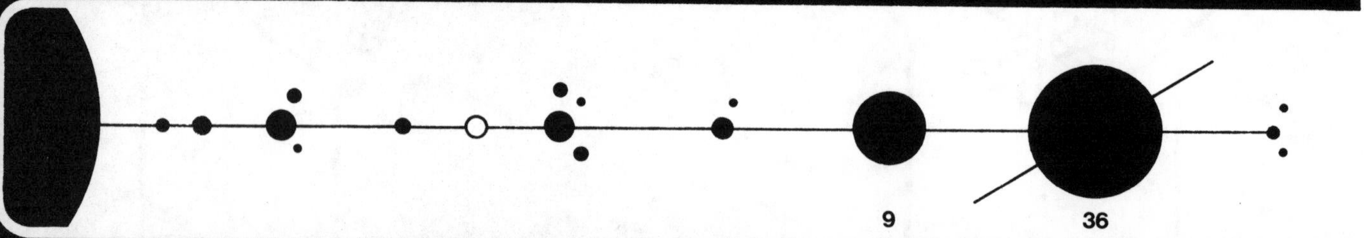

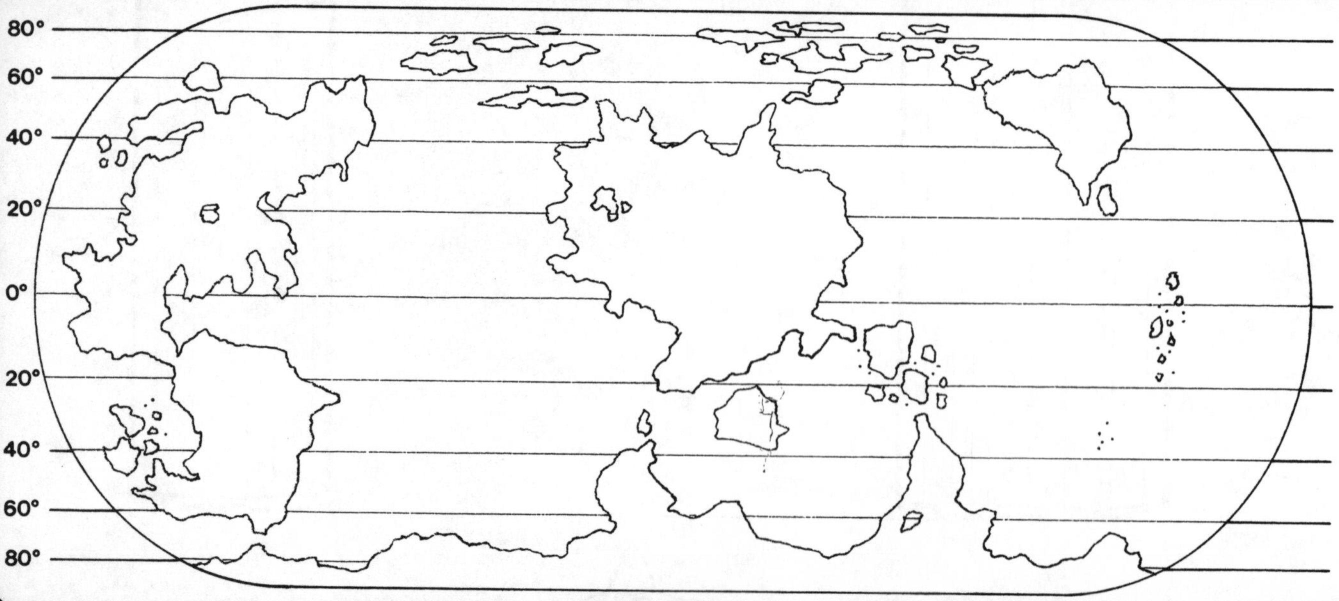

MEMORY ALPHA HISTORICAL ARCHIVE
DATABANK EXTRACT (HARDCOPY)

SUBJECT: STARMAP — PATH OF YONADA

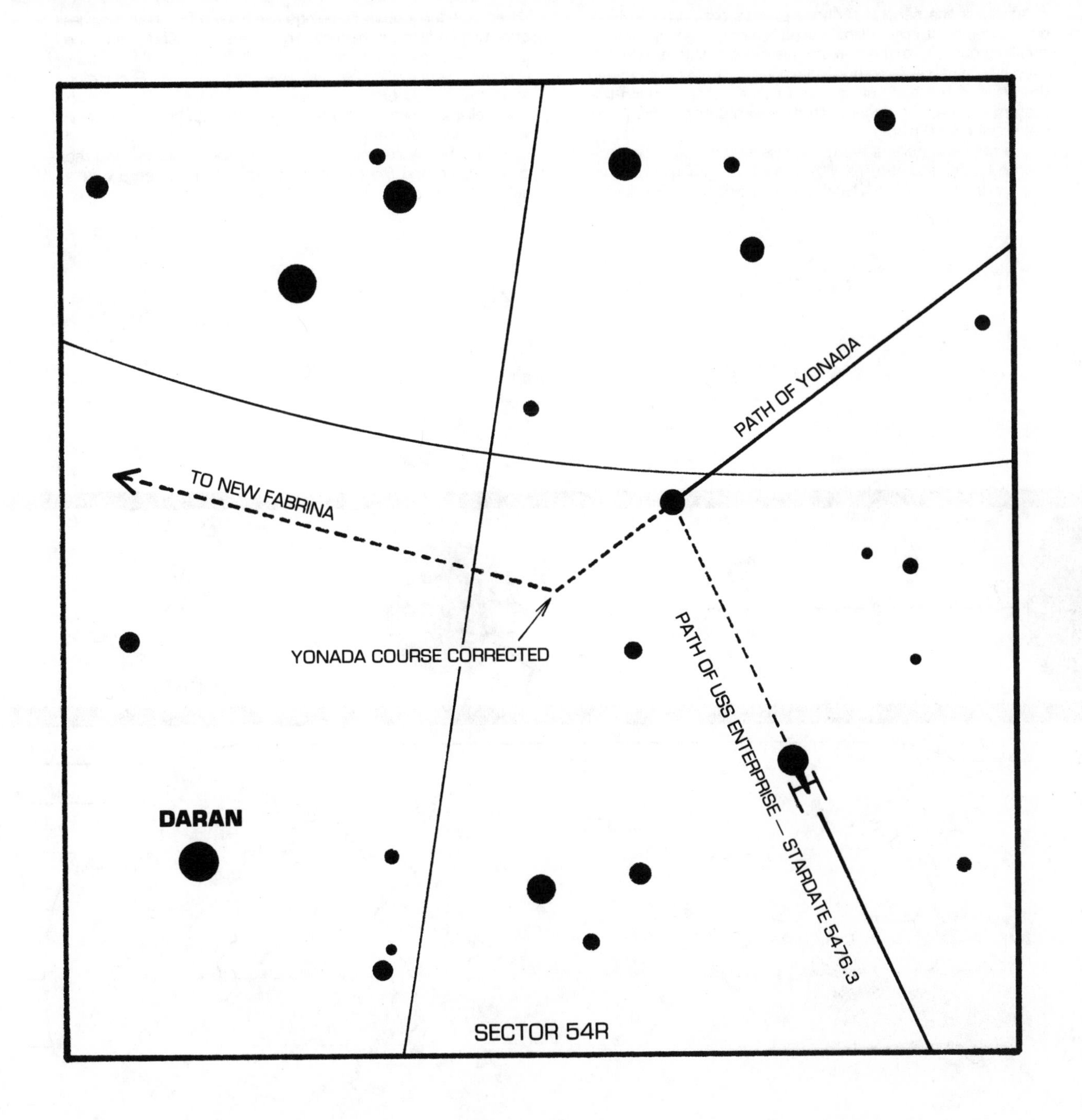

19

886

260

AURELIA (L)

MERIABII

XI HERCULIS

[176.7, 44.5, −63.3]

Aurelia is the second of three planets that orbit XI Herculis, a red giant star. Planet three is a ringed gas giant with twelve moons, two of which provide most of the mineral ore used by the native Aurelians. A vast asteroid belt lies beyond the orbit of the third planet. The belt revolves around the system's sun at an angle of thirty-seven degrees from the planetary orbital plane.

The native Aurelians live on the second planet. They are graceful, birdlike creatures with an adult wingspan of approximately three meters. Roughly humanoid in configuration, these bipedal, intelligent beings are known for their fascination with Federation history. They have amassed one of the largest and most comprehensive libraries of UFP history anywhere, providing a valuable record for Federation scholars.

Aurelians make their homes in the high peaks of their world's mountain ranges, constructing deep, interconnected caverns. The Aurelians are excellent stonecrafters, and the polished, flowing lines of their deep-rock architecture is a delight to visitors.

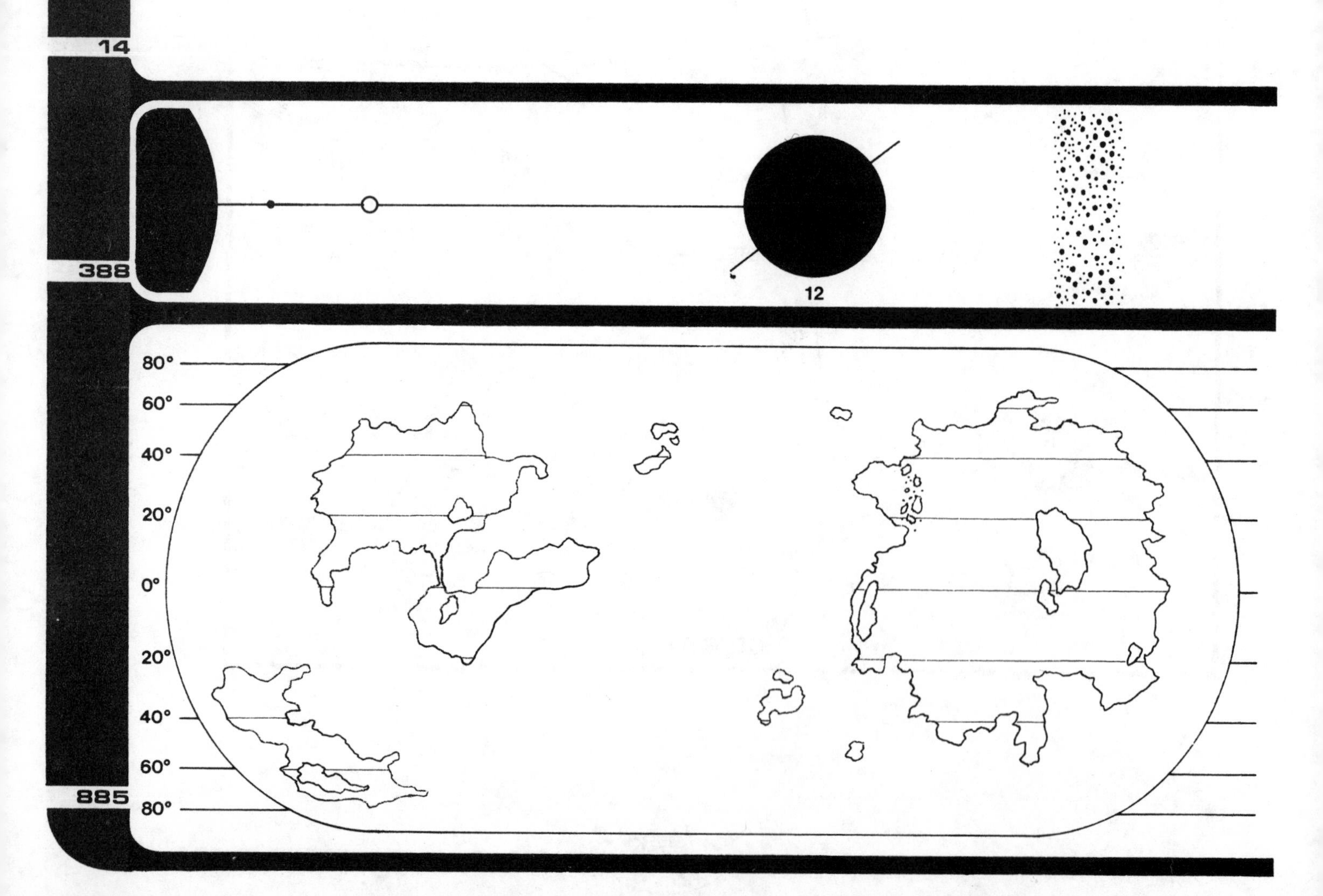

MEMORY ALPHA HISTORICAL ARCHIVE
DATABANK EXTRACT (HARDCOPY)

SUBJECT: AURELIAN

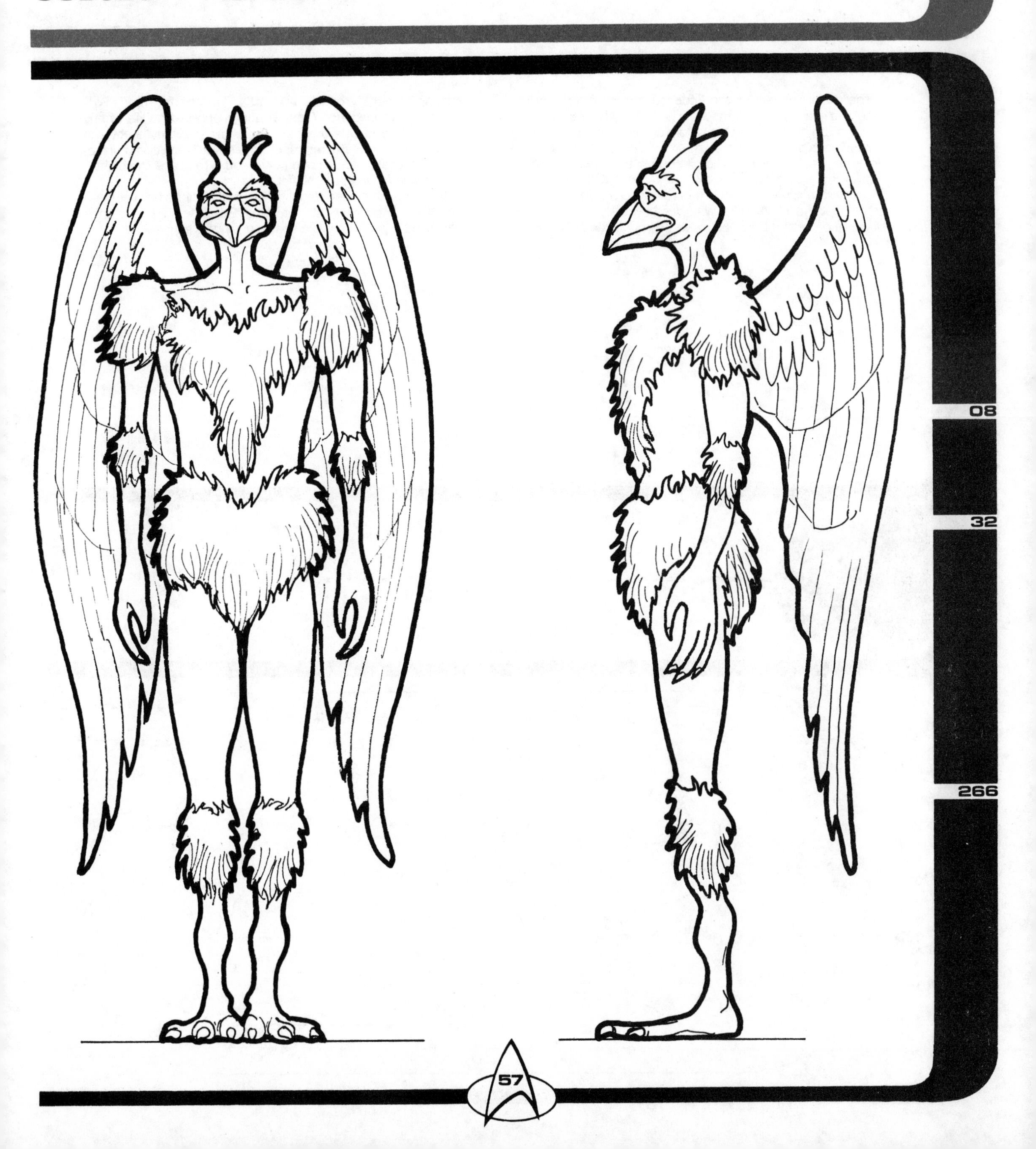

MANTILLES (M)
NO INDIGENOUS NAME
PALLAS XIV
[245.5, 188.3, –56.1]

The most remote of the Federation's inhabited worlds, Mantilles is one of two planets in the Pallas XIV star system. The system consists of twin yellow dwarf stars that revolve around each other. The system's two planets, Mantilles and Bezaride, revolve around the binaries in an elliptical orbit.

It is important to note that, until recently, there was another planet named Alondra in the system. The system's outermost world, Alondra was destroyed by an immense, cloudlike organism that had moved through the galaxy, consuming planetary bodies and other matter for food. Fortunately, Alondra was Class J and supported no life of any kind. The cloud was stopped just short of Mantilles by the crew of the USS **Enterprise**, who established communication with the organism and convinced it to spare the eighty-two million lives on the planet.

Bezaride, the inner planet, is Class K but has not yet been colonized. Marslike in atmosphere, Bezaride may have once harbored a native culture that has since disappeared.

205

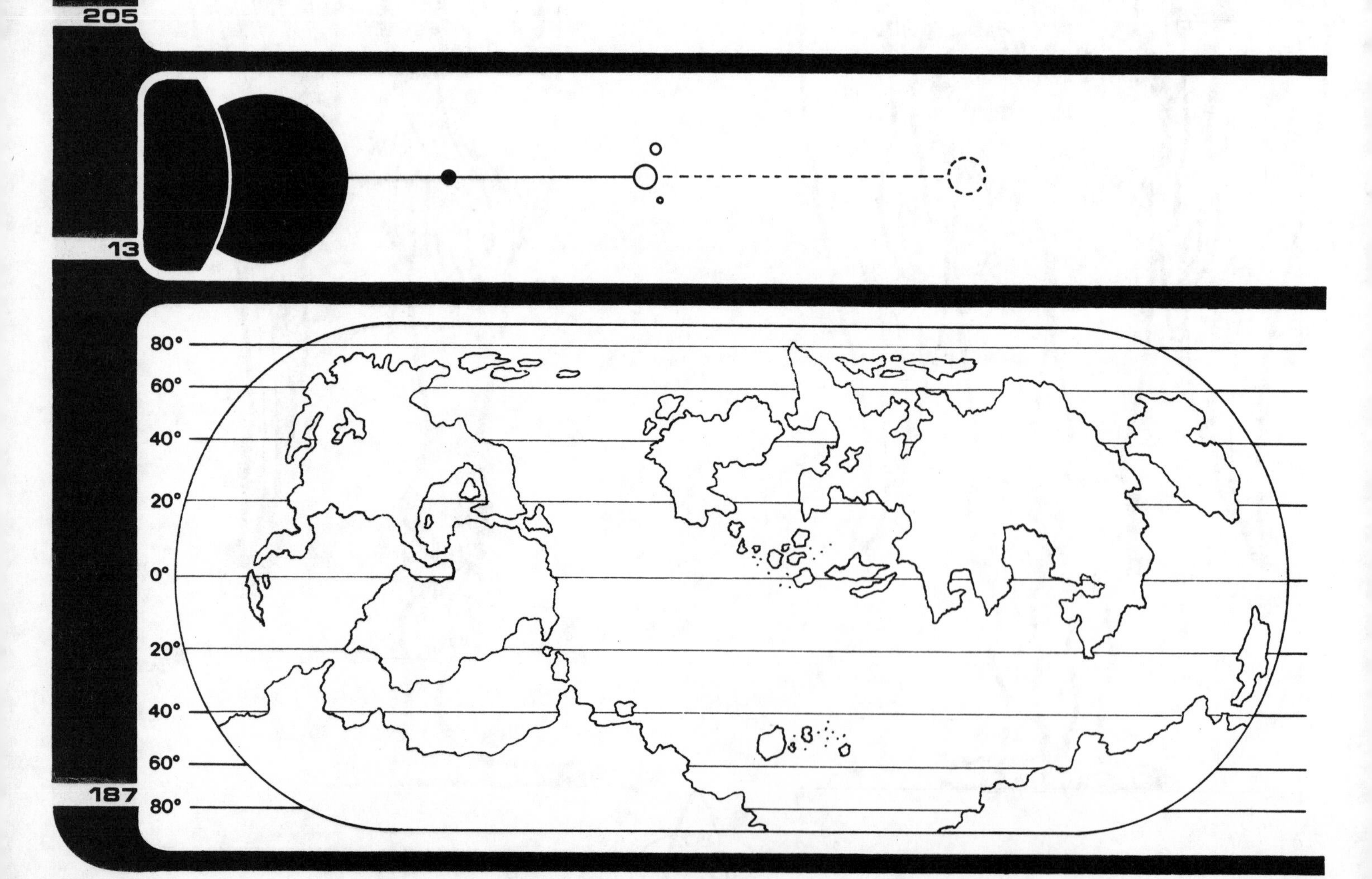

MEMORY ALPHA HISTORICAL ARCHIVE
DATABANK EXTRACT (HARDCOPY)

SUBJECT: STARMAP — PATH OF CLOUD ORGANISM

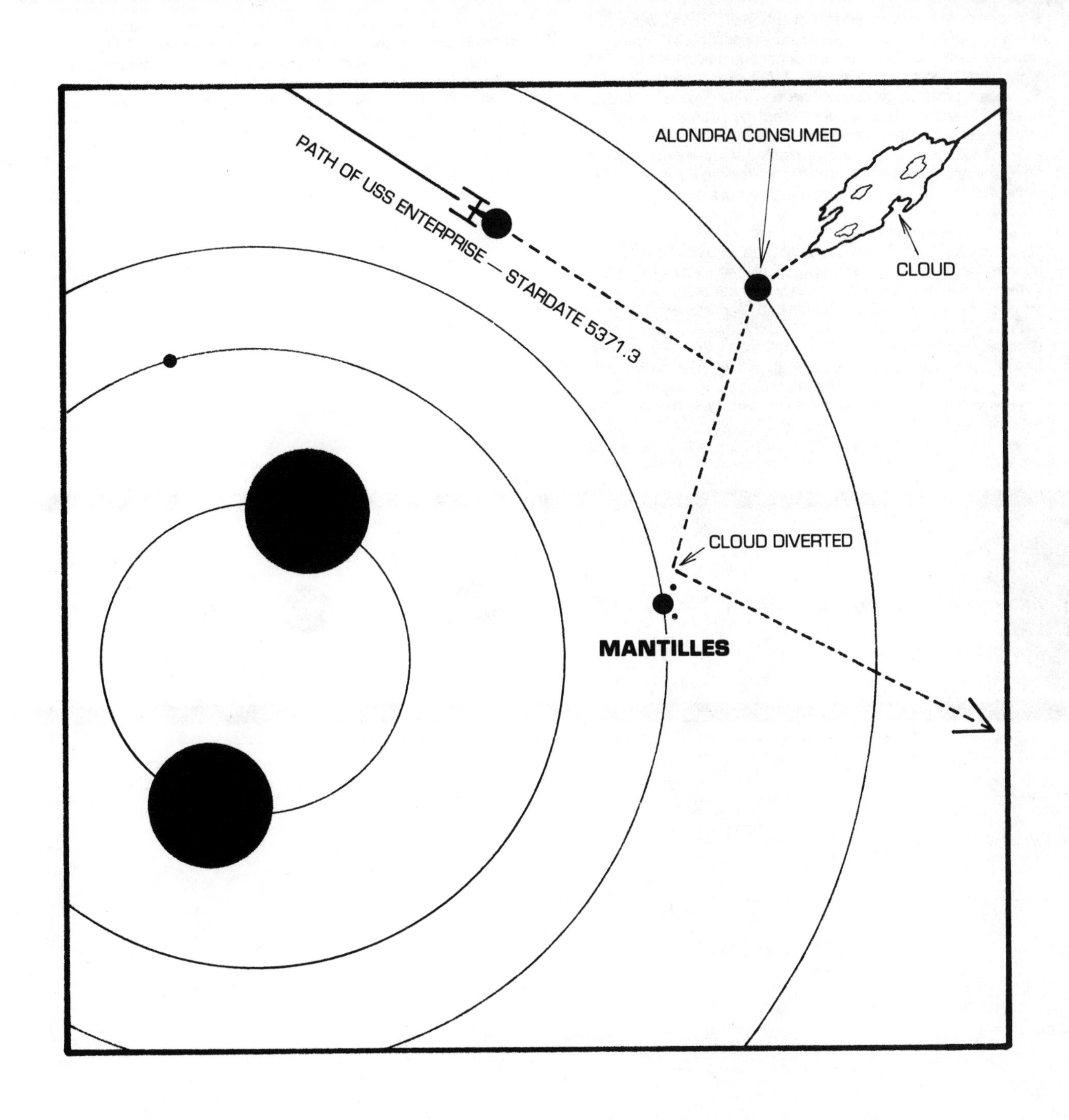

32

54

776

23

MEDUSA (C)
VISALAYAN
XI HYDRAE
[27.2, 137.6, −41.3]

A binary system composed of a brilliant white star and a yellow dwarf companion, Medusa supports eight planets, none of which is capable of supporting carbon-based life. Only the fourth is inhabited, by a noncorporeal race. Surveyed only by unmanned probes, Medusa is a typical Class C world, heavily blanketed by dense clouds of superheated carbon dioxide.

The Medusans are a race of highly intelligent, nonphysical beings that are electromagnetic in composition. Contact between the Medusans and the Federation has been extremely limited.

The native Medusans have demonstrated vastly advanced scientific abilities and possess telepathic capabilities far more advanced than those of any other Federation member race. When necessary, Medusans can travel aboard UFP vessels by remaining within highly specialized electromagnetic containers. However, there is a risk involved in such close contact with humanoid races; while their thoughts are sublime in nature, the Medusans' physical appearance is so hideous that a humanoid viewer will be immediately rendered insane. Special eye shields can filter out the damaging frequencies, lessening the risk to those nearby.

Medusans have developed interstellar navigation into a fine art and are extraordinary starship navigators. Their talent is the result of their radically different sensory system. One theory holds that they are able to electromagnetically identify and lock onto thousands of guide stars simultaneously, including those beyond deep sensor range.

These life forms have a distinct sense of beauty and have delighted in the many forms of art available to them since their entry into the Federation.

110

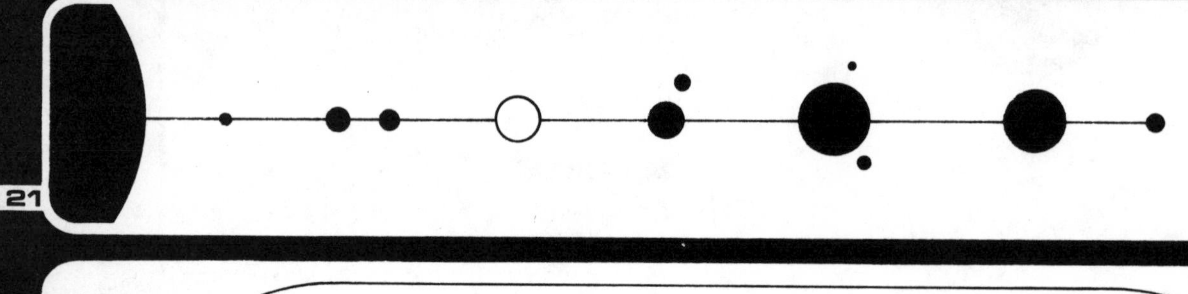

21

96

MEMORY ALPHA HISTORICAL ARCHIVE
DATABANK EXTRACT (HARDCOPY)

SUBJECT: MEDUSAN ELECTROMAGNETIC CONTAINER

HEIGHT:
.78 METERS
COMPOSITION:
OUTER SHELL — TRITITANIUM ALLOY

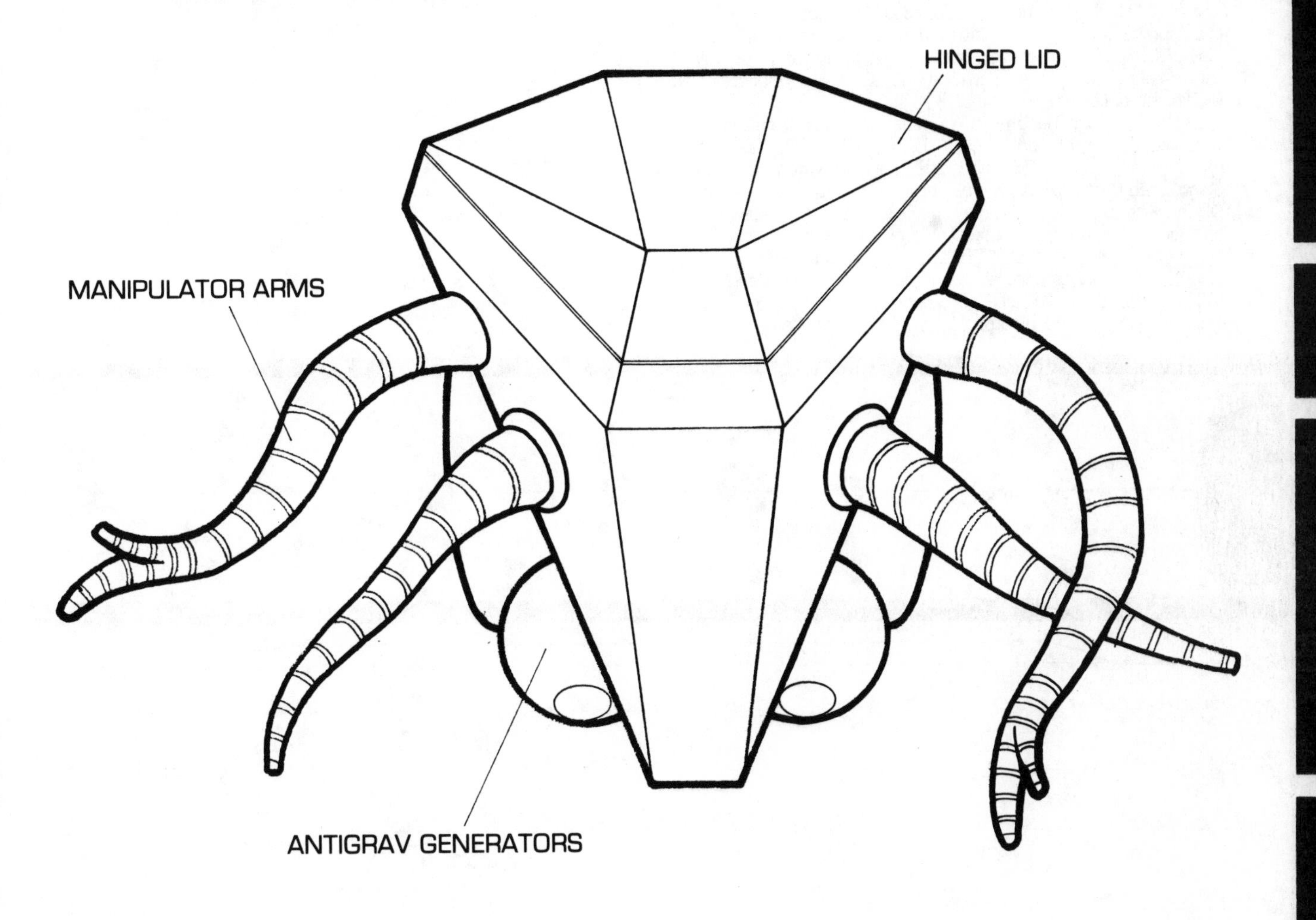

CORIDAN III (M)

DESOTRIANA

CORIDAN

[29.7, 64.3, 29.9]

The Coridan system has a total of four inhabited worlds, more than any other Federation system with the exceptions of Rigel and Terra. While Coridan III is the primary population center, the entire system is a single entity, unified under one ruling government. The star, Coridan, itself is a red dwarf that supports ten planets. Asteroid belts lie in the spans between the second and third and the eighth and ninth worlds. The outer belt is rich in many rare mineral ores.

Following their development of interplanetary flight, the natives of Coridan III moved outward and formed colonies on the fourth, seventh, and ninth planets. The humanoid Coridans have spread themselves rather thinly, inviting raids by other races who often establish illegal mining operations within the outer asteroid belt.

Before Coridan became a member of the Federation, it was the center of controversy during a Babel Conference many years ago. The difficulties arose when it was discovered that Coridan IX was very rich in dilithium crystals. Mining was secretly initiated by the Orions and the Tellarites, sparking an initiative to take the Coridan system into the Federation fold so that UFP authority could protect the planet's rights to its mineral resources. Ambassador Sarek of Vulcan led the vote for UFP admission and was followed by a vast majority of the electoral body. Orion and Tellar voted against the admission in a vain effort to protect their clandestine interests in the system.

87

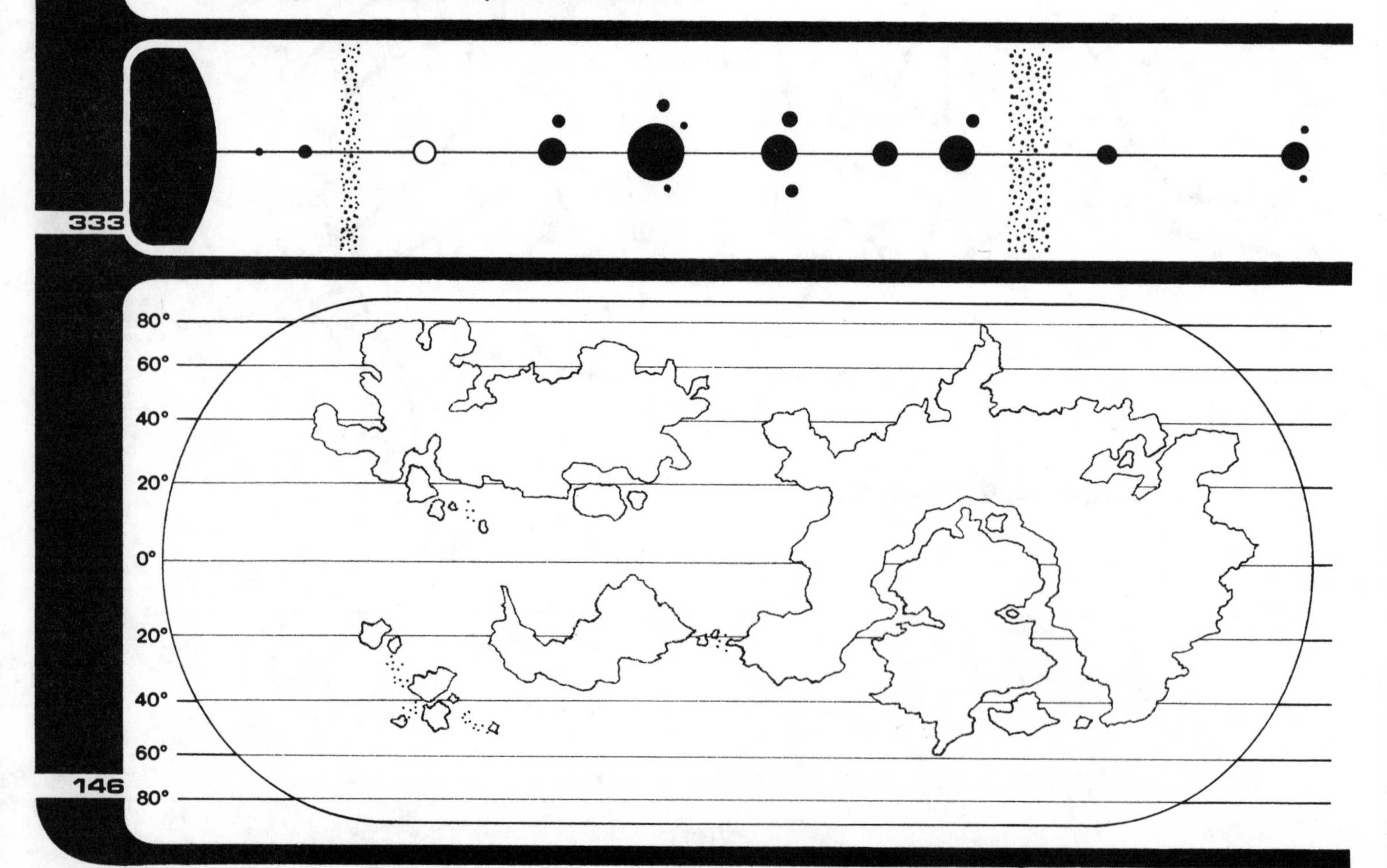

MEMORY ALPHA HISTORICAL ARCHIVE
DATABANK EXTRACT (HARDCOPY)

SUBJECT: CORIDAN

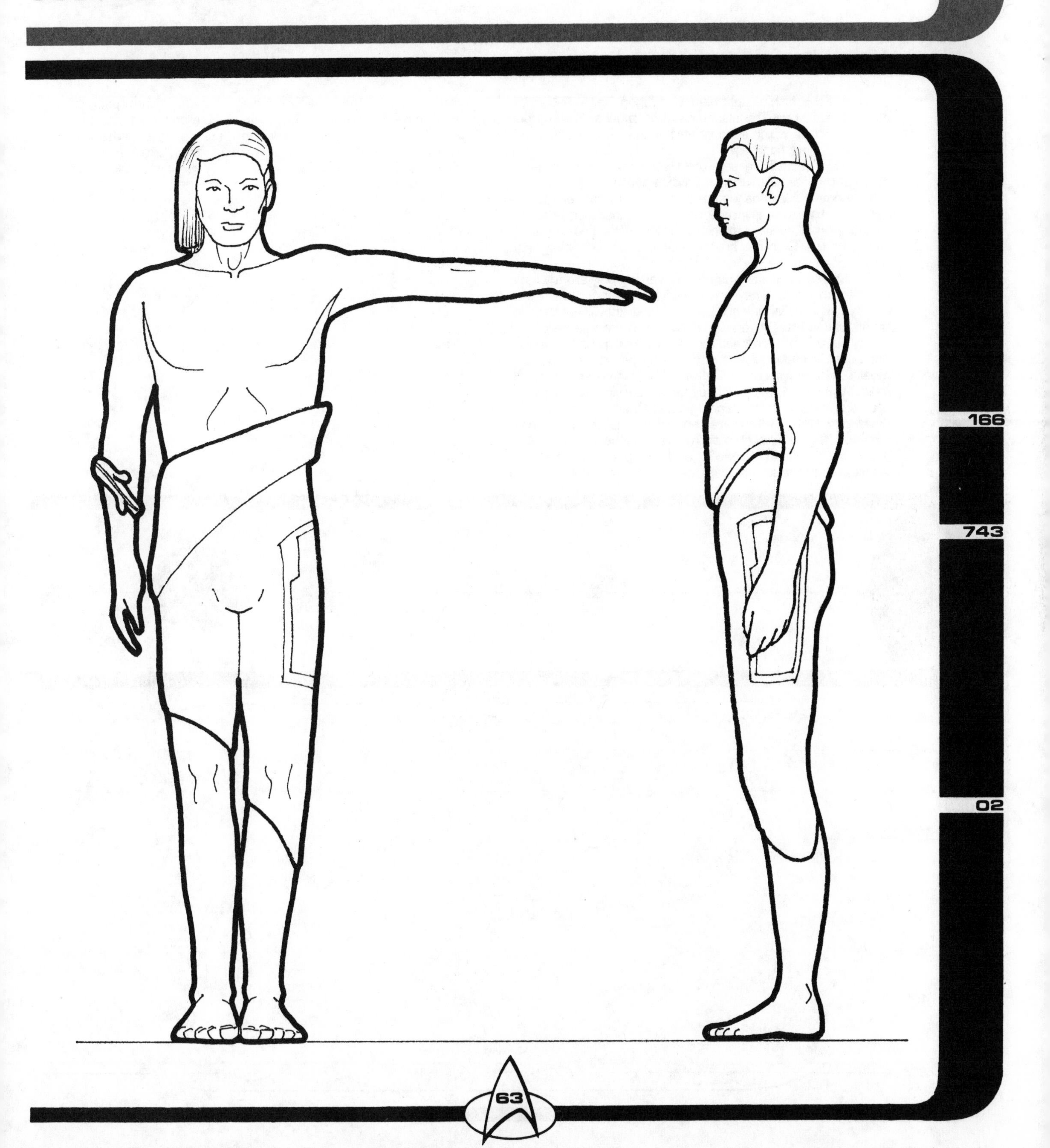

DELTA (M)

SEYALIA

DELTA TRICIATU

[187.3, 89.9, −17.3]

Delta is the fifth of eight planets orbiting Delta Triciatu, a white dwarf star. The planet has two moons, Seyann and Cinera, both of which support large underground cities with Federation port facilities.

Delta is a beautiful, green world with vast forests covering much of the planet's surface. Environmental conservation of the abundant flora has long been of primary concern to the native population. It is interesting to note that Delta has the lowest animal species extinction rate in the Federation, a result of the Deltans' artistic blending of technology and nature.

The Deltan people are humanoid, varying only slightly from the Terran norm. They are hairless, except for eyebrows and eyelashes. Deltans are perhaps best known for their intense sexual attractiveness. Both sexes emit some of the most potent pheromones known to Federation science. These natural aphrodisiacs affect all humanoid races but are most effective with other Deltans. For this reason, Deltans must swear an oath of celibacy before serving at any facility that employs other humanoid races. Chemical applications developed by the Deltans are capable of diminishing the pheromonal effect, and such treatments have been made mandatory within confined spaces, such as aboard a starship.

Deltans are also naturally empathic, allowing them to deliver medical aid by absorbing and minimizing pain in humanoid life forms. They make excellent doctors and nurses and can provide a form of "mind-meld anesthesia" during emergency surgical procedures. Like Vulcans, Deltans are talented telepaths and can easily sense the emotions of others.

34

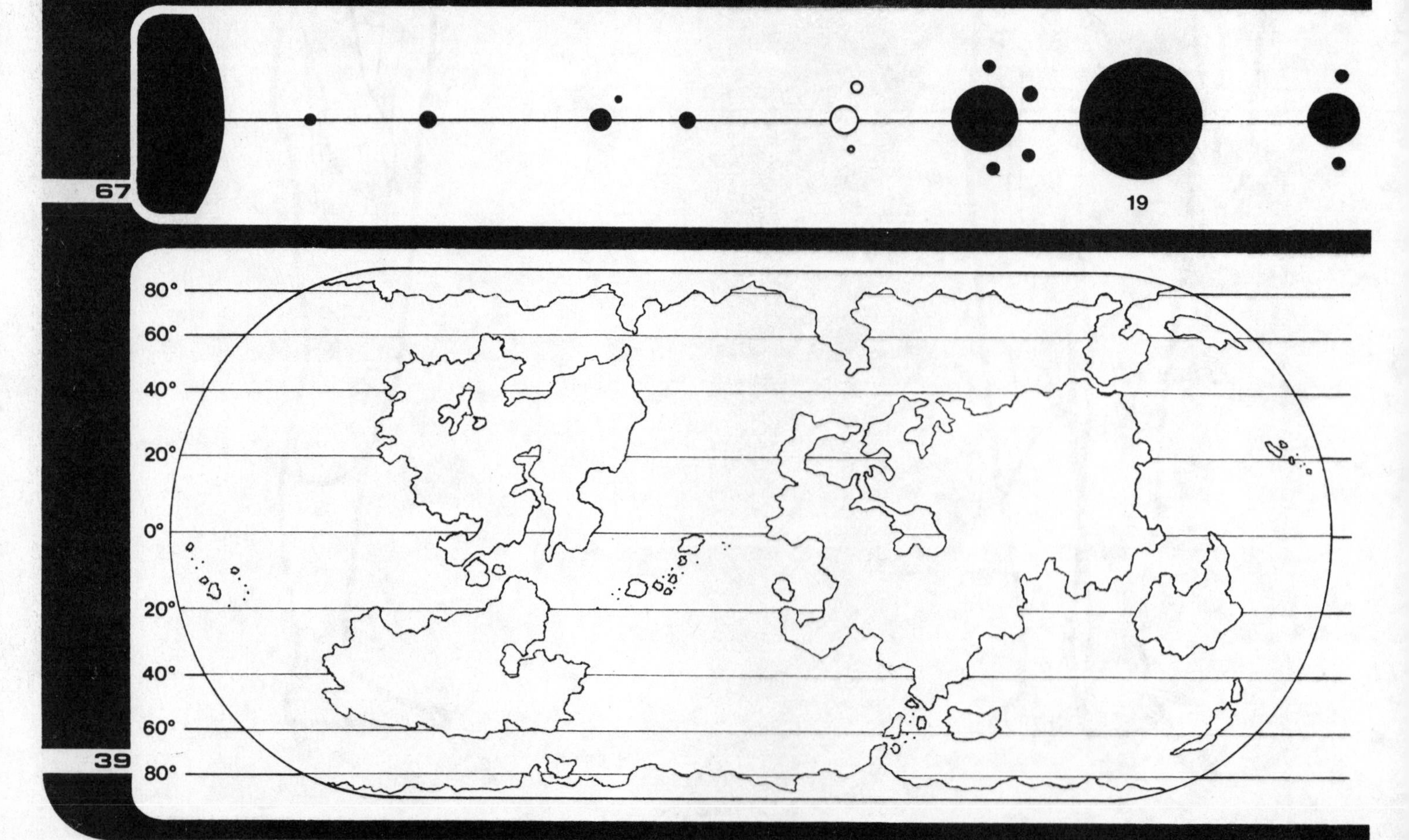

SUBJECT: DELTAN

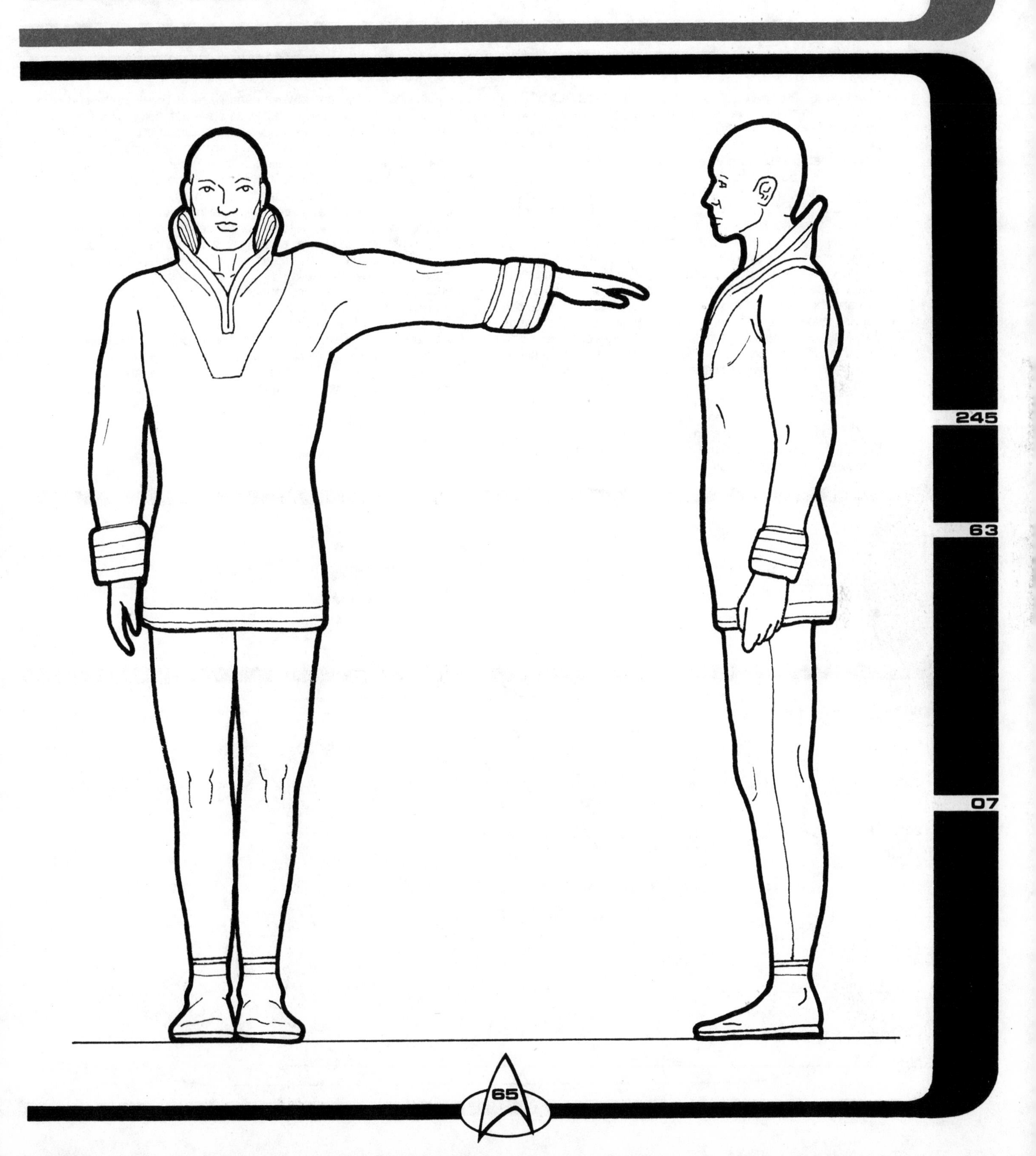

26

SAURIA (L)
LYAKSTI'KTON
UFC 512
[−166.3, −43.3, 62.1]

Sauria is the fourth planet of nine orbiting UFC 512, a white star in an outer sector of Federation space. A world of moderate climate, Sauria's surface is evenly divided between land mass and open sea. There are no continents, only major islands that create a network of habitable terrain.

The native Saurian race is reptilian and bipedal. Humanoid in shape, they have ruddy skin and large, yellowish eyes. Their four hearts give them great strength and endurance.

When first contacted by a Federation diplomatic envoy, the Saurians possessed the technology necessary for interstellar travel. However, they showed no interest in moving out among the stars, assuming that life did not exist there. Instead, all of their creative energies were channeled into art and music. Religion was a concept totally alien to the Saurian race, and they were so intrigued by theology that they insisted a chaplain be included in all negotiation sessions with the UFP. The Saurian name for the Terran race became "Kyrrstn'Kwynn," which translates as "those created in the image of God."

The Saurians have an intricate, almost musical native language that is sung and cannot be spoken by most humanoids due to differences in laryngeal structure. However, Saurians have no trouble pronouncing phonetic languages, such as English.

Saurian names are always comprised of three parts and translate into written English with some difficulty. The first two components, the birthname and the clan name, closely resemble the first and surnames common on Terra; the last name is a historical reference that changes continually throughout each Saurian's lifetime. It reflects such things as date of birth, gender, personal achievements, marital status, occupation, and even personal interests. As a result, Saurian last names are often more than fifty letters long and for common usage are abbreviated into three representative letters, divided by apostrophes. Saurians often modify their names when dealing with other races, giving them a phonetic structure pronounceable by humanoids. The Saurians' name for their world, "Lyaksti'kton," most closely translates as "supporter of precious life."

Sauria is also well known as the producer of Saurian brandy, a delicious alcoholic beverage that enjoys a wide reputation as one of the best drinks in known space. The Saurians themselves are immune to its highly intoxicating effects.

056

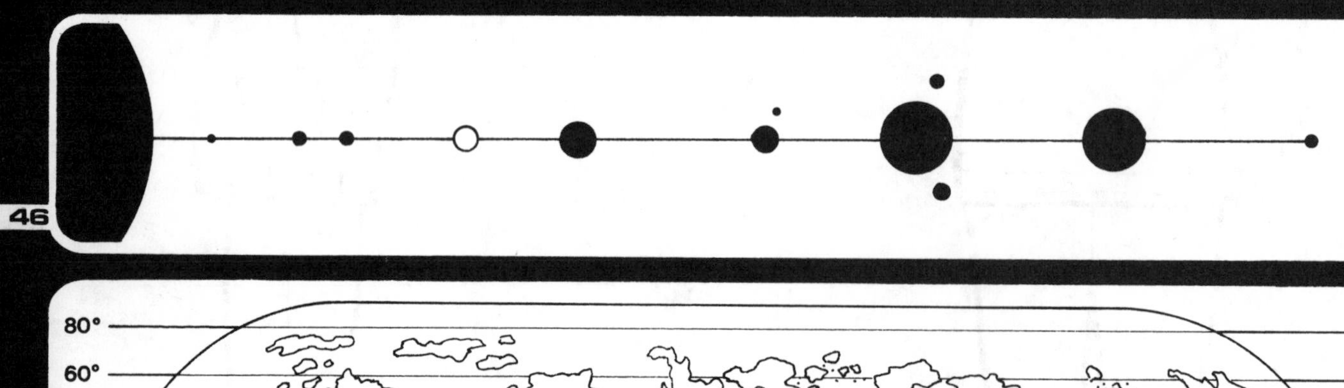

46

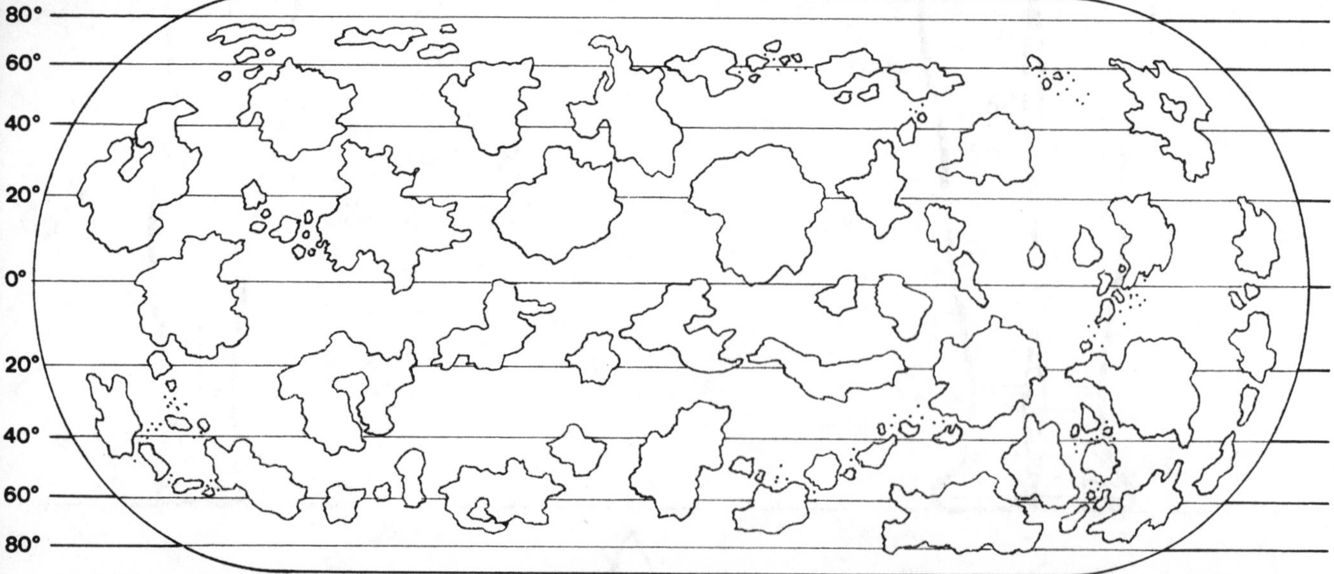

218

MEMORY ALPHA HISTORICAL ARCHIVE
DATABANK EXTRACT (HARDCOPY)

SUBJECT: SAURIAN

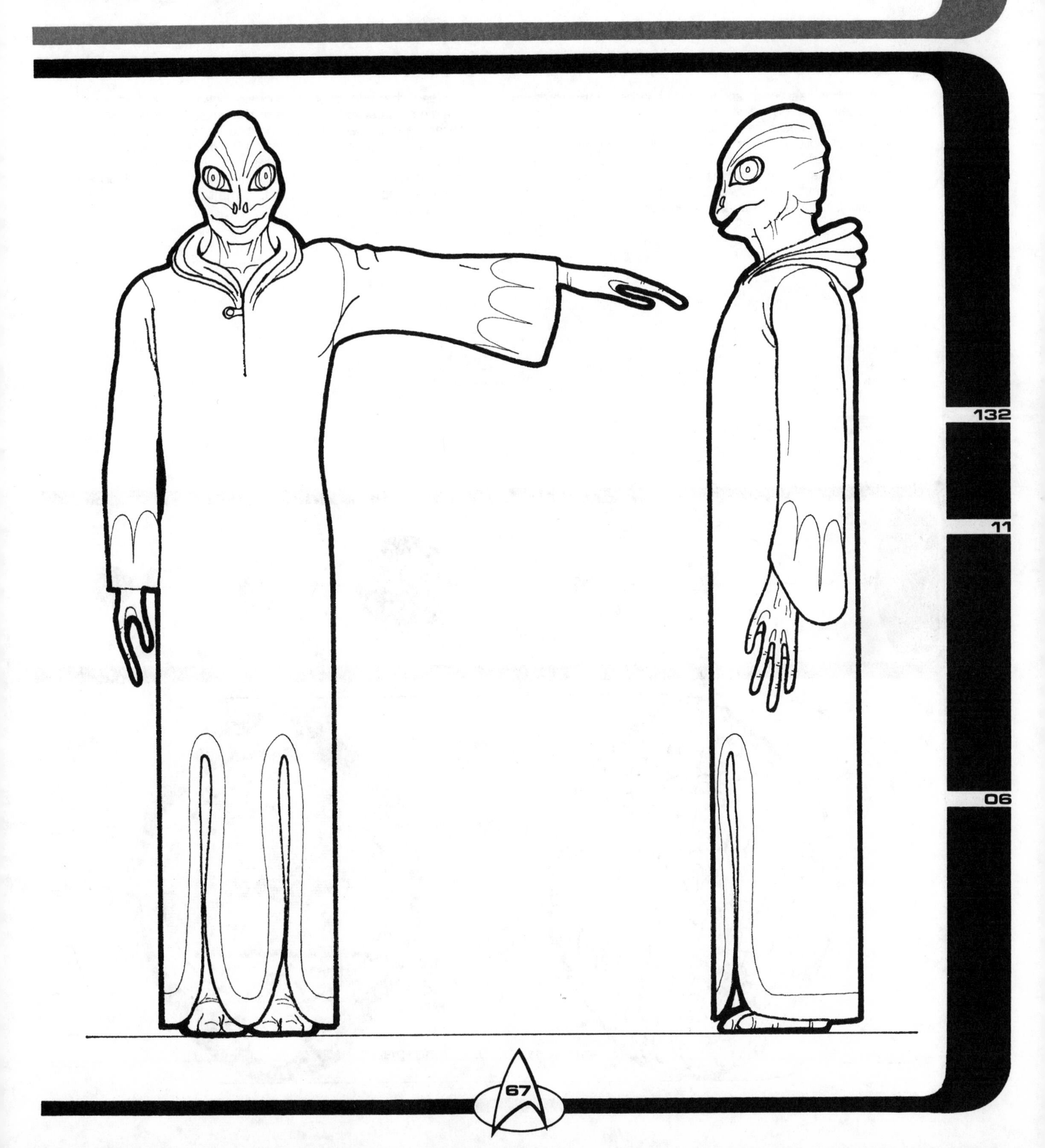

YONADA (UNCLASSIFIED)
NEW FABRINA
UFC 376082
[−51.1, −93.6, −91.4]

A hollow asteroid about one hundred fifty miles in diameter, Yonada is not a planet but a spaceship constructed to appear as a natural body. Its inhabitants, who live within a protective inner shell unaware that their world is artificial, are the descendants of the ancient Fabrini race. Knowing that their sun was going nova, the Fabrini built Yonada, a vast ship powered by a form of nuclear propulsion, and sent it out on its ten-thousand-year voyage.

Near the end of the journey, however, a computer malfunction caused a change in the vessel's trajectory and threatened to send it crashing into Daran V. Fortunately, Federation intervention prevented the disaster. Returned to its original course, Yonada assumed orbit around its programmed destination, a planet now known as New Fabrina. New Fabrina, a Class M world, is the third planet of seven that orbit UFC 376082.

19

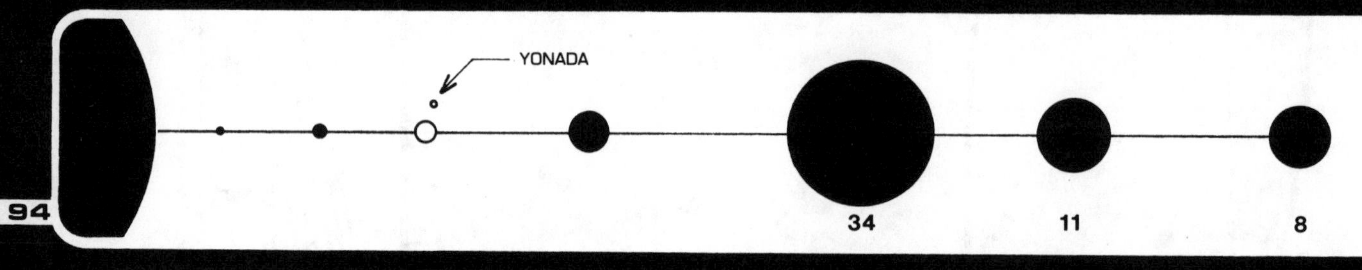

94

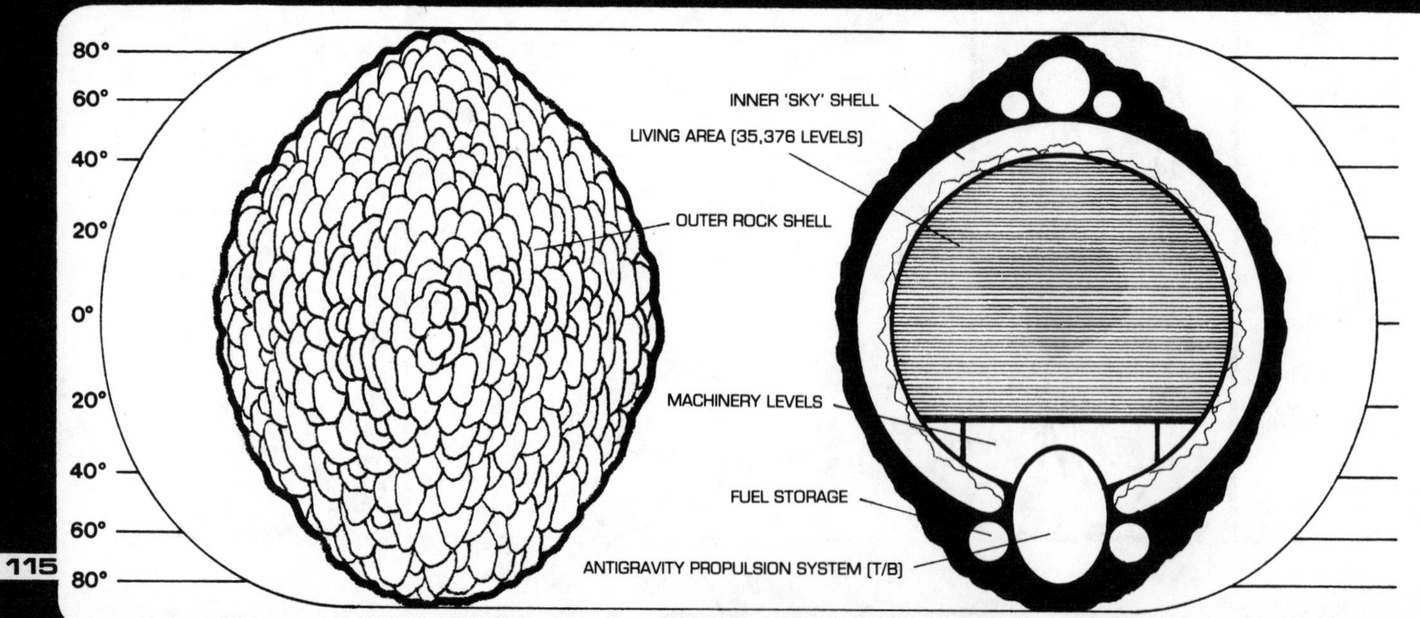

115

MEMORY ALPHA HISTORICAL ARCHIVE
DATABANK EXTRACT (HARDCOPY)

SUBJECT: FABRINI

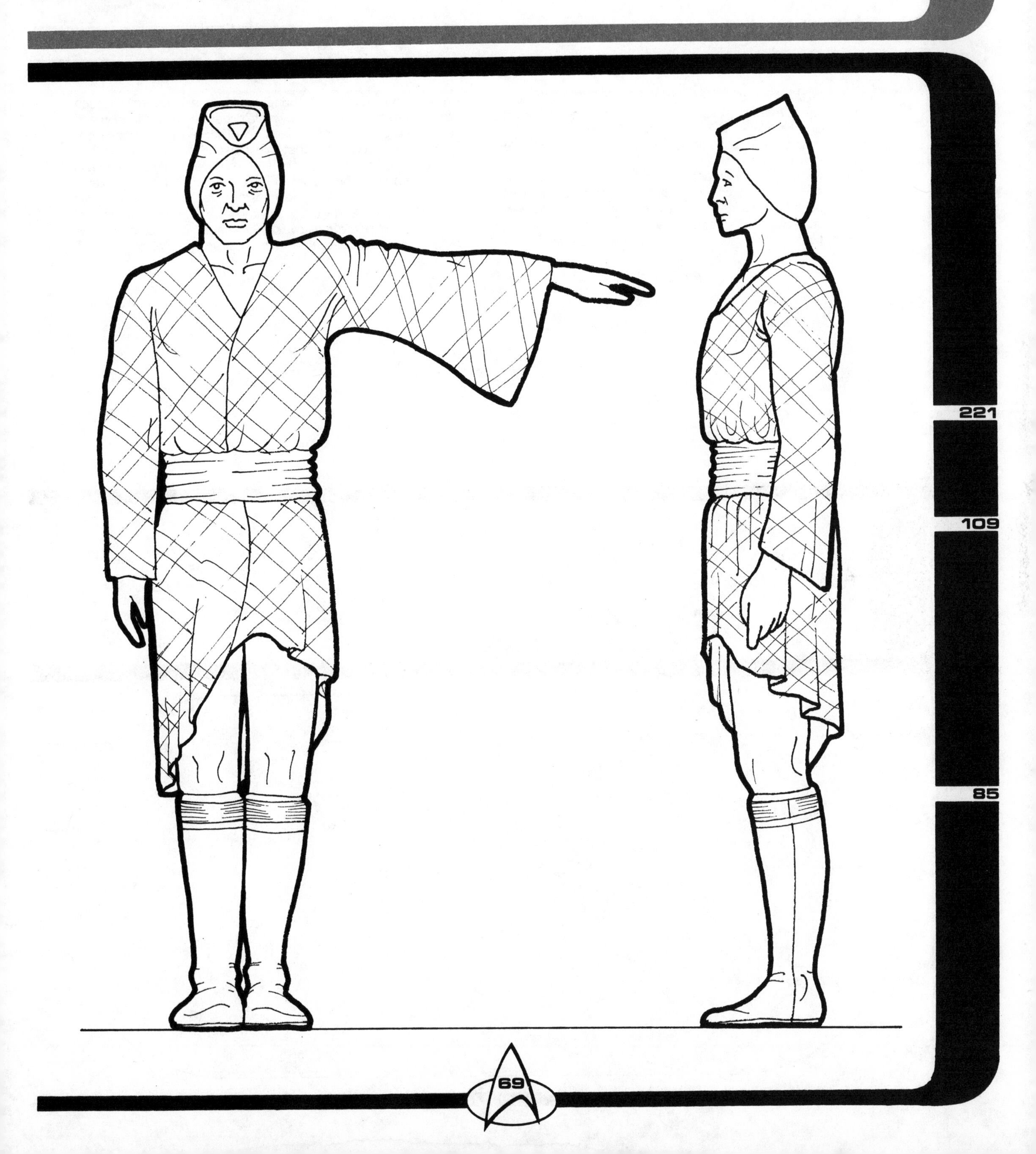

282

THETA KIOKIS II (M)
MELKOT
THETA KIOKIS
[−76.9, −145.9, −12.7]

Melkot is the second of six planets that orbit Theta Kiokis, a yellow star of moderate size. Although it has been surveyed only briefly, the planet exhibits Class M conditions in the lower atmosphere, in contrast to the dense carbon dioxide cloud layers at higher altitudes.

The Melkot, or "Melkotians," as they are sometimes referred to, have limited physical bodies and perform all tasks using advanced psionic powers. They have squarish heads and thick, rough necks that narrow into small abdominal areas with multiple tentacles. Observation seems to indicate that the Melkot hang in midair and move from place to place by telekinesis. They have great powers of illusion and can create within the minds of other races intricate environmental scenarios that are indiscernible from reality.

Xenophobic in nature, the Melkot have established a vast array of marker buoys beyond the limits of their star system. These serve as warning beacons to those who approach and provide mental communication with the intruder spacecraft. Only determined effort by the Federation has convinced the Melkot to participate in a limited cultural exchange.

44

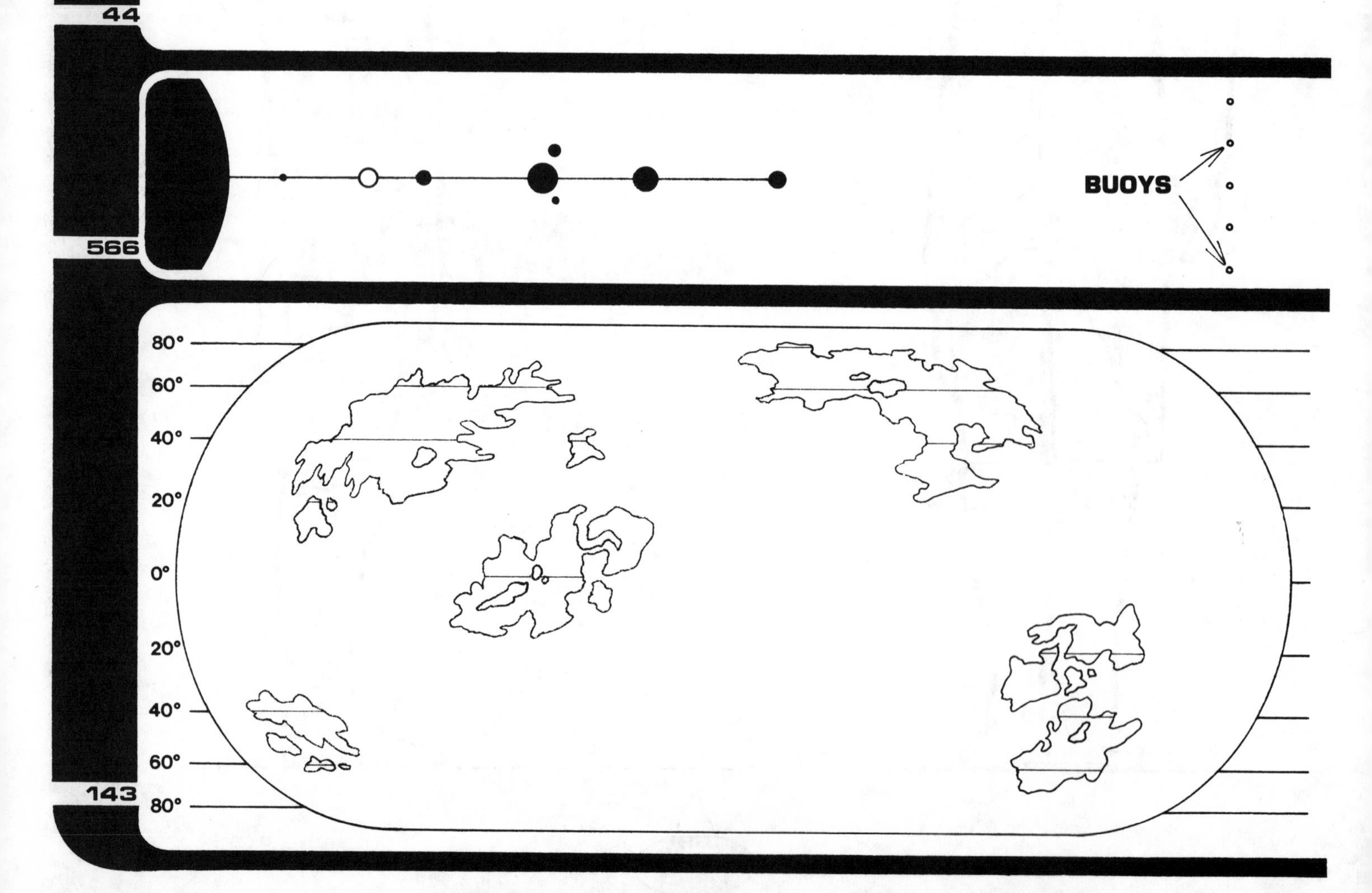

SUBJECT: MELKOTIAN

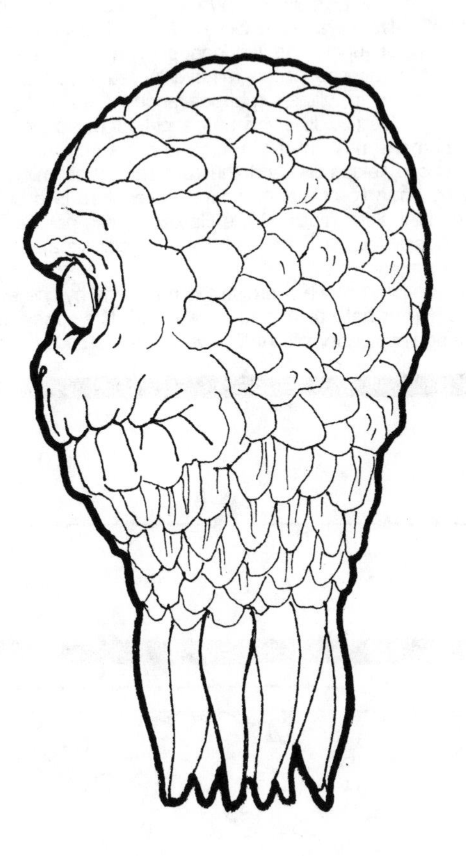

29

BETAZED (M)

CYNDRIEL

BETA VELDONNA

[−292.3, −93.3, −88.1]

Betazed is the fifth world in an eight-planet system and orbits a medium-size yellow star known as Beta Veldonna. Betazed is also the only planet to support life or have a moon. This large body, named Lonita, is Class K and supports a large colony of Betazoids.

Betazed is a remarkably beautiful world and is sometimes referred to as "the jewel of the outer crown" by traders and other visiting personnel. Great expanses of natural wilderness cover much of the planet, home to thousands of forms of native wildlife. High mountain peaks of multicolored crystal catch the rays of the Betazed sun, throwing delicate layers of color upon the landscape. The soil possesses crystals of a faceted green mineral called versina, which gives it a sparkling, glittering appearance.

The native Betazoids are a humanoid race, so similar to Terran humans that intermarriage is quite common. They are advanced telepaths, and the fact that their minds are constantly open to one another's has resulted in a culture based on complete truth. While Betazoids are not easily insulted, other races sometimes have a difficult time adjusting to such veracity.

Betazoid children are promised in marriage by the age of four and do not date or mingle socially with the opposite sex until the age of twenty-six. At this time, the betrothed couple is reintroduced and marriage takes place. If one partner dies before the proper age is reached, the survivor is allowed to select a new marriage partner of his or her own choosing.

22

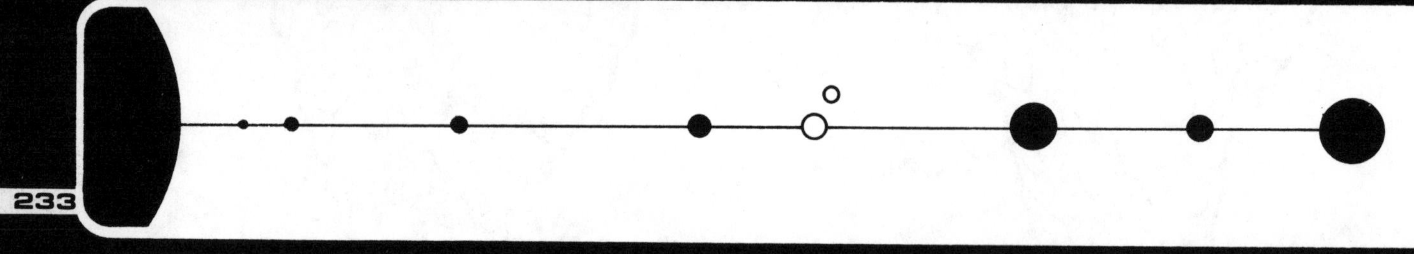

233

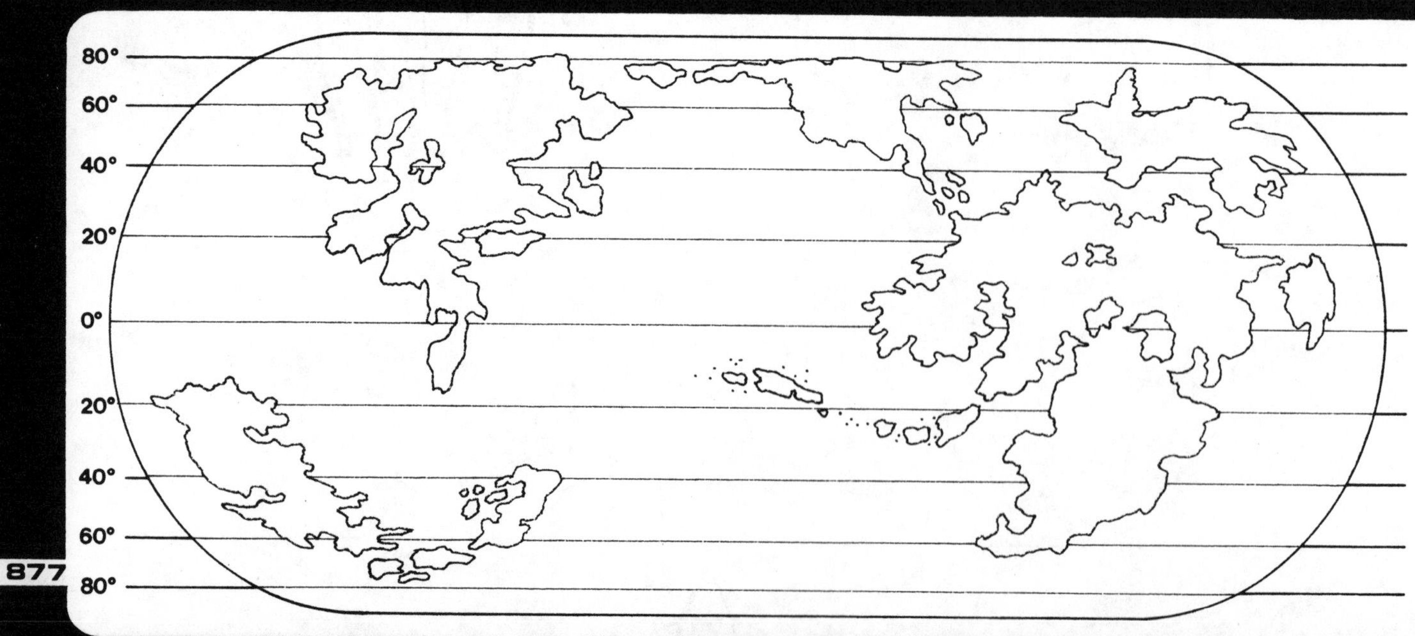

877

MEMORY ALPHA HISTORICAL ARCHIVE
DATABANK EXTRACT (HARDCOPY)

SUBJECT: BETAZOID

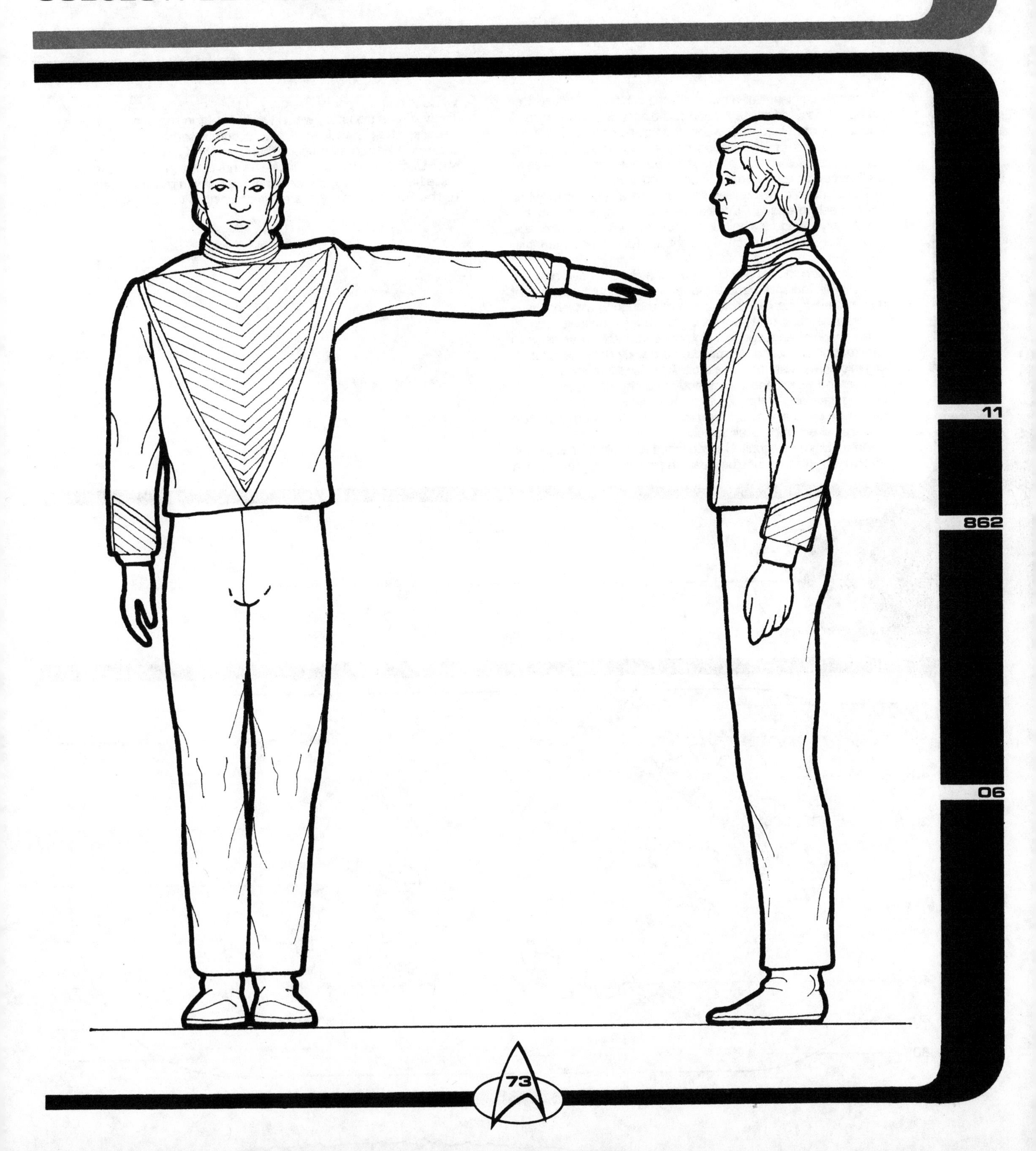

30

BYNAUS (M)

101100010100110

SIGMA REGONIS

[−296.4, 98.9, −46.3]

The fourth planet of a system once orbiting a trinary star group, Bynaus revolves around the binary Sigma Regonis A and C. Sigma Regonis B went nova quite recently, but the nova's sphere of destruction only extended as far as the second planet's orbital path. The two inner planets, lifeless and barren of atmosphere, were vaporized.

The Bynars are a unisexual race and all give birth when they reach maturity. Children are born in pairs and are psychically linked for their entire lives. Small for a humanoid race, the Bynars reach a height of four feet when fully developed.

Over a period of many centuries the Bynars have become mentally linked to a central planetary computer complex of unmatched intricacy. In fact, their thought patterns have become as near to binary as is possible for organic beings. Their primary language is a high-speed chatter that delivers information at incredible speeds, so quickly that the Bynars' organic brains cannot store it all. A buffer memory unit, carried at the waist and tied directly into the brain, stores incoming data and transmits it to the brain as needed. Fraternal Bynar pairs are so strongly linked that they communicate in pairs, alternating their speech.

When Sigma Regonis B threatened to explode, the people of Bynaus knew that the resulting electromagnetic pulse would erase the entire memory of their planetary computer. To avoid this disaster, which would result in the deaths of all Bynars, they downloaded the accumulated knowledge of their world into the computer banks of the Galaxy class starship USS **Enterprise**. Once the nova detonated and the pulse had died down, the **Enterprise** relayed the information to the Bynar memory system, returning it to normal.

39

04

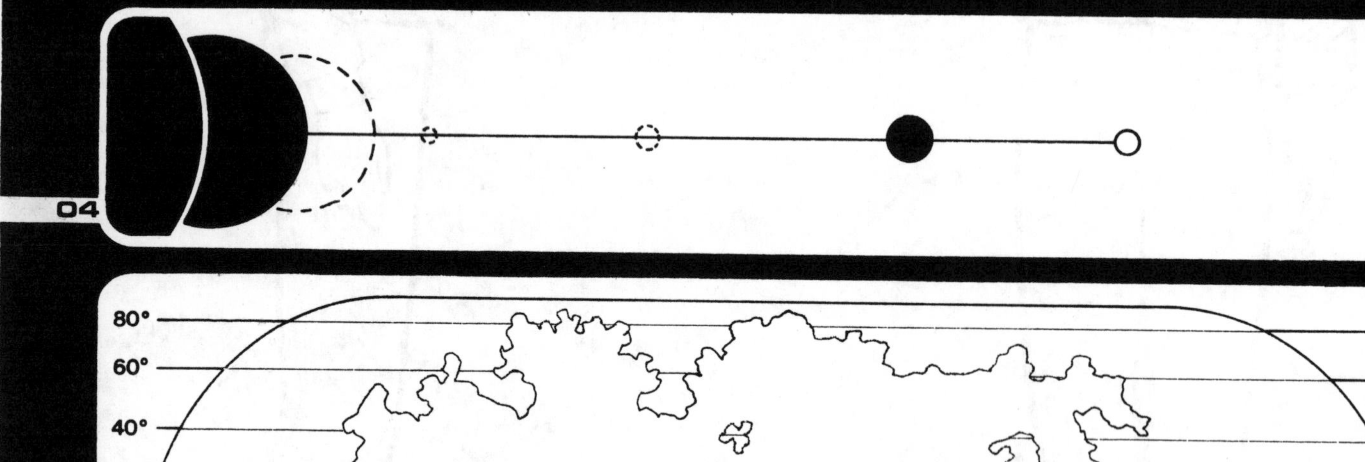

80°
60°
40°
20°
0°
20°
40°
60°
80°

677

MEMORY ALPHA HISTORICAL ARCHIVE
DATABANK EXTRACT (HARDCOPY)

SUBJECT: BYNAR

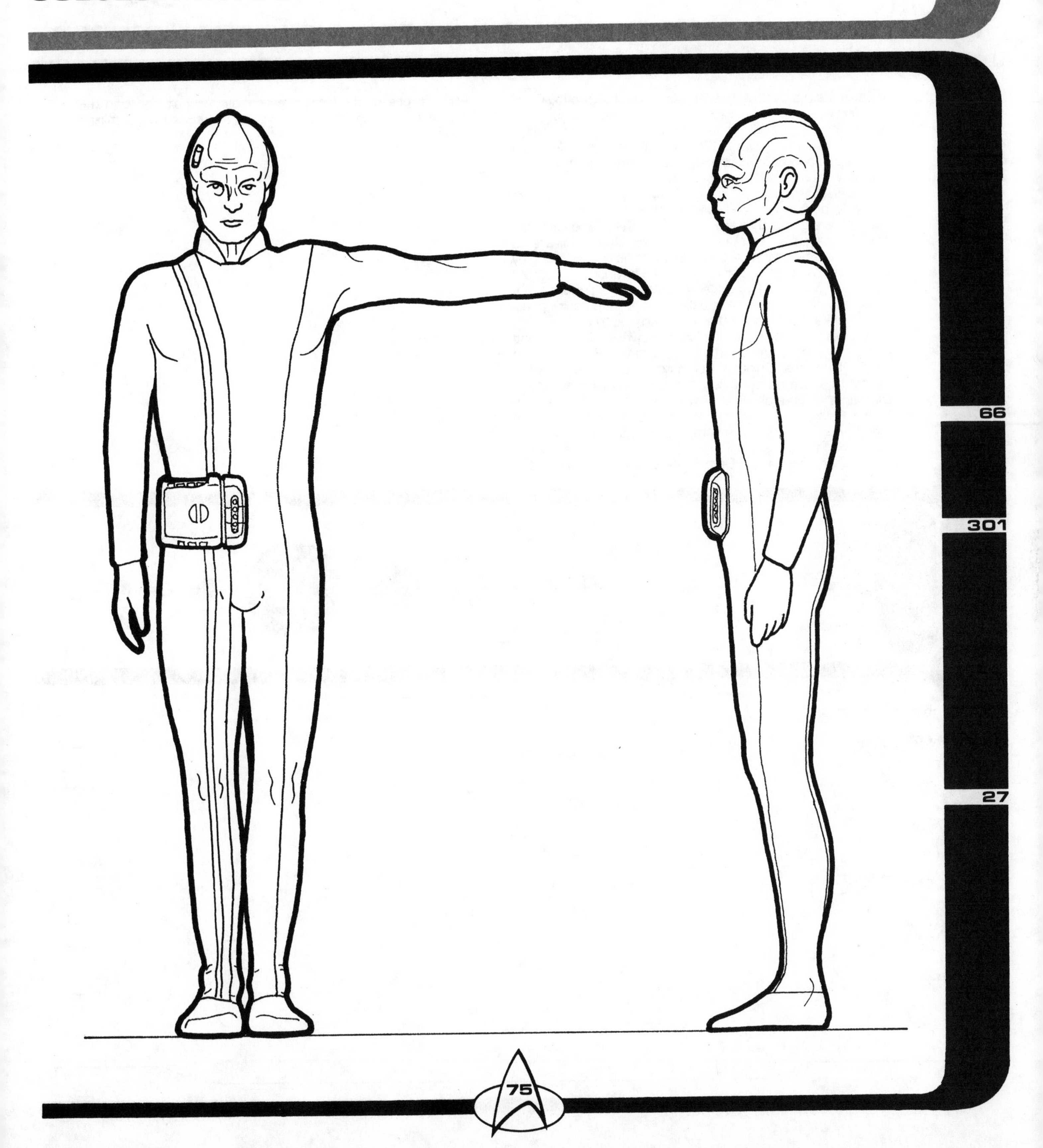

3
1

BENZAR (M)
PHERADON
GAMMA XERTIA
[301.4, –57.4, 84.4]

Benzar is the third of thirteen planets in orbit around Gamma Xertia, a red giant star. Benzar has two moons, Herti and Dwora, and harbors a massive orbiting space station with 2.3 million inhabitants. This spaceborne city, Merria, is the major Federation port and repair center for the sector and may soon be given starbase status.

Benzar's atmosphere is classically Class M, comprised primarily of nitrogen and oxygen, though it also contains several rare gases that are essential to Benzite respiration. These gases, inert to all other humanoid life forms, are so vital to Benzite existence that they must be carried along by Benzar natives who journey upon Federation vessels or serve on other UFP worlds. A small, timed-release apparatus worn at the neck delivers the life-sustaining atmosphere supplement to the nostril area automatically.

Benzites are well known for their prowess at gaming and computer programming. Mordock, a native Benzite and a recipient of the Galactic Computer Network's Vedallus Award, created a now widely employed attack method for the game of della-chess known as the Mordock Strategy. Other Benzite technological contributions have led to the memory expansion of the computer system used at most Federation starbases.

No other planet in the Gamma Xertia system is habitable, though one of the largest asteroids in a belt between the ninth and tenth planets contains an underground mining facility.

107

343

089

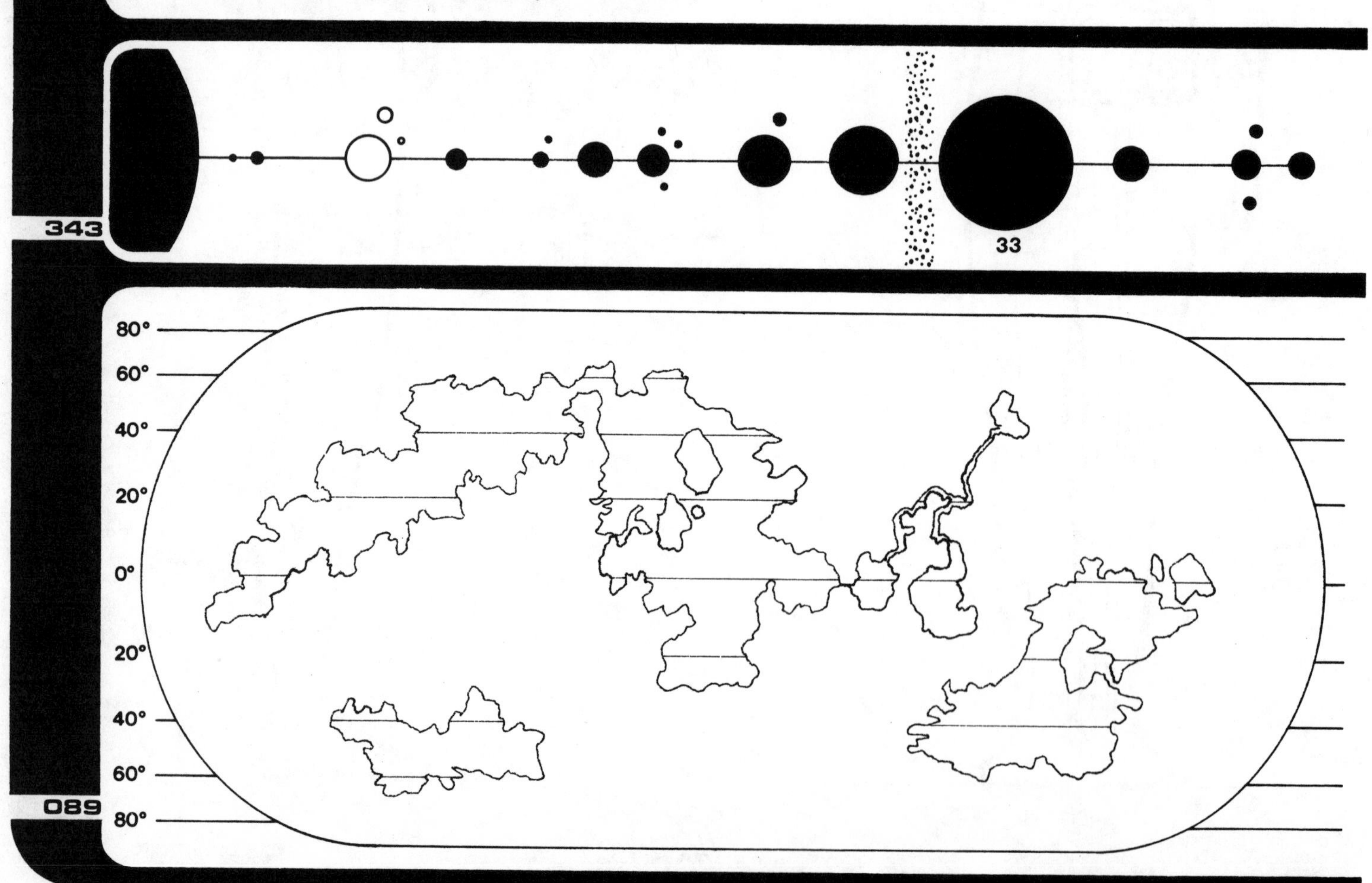

SUBJECT: BENZITE

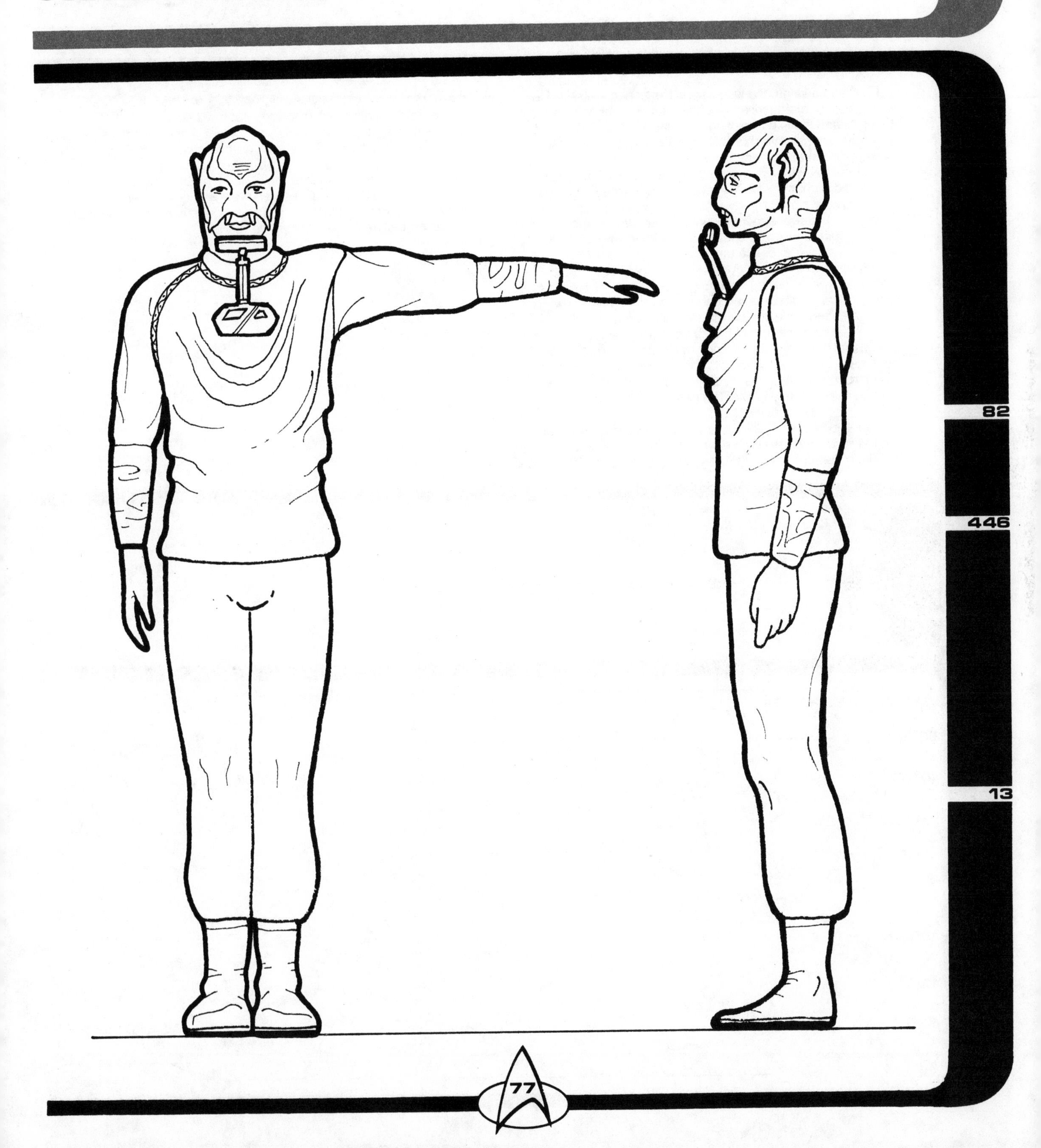

PHYLOS II (M)
MERARI
PHYLOS
[306.5, –98.9, 187.4]

Phylos is a large orange star at the upper, outer edge of the Federation's quadrant-three-south. Its second planet is Class M and is the home of an abundance of plant life, though no native animals live there. Phylos II's flora gives the world a brilliant green appearance from space.

The native Phylosians are intelligent plant beings, roughly humanoid in shape, with heads, eye stalks, bipedal leg projections, and a central body with many vinelike appendages. They are passive and have an intense desire for galactic peace. They share a planetwide dream of moving out into space to serve as peace enforcers.

The race is, sadly, a dying one. Dr. Stavos Keniclius, an Earth scientist during the Eugenics Wars, migrated to Phylos after a bitter disagreement with Terran authorities over the need for a genetically superior human master race. The Phylosians greeted him with open arms and aided him in his quest to perfect the science of genetic cloning. Unknown to them, he had inadvertently brought with him a staphylococcus bacterial strain against which the Phylosians had no resistance. Many of the natives died in the worldwide plague, and the spore cells of the survivors were rendered sterile. Much later, Keniclius and a specially assigned Federation scientific team set out to artificially produce a healthy group of seed individuals using genetic information taken from the surviving Phylosians. While progress has been made, it is unknown whether the race will survive.

Other indigenous life includes a plant known only as a swooper, a mindless flying attack creature approximately fifteen feet long. Phylos' retlaw plant, a seemingly harmless flower about seven inches high, is a mobile, highly toxic organism. Its sting produces paralysis and quickly results in death unless counteracted by a chemical antidote, which is secreted by the native Phylosians' bodies.

612

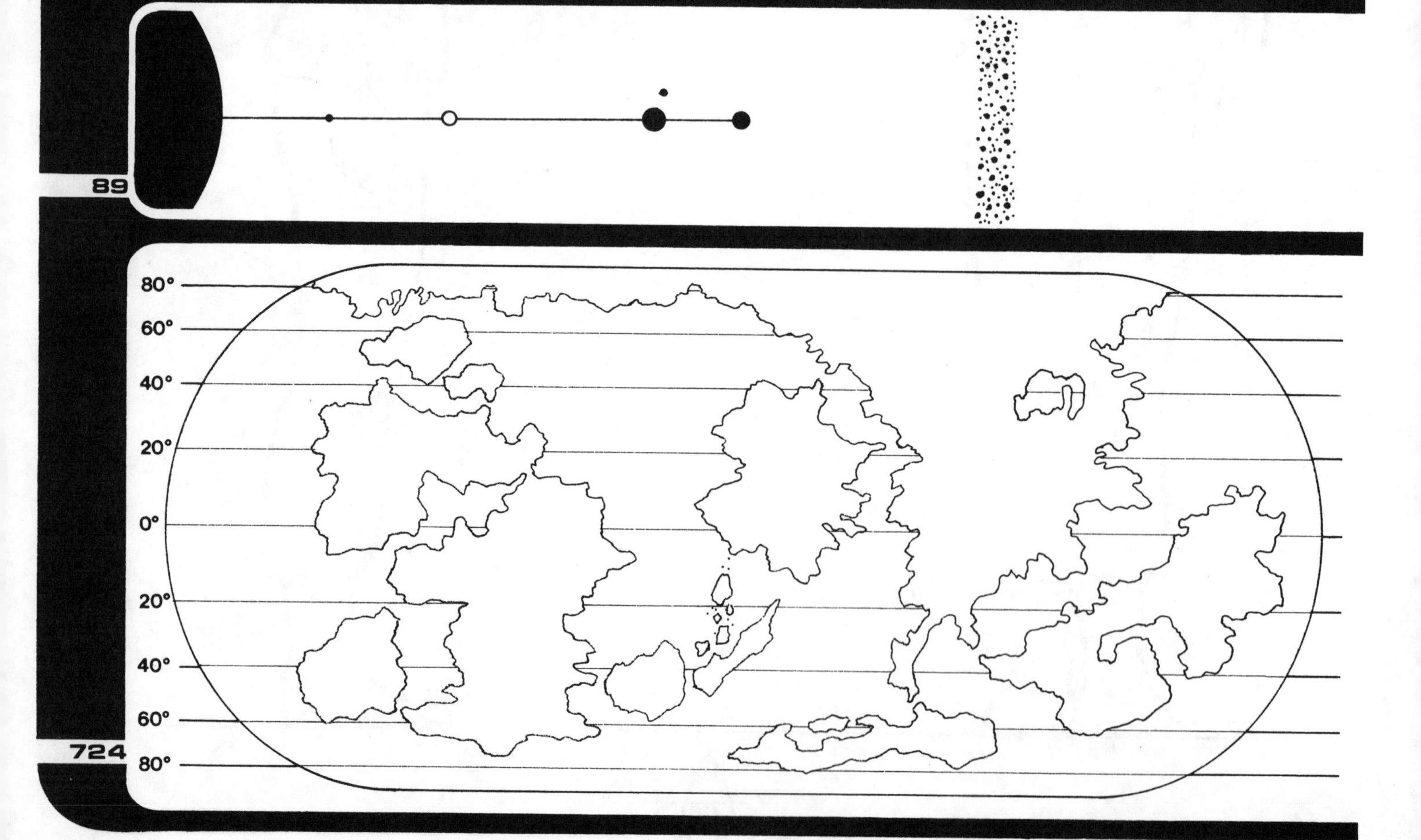

MEMORY ALPHA HISTORICAL ARCHIVE
DATABANK EXTRACT (HARDCOPY)

SUBJECT: PHYLOSIAN

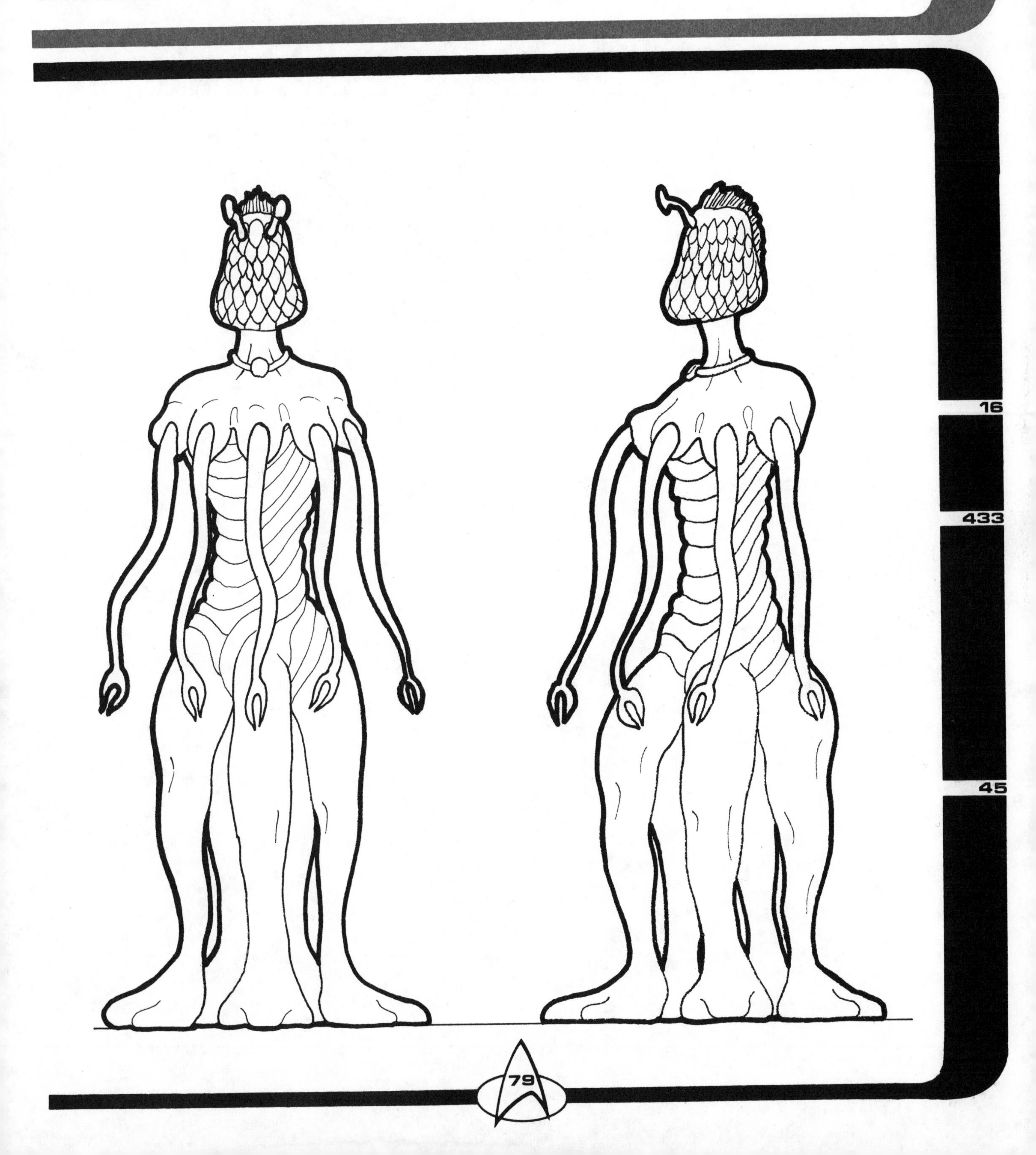

NEUTRAL AND/OR INDEPENDENT WORLDS

ANTARES B III (L)
NO INDIGENOUS NAME
ANTARES
[172.1, 118.9, −13.9]

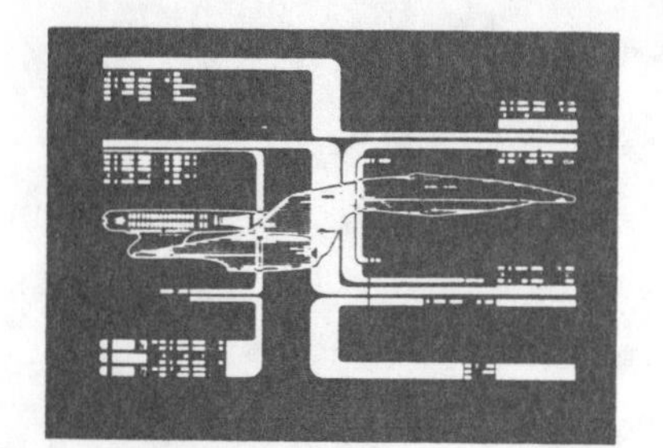

Antares is the name given to a binary system that consists of a red giant primary star and a small yellow secondary. The system supports a total of nine planets, with four orbiting the primary and five revolving around the secondary. None of the worlds is inhabited.

Antares B III is the home of many interesting lower life forms, such as the Antarean dryworm. A popular trade item, Antarean "glow water" is actually dryworms suspended in a life-supporting liquid.

Phentora, a grain that grows only on Antares B III, is used in the distillation and production of Antarean brandy. A favorite beverage on many Federation worlds, it is known for its pale blue color.

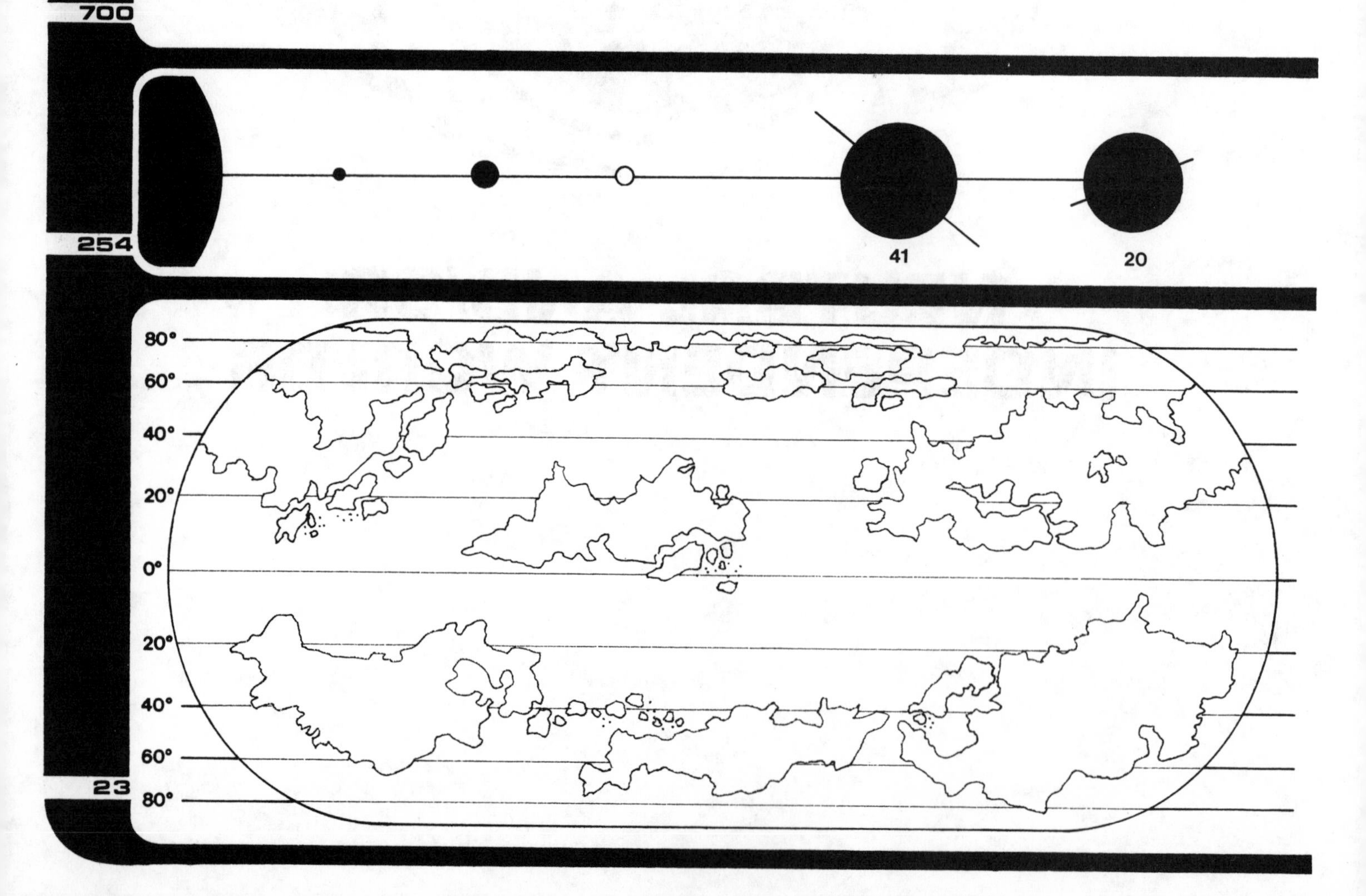

LIBRARY COMPUTER — USS ENTERPRISE (NCC-1701-D)
DATABANK EXTRACT (HARDCOPY)
SUBJECT: ANTAREAN DRYWORM

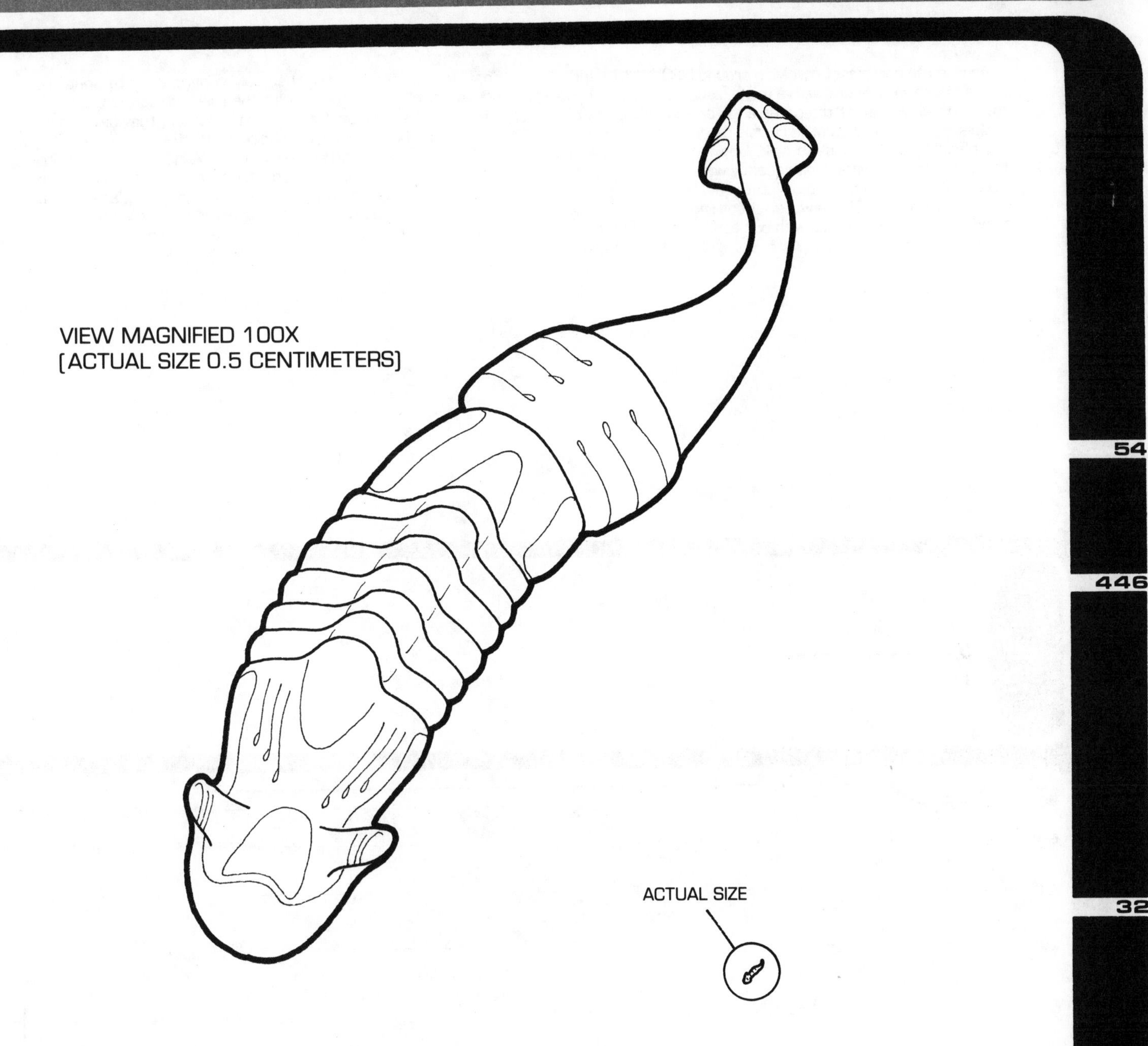

ARGO (N)
HESTALOR
UFC 78856
[133.4, −45.5, 32.9]

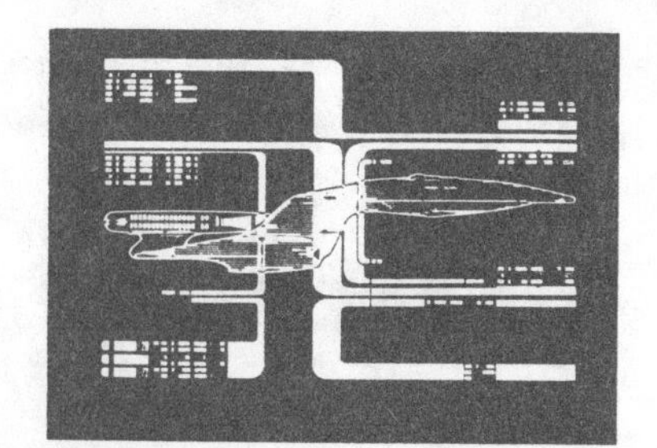

Argo is the only planet revolving around UFC 78856 and is a blue-green waterworld with a misty cloud cover. Its sun is a medium yellow star at the outer edge of Federation space.

Seismic disturbances of incredible magnitude once caused the planet's land masses to sink, leaving only spotty islands to dot the vast oceans. Only recently was it learned that the oceans of Argo are host to an intelligent, city-dwelling people known as Aquans. These water-breathing inhabitants are a handsome, humanoid race with webbed hands and feet, dorsal fins, and greenish hair. Air-breathers at one time, Argo natives decided to alter themselves genetically to adapt to ocean dwelling. Advanced Argo medical techniques made this artificial change possible. In the years since, they have come to fear and hate all aerobic beings.

Some of the creatures that inhabit Argo's seas are quite large and dangerous. One, the duitra, resembles a Denebian whale and is aggressive in nature. The sur-snake, as it is also known, is a rare and protected creature, and the capture of specimens is prohibited by the natives of Argo.

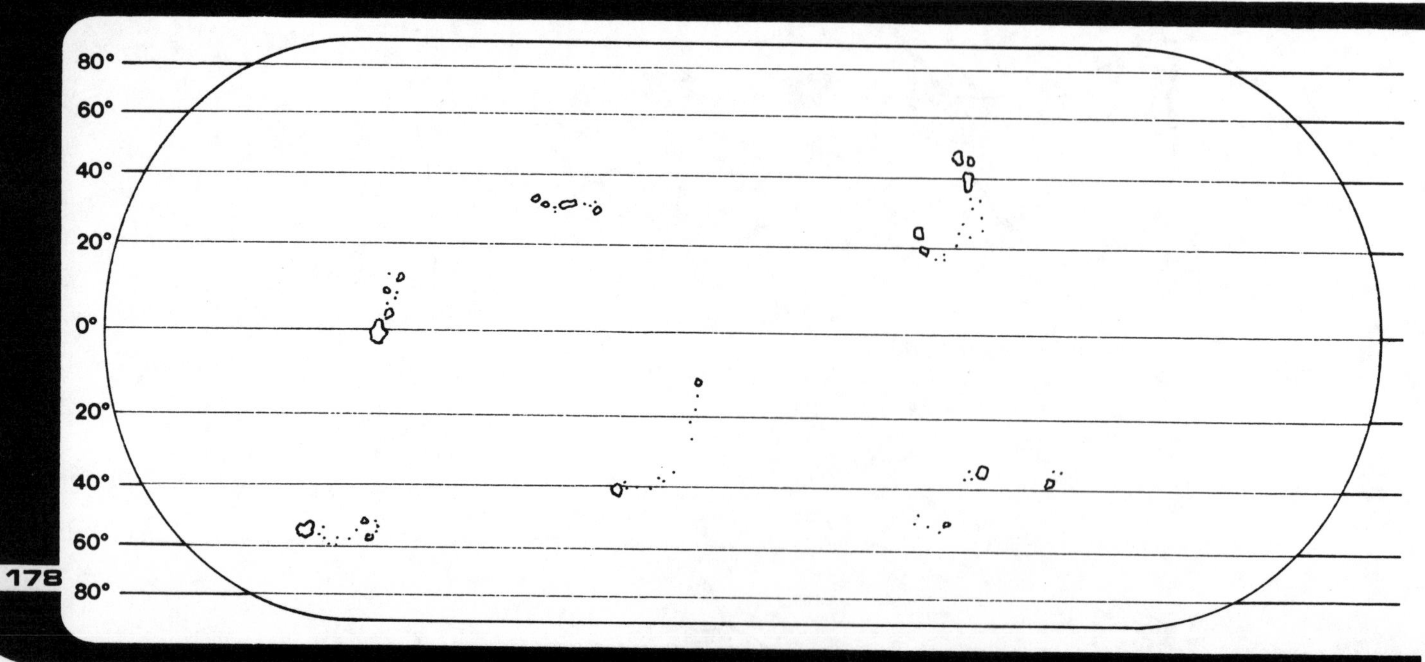

LIBRARY COMPUTER — USS ENTERPRISE (NCC-1701-D)
DATABANK EXTRACT (HARDCOPY)
SUBJECT: ARGOAN AQUAN

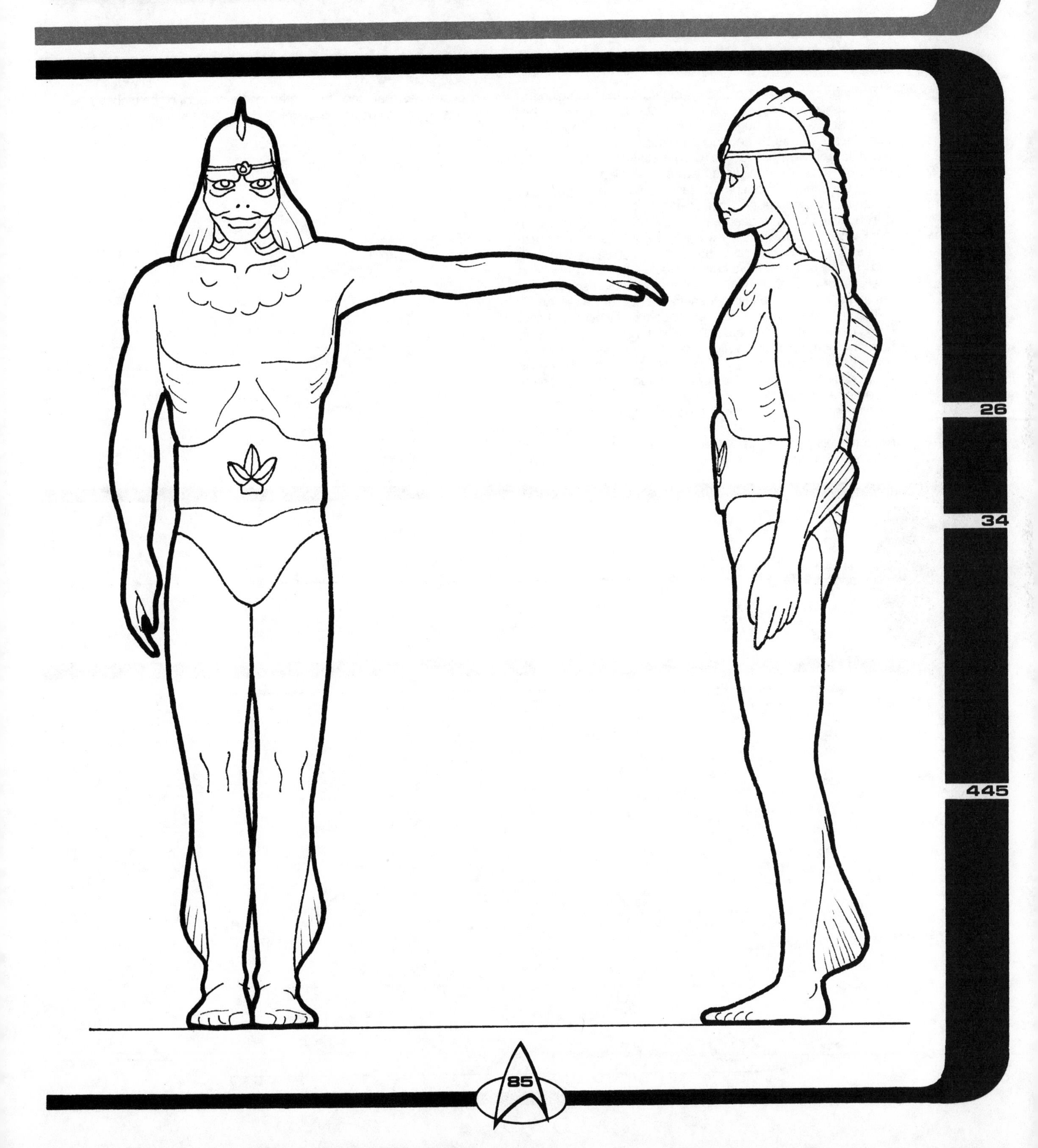

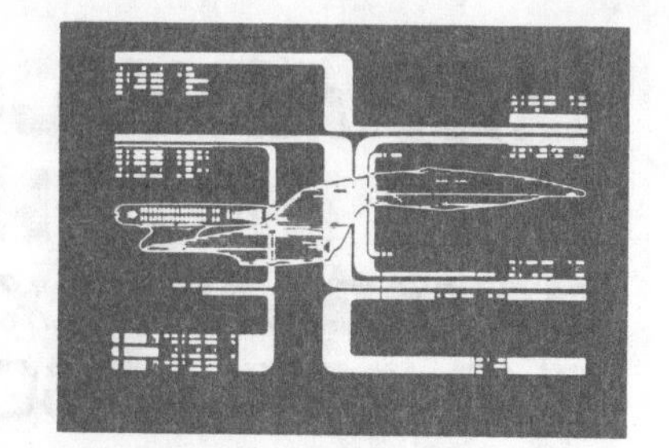

BERENGARIA VII (M)

NO INDIGENOUS NAME

BERENGARIA

[−21.4, −51.8, −60.3]

Berengaria is a giant red star orbited by thirteen planets. The seventh and eighth are both Class M, but the other eleven are actually huge asteroids with no atmosphere. Berengaria VII has three moons named simply Alpha, Beta, and Gamma which are the only natural satellites in the system. None of the planets have sentient life.

The dominant inhabitants of Berengaria VII are species of beautiful, winged reptiles referred to as the "dragons of Berengaria," which measure from nine to fifty feet in length. While their life spans are a mystery, many believe that these animals live more than seven hundred Terran years. Docile in nature, the dragons have never attacked researchers, and observation indicates that they are strictly herbivorous, feeding only upon the lush greenery of their native world.

The dragons' wings were long considered incapable of providing enough lift to achieve flight. Recent analysis, however, has revealed a complex system of highly specialized internal organs that draw hydrogen from water and store the gas in sacs that run along the sides of the abdomen and tail. These sacs serve the same basic function as the swim bladder in Terran fish, and much of the dragon's weight is offset by the buoyancy of these light-than-air compartments. Later, the excess hydrogen travels to the dragons' mouths, where it is exhaled and ignited by electrochemical means. Similar creatures may once have lived on Earth during the dinosaur age, giving birth to the planet's many dragon legends.

66

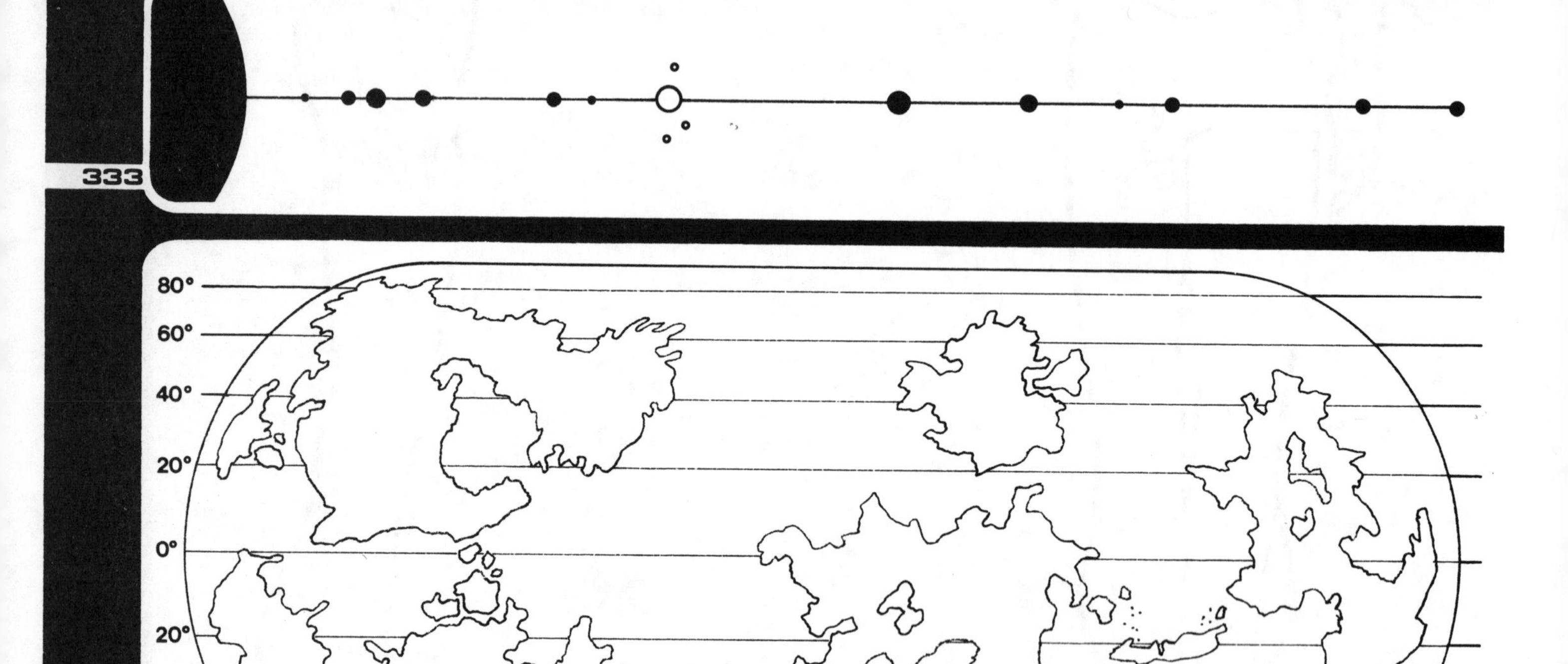

LIBRARY COMPUTER — USS ENTERPRISE (NCC-1701-D)
DATABANK EXTRACT (HARDCOPY)
SUBJECT: BERENGARIAN DRAGON

BETA III (M)
LANDRU
UFC 611-BETA
[90.1, 71.9, −2.4]

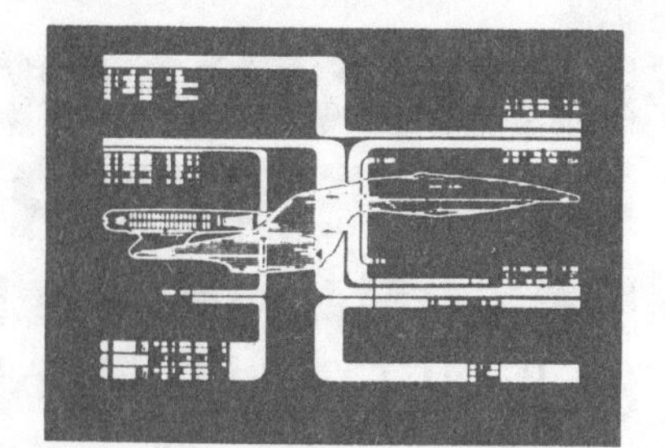

UFC 611 is a binary system comprised of two bright yellow stars, designated 611-Alpha and 611-Beta. 611-Alpha has no planets, but Beta supports a system of five worlds.

The third planet, Beta III, is a Class M world with two major continents and several large oceans. At one time the planet harbored a sophisticated technological society of humanoid beings who were governed by a vast artificial intelligence network. Six thousand years ago, however, the culture ceased to grow, and, it progressed no further due to a malfunction in the planet's primary computer. Programmed by the civilization's foremost cultural scientist, Landru, the computer was originally intended to carry on Landru's teachings after his death and lead the culture to a peaceful, stable society. However, a misinterpretation of the programmed data produced a stagnant, controlled people. Technology was lost as the inhabitants fell into a more primitive culture. Outsiders who came to the planet were "absorbed" into the mind-controlled society.

A Federation landing party, investigating the disappearance of the USS **Archon**, encountered the culture. They convinced the computer system that damage was being done to the people by the imposition of such rigid constraints. The computer finally released the people of Beta III to create their own society.

The once-arrested culture has sought Federation aid and is well on the way toward self-government. Growth and progress have become evident planetwide.

90

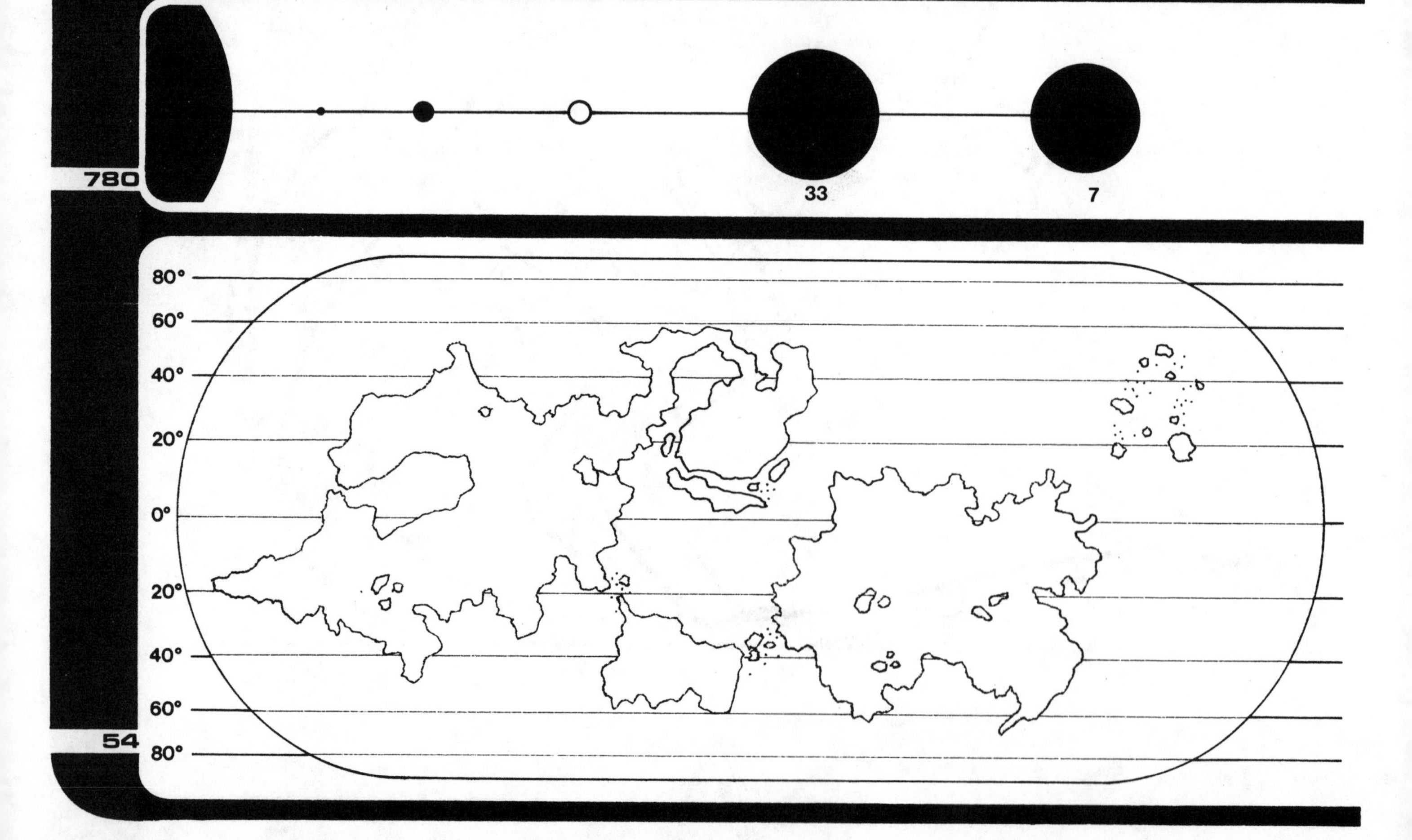

LIBRARY COMPUTER — USS ENTERPRISE (NCC-1701-D)
DATABANK EXTRACT (HARDCOPY)
SUBJECT: BETAN (ENFORCER)

CAPELLA IV (G)
KOHATH
CAPELLA
[11.1, 60.0, 4.6]

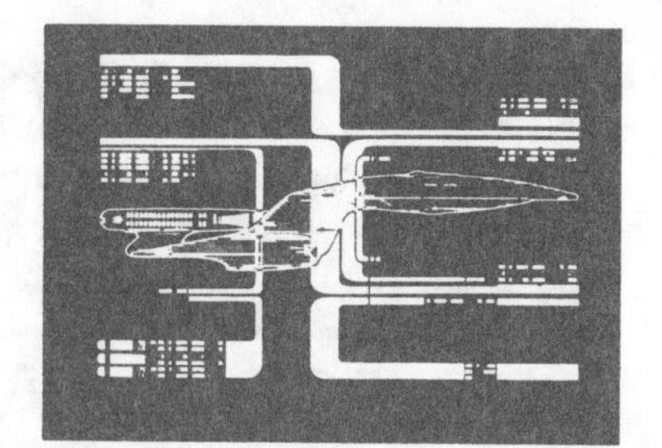

The Capella system contains four stars. Two of these, both moderate-size yellow stars, form a binary pair that revolve around each other. They are orbited, at a distance of 0.17 light years, by a pair of binary red dwarf stars. This double-binary system is unique in Federation space and is a focal point for astrophysical research.

The only inhabited planet in the system is the outermost of the four worlds that orbit the central yellow binary pair. A Class G desert world, Capella IV has a small population of native nomadic humanoids who are believed to be the descendants of the lost USS **Ceres** expedition, which disappeared over one hundred years ago.

The planet is rich in the rare element known as topaline, a key element in the life-support systems of many planetoid colonies. After a long period of negotiation, the Federation and the Klingon Empire have decided to share mining rights.

This world is also the home of the Capellan power-cat, the fiercest and most untamable creature in the known galaxy. About the size of the Terran brown bear, the power-cat has brick-red fur, golden eyes, a short tail, and brown spines running down its back. While in motion, the creature emits a highly charged white aura of electricity and can move as quickly as the Terran cheetah. They have been known to throw an electrical jolt of more than two thousand volts, with a range of twenty feet. A power-cat has never been kept alive in captivity for more than a few days.

The native Capellans live in tents and move from place to place continually. They believe that only the strong should survive and therefore have never developed medical treatment. Like the Vulcans, they are born with the innate ability to control pain.

Their culture relies heavily upon tradition, and they are an extremely honest people who keep their word without fail. Early Federation contact teams found that the Capellan people regard any show of weakness as disgusting, any show of force as a declaration of war. To them combat is a source of great pleasure.

05

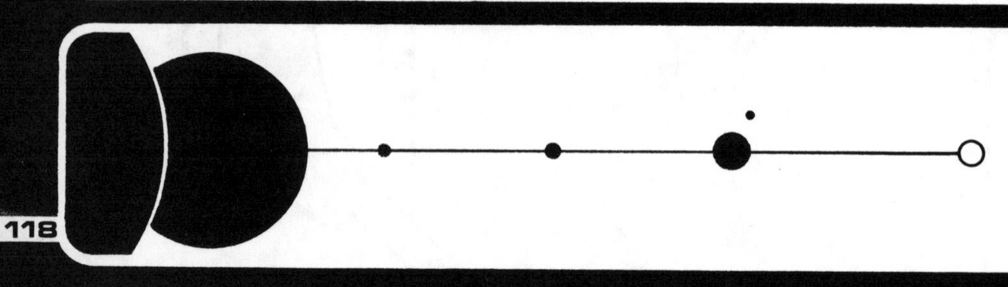

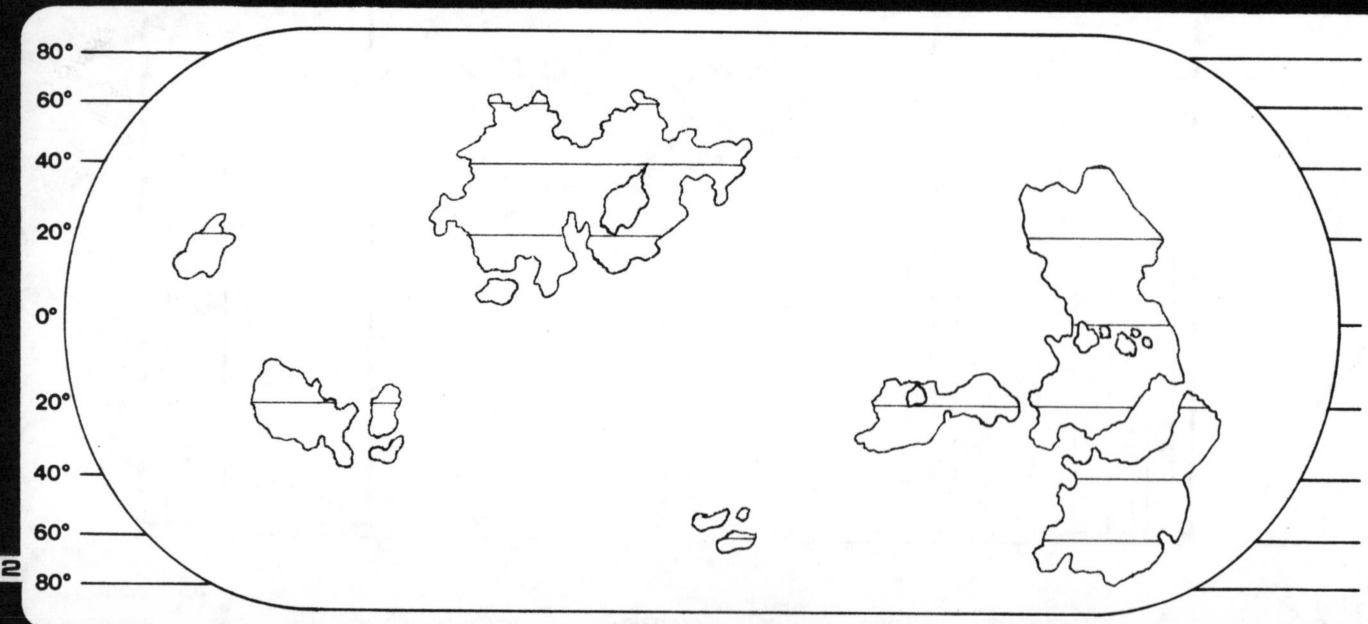

LIBRARY COMPUTER — USS ENTERPRISE (NCC-1701-D)
DATABANK EXTRACT (HARDCOPY)
SUBJECT: CAPELLAN

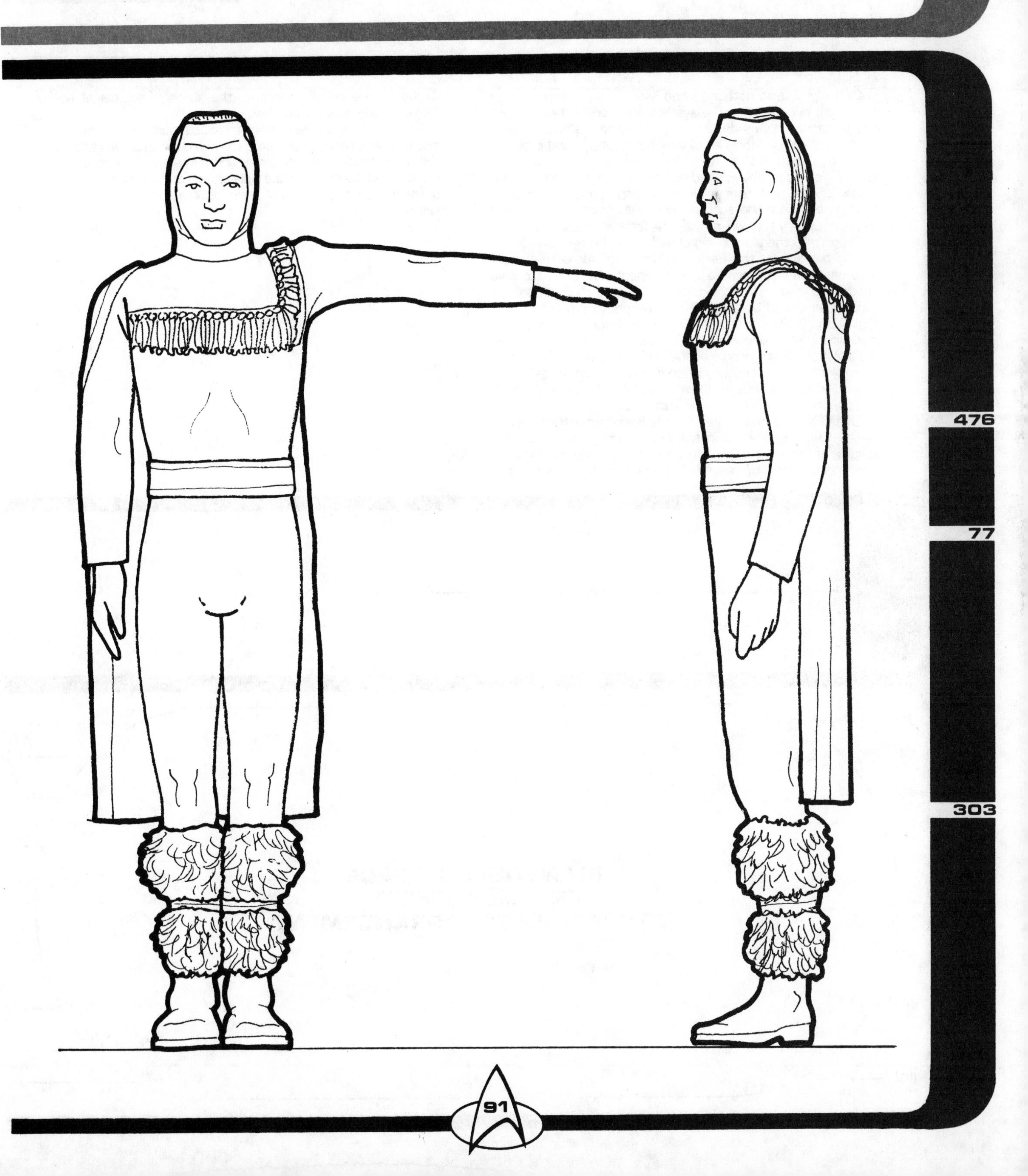

CETI ALPHA V (G)
NO INDIGENOUS NAME
CETI ALPHA (MENKAR)
(12.4, 49.5, −19.7)

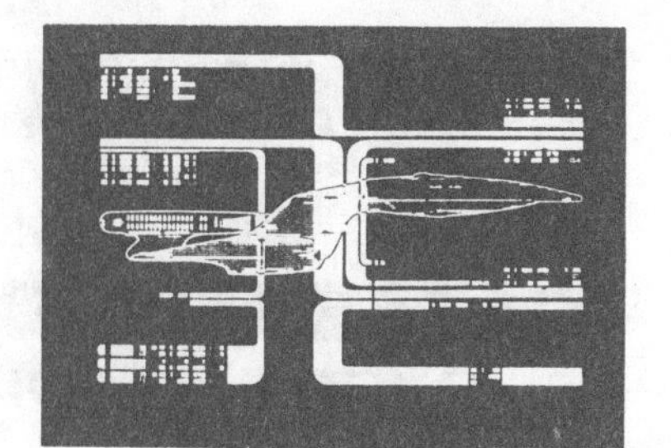

Ceti Alpha, also catalogued as Menkar, is a large orange star with five planets. The system once supported six, but the outer world was destroyed in a natural disaster.

Belts of rocky debris lay closely both outside and inside of the orbital path of Ceti Alpha VI — so close, in fact, that the planet was constantly pelted by meteorites of varying sizes. Some of the rock that fell into the atmosphere was large enough to reach the surface, and dust from such impacts was continually thrown into the planet's atmosphere.

Eventually, the planet was struck by an immense asteroid nearly the size of the Earth's moon. Ceti Alpha VI's crust was practically obliterated on the impact side, and extensive fracturing of the planet's substrata caused the sudden, explosive release of the planet's internal geothermal pressure. Ceti Alpha VI blew apart, sending large sections of the planet outward in all directions.

Ceti Alpha V suffered a sudden tidal shift when Ceti Alpha VI exploded. As a result, planet five slipped on its axis, and the planetary climate fell from Class M to Class G. All plant life perished, and few animals survived.

One of the few native life forms to live on after the disaster is the Ceti eel, a small insectoid creature. Adults reach a length of approximately fourteen inches and carry their young in the folds of tissue between their dorsal armor shell sections. The eels live beneath the sands of the planet and move quickly as they burrow.

The young have been known to attack humans by crawling into the body through the ear. They wrap themselves around the cerebral cortex, rendering the human subject susceptible to mind control. As the eels grow to adulthood they put pressure on the victim's brain until madness and death result.

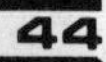

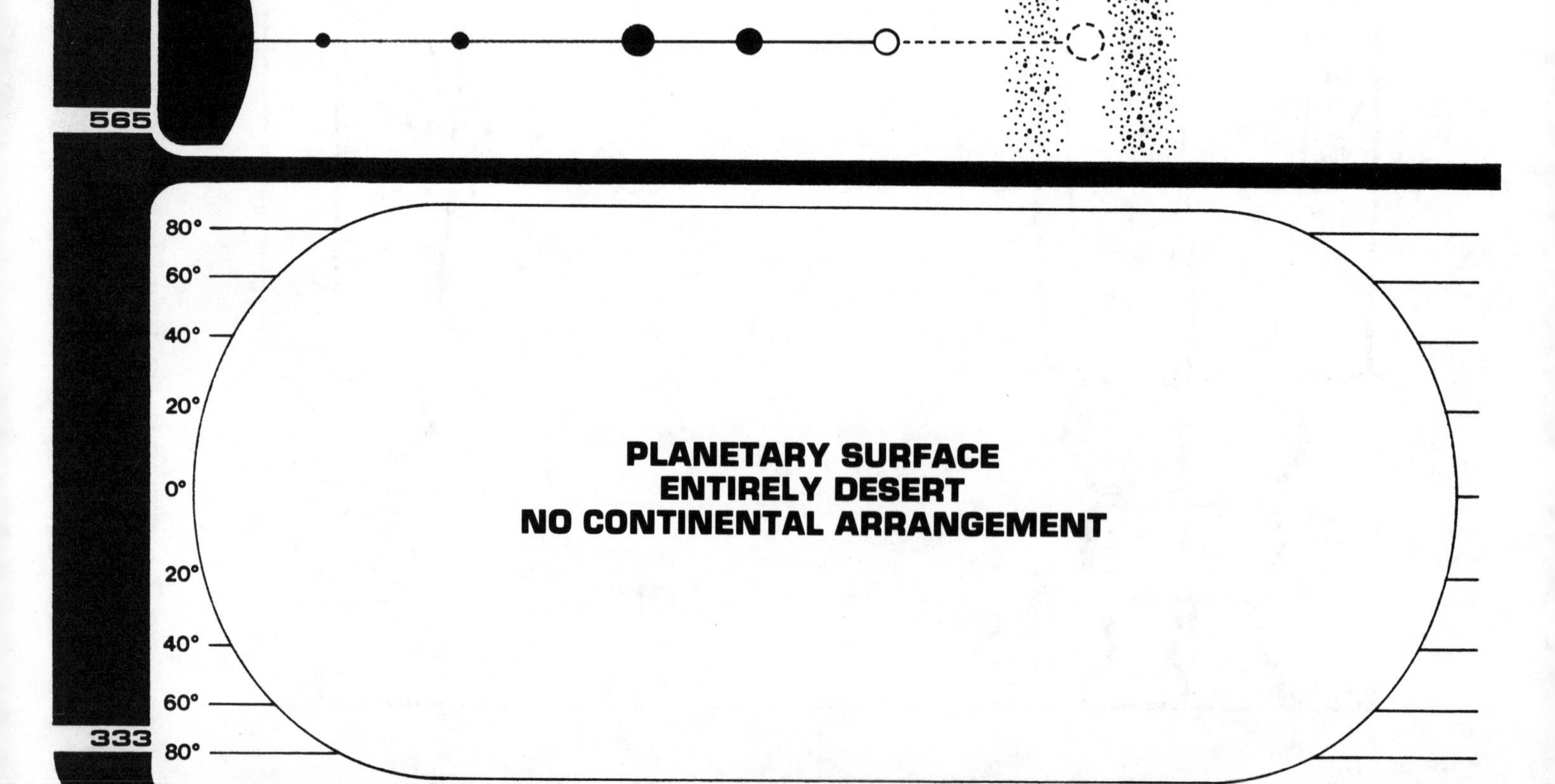

LIBRARY COMPUTER — USS ENTERPRISE (NCC-1701-D)
DATABANK EXTRACT (HARDCOPY)
SUBJECT: MENKARAN CETI EEL

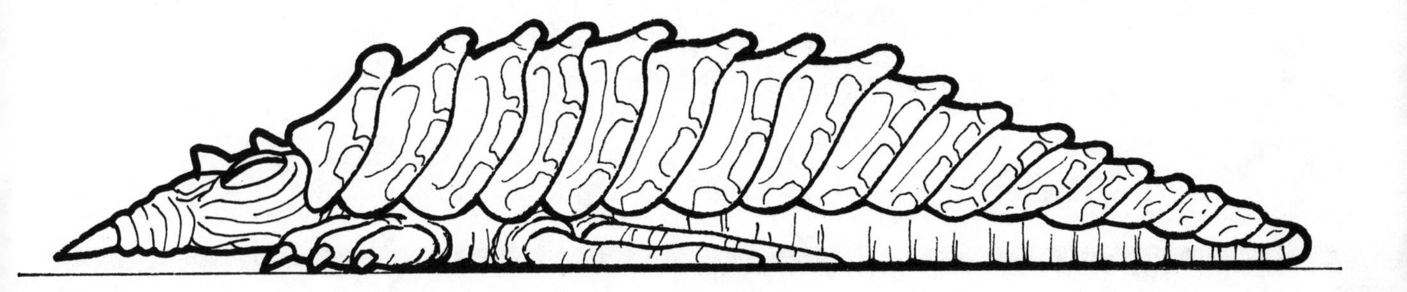

LENGTH:
0.36 METERS

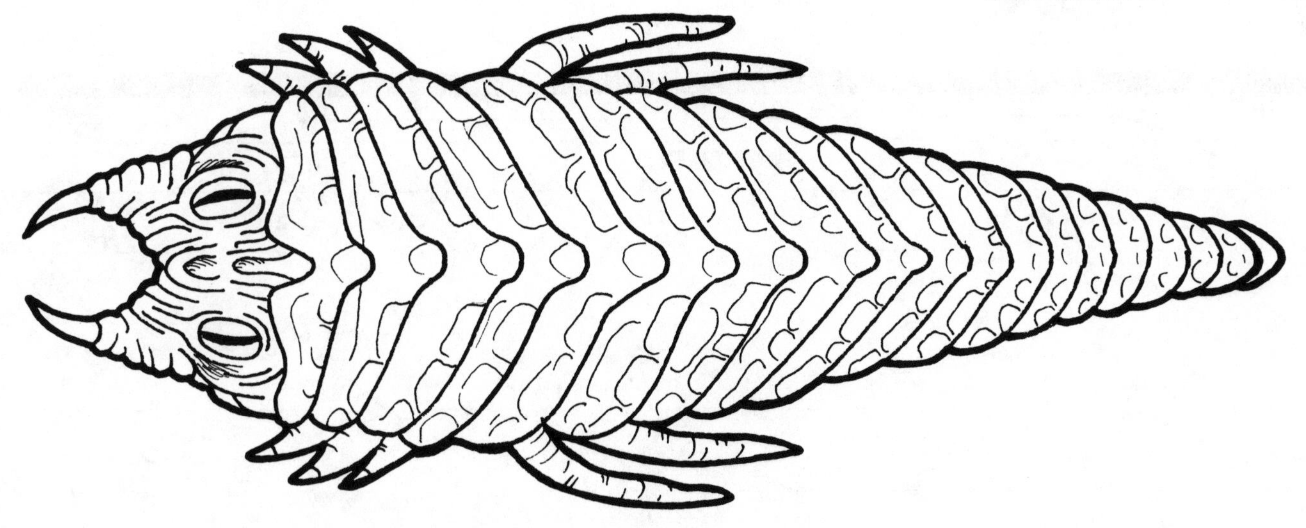

76

39

755

DELOS III, IV (M)
ORNARA, BREKKA
DELOS
[262.3, −43.2, −93.5]

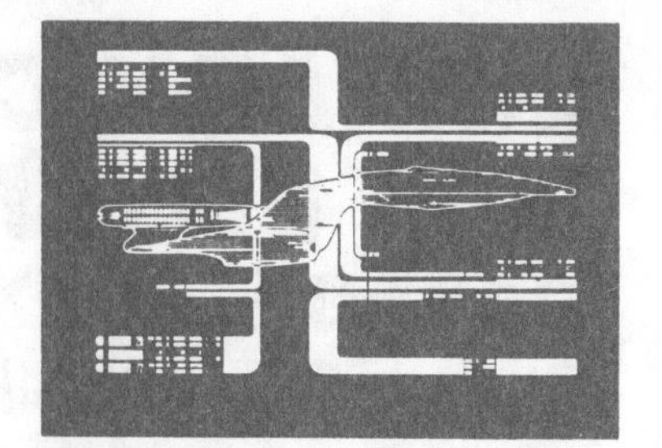

Delos is a moderate-size yellow star with an unremarkable system. The star is subject to massive magnetic field changes, which occur frequently and produce intense disturbances on the stellar surface.

Only two of the system's planets are habitable. The third, Ornara, and the fourth, Brekka, are both Class M and support humanoid cultures rated F plus on the Richter Scale of Culture. Both worlds are capable of rudimentary interplanetary travel.

These two cultures have developed a strange symbiosis and rely upon each other for survival. Ornara supplies all industrial needs for both planets, including food, clothing, building materials, and limited transportation. In exchange, Brekka provides the Ornarans with a highly narcotic drug to which the Ornarans are addicted. Originally created as a cure for a plague that swept Ornara two centuries ago, the chemical substance, Felicium, was so immediately addictive that its grip on the Ornaran natives was established before the side effect was realized. Many Ornarans still believe that they will die of the long-extinct plague if they do not receive their Felicium. The Brekkians are aware of the true nature of the drug, but they know that their economy would suffer greatly if the Ornarans managed to detoxify themselves. The Brekkian desire to keep their fellow beings addicted has resulted in the forfeiture of Federation contact.

889

56

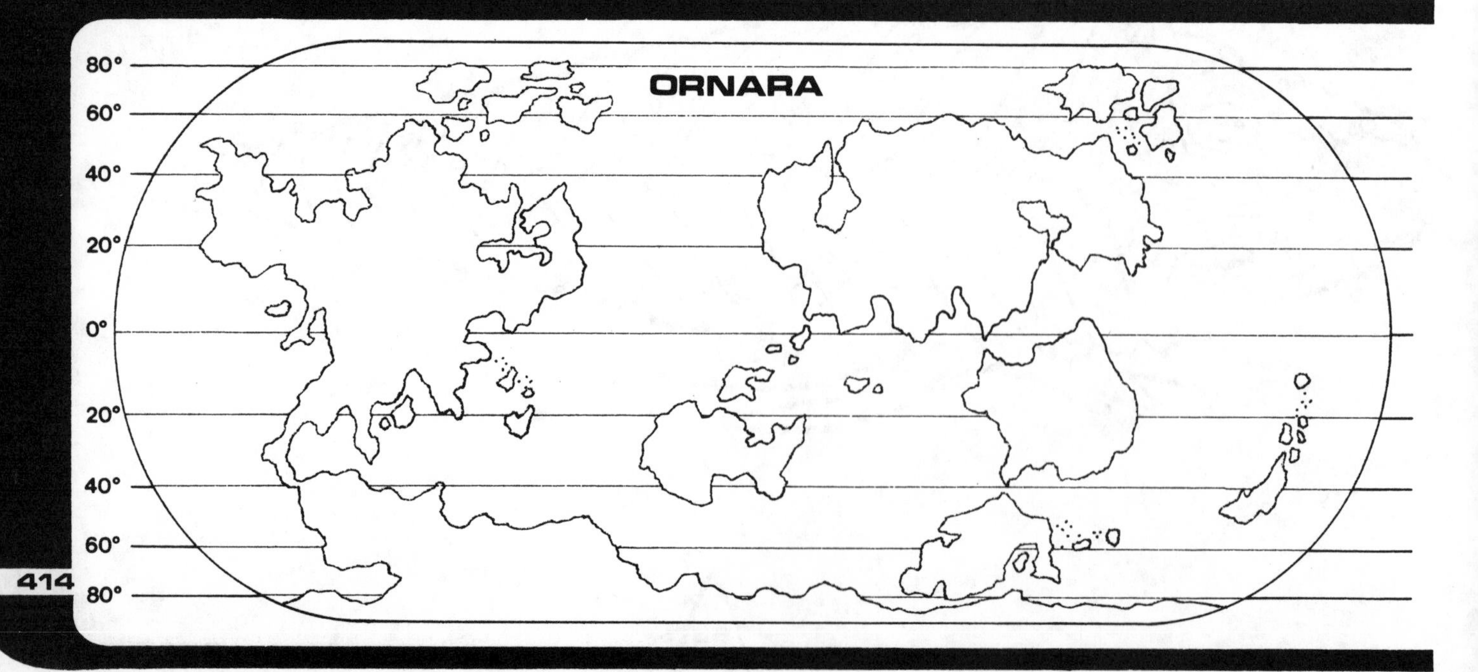

414

LIBRARY COMPUTER — USS ENTERPRISE (NCC-1701-D)
DATABANK EXTRACT (HARDCOPY)
SUBJECT: DELOSIAN

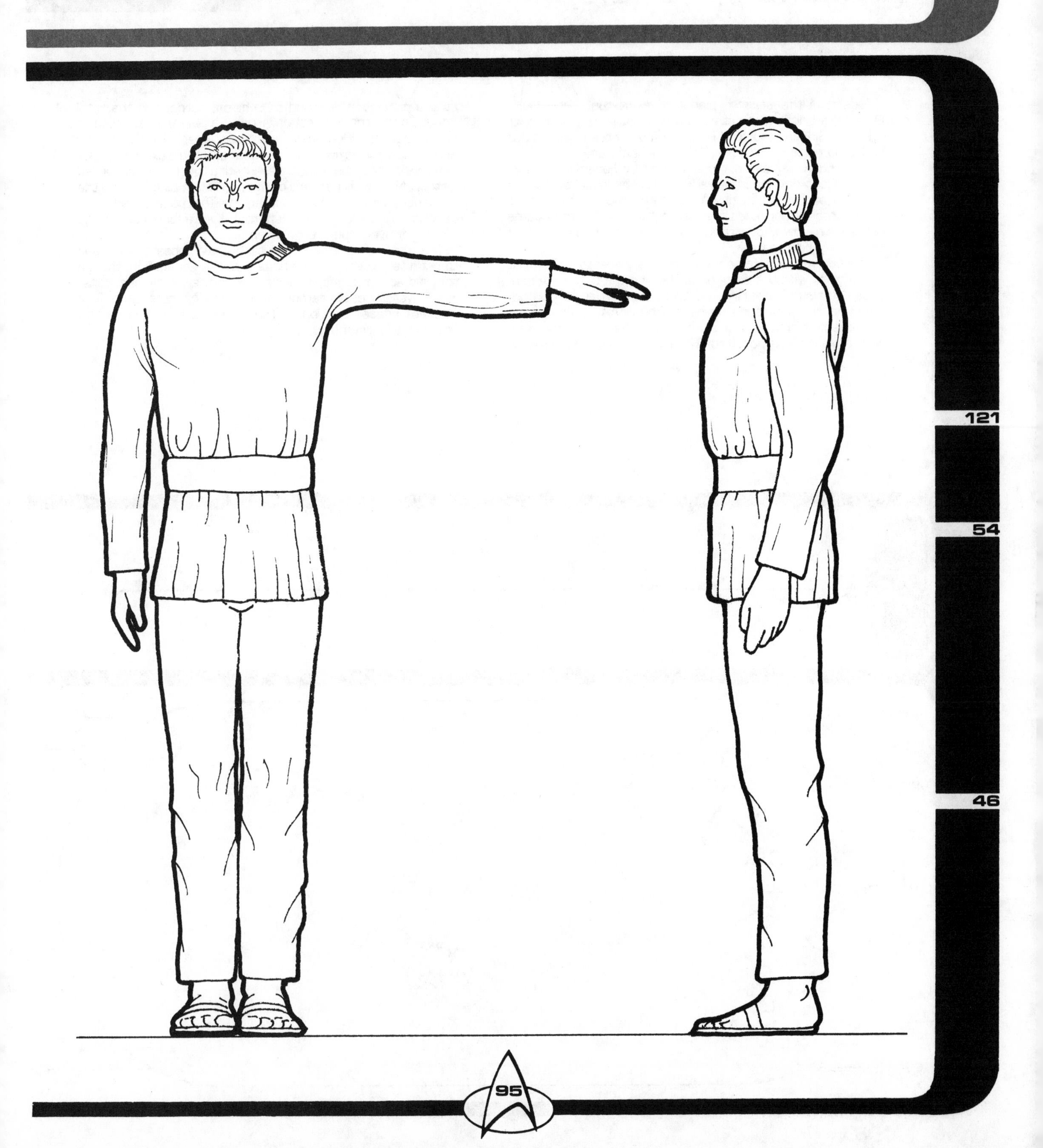

DELTA DORADO VII (M)
GIDEON
DELTA DORADO
[54.5, 42.7, −242.9]

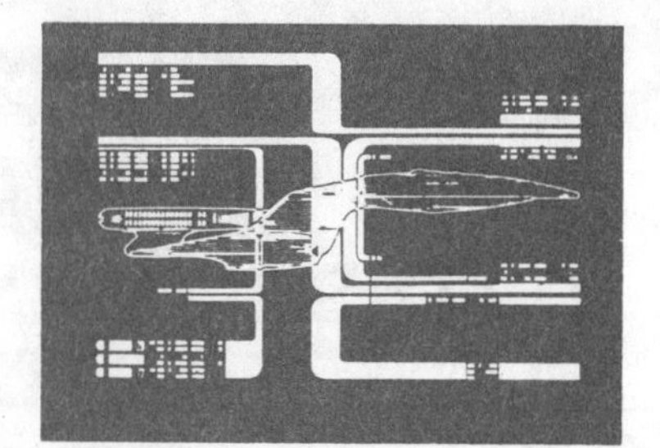

Gideon is the seventh planet of eight that orbit Delta Dorado, a bright white star. The only habitable planet in its system, Gideon's surface is eighty-four percent land mass and is home to an advanced humanoid species.

Through a process not understood by Federation scientists, Gideon developed into a world totally devoid of disease bacteria and viral strains. As a result, the inhabitants' life spans steadily increased over the centuries. Death became virtually unknown, occurring only when the body could no longer regenerate itself.

The people loved life so much that they absolutely refused to interfere with the creation of life, and the birth rate continued to rise. Eventually, the Gideonites developed an unmatched overpopulation problem. The crisis reached such extreme proportions that every square meter of land area on the planet was occupied. The natives longed for release as the population reached 500 billion, surpassing the total population of the Federation. Finally, a plan was enacted to bring Vegan choriomeningitis to the planet. The Gideonites had no natural immunity to disease, and the sickness quickly developed into the most devastating plague in recorded history. Ninety-six percent of the population died, leaving the hardened survivors to start again. The people had such devotion to their fellow men that to die and relieve the burden of overpopulation was an honor.

The planet's remaining inhabitants have repeatedly refused to establish diplomatic relations with the Federation, though they did accept a gift of many phaser-energy disposal units, which were used to remove the bodies of the dead before further diseases developed. Today the planet is a very lonely one and largely empty.

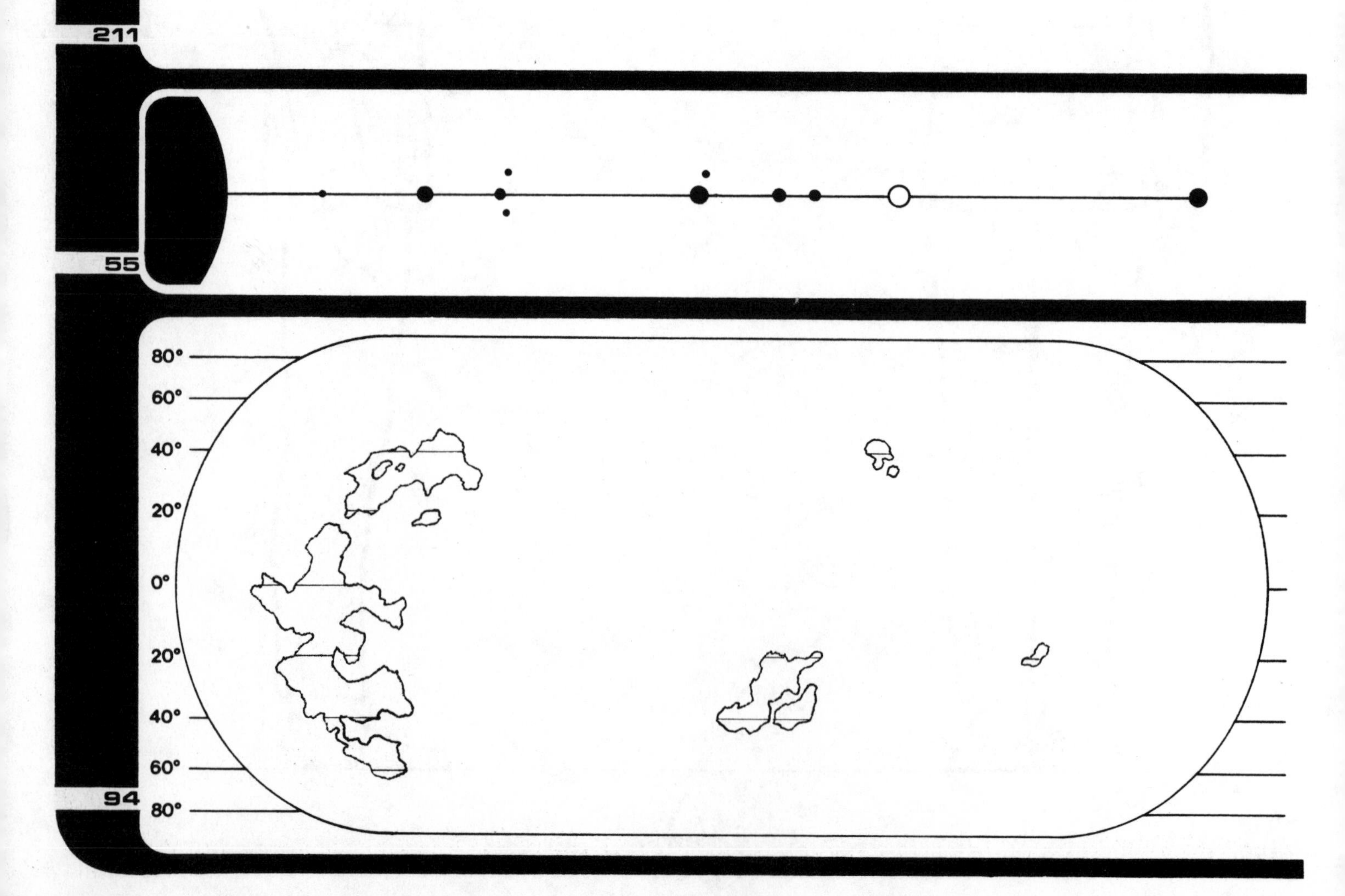

EXCALBIAN
EXCALBIA I
THOLIAN
THOLIA
HORTA WITH EGG NODULES
JANUS VI

MUGATO
ZETA BOOTIS III
M-113 CREATURE
PLANET M-113

TARG
KLING
SCORA
VEGA IX
DENEBIAN SLIME DEVIL
DENEB IV

PUNCHATZ

CAPELLAN POWER CAT
CAPELLA IV
BERENGARIAN DRAGON
BERENGARIA VII

EELBIRD
REGULUS
LE-MATYA
VULCAN
SEHLAT
VULCAN

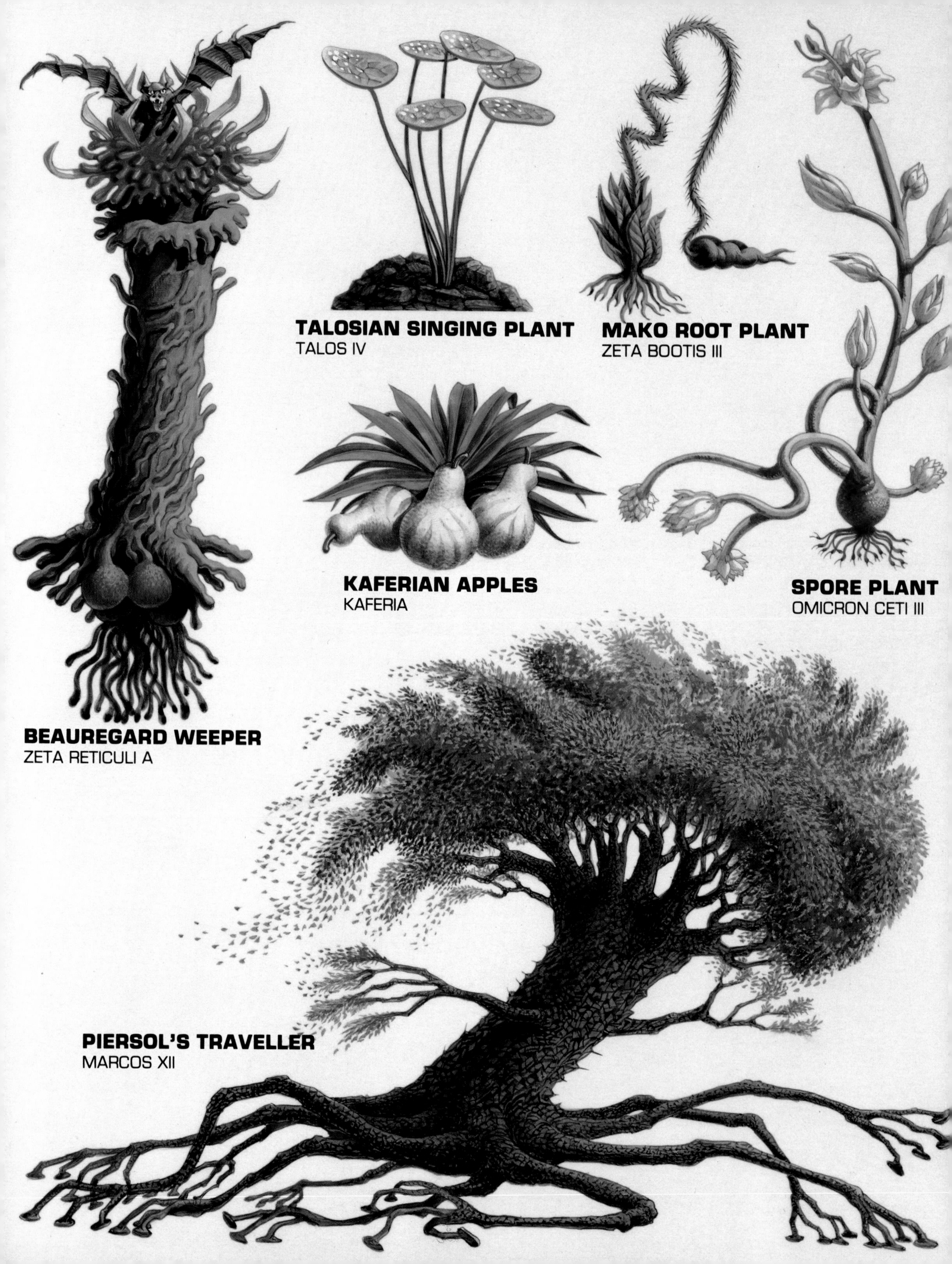
TALOSIAN SINGING PLANT
TALOS IV
MAKO ROOT PLANT
ZETA BOOTIS III
KAFERIAN APPLES
KAFERIA
SPORE PLANT
OMICRON CETI III
BEAUREGARD WEEPER
ZETA RETICULI A
PIERSOL'S TRAVELLER
MARCOS XII

LIBRARY COMPUTER — USS ENTERPRISE (NCC-1701-D)
DATABANK EXTRACT (HARDCOPY)
SUBJECT: GIDEONITE

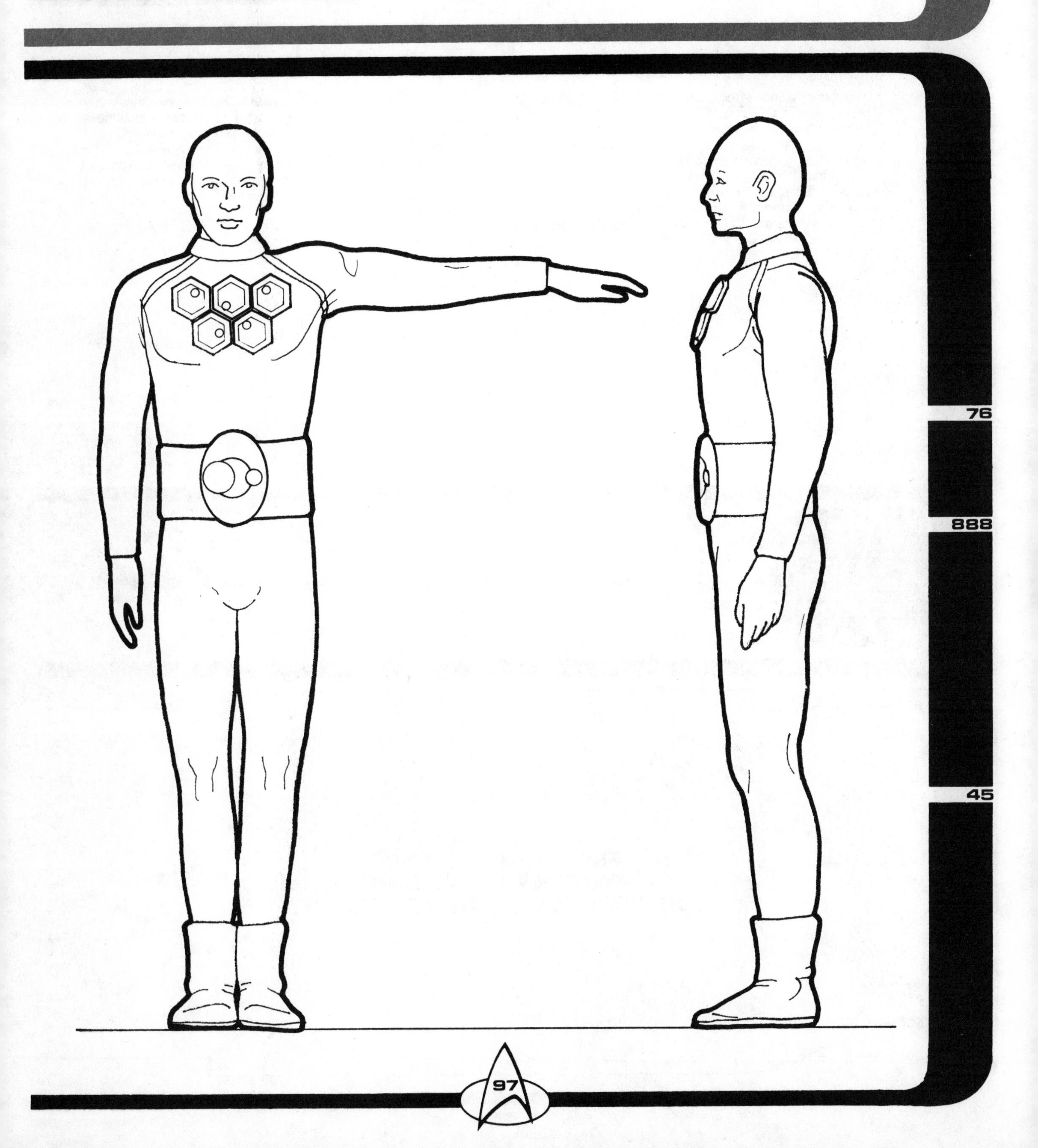

DIMORUS IV (M)
INDIGENOUS NAME UNKNOWN
DIMORUS

[−26.7, −18.8, −27.9]

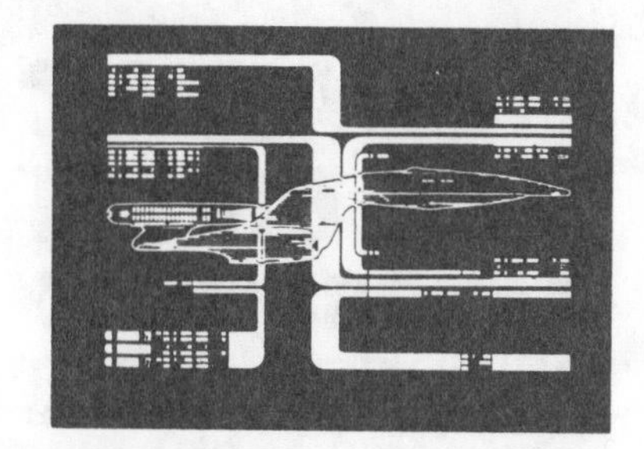

The fourth planet of eight that orbit a pair of moderate-size orange stars, Dimorus IV is entirely covered by massive forests with dense underbrush. Fed by an intricate network of underground reservoirs, these timberlands support thousands of indigenous life forms.

The planet has a native population of sapient, rodentlike creatures. Bipedal, they stand approximately half as tall as humanoids. Dimorus was once used as a research facility and living laboratory for botanists but was placed under Federation quarantine when researchers learned that the intelligent rodent creatures were extreme xenophobes. Several early expedition members died when hit by the highly toxic "darts" thrown by the rodents, which are similar to the quills of the Terran porcupine. An antidote was eventually developed, but the constant threat to landing parties and the unnecessary stress on the natives led to the cancellation of all expeditions to the planet.

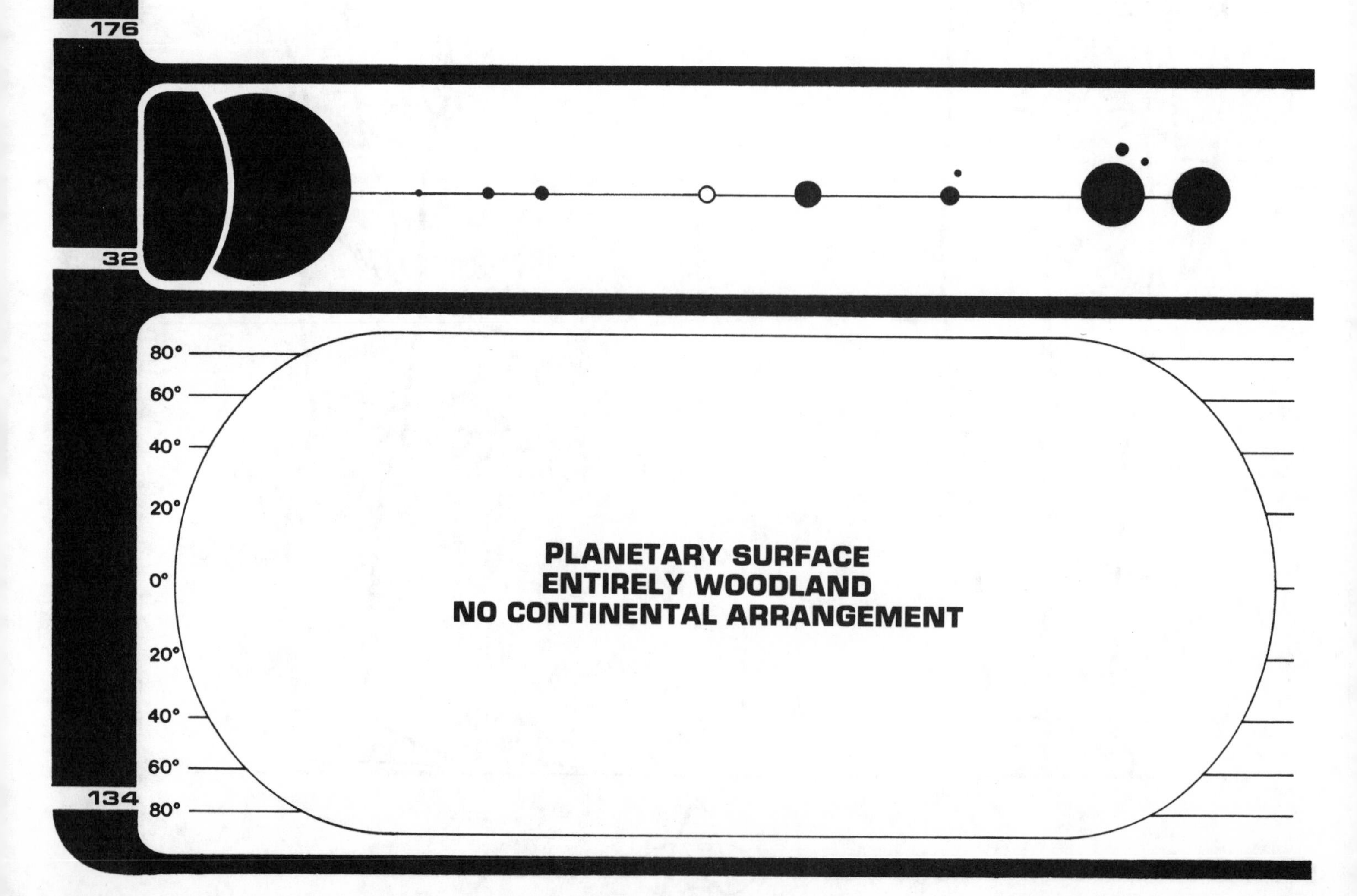

LIBRARY COMPUTER — USS ENTERPRISE (NCC-1701-D)
DATABANK EXTRACT (HARDCOPY)
SUBJECT: DIMORUSIAN

HEIGHT:
0.7 METERS
WEIGHT:
32 KILOS
AVERAGE LIFESPAN:
14 YEARS

912
65
01

892-IV (M)
MAGNA ROMA
UFC 892
[−132.1, −101.1, −56.7]

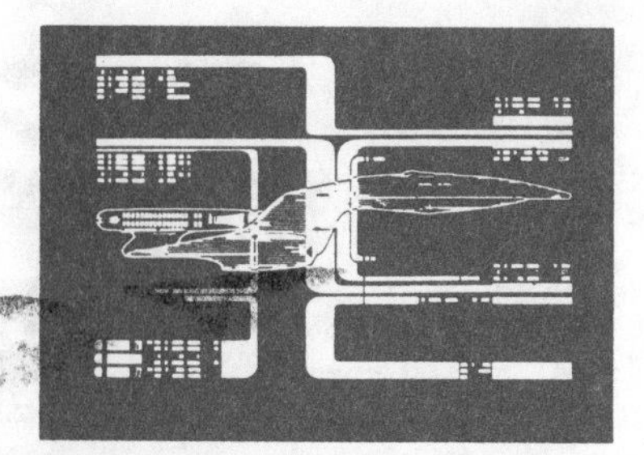

A yellow dwarf star, UFC 892 supports a system of eleven planets that very closely parallels that of Sol, Terra's primary. Unlike Sol, UFC 892 has an additional planet in an extremely close orbit around its star, so near that the world is virtually molten.

Planet four of the system is nearly identical to Terra, a perfect example of Hodgkin's Law of Parallel Planet Development. It is Class M, with the same proportions of land to water as Earth, a mean density of 5.5, a diameter of 7917 miles, and an atmosphere that is seventy-eight percent nitrogen and twenty percent oxygen. In effect, it is both physically and culturally a duplicate of twentieth-century Earth, with a few notable exceptions.

On Magna Roma, the Roman Empire didn't fall as it did on Terra. When the planet was first encountered it was an unusual combination of technological advancement and cruelty, with slavery and killing-for-entertainment as accepted practices. Like Earth, Magna Roma had known Caesarean rule and the coming of Christ, but it was not until nearly two thousand years after the advent of Christianity that the grip of the Roman dictatorship was finally broken.

Since then, the Magna Romans have developed very quickly. After abandoning their gladiator-style entertainment, their culture and technology advanced at an accelerated rate. Magna Roma is in the process of becoming a Federation member world, contributing valuable goods, services, and personnel.

499

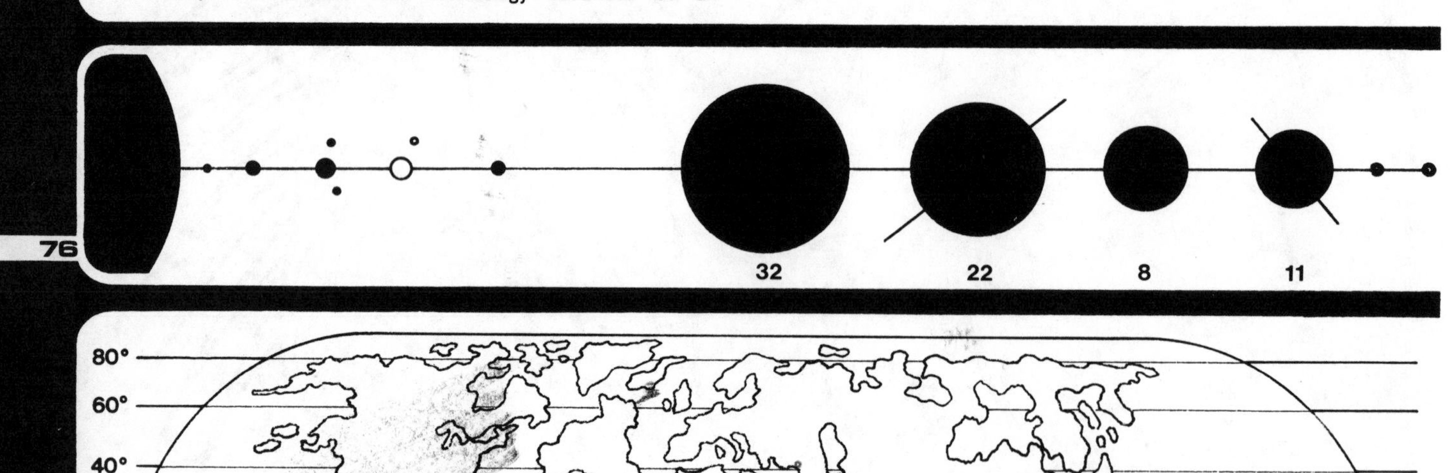

80°
60°
40°
20°
0°
20°
40°
60°
128
80°

LIBRARY COMPUTER — USS ENTERPRISE (NCC-1701-D)
DATABANK EXTRACT (HARDCOPY)
SUBJECT: MAGNA ROMAN (SLAVE)

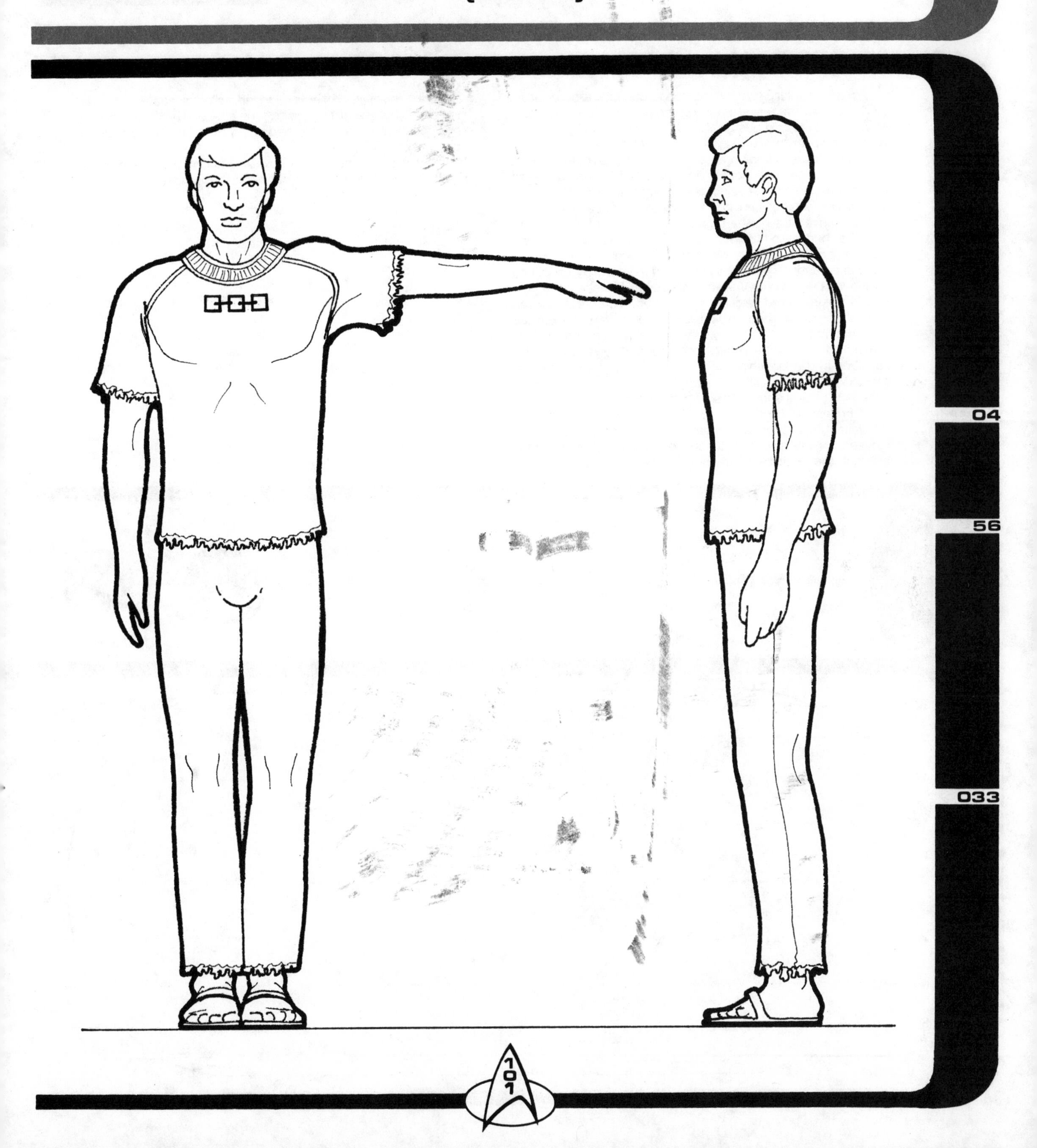

EMINIAR III, VII (M)
VENDIKAR, EMINIAR
EMINIAR
[−37.0, 222.3, 25.1]

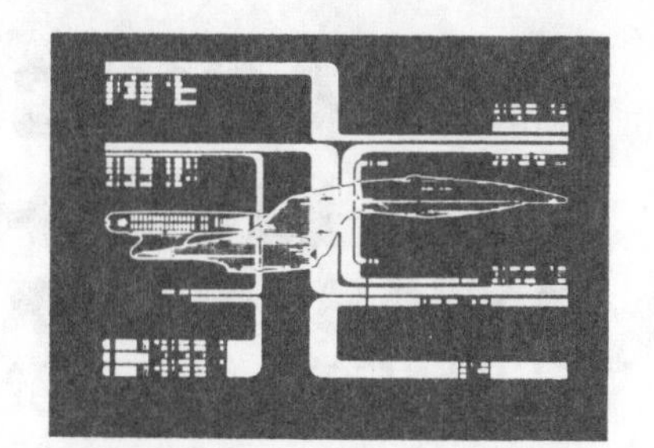

Eminiar is a large yellow star in a dense stellar cluster, NGC 321. It has a system of eleven planets, the outer two of which are ringed gas giants. Of the solid worlds, only the third and seventh are Class M and inhabited.

Eminiar III, also known as Vendikar, originally began as a colony of Eminiar VII. Both are home to advanced humanoid civilizations, who possess some of the most extensive and intricate computer technology known to the Federation.

The inhabitants of the two worlds recently halted a civil war that had lasted for more than five hundred years. Their war had become a clean, bloodless one fought by computers and based entirely upon data obtained from their interlocked intelligence systems. When an attack was launched, the projected target would register a "hit," and computer-chosen casualties were then expected to report to designated disintegration stations where they would be neatly eliminated. Failure to report constituted breach of treaty, resulting in the launching of actual weapons against the offending party.

When a Federation starship was declared "hit" as it orbited Eminiar VII, the Eminians demanded that the crew of the vessel report for disintegration. When the ship's captain refused to comply, the threat of actual impending war brought the inhabitants of the two warring planets to the negotiation table. After prolonged talks, a cease-fire was reached that eventually led to true peace. Their war ended, but only after millions had died in the disintegration chambers.

At this time, the Eminian system enjoys a trade alliance with the Federation and is considering membership.

211

03

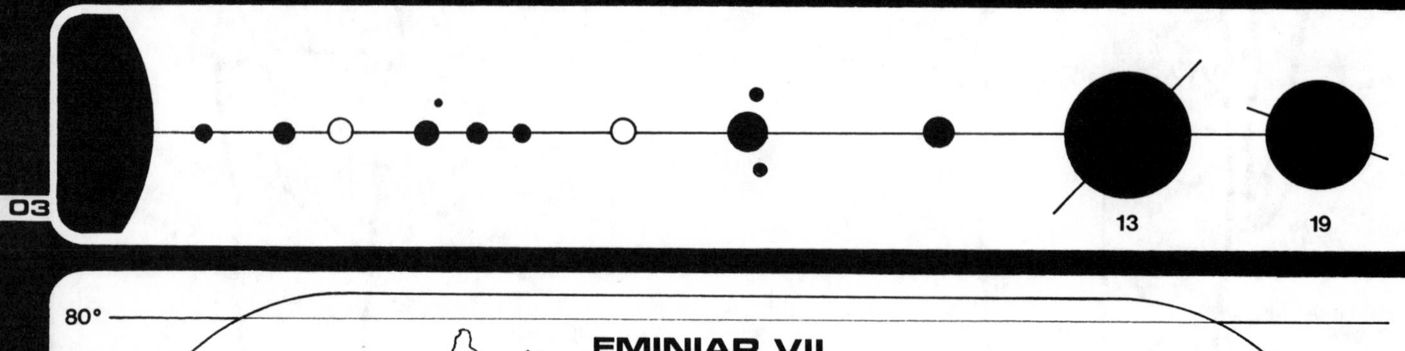

67

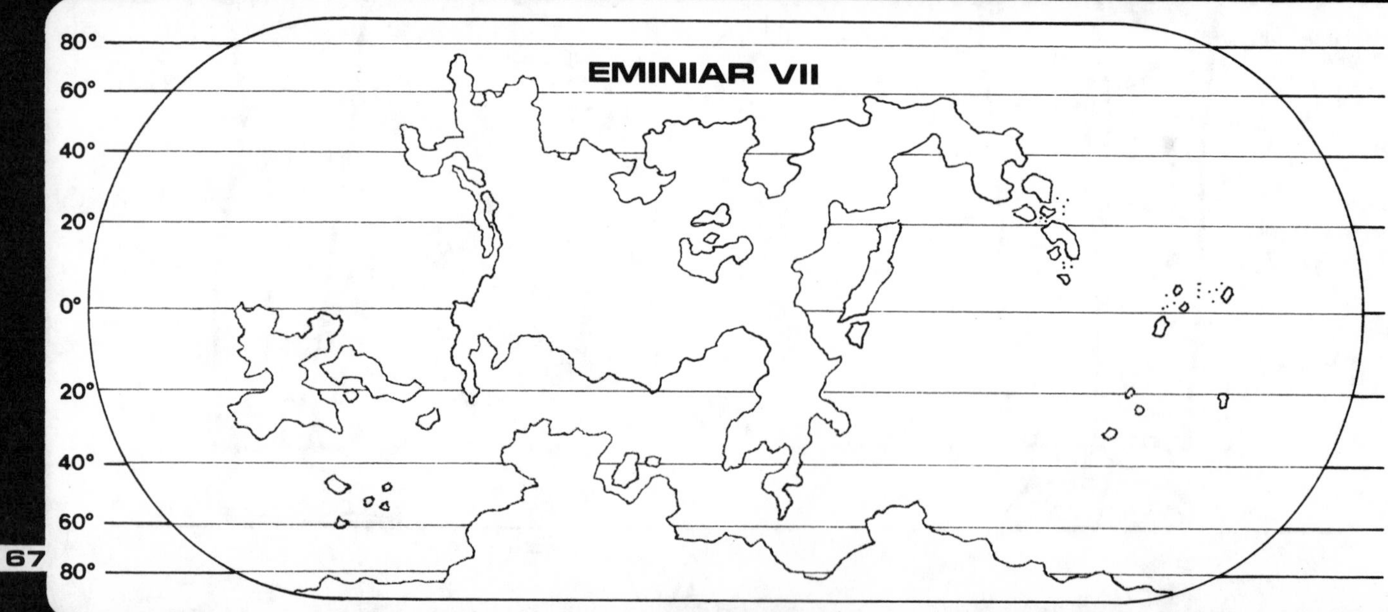

LIBRARY COMPUTER — USS ENTERPRISE (NCC-1701-D)
DATABANK EXTRACT (HARDCOPY)
SUBJECT: EMINIAN

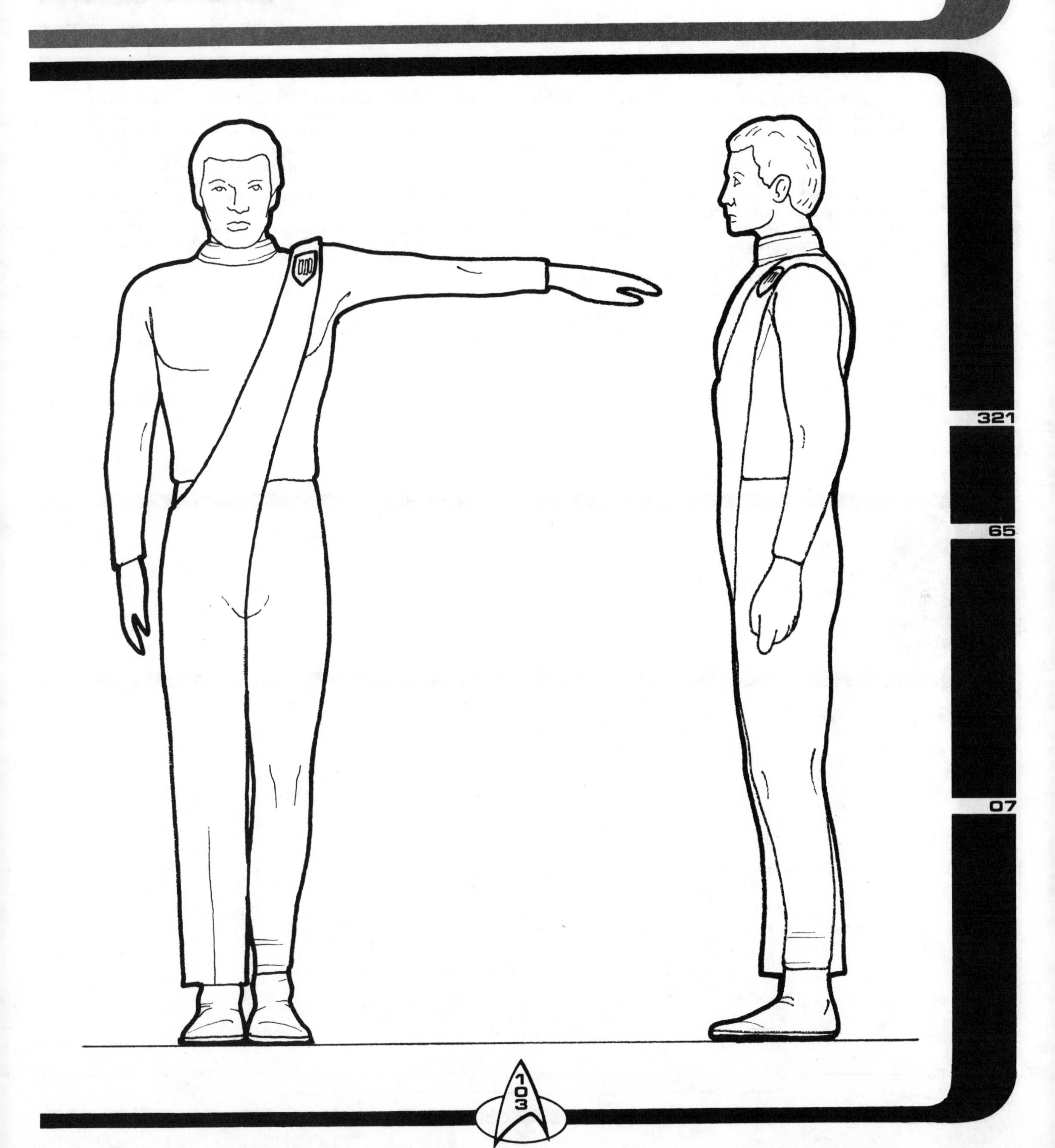

EXCALBIA I (I)
INDIGENOUS NAME UNKNOWN
EXCALBIA

[−54.8, −157.7, −193.4]

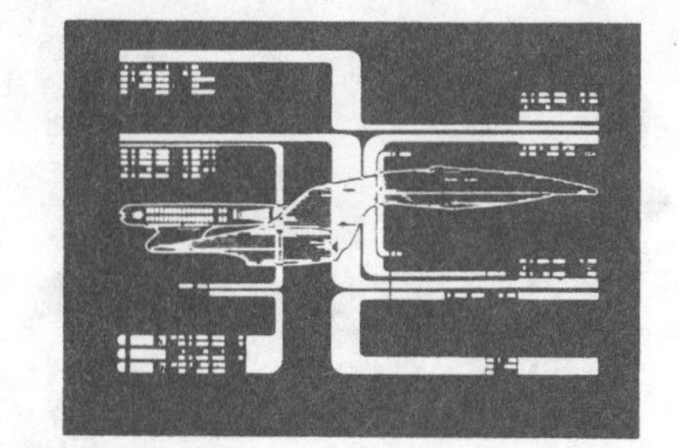

Excalbia is the first of three planets orbiting a blue-white giant star. Like many Class I planets, its surface consists entirely of molten lava and primeval gases. Unlike other Class I worlds, however, Excalbia has produced a sentient native life form.

The Excalbians are a carbon-cycle race of beings with a body chemistry based upon calcium carbonate. While little is known about their society or capabilities, they have shown the ability to alter their planet in order to produce other environments for research purposes.

Excalbians are creatures of "living rock," with no apparent internal organs and incredibly high body temperatures. They can draw minerals from within themselves to form quartz lenses for seeing or mineral claws for crushing, with no apparent limit to the variety in their external configurations.

Excalbia is under general quarantine due to an event that nearly caused the deaths of Captain Kirk and Commander Spock of the Constitution class USS **Enterprise**. These two officers were forced to fight for their lives in an Excalbian "theater" display through which the Excalbians hoped to learn the difference between good and evil. To avoid further incidents, the planet has been declared off limits to Federation personnel.

51

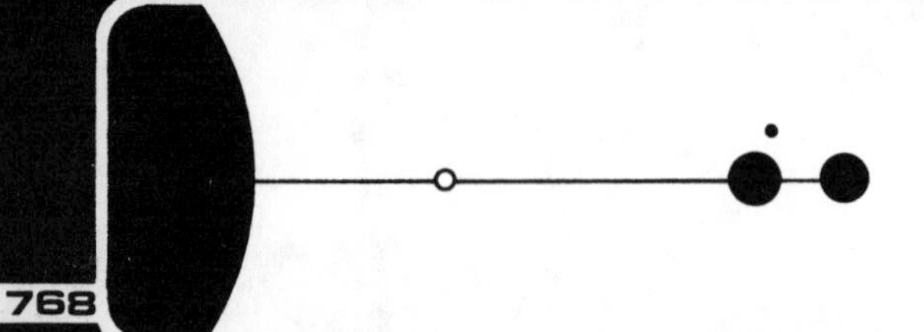

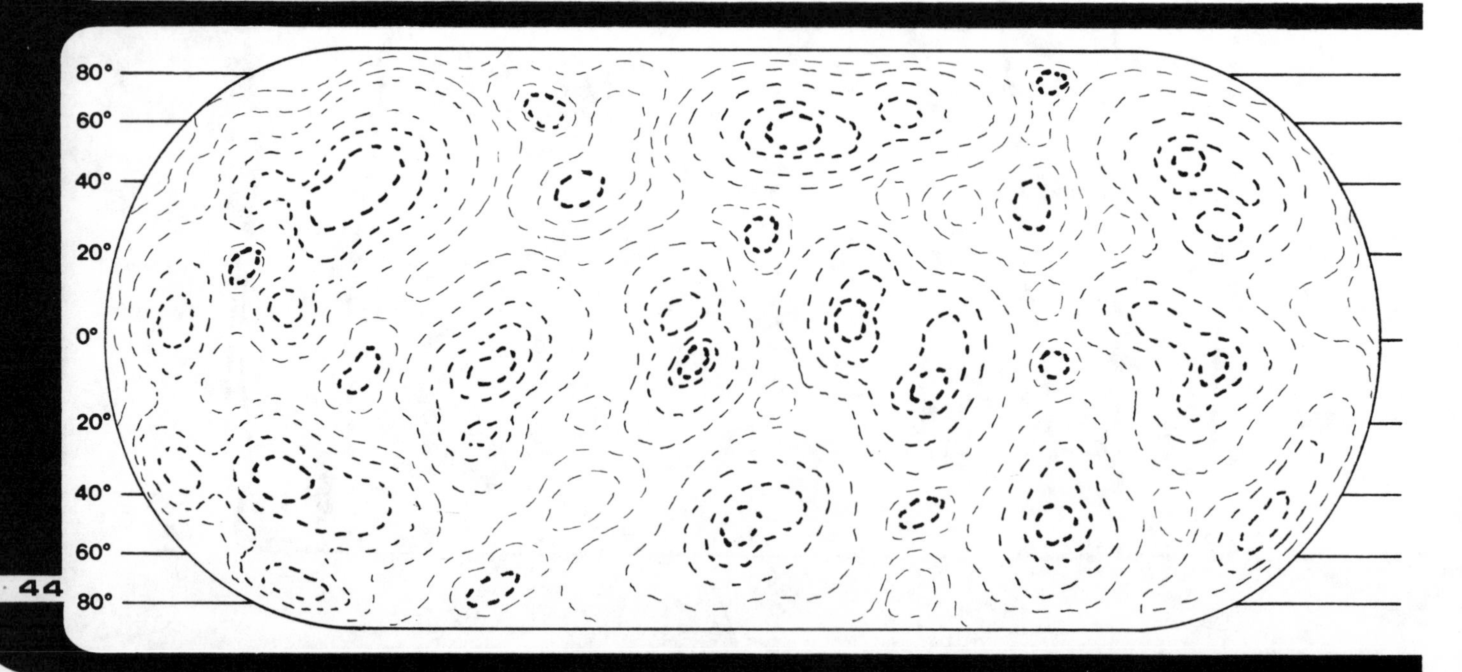

LIBRARY COMPUTER — USS ENTERPRISE (NCC-1701-D)
DATABANK EXTRACT (HARDCOPY)
SUBJECT: EXCALBIAN

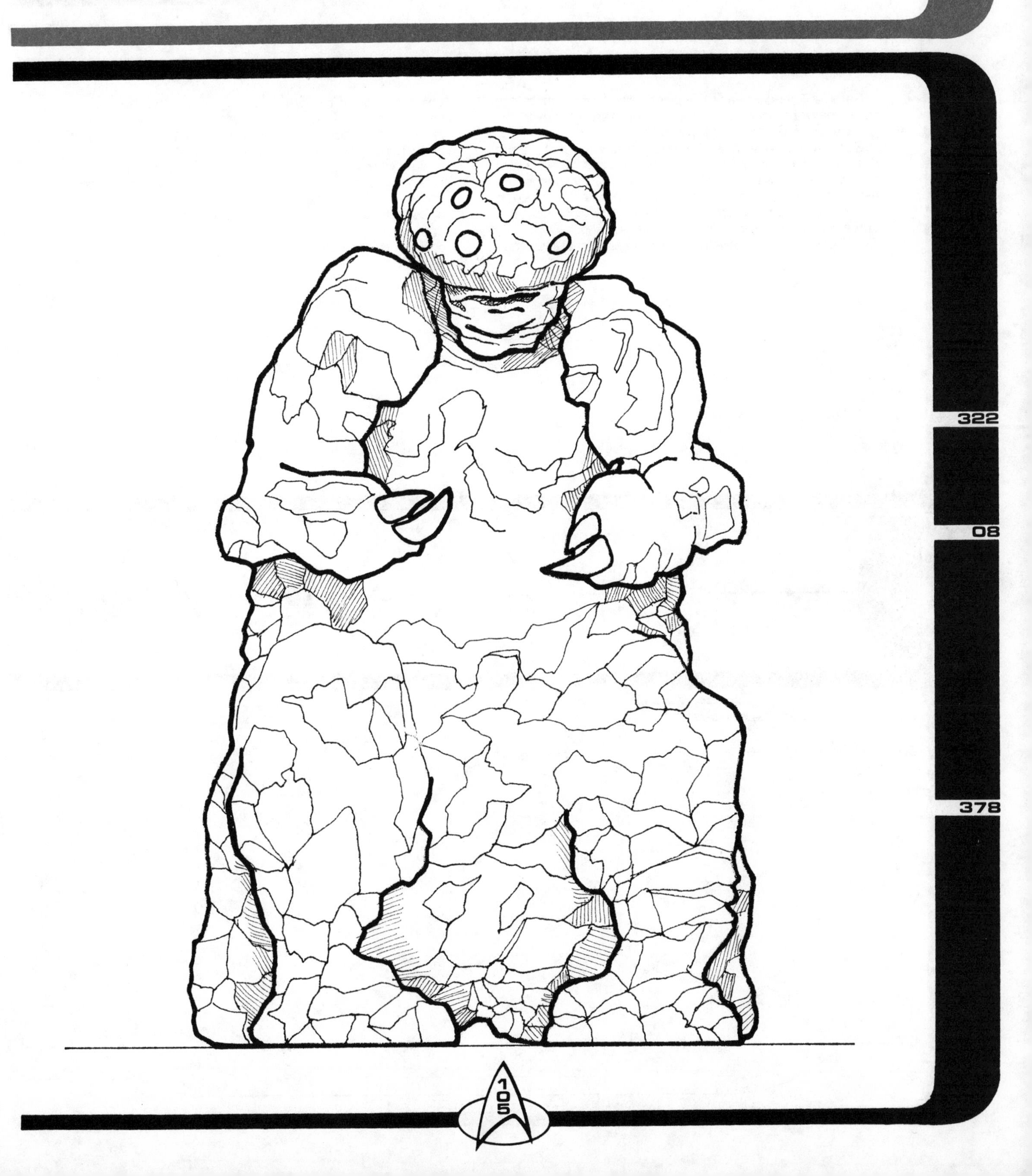

GAMMA TRIANGULI VI (M)

VAALEL

GAMMA TRIANGULI

[–170.5, –126.0, 91.6]

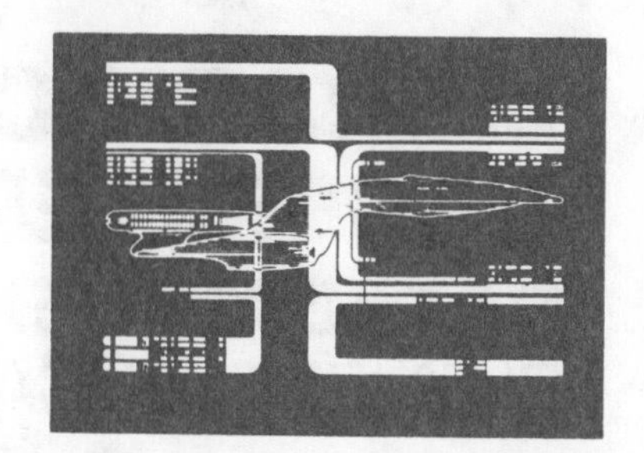

Gamma Trianguli is a yellow giant with eleven planets and three major asteroid belts. Planets eight through eleven are gas giants, while nine and ten are ringed.

Gamma Trianguli VI is the only inhabited planet in the system. A tropical jungle world, it has a mean temperature of seventy-six degrees, even at its poles. One dangerous native feature is a common, rainbow-hued mineral containing a mixture of elements that make the rock violently unstable and explosive when treated to any sudden shock.

The planet has a native humanoid population of less than one thousand, with life spans approaching two hundred and fifty years. Rather simple in their ways, these people are primitive in culture and have no native technology beyond basic hand tools. At one time, the lives of the population were controlled by an underground computer system called "Vaal" by the natives. Built by whatever civilization planted the humanoids on the planet, this supercomputer-controlled all aspects of the natives' lives, including their environment. The system was destroyed before Federation researchers could learn the computer's methods of climate control.

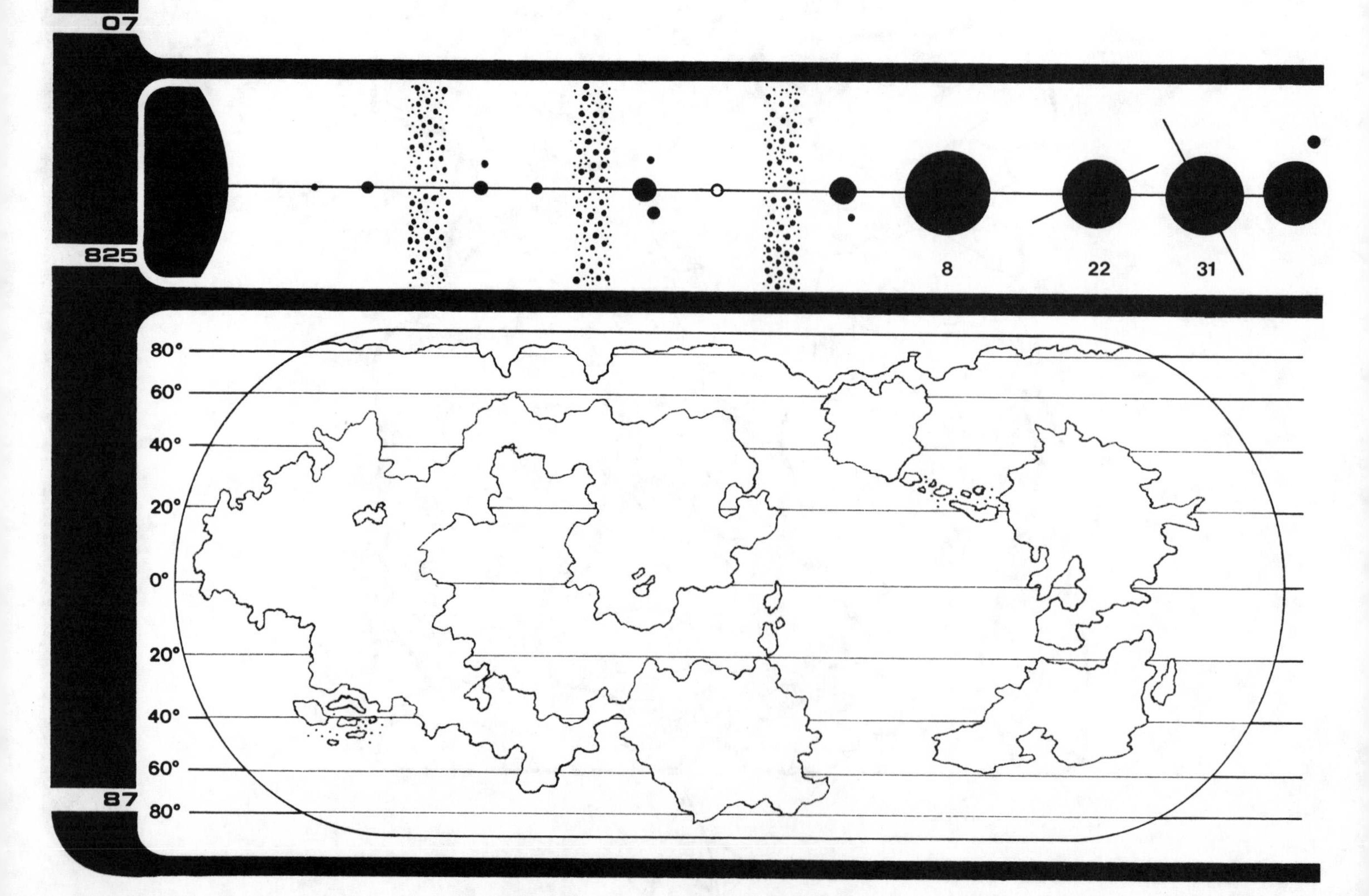

LIBRARY COMPUTER — USS ENTERPRISE (NCC-1701-D)
DATABANK EXTRACT (HARDCOPY)
SUBJECT: VAAL COMPUTER ENTRYWAY

IOTIA (M)
OXMYX
SIGMA IOTIA

[−5.7, −144.2, −109.1]

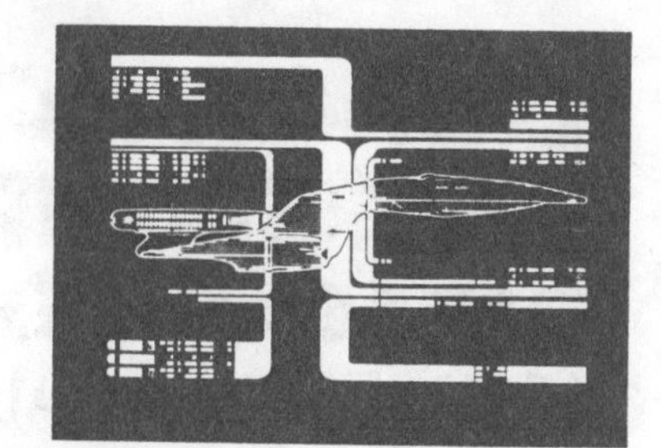

The planet Iotia has become a textbook example of the importance of the Prime Directive. Through an inadvertent act, Iotia's course of history was forever changed by a visit from the USS **Horizon** nearly two hundred years ago.

The planet is the second of nine that orbit a large yellow star. It is the only world in its system capable of sustaining life and harbors a race of intelligent humanoids with a distinct talent for imitation.

The **Horizon** contamination came from a single printed volume, entitled **Chicago Mobs of the Twenties**. Accidentally left behind when the starship broke orbit, the book gave a complete history of crime gang rule on Earth of the 1920's. It soon became the cultural instruction manual for a bright people who felt that stagnation was creeping into their society. The populace quickly embraced the new crime philosophy, and Iotia became a planet led by gangs and crime bosses as radio, automobiles, and projectile weapons were developed in a burst of technological growth. The planet's official language became English, including the gangland slang commonly used by the historical figures noted in the book.

During a second mission to Iotia to undo the damage of the first, the Constitution class USS **Enterprise** inadvertently left another article behind that would cause further contamination. A communicator, built using transtator physics, was discovered by the Iotian inhabitants. They quickly abandoned their mobster culture and jumped at the opportunity presented by the new treasure. The next vessel to orbit Iotia found what at first appeared to be a Federation starbase, complete with uniformed personnel and communications on Starfleet frequencies.

The planet is now a Federation Protectorate with a current cultural rating of E plus. While the planet is not under quarantine, all visiting personnel must first be cleared through a new orbital customs facility.

211

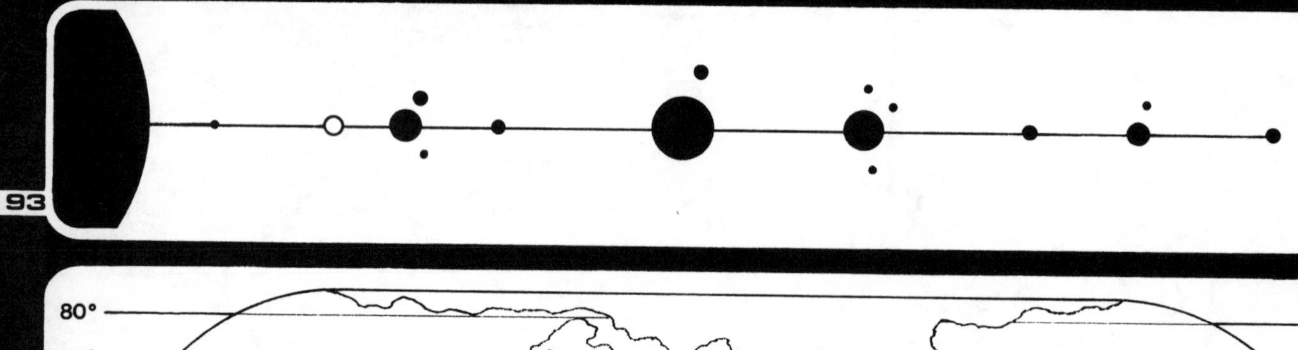

93

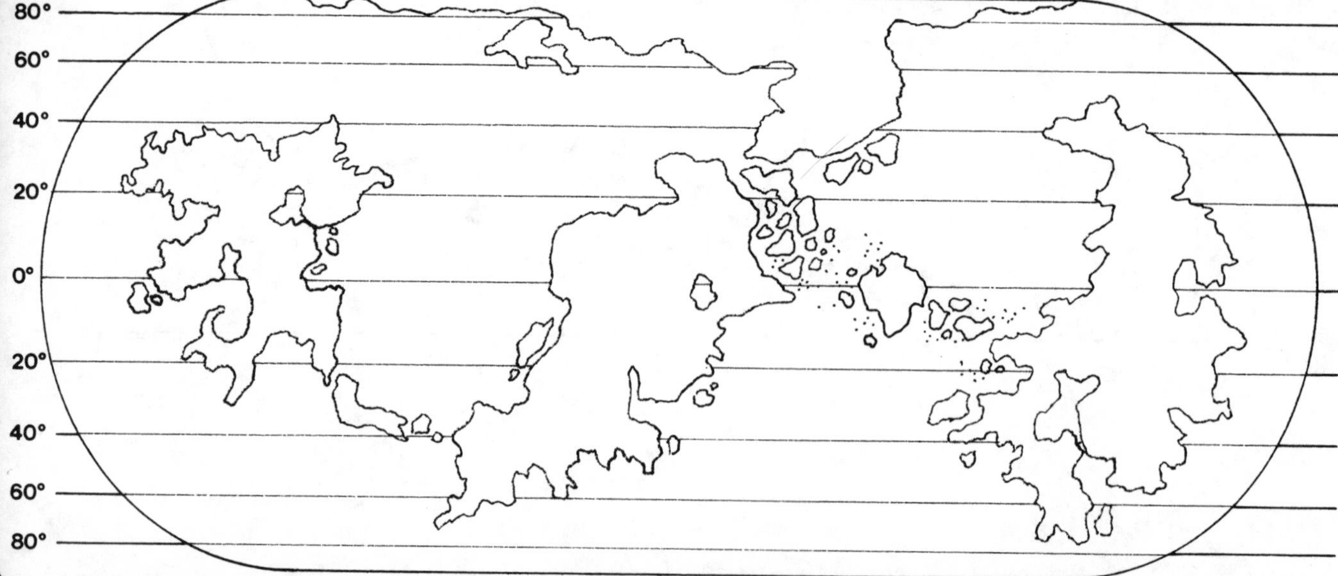

768

LIBRARY COMPUTER — USS ENTERPRISE (NCC-1701-D)
DATABANK EXTRACT (HARDCOPY)
SUBJECT: IOTIAN

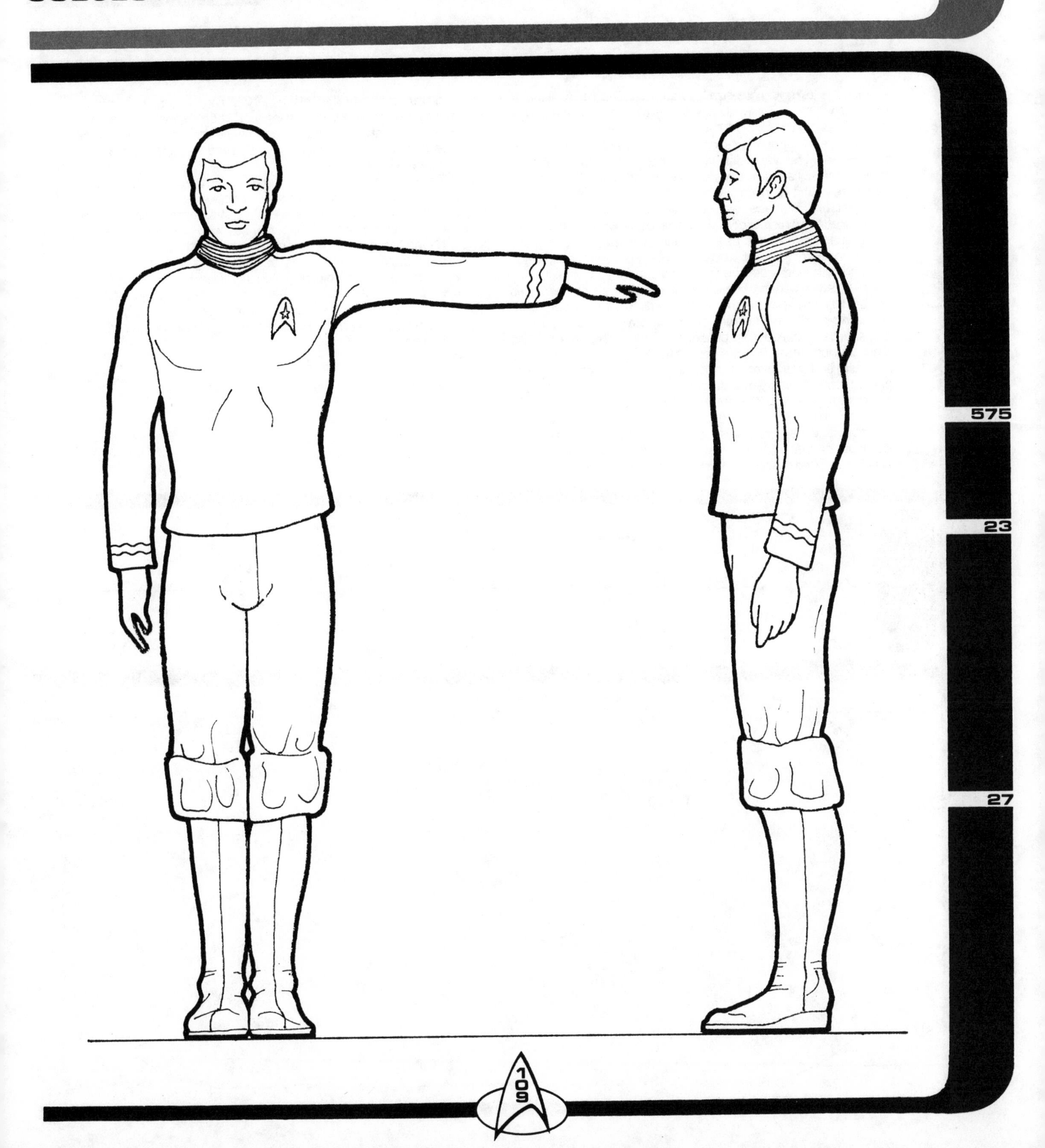

JANUS VI (E)
SHAUL
JANUS
[−123.8, −30.1, −15.8]

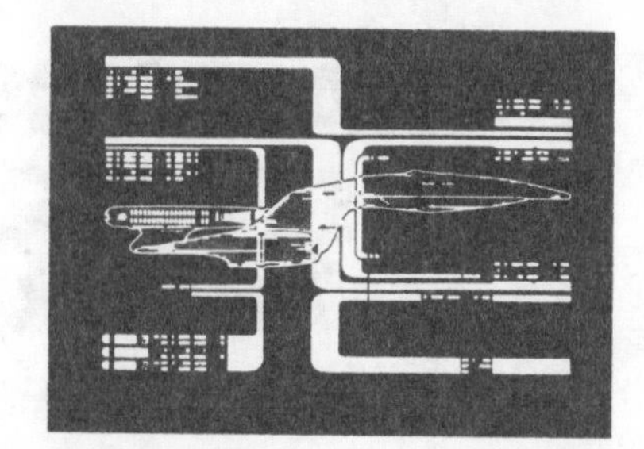

Janus is a moderate-size orange star with ten planets, none of which is Class M. It was believed that none of the planets supported life until the recent discovery of the Horta.

Orbital sensor scans indicated that the sixth world of the system was heavily laden with pergium and other super-heavy elements, which were used in most of the nuclear reactors found at ground-based Federation colonies. While the planet's surface was hostile and uninhabitable, an underground mining facility was built that, when completed, could supply the needs of a thousand planets. An extensive subsurface network of tunnels was eventually created and mining continued smoothly for more than fifty years.

Then, after penetrating a new lower-level cavern, miners began to die mysteriously, the victims of an unseen acid-throwing monster. Pergium production was halted, causing the shutdown of reactors on a dozen Federation planets. The Constitution class USS **Enterprise** was assigned to halt the menace and reactivate the mining facility. Upon investigation, they discovered that the miners had inadvertently broken into the egg chamber of the Janus system's only indigenous life form, the Horta. The only known intelligent silicon-based life form, the Horta had attacked the miners in defense of her children, yet unhatched. The last of her species, she had shared her planet peacefully for more than half a century, intentionally staying clear of those areas used by the miners. Researchers later learned that following a life span of approximately sixty thousand years the entire Horta race dies out, leaving a single Horta to tend the eggs and insure their safe hatching.

Fifty-six miners died before a Vulcan telepath communicated with the creature. Peace was made once the mother Horta was convinced that the damage to some of the eggs was unintentional. In fact, the Horta proved to be such an intelligent and forgiving being that she and the babies, once hatched, assisted the mining operation by using their acid spray to dig new tunnels. Pergium production increased dramatically since the Hortas move through stone as men move through air. Since that time a true partnership has developed, and the Hortas own a half interest in the mining colony.

216

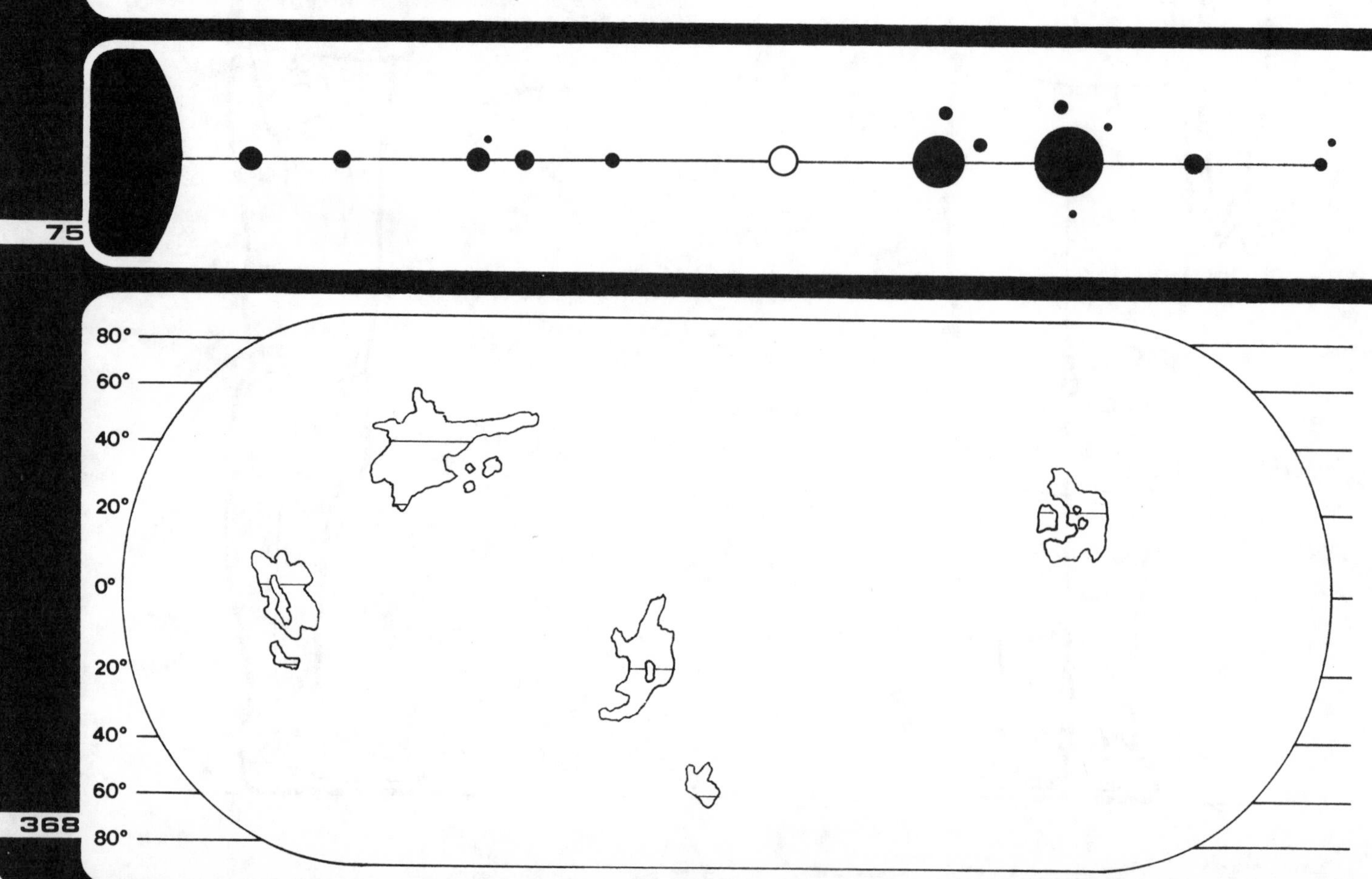

LIBRARY COMPUTER — USS ENTERPRISE (NCC-1701-D)
DATABANK EXTRACT (HARDCOPY)
SUBJECT: JANUSAN HORTA

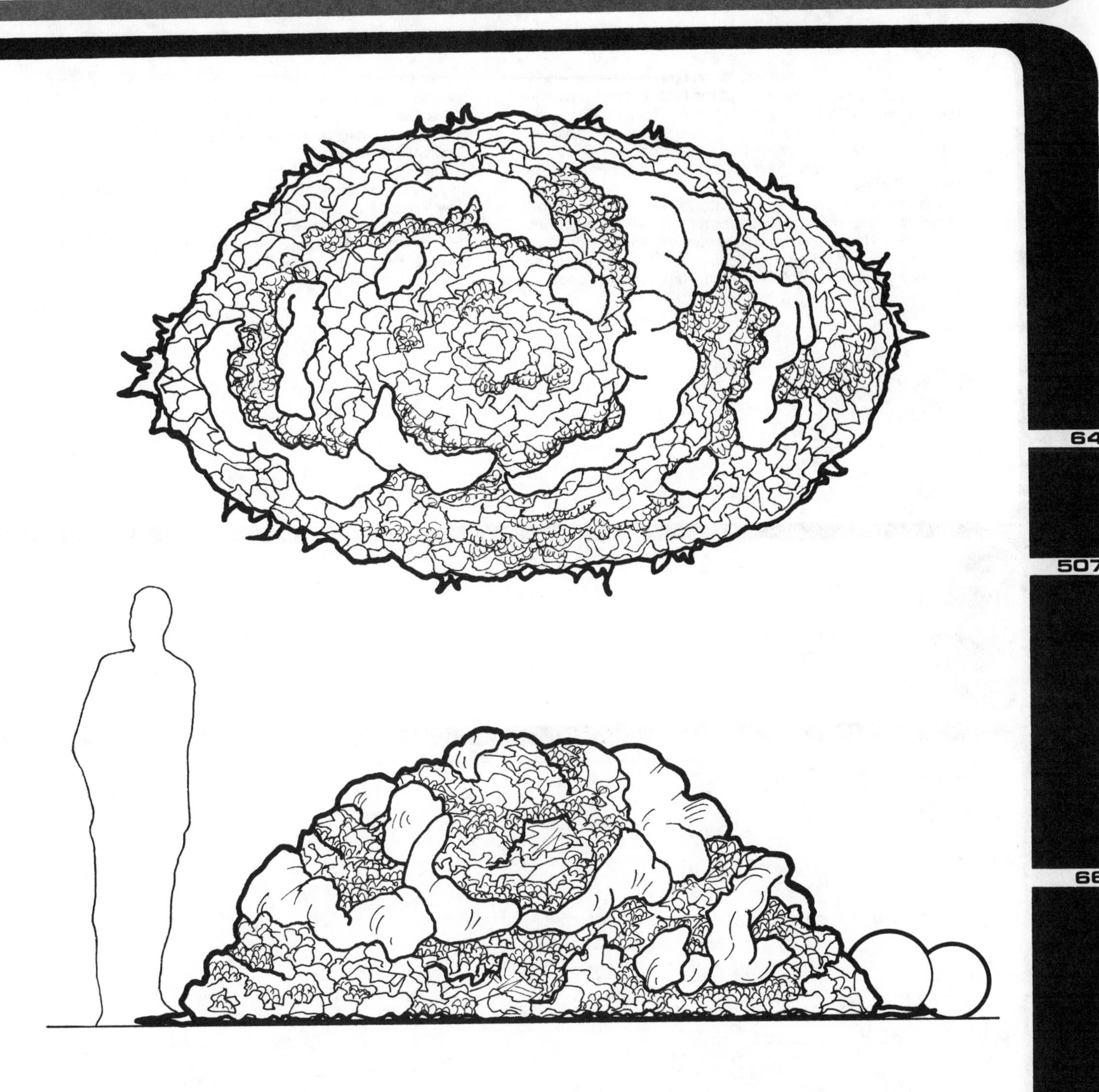

KAFERIA (M)
KOHATH-SEREDI
TAU CETI
(22.8, 58.7, −1.5)

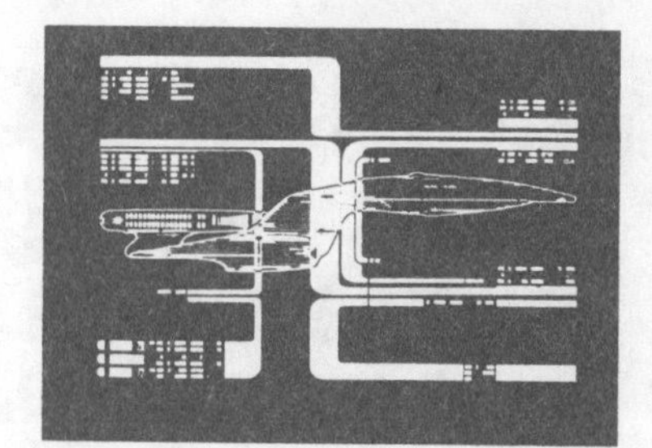

The third planet of five orbiting the moderate-size yellow star Tau Ceti, Kaferia was one of the first nonhuman civilizations contacted by Federation explorers. Travel through the system is difficult, as Tau Ceti supports the greatest interplanetary cloud of debris ever seen. Rock and ice fill the transorbital voids to such an extent that the planet must be approached from the poles.

The native Kaferians are insectoids who have humanoid shape and build their dwellings from gathered soil and plant materials. Their structures sometimes reach heights of eight to nine hundred feet and are interconnected by slideways, which the Kaferians spin from their own bodies.

The Kaferians have enjoyed a highly profitable trade relationship with the Federation for more than two hundred years and are extremely friendly toward visiting races. They prefer, however, to remain a trusted ally rather than a Federation member.

These talented insectoids are expert geneticists. Their primary planetary exports are the plant and animal types they create to thrive on colony worlds with demanding climates. Some of their greatest successes have come in the area of food production, yielding many of the most delicious fruits in the galaxy.

119

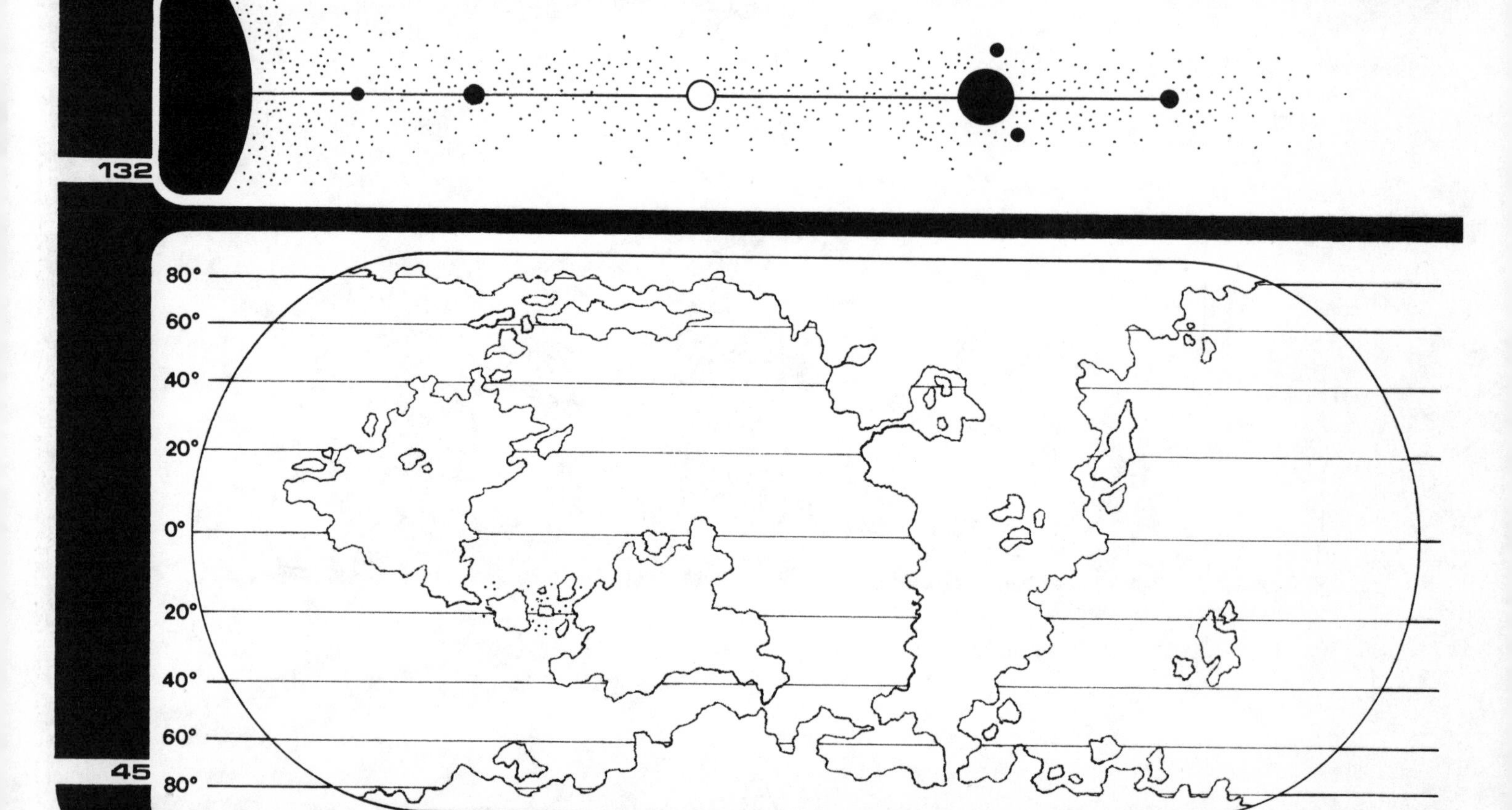

LIBRARY COMPUTER — USS ENTERPRISE (NCC-1701-D)

DATABANK EXTRACT (HARDCOPY)

SUBJECT: KAFERIAN INSECTOID

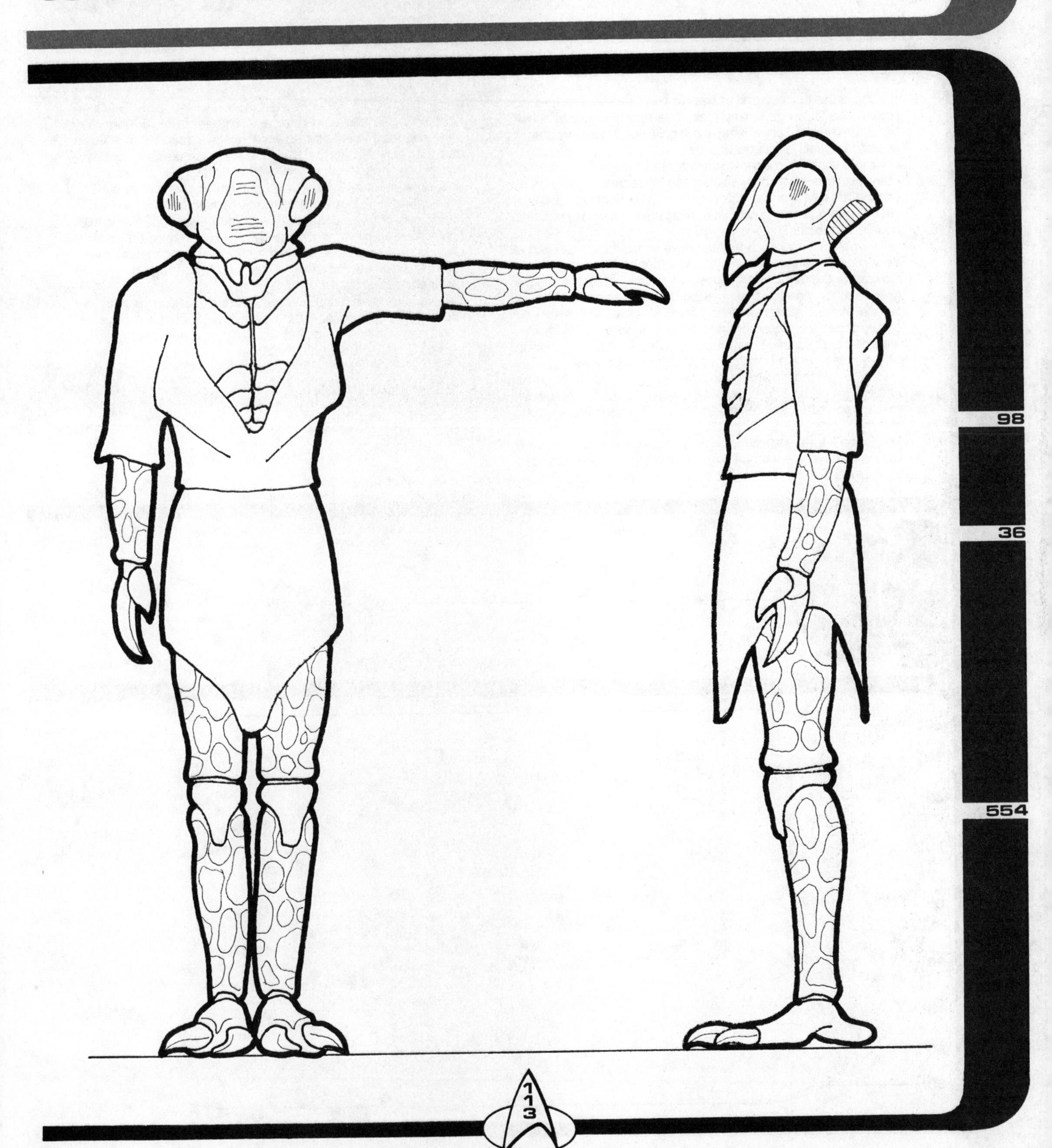

KLING (M)
KLING
KLINGON

[−321.5, 48.6, −87.9]

Kling is the home world of the Klingon Empire. The second planet of an orange binary star, it is nearly one and a half times the size of Terra. Kling is the only world in its five planet system capable of supporting life.

Kling's surface is almost entirely land mass, with shallow, heavily salted seas thinly dotting the landscape. Unlike most other Class M worlds, there is very little vegetation. As a result, nearly every native animal species is carnivorous and hostile in nature.

The planet tilts only a few degrees on its axis, resulting in very little seasonal change. A high, dense layer of carbon dioxide in the upper atmosphere retains heat, creating a greenhouse effect that renders the planet's overall temperature high for a Class M world. Since there are no great bodies of water or variations in land area elevation, weather across the planet is consistent with the exception of the poles, which average a few degrees cooler.

Only in recent history did the Klingon people become Federation allies. In the past they were the UFP's greatest military threat. It is interesting to note that for many years the true appearance of the Klingon race was unknown. The "Klingons" encountered along the Federation border with the Empire were a Klingon-human fusion, genetically created to make infiltration into Federation areas easier. The interception of the Amar transmission during the V'Ger incident revealed the true nature of the Imperial Klingon race and stunned Federation science. Before that time, no one had suspected that the Klingons were capable of such advanced genetic engineering, and a great deal of rethinking was done concerning the level of Klingon technology.

Following the Swift War, many Federation leaders were suspicious of the Klingons' desire for peace, but the virtual annihilation of many worlds on both sides inspired a genuine change of attitude. Scattered factions of Klingons still maintain the old ways, but their limited numbers make them little more than pirates.

Federation and Klingon starship crews still serve primarily within the confines of their respective fleets, but new exchange programs have met with success and may one day lead to a unified space fleet.

165

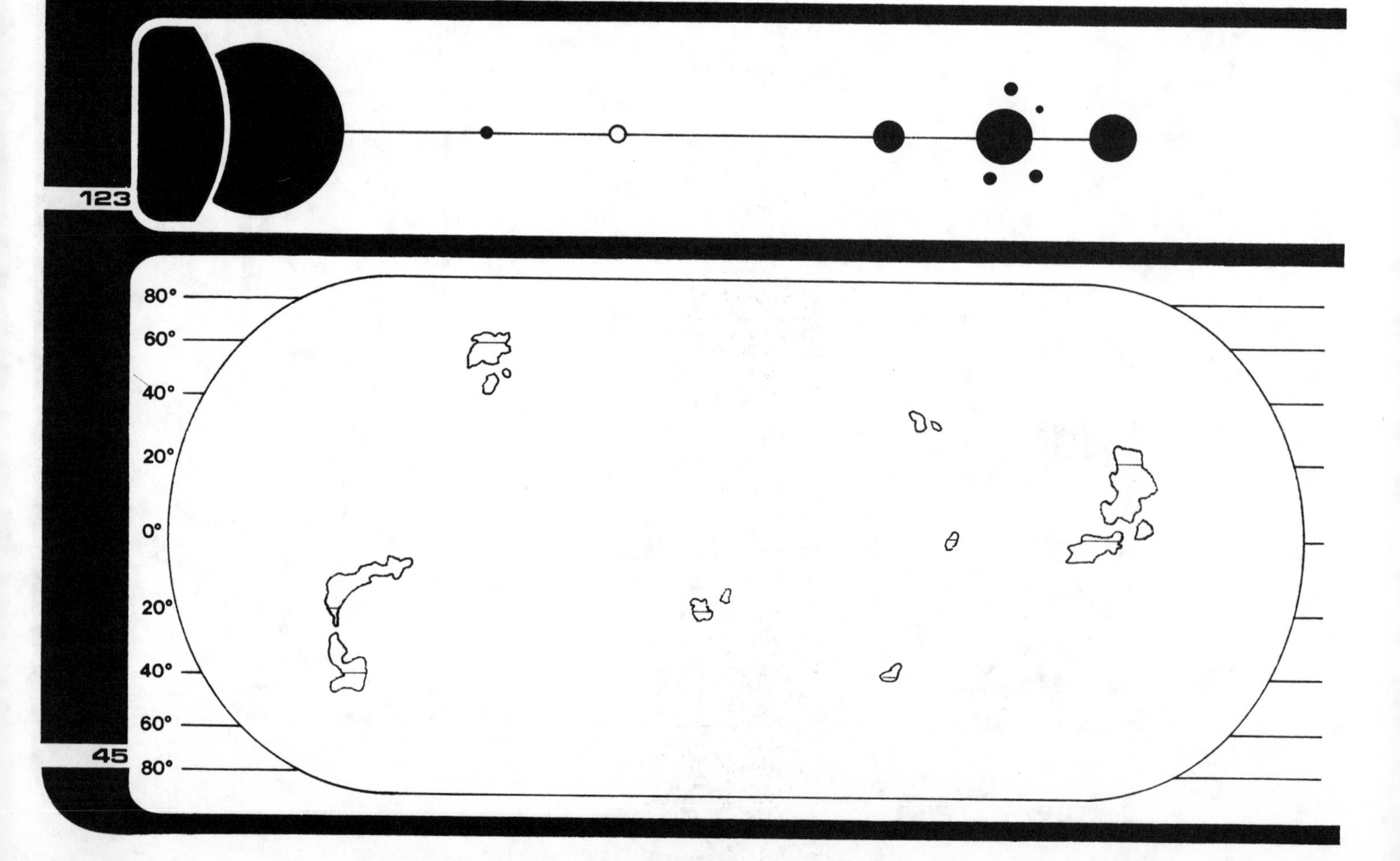

LIBRARY COMPUTER — USS ENTERPRISE (NCC-1701-D)
DATABANK EXTRACT (HARDCOPY)
SUBJECT: KLINGON

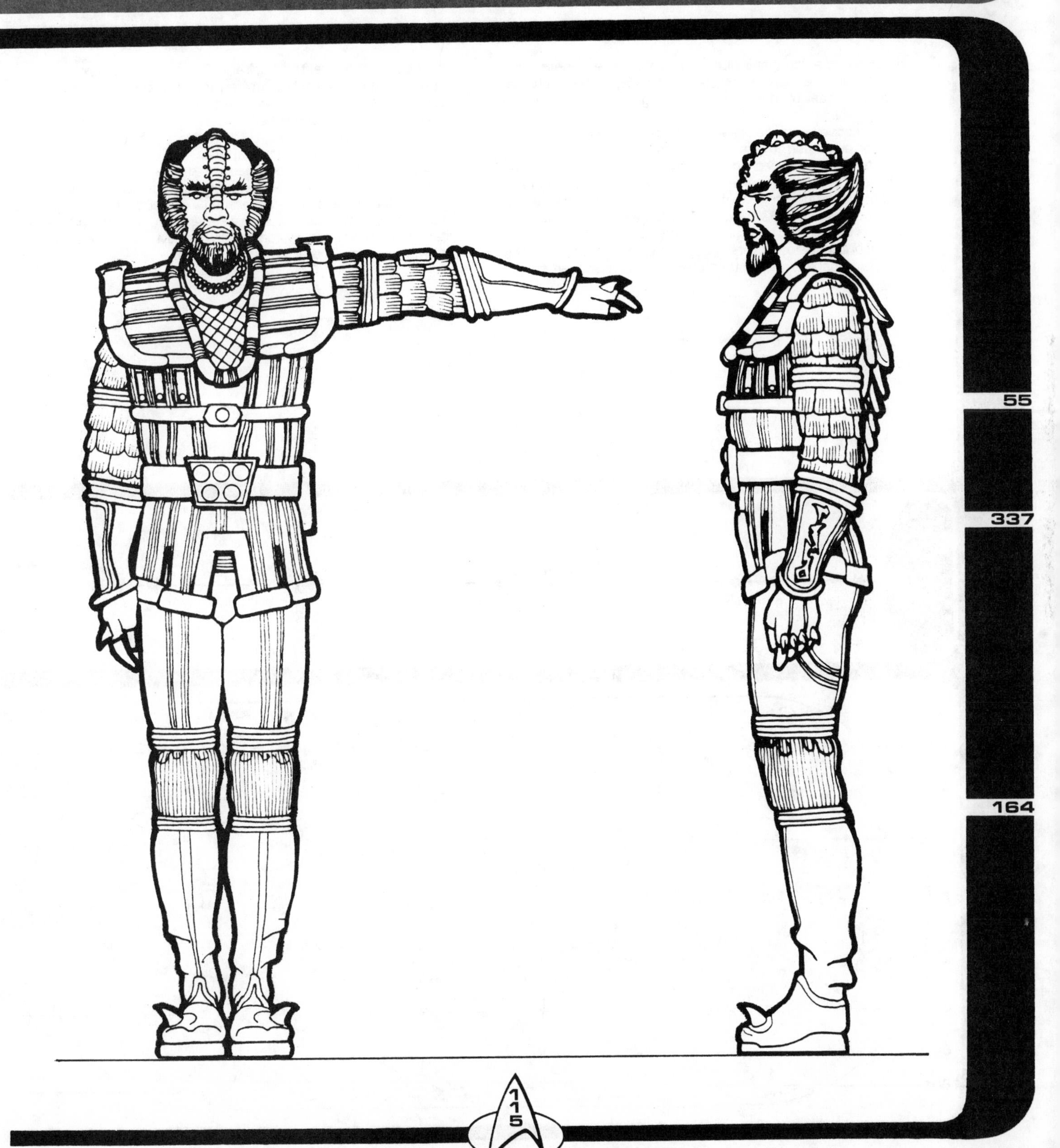

LACTRA VII (M)
SESSALINE
LACTRA
[264.7, 65.4, 98.1]

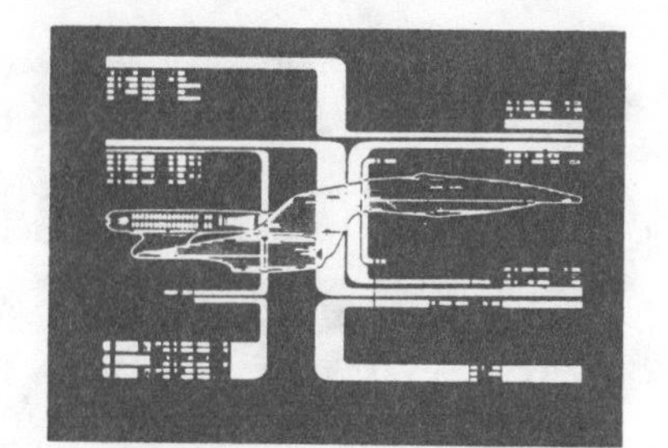

Lactra is a red giant with a system of nine planets. Only the seventh is capable of supporting life, and a highly intelligent race of non-humanoid beings has an extensive culture there.

The native Lactrans are a fascinating species. Twenty feet long at adulthood, these sluglike creatures possess incredible telepathic powers and communicate mentally using an intricate, mathematics-based language. The Lactrans have large eyes and a long, thin trunklike appendage with which they perform intricate tasks, although the majority of Lactran labor is carried out through the use of telekinesis.

A worldwide zoo covers much of Lactra VII. Some of the wildlife is caged, while other creatures are allowed to run free in specially created habitats. Ecologies as different as desert and rain forest are often found sharing a common border, demonstrating the Lactrans' ability to control planetary climate. Early sensor readings of the planet showed no signs of life, although the many different climatic regions suggested terraforming by an intelligence. Since that time researchers have learned that the Lactrans can even manipulate and control sensor readings of passing ships.

The Lactran race has an average IQ of well over nine thousand. They know much about the Federation, having read the data in a starship library computer, but have decided against membership or further communications.

15

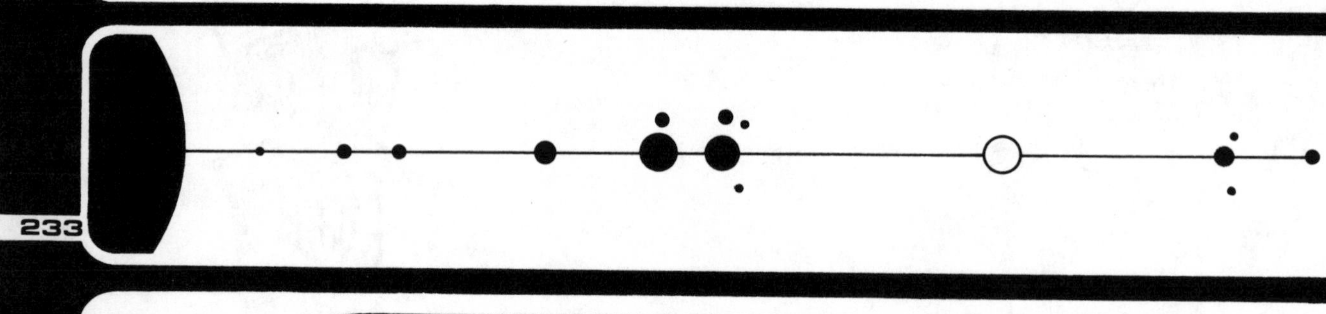

233

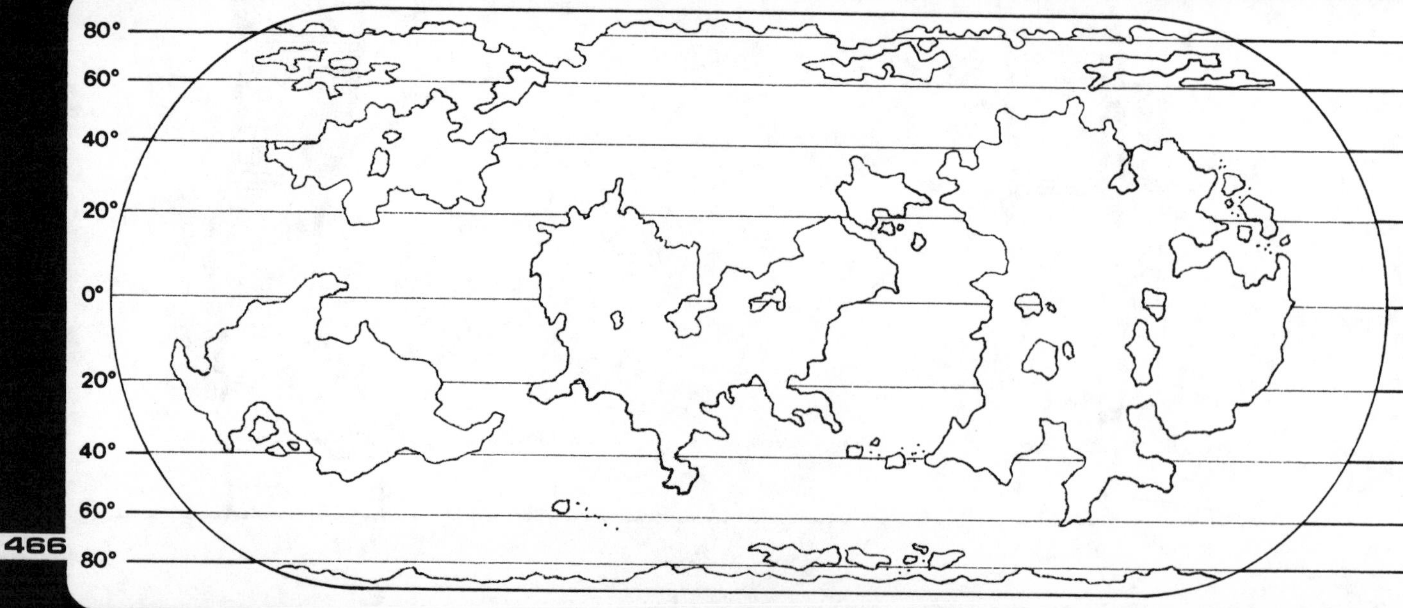

466

LIBRARY COMPUTER — USS ENTERPRISE (NCC-1701-D)
DATABANK EXTRACT (HARDCOPY)
SUBJECT: LACTRAN

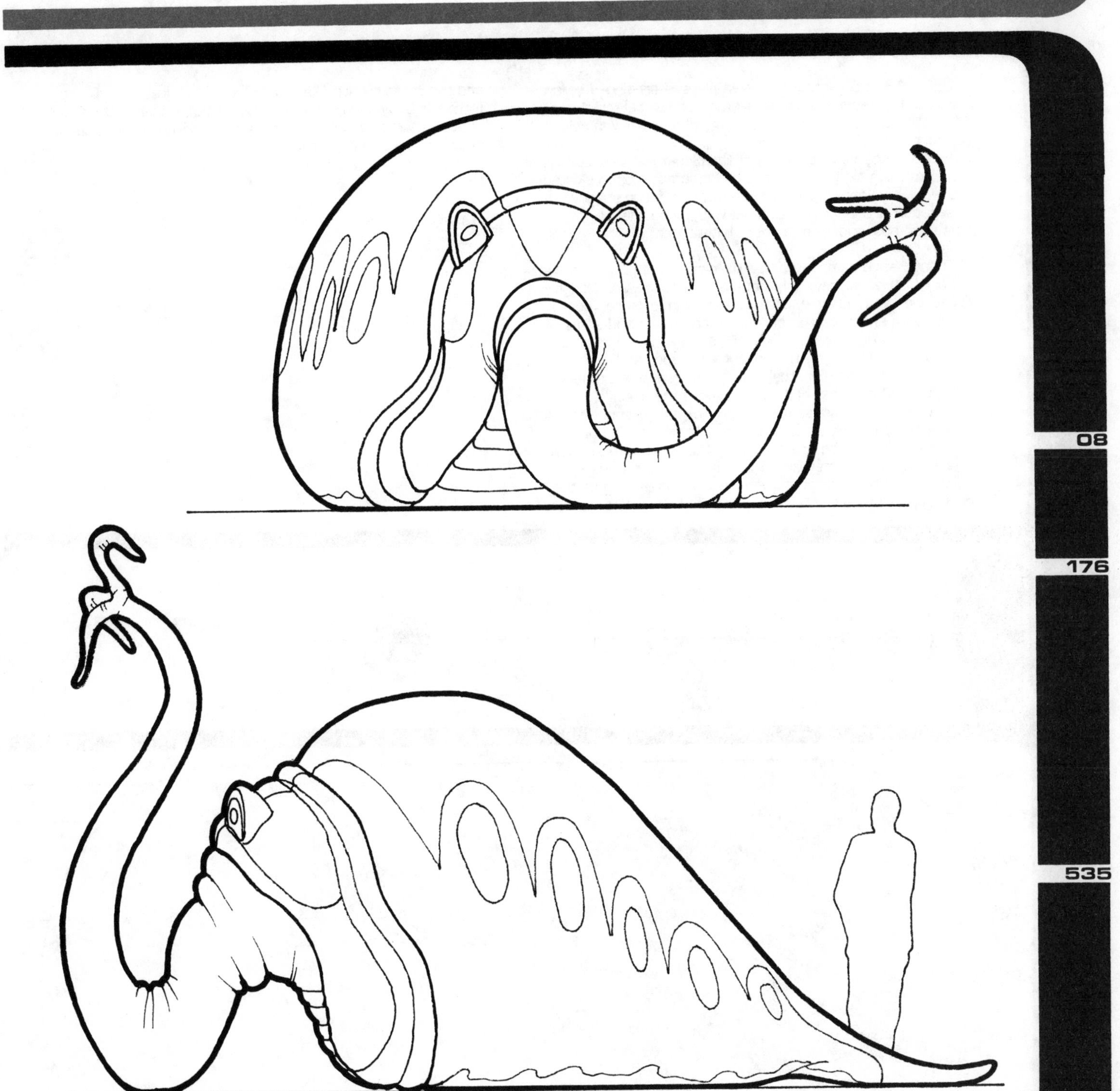

M-113 (M)
FOTIALLA
UFC 113

[−23.6, −81.9, 0.7]

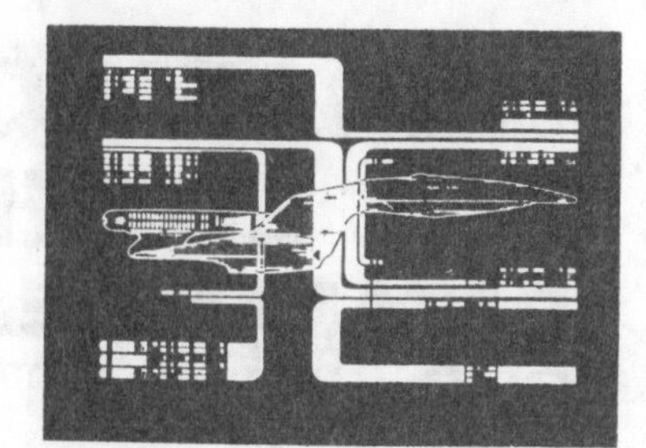

UFC 113 is a system of seven planets orbiting a yellow dwarf star. Planet four in the system, usually referred to as M-113, is Class M and is the only world of the seven able to support life.

Extensive ruins cover much of the planet's land area, the last remaining sign of the great civilization that once existed there. Eighty years ago a sole survivor was found still alive. A Federation archaeologist and his wife found the being in a state of suspended animation within one of the ruined buildings.

These native inhabitants had developed the power of illusion, which was their only defensive mechanism. Roughly humanoid, with coarse, shaggy hair and a large, conical mouth with sharp teeth, this race lived on salt and some of the native vegetable life. The salt, an essential part of the creatures' diet, began to run out long ago, and the race started to die out. Eventually, only one creature remained out of the billions that had once covered the planet.

This survivor demonstrated a complex native language but generally communicated by direct telepathy. Through its power of illusion, the creature would assume human form. The being, later referred to as the "M-113 Creature", coexisted with the scientist and his wife for as long as they could supply it with salt tablets. These soon began to run out, and the creature attacked the woman and drew salt directly from her body, killing her instantly. Later, a Starfleet vessel arrived at the planet and destroyed the creature after it attacked several crew members.

65

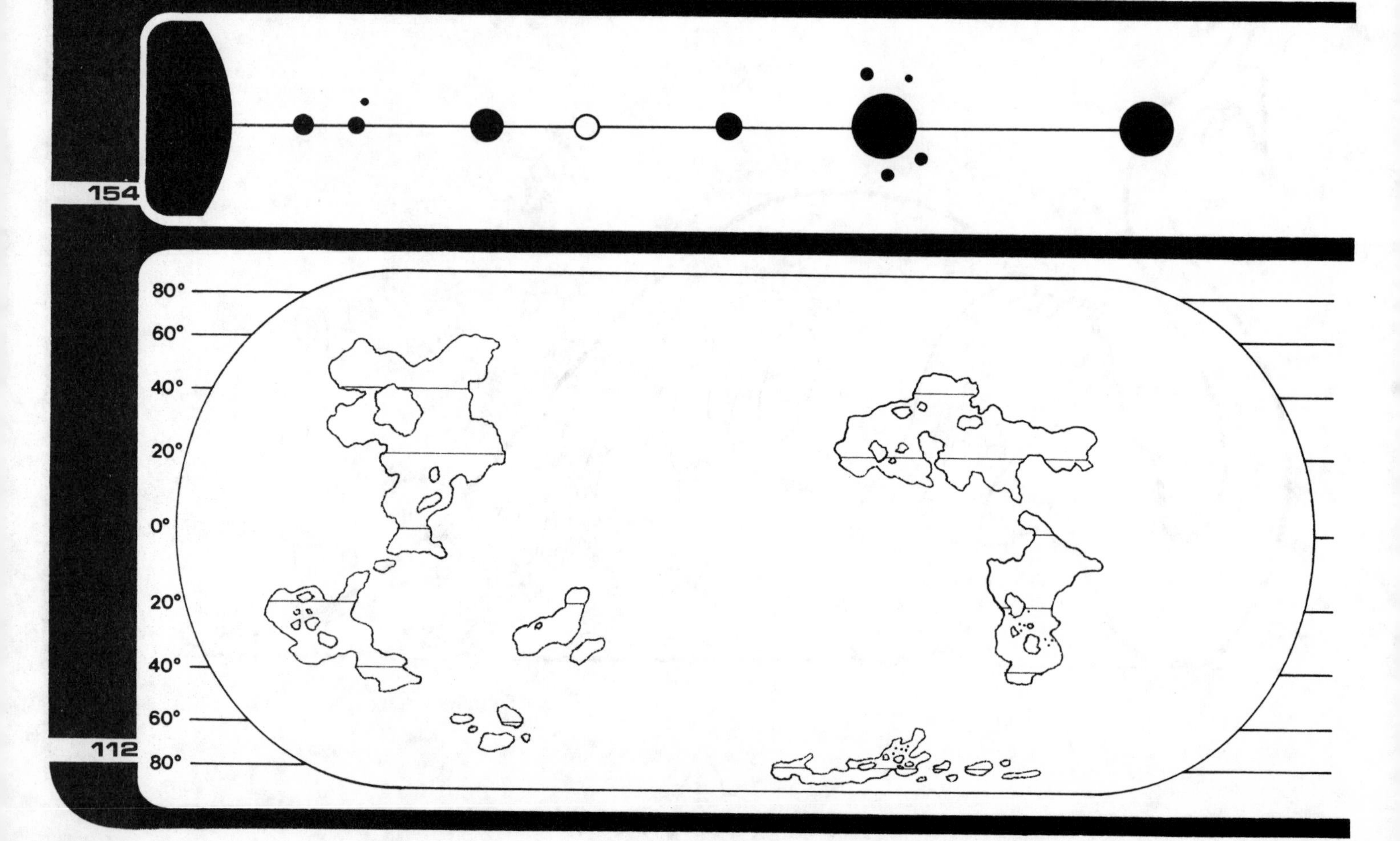

LIBRARY COMPUTER — USS ENTERPRISE (NCC-1701-D)
DATABANK EXTRACT (HARDCOPY)
SUBJECT: M-113 CREATURE

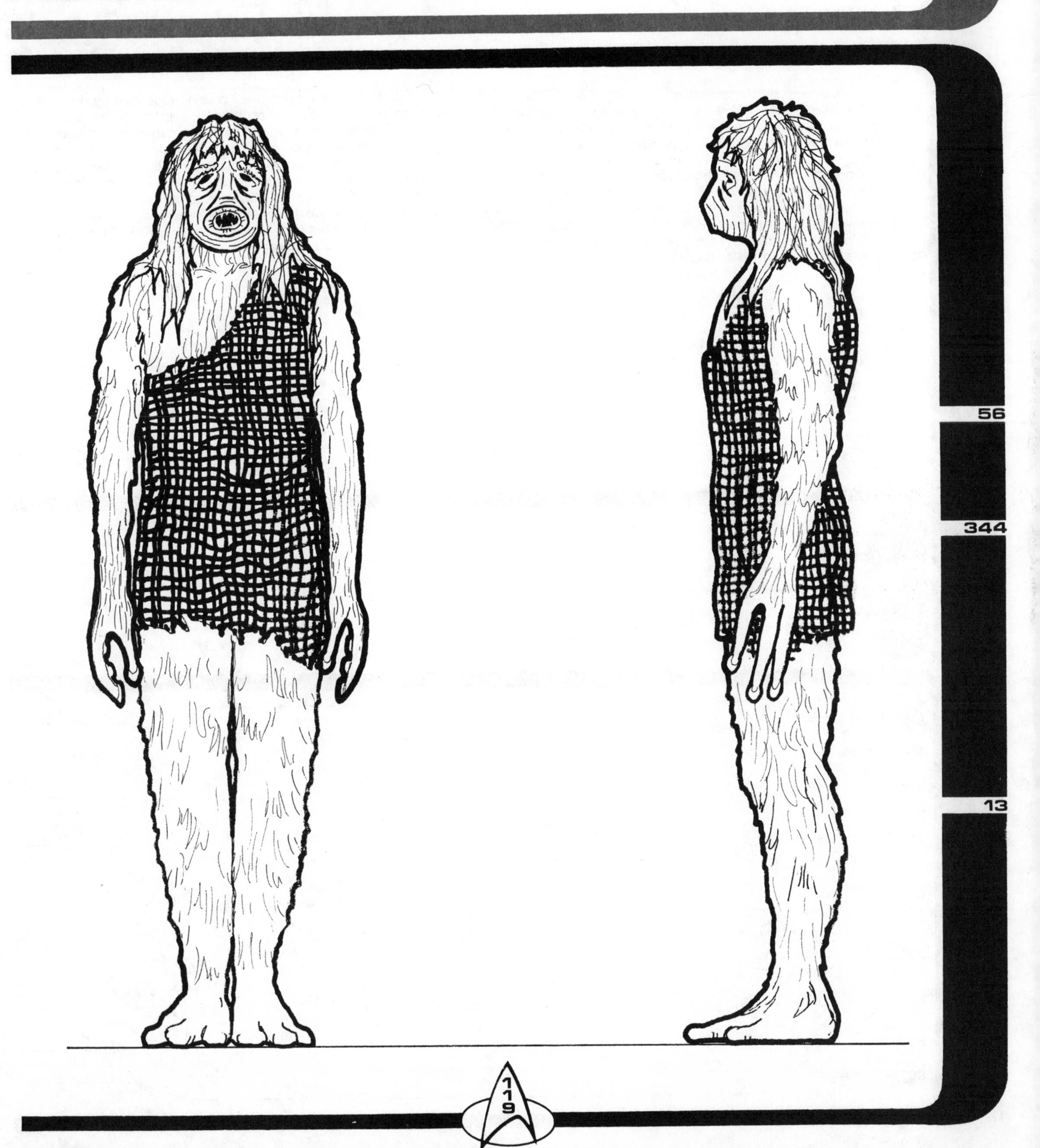

M24-ALPHA II (M)

TRISKELION

M24-ALPHA

[−85.5, −59.1, −75.8]

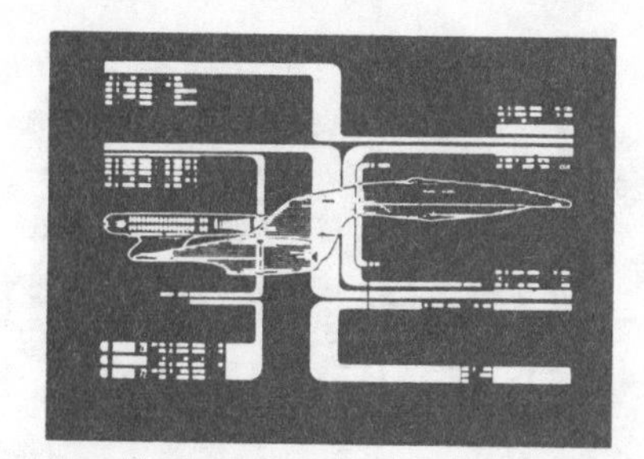

Triskelion is the second planet orbiting a moderate-size yellow star — one of three in a trinary system comprised of two yellow stars and a white dwarf that orbit a common center of gravity. This configuration is most uncommon, and Triskelion is one of only two such systems ever charted.

Once the home of a highly advanced technological civilization, Triskelion is now virtually barren on its surface. Ruins of once-great structures cover the landscape, displaying great knowledge of architecture and advanced physics. The Triskelion race, destroyed in an ancient, unknown planetary catastrophe, now exists only in subterranean vaults. They are maintained as disembodied brains, kept alive by an intricate biological matrix of artificial life-support machinery.

The Triskelions have a penchant for gambling and once amused themselves by staging combat between specially trained slaves on the planet's surface. These fighters, kidnapped from surrounding systems, would fight to the death as their owners underground wagered on the outcome.

These slaves were given self-government when the Triskelions lost a bet with Captain James T. Kirk of the Constitution class **USS Enterprise**.

908

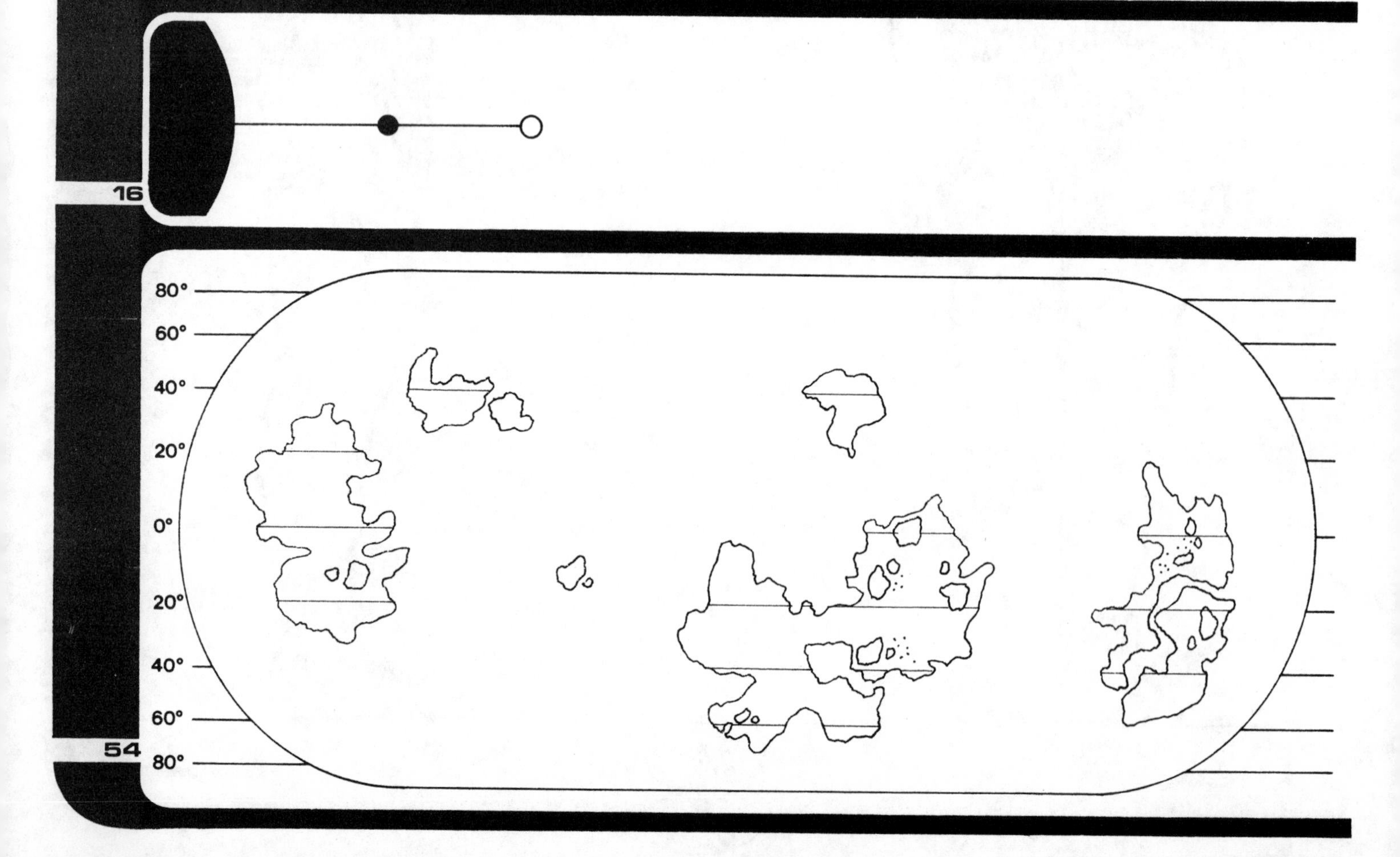

LIBRARY COMPUTER — USS ENTERPRISE (NCC-1701-D)
DATABANK EXTRACT (HARDCOPY)
SUBJECT: TRISKELION DRILL THRALL

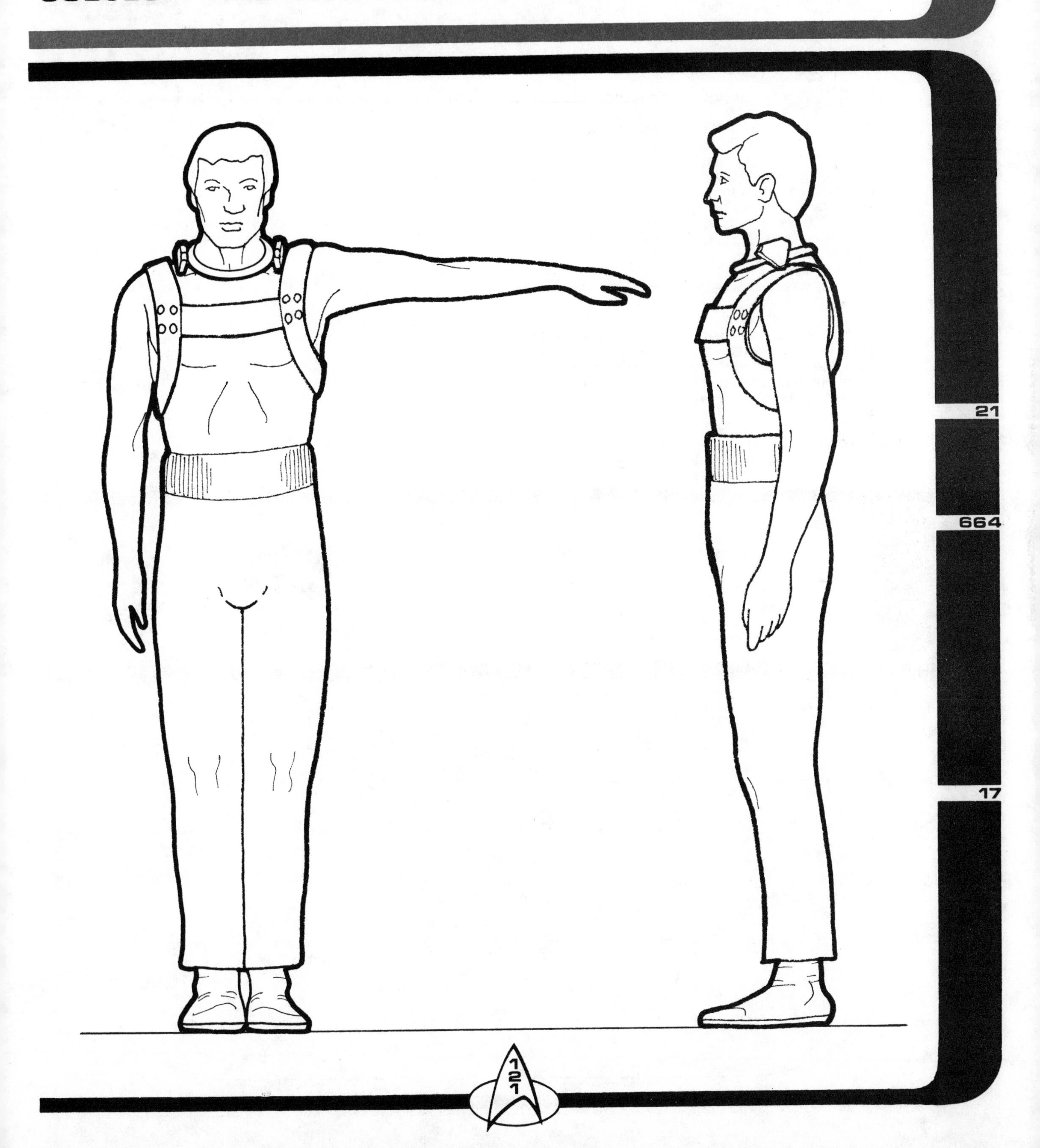

M43-ALPHA IV, V (M)
EKOS, ZEON
M43-ALPHA
[72.8, −29.1, −68.7]

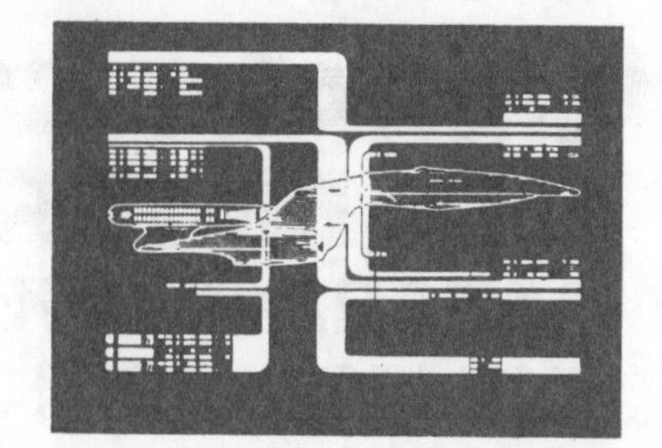

M 43-Alpha is a trinary system with ten planets orbiting the moderate-size yellow primary star. The two outer planets are both ringed gas giants. The others, except for the fourth and fifth, are massive asteroids in stellar orbit.

The fourth planet, Ekos, and the fifth, Zeon, are Class M and have large humanoid populations, both descendants of a native Zeon race. Only recently, however, did either develop interplanetary travel, indicating third-party intervention at some point in the ancient past. More recently, the Zeons traveled to Ekos in order to teach the peaceful Ekosian people how to utilize advanced technology.

John Gill, a noted Federation historian, decided that the backward Ekosian people needed a common goal in order to unify them. He introduced a modified version of twentieth-century Earth's Nazi culture, noting that the Nazis developed the most efficient state Earth ever knew. A power-hungry subordinate named Melakon drugged Gill and turned the Ekosians against the people of Zeon. Holocaust resulted. The Ekosians began an extermination process with the ultimate goal of eradicating the Zeon people.

At that point, a routine check of the planet Ekos revealed the nature of the contamination to Federation officials. The Nazi state was quickly halted following a television announcement by Gill, who had been freed of his drug-induced stupor. Melakon was executed, and the two cultures began to build a joint civilization based upon trust.

70

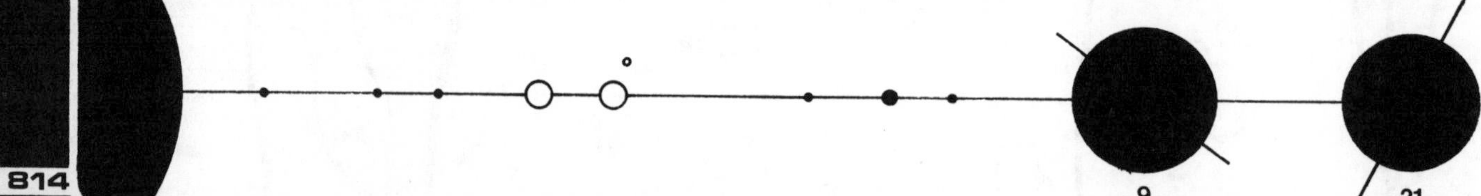

814

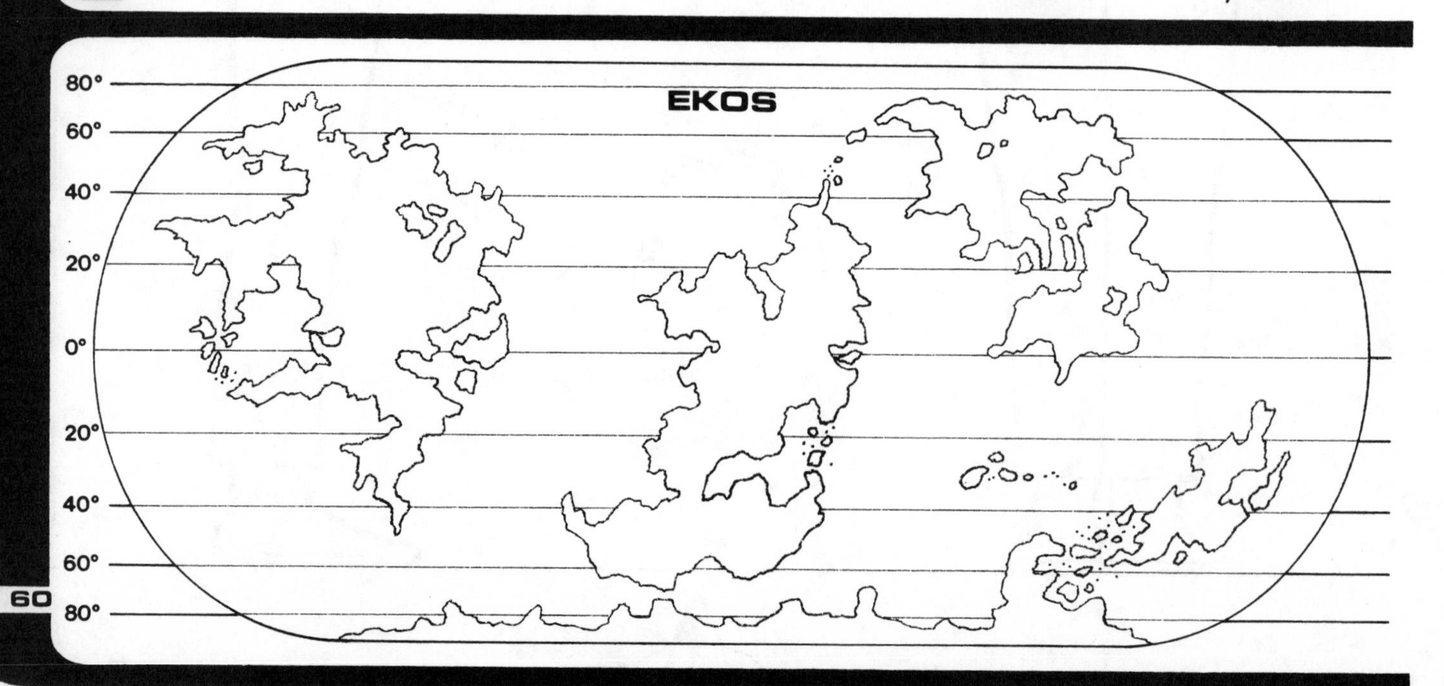

60

LIBRARY COMPUTER — USS ENTERPRISE (NCC-1701-D)
DATABANK EXTRACT (HARDCOPY)
SUBJECT: EKOSIAN

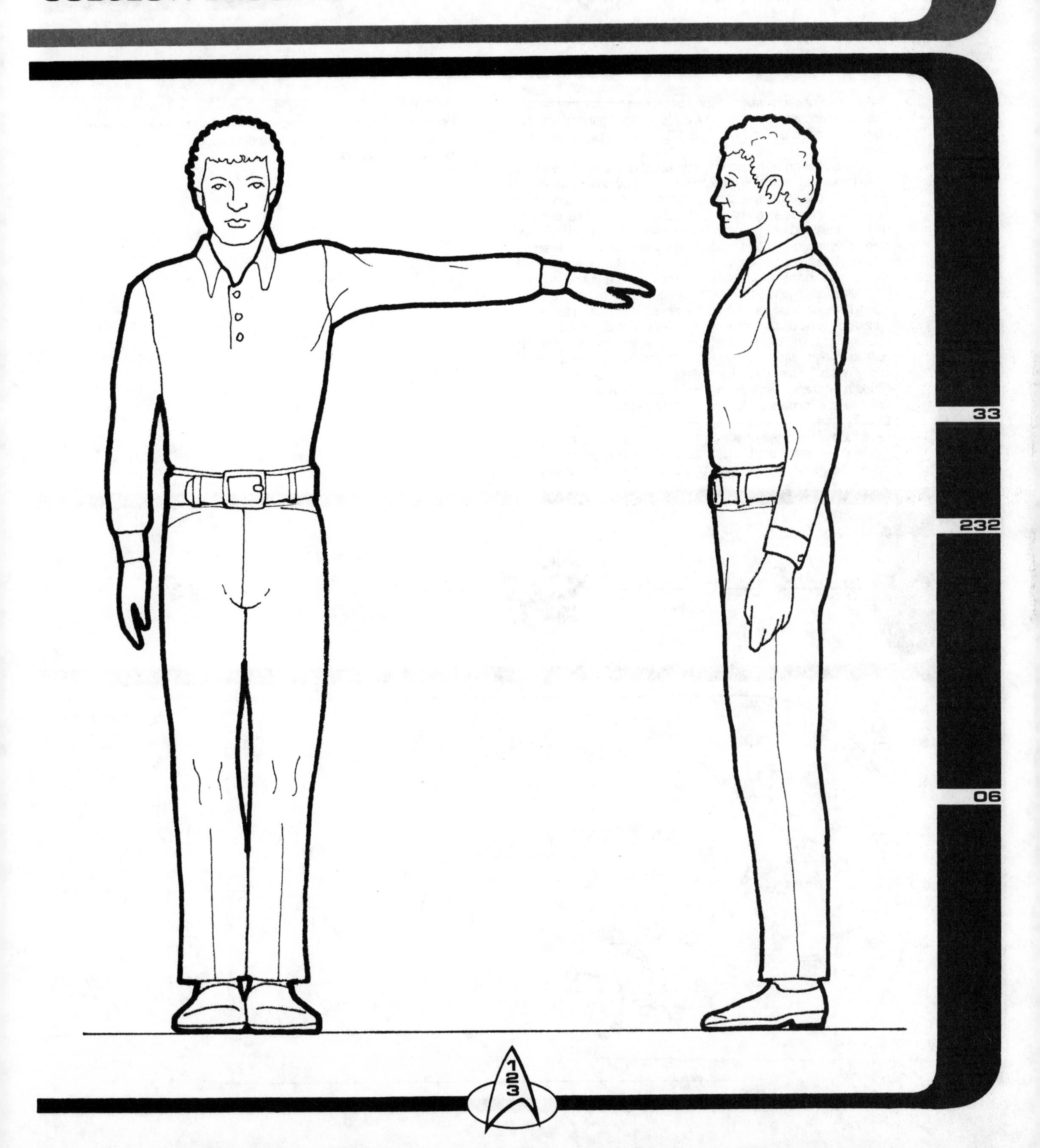

MUDD (K)
NO INDIGENOUS NAME
UFC 257704
[−13.3, 225.1, −45.5]

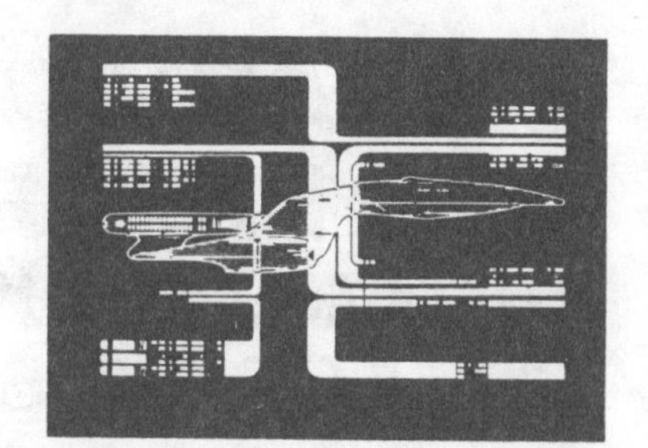

A rather unusual world, Mudd is named for its only human citizen, Harcourt Fenton Mudd. It is the second of five planets in orbit around UFC 257704, a moderate-size red star.

The population of Mudd is made up of more than two hundred thousand androids, which were built by an extragalactic civilization that became extinct more than one million years ago. The androids, humanoid in appearance, were created as servants and are programmed to serve the needs of living beings. Harcourt Mudd inadvertently landed his spacecraft on the planet in an effort to evade a Federation trade patrol. Sensing his inability to stay out of trouble, the dutiful android population dismantled Mudd's spacecraft to protect him from his own nature. Mudd became a virtual prisoner in paradise, with all of his material needs met to excess.

Living in an extensive and comfortable underground city built long ago, Mudd became Mudd the First, a king whose every wish [save that for freedom] was obeyed. Planet Mudd's existence was discovered when the androids, following Mudd's orders, hijacked the Constitution class USS **Enterprise** and brought its crew to the planet as company for Mudd. The crew of the **Enterprise** escaped, but Mudd was held on the planet, again for his own protection.

Mudd eventually managed to escape himself, leaving the android servants to search for other ways to fulfill their programming. Federation traffic was rerouted to avoid the area, but the androids have space travel capability, and another encounter is expected.

45

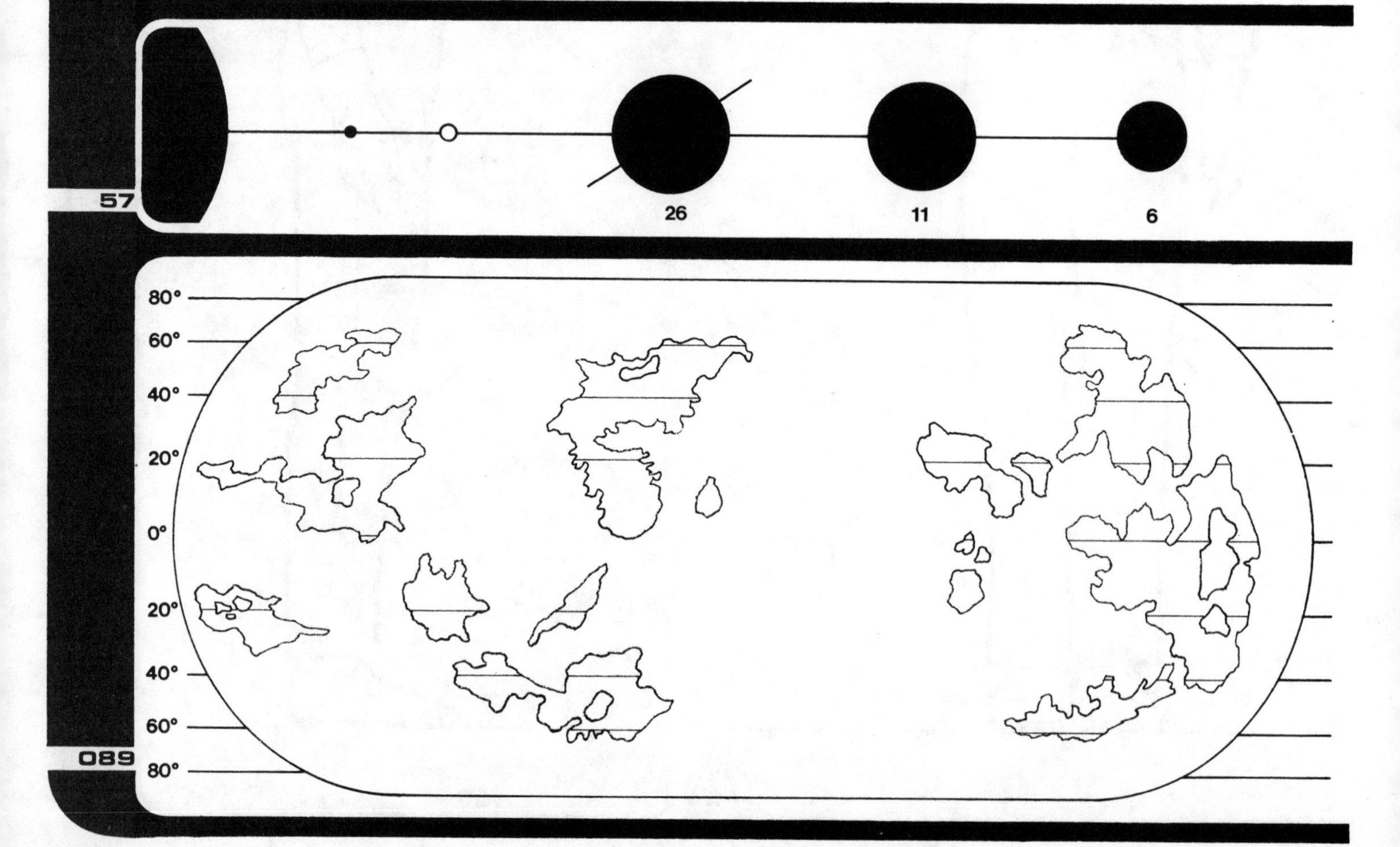

LIBRARY COMPUTER — USS ENTERPRISE (NCC-1701-D)
DATABANK EXTRACT (HARDCOPY)
SUBJECT: MUDDIAN ANDROID

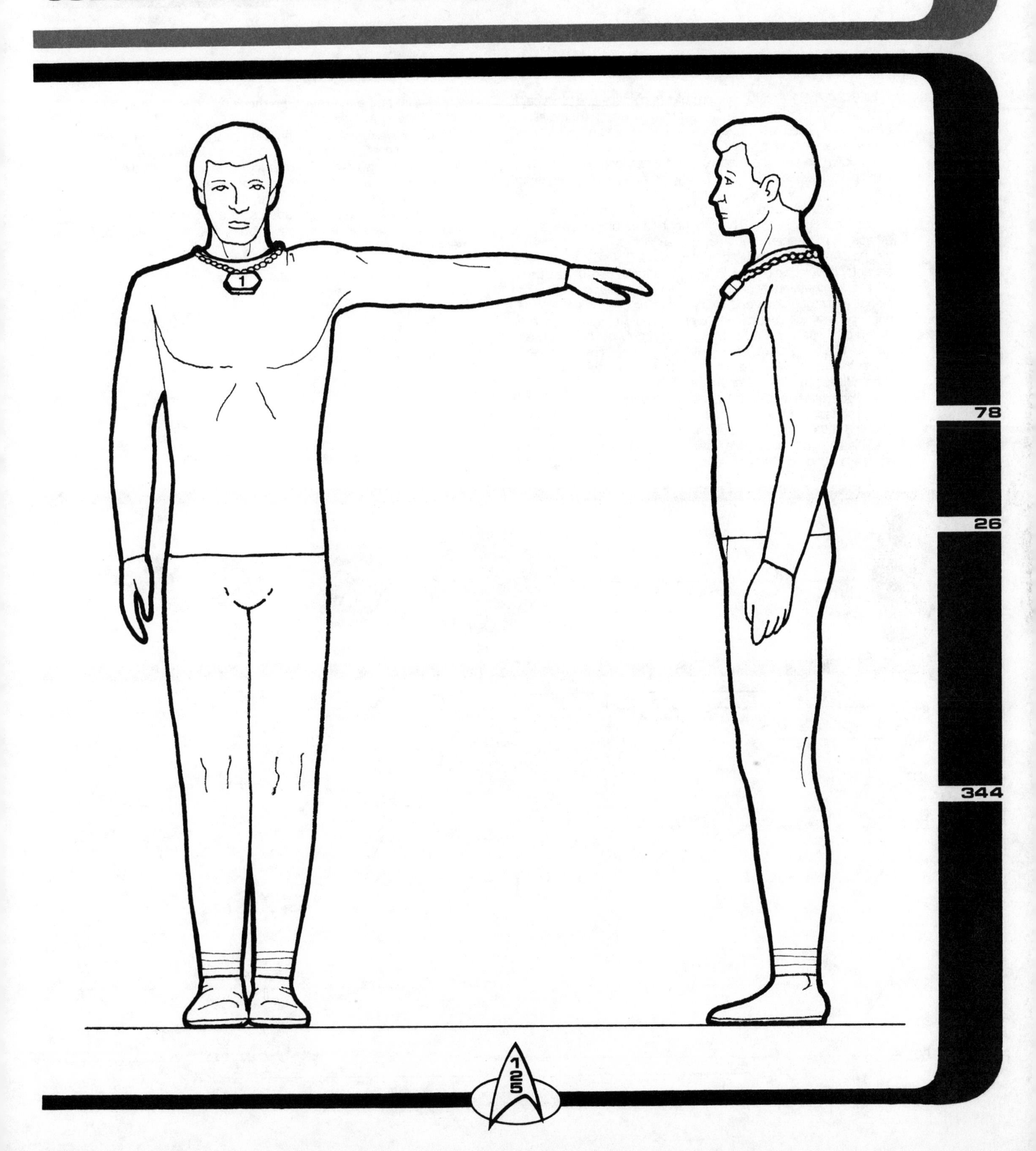

ONLIES (M)

EARTH

UFC 347601

[−43.3, −103.5, −82.3]

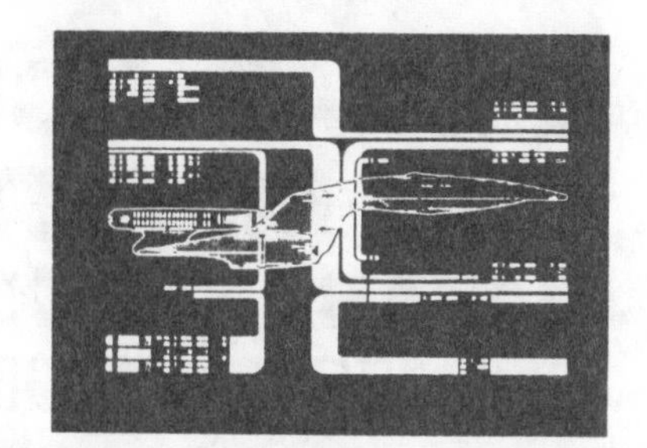

UFC 347601 and its system of ten planets are physically indistinguishable from the Sol system in every measurable parameter. The mass, size, orbital speed, and even color of every planet in the system is identical to Sol's counterparts, right down to surface features and weather patterns. The third planet, once called "Earth" by its inhabitants, has been named Onlies by the Federation.

Onlies is an exact duplicate of Terra, right down to its continental configurations. The only inhabitants of the planet are a race of adolescent humans, the survivors of a planetwide plague. A filterable virus of the order 2250-67A was apparently developed during Onlies' twentieth century as part of a life-extension research project. It escaped into the planet's atmosphere, and everyone at or beyond the age of puberty was killed. Children were given life spans on the order of three hundred fifty years and only died when their bodies finally aged to the point of puberty. The planetary name "Onlies" was taken from the childrens' name for themselves, the "only" ones left alive.

A Federation exploration team encountered the planet when sensors revealed its incredible similarity to Earth and showed a very small population. A landing party contracted the disease but was able, using the ship's computer, to derive a cure to the viral infection. That cure was applied worldwide, and since that time the Federation has begun colonizing the world.

The very existence of the planet and its system holds uncertain ramifications for both the scientific and religious communities on Terra. One theory holds that the system is a result of a massive tear in the space-time continuum through which, at some point long ago, the Sol system passed, somehow resulting in replication at the subatomic level. The Judeo-Christian line of thought implies a simultaneous, separate creation by God.

06

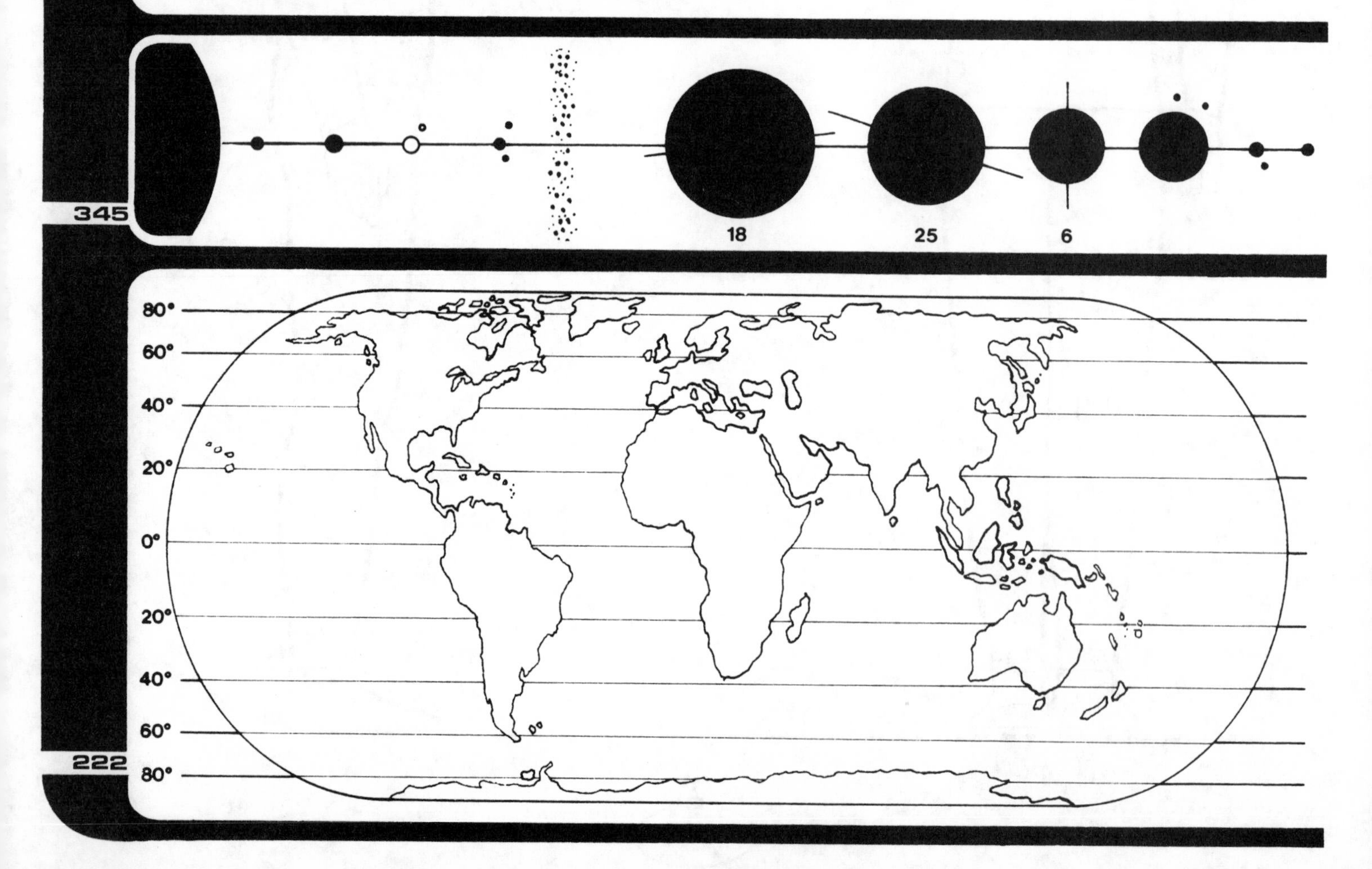

LIBRARY COMPUTER — USS ENTERPRISE (NCC-1701-D)
DATABANK EXTRACT (HARDCOPY)
SUBJECT: ONLIESIAN

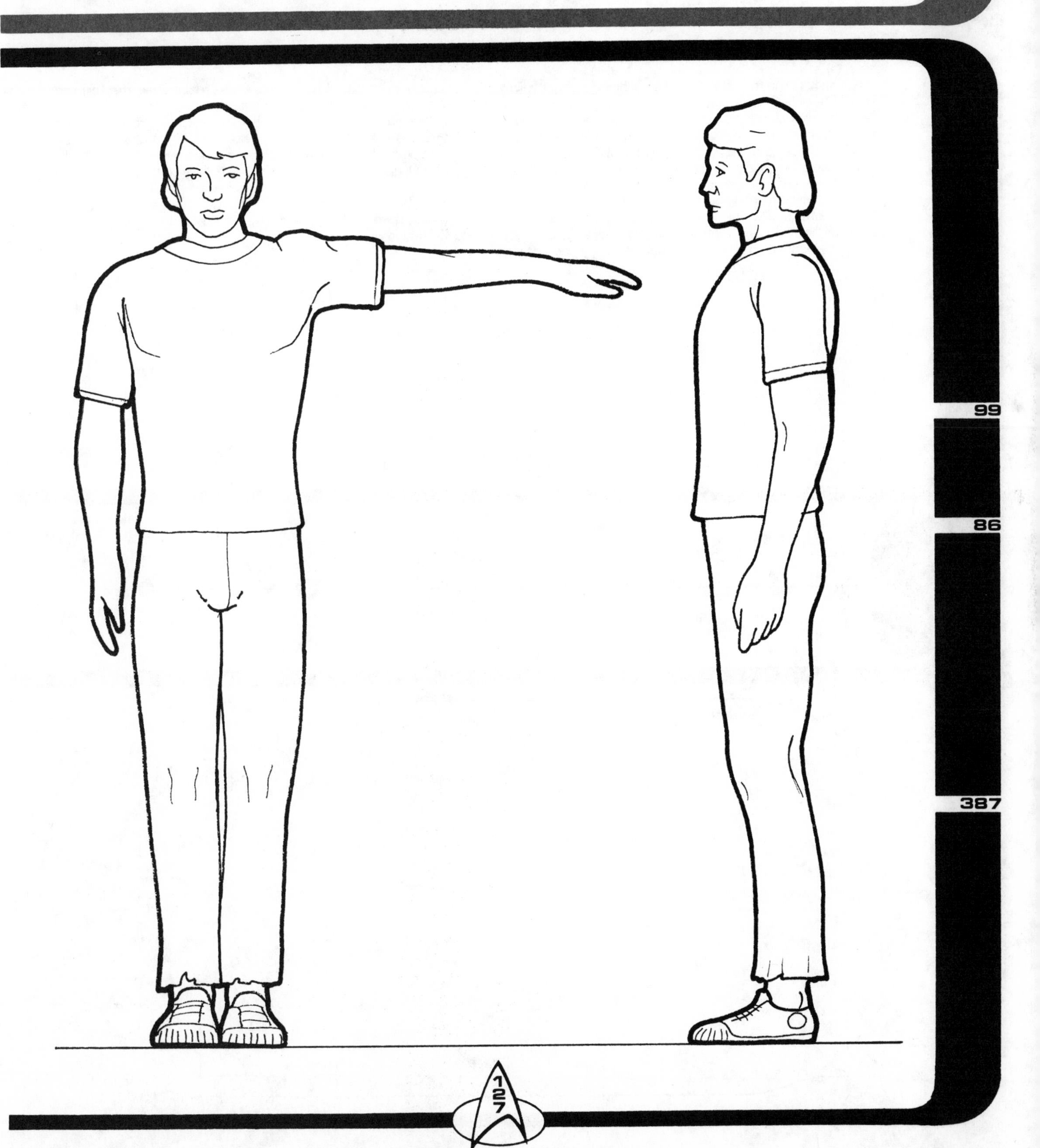

ORGANIA IV (M)
INDIGENOUS NAME UNKNOWN
ORGANIA

[−112.6, 186.3, −12.1]

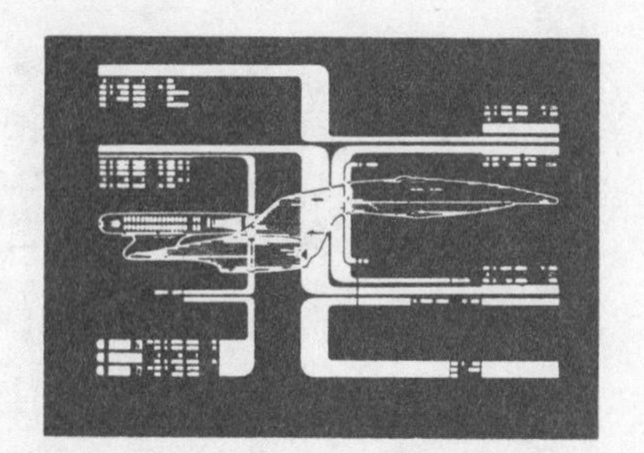

Organia IV is the fourth planet of six orbiting a bright yellow dwarf. The only Class M world within a strategic sector of space that lies along the Federation/Klingon border, it was sought after as a base by both sides during early UFP/Klingon conflicts. Since that time, the two governments have become allies, largely due to the intervention of the Organians.

The Organians originally appeared to be a simple, nontechnological farming people with culture rated D-minus on the Richter scale. This illusion quickly vanished, however, as it was learned that the inhabitants were actually immensely advanced, noncorporeal beings. They had little interest in the affairs of others and maintained the farming culture illusion solely for the benefit of visitors.

Despite their aversion to extraplanetary contact, the Organians became involved in the UFP/Klingon conflict when it appeared that a war would take place upon Organia itself. The Organians revealed their true nature to the warring parties and made war impossible by rendering all shipboard and hand-held weapons useless. The war was averted, and a pact known as the Organian Peace Treaty was imposed upon both sides.

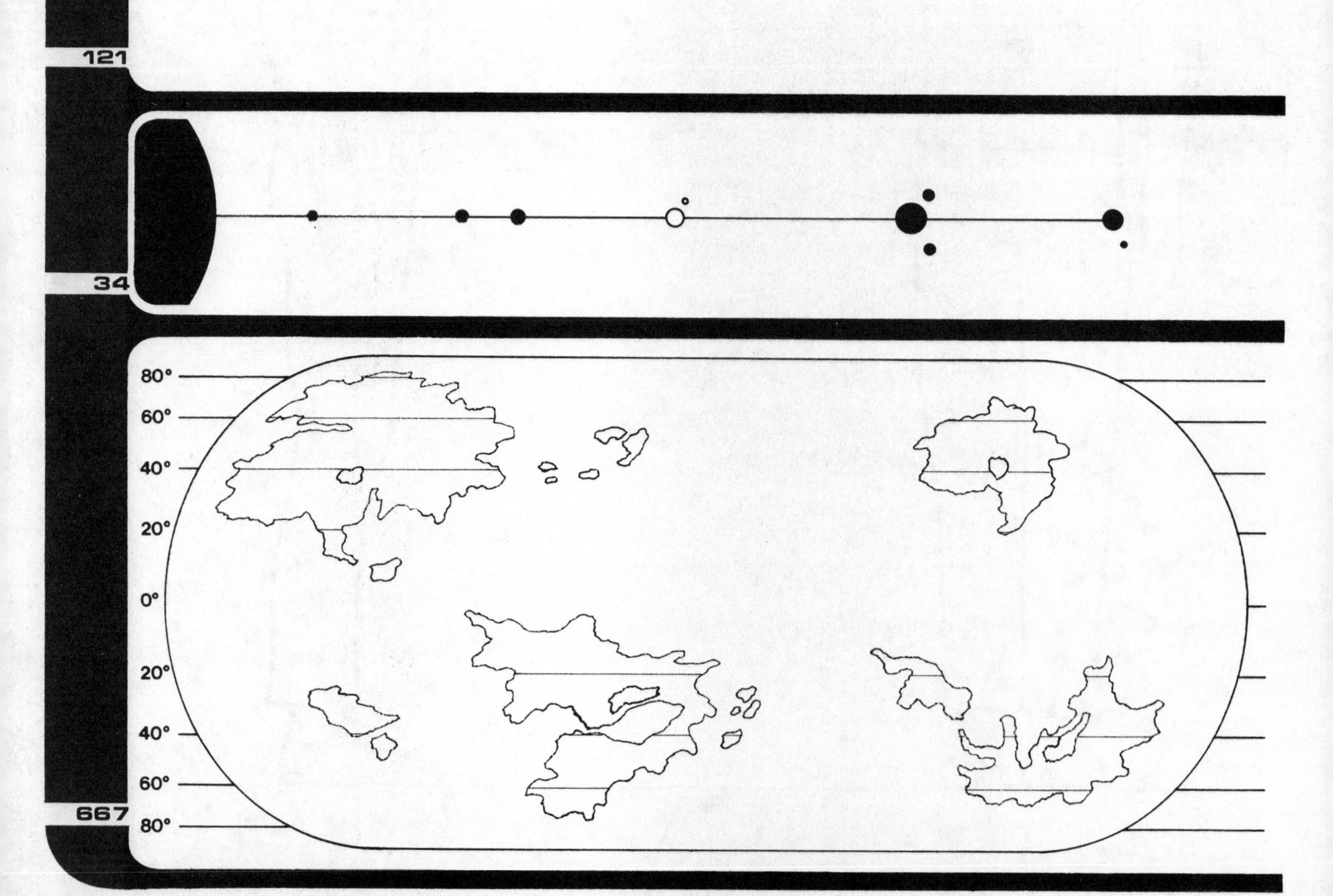

LIBRARY COMPUTER — USS ENTERPRISE (NCC-1701-D)
DATABANK EXTRACT (HARDCOPY)
SUBJECT: ORGANIAN (HUMAN FORM)

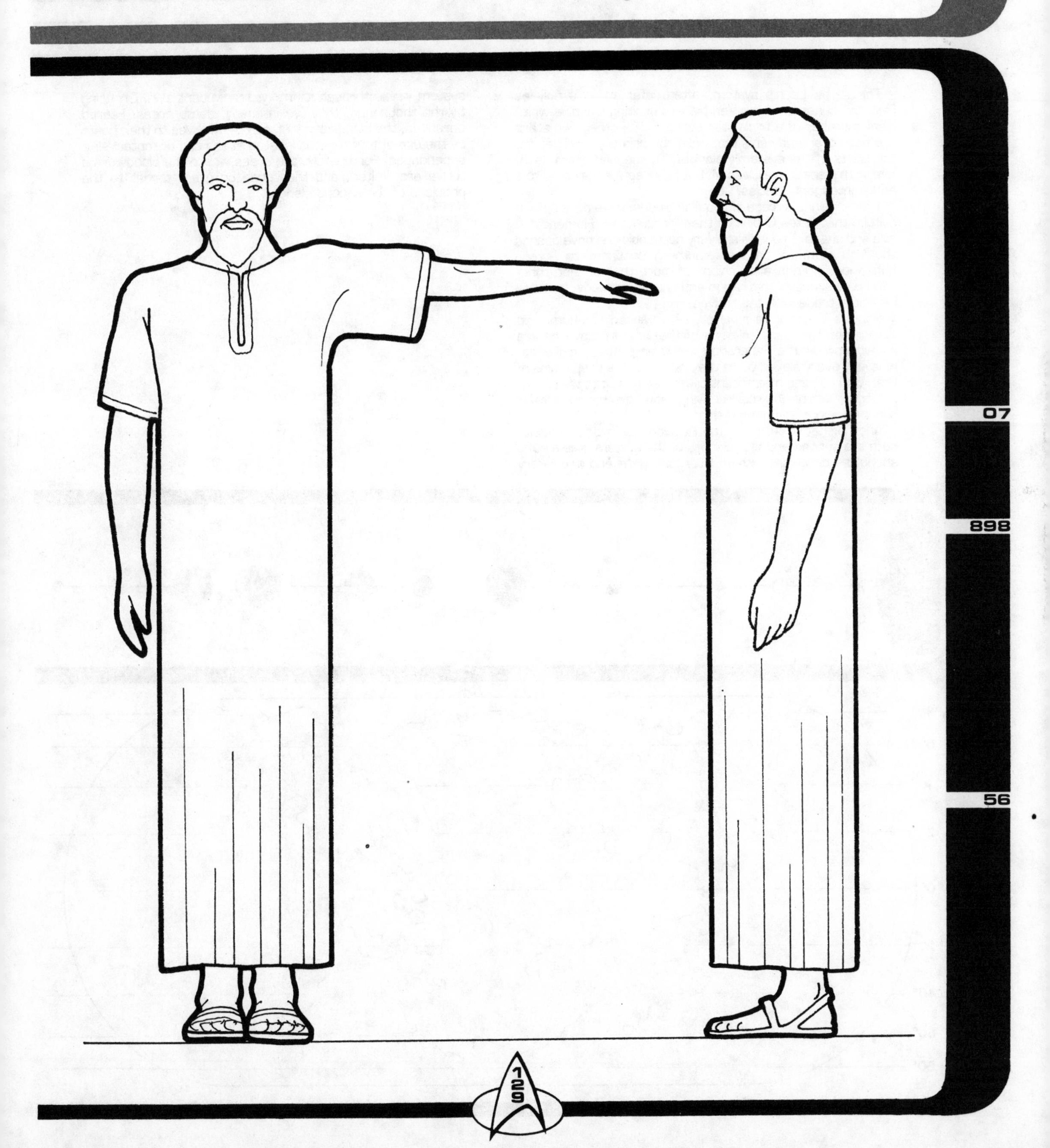

REGULUS (M)

ARODI

ALPHA LEONIS

[10.7, 83.9, 0.7]

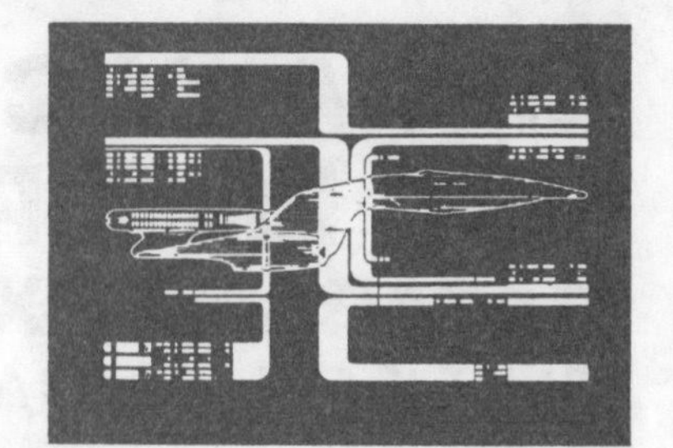

The Alpha Leonis system, often referred to simply as Regulus, consists of thirteen planets orbiting the blue-white giant member of a triple star system. The other two stars are both orange dwarfs that orbit the primary, well beyond the orbits of the system's planets. The second, third, fifth, and sixth planets are Class M, but only Regulus II is home to a native intelligent species.

The Regulans, a race of reptilian bipeds, have developed a culture that rates G plus on the Richter scale. Humanoid in size and shape, Regulans are very hospitable and have opened the lush plateaus on their southern continent to human habitation. A Federation colony of more than sixteen thousand now occupies this region and shares a steady, mutually beneficial trade with the natives.

Regulus V supports a variety of advanced non-humanoid life forms. The giant eel-birds of the western caverns are known across the Federation for their precise migration, whereby every eleven years they return to the deep caves of their birth. These magnificent creatures are up to thirty feet in length, with brightly colored wings and tails that reflect the sun's rays in a prismatic fashion.

Another native life form, the Regulan bloodworm, inhabits both the second and fifth planets of the system. It is a soft, shapeless organism with its internal organs and circulatory system visible through its milky, translucent skin. Grouping by the thousands, they live in shady, damp areas. Feared parasites, the bloodworms attach themselves to their hosts by the use of four mouths located at the end of tentacle-like appendages. Fortunately, the areas where the bloodworms thrive are limited, and they pose no great threat to the populace of the second planet.

33

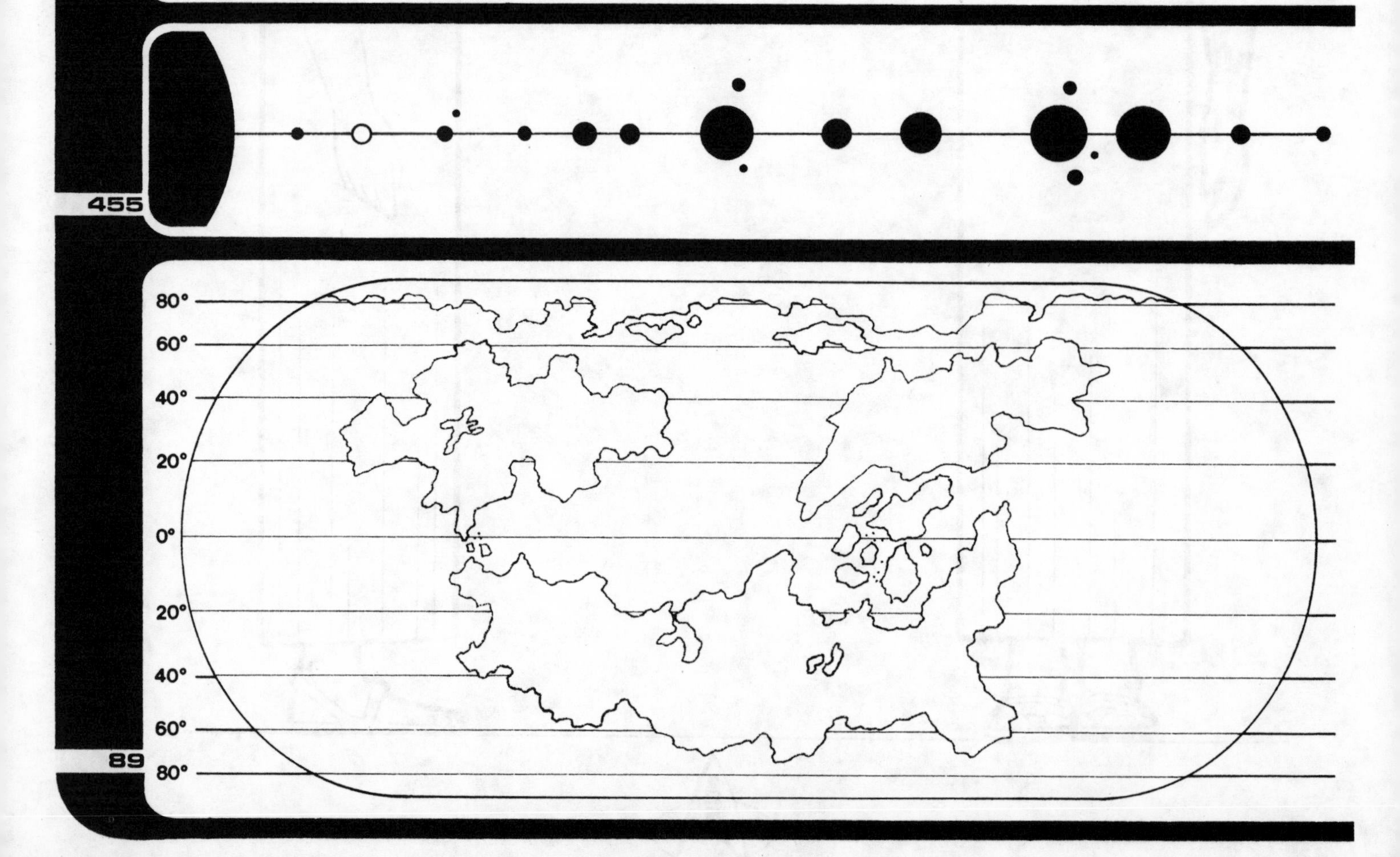

LIBRARY COMPUTER — USS ENTERPRISE (NCC-1701-D)
DATABANK EXTRACT (HARDCOPY)
SUBJECT: REGULAN BLOODWORM

LENGTH:
2.4 - 5 CENTIMETERS

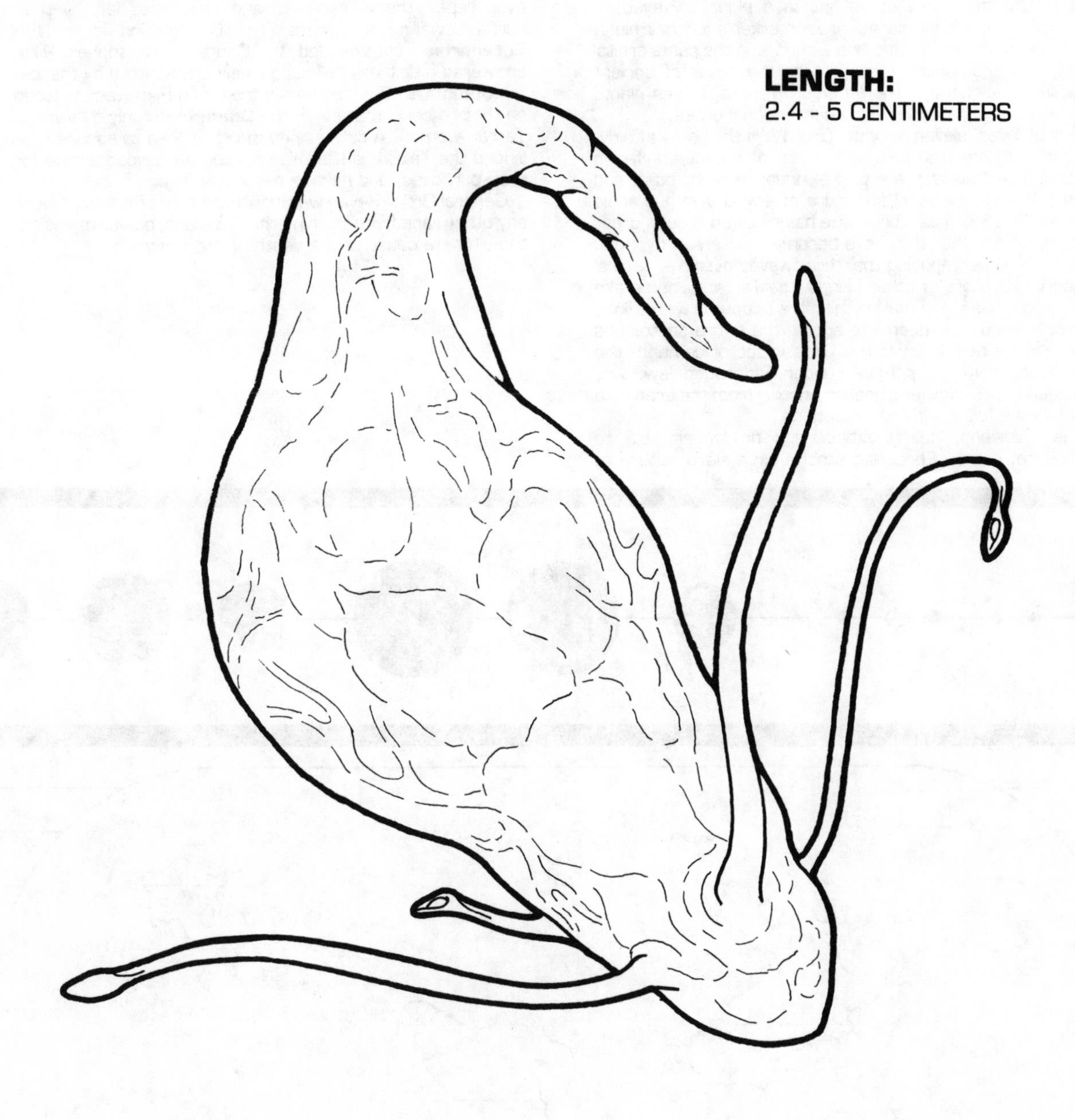

TALOS IV (M)
CLESIK
TALOS
[−119.4, −43.7, −24.0]

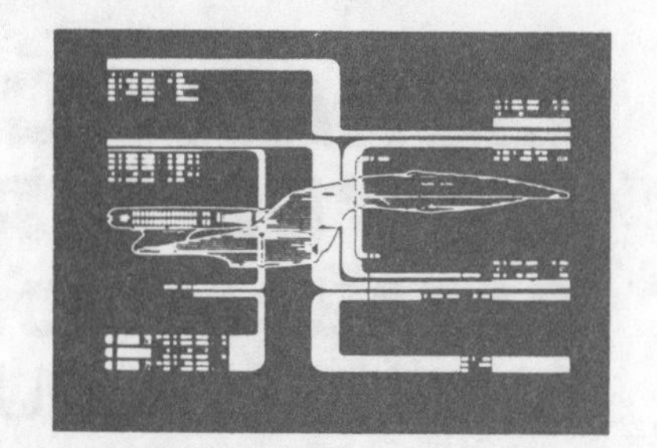

The Talos star group is comprised primarily of white dwarf stars and "stellar corpses," which are systems now devoid of life. One red giant still supports a planetary system, however. Its five inner planets are remarkable for their highly eccentric orbits. In fact, no two worlds lie in the same orbital plane, a phenomenon believed to be the result of ancient planetary engineering. The other six planets, all gas giants with no natural satellites, have conventional orbits.

One of Talos' eleven planets, Talos IV, is the home of a dying race of humanoid beings, the last of a once-starfaring culture. The Talosians are pale-skinned, of slight build, and have the largest cranial structure of any known humanoid species. This increased brain size has resulted in such great mental powers that they have become masters of hypnotic illusion. By superimposing their brainwaves over the natural sensory receptors of other beings, the Talosians can make others see, hear, and feel anything the telepaths wish. Since this power extends deep into space, the entire sector has been quarantined. Entry to the Talosian sector demands the only death penalty applicable under Federation law. Any emergency call or other signal emanating from the area is to be assumed false, with no exceptions.

The Talosians, nearly extinct and no longer able to reproduce, sought "breeding stock" for a slave culture to rebuild their planet, devastated in a nuclear war thousands of years ago. They had lost the ability to build and could not even repair those machines and structures left by their surface-dwelling ancestors. The Constitution class USS **Enterprise**, commanded by Captain Christopher Pike, answered a distress call supposedly transmitted by the lost SS **Columbia**. The plea was a trap, and Pike was captured so that he could mate with the **Columbia's** only survivor, a Terran woman. A determined effort by Pike to escape convinced the Talosians that his was too dangerous a race for their purposes, and he was eventually freed.

General Order Seven was instituted in an effort to prevent any other race from learning the Talosians' power of illusion, the ultimate cause of the death of their race.

87

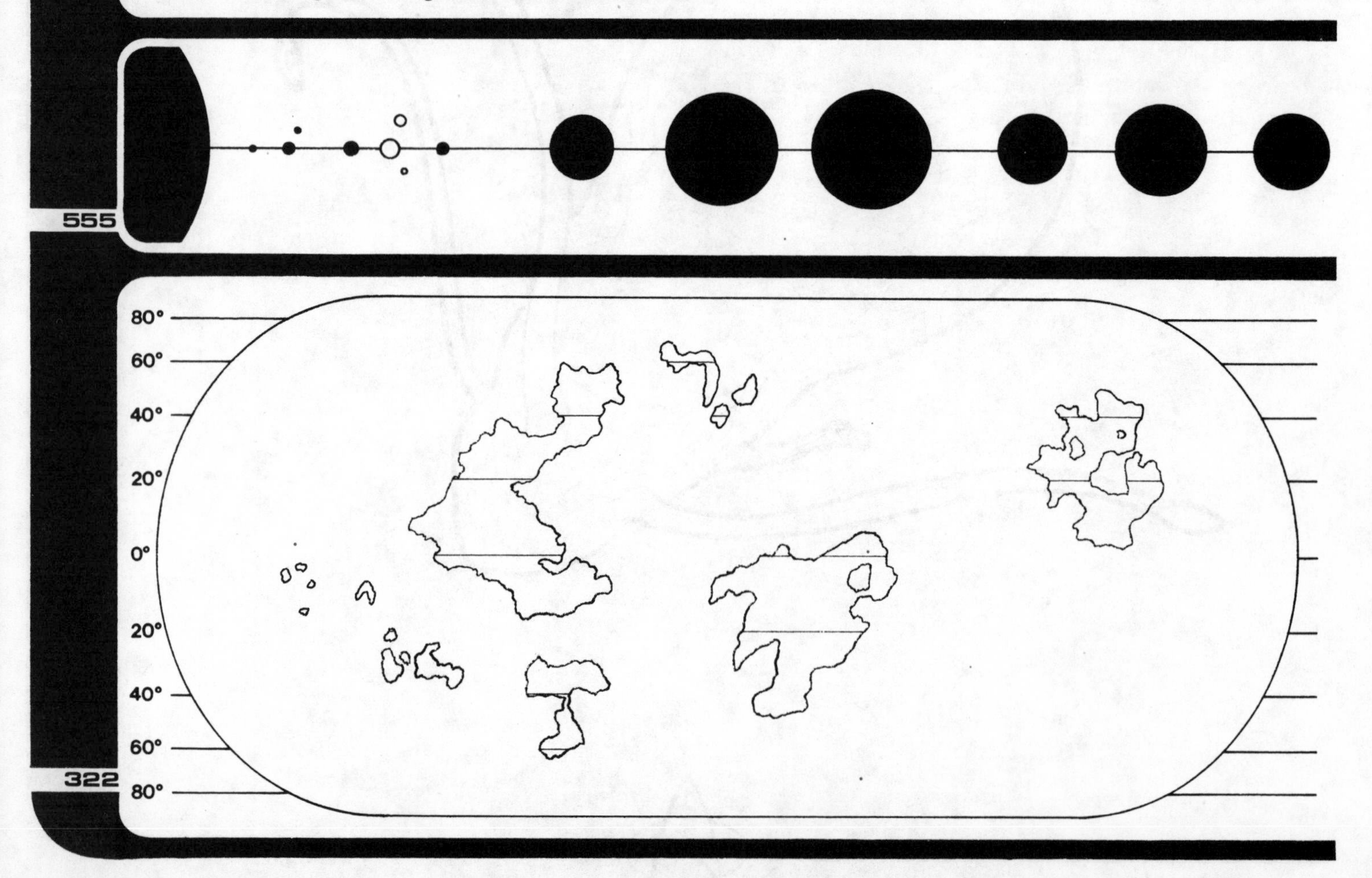

LIBRARY COMPUTER — USS ENTERPRISE (NCC-1701-D)
DATABANK EXTRACT (HARDCOPY)
SUBJECT: TALOSIAN

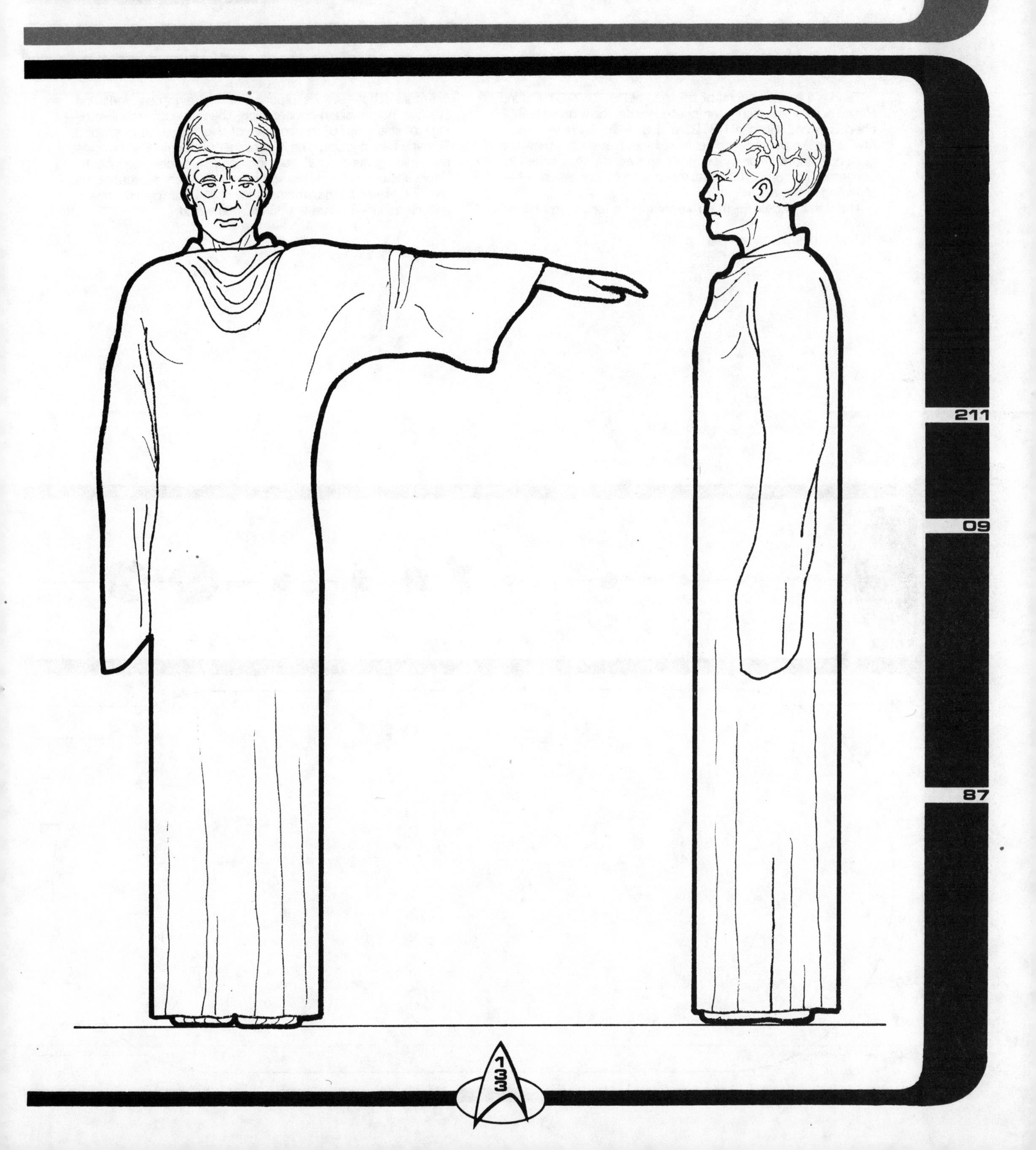

TAURUS II (G)
NO INDIGENOUS NAME
BETA TAURI
[−66.5, 47.4, 8.1]

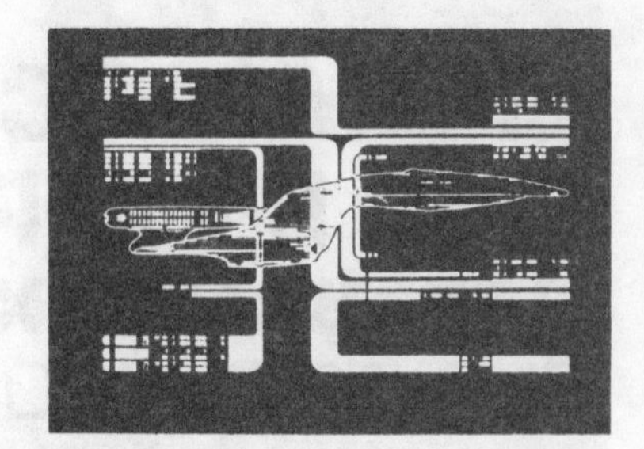

Taurus II is the second of thirteen planets in orbit around Beta Tauri, a blue giant star located within the Murasaki 312 phenomenon. Murasaki 312, a quasar-like nebular cloud, has been known to interfere with and even destroy the guidance and sensor systems of spacecraft that cross its borders. Therefore, utmost care should be taken when traveling in the area.

The dominant life form on Taurus II is a large, anthropoid creature that stands approximately eighteen feet tall. Roughly humanoid in appearance, these Neanderthaloid beings inhabit most of the surface of this rocky, desert world. Primitive in culture, the Taurean creatures live in small, nomadic groups that attack one another constantly. Taureans use crude tools and hunt with spears, wearing the furs of other animal forms they kill. Their overtly hostile nature makes Taurus II a dangerous world.

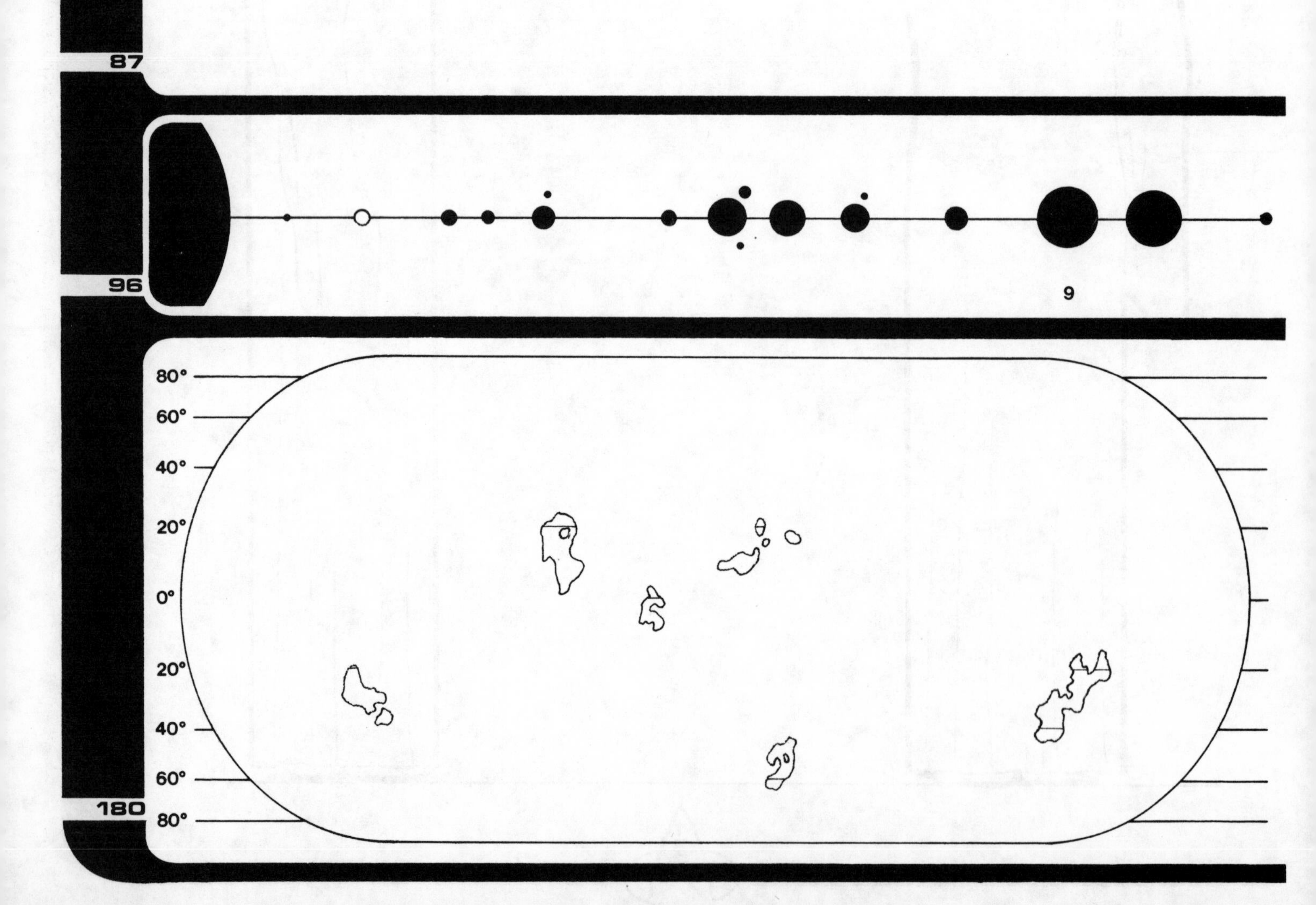

LIBRARY COMPUTER — USS ENTERPRISE (NCC-1701-D)
DATABANK EXTRACT (HARDCOPY)
SUBJECT: TAUREAN

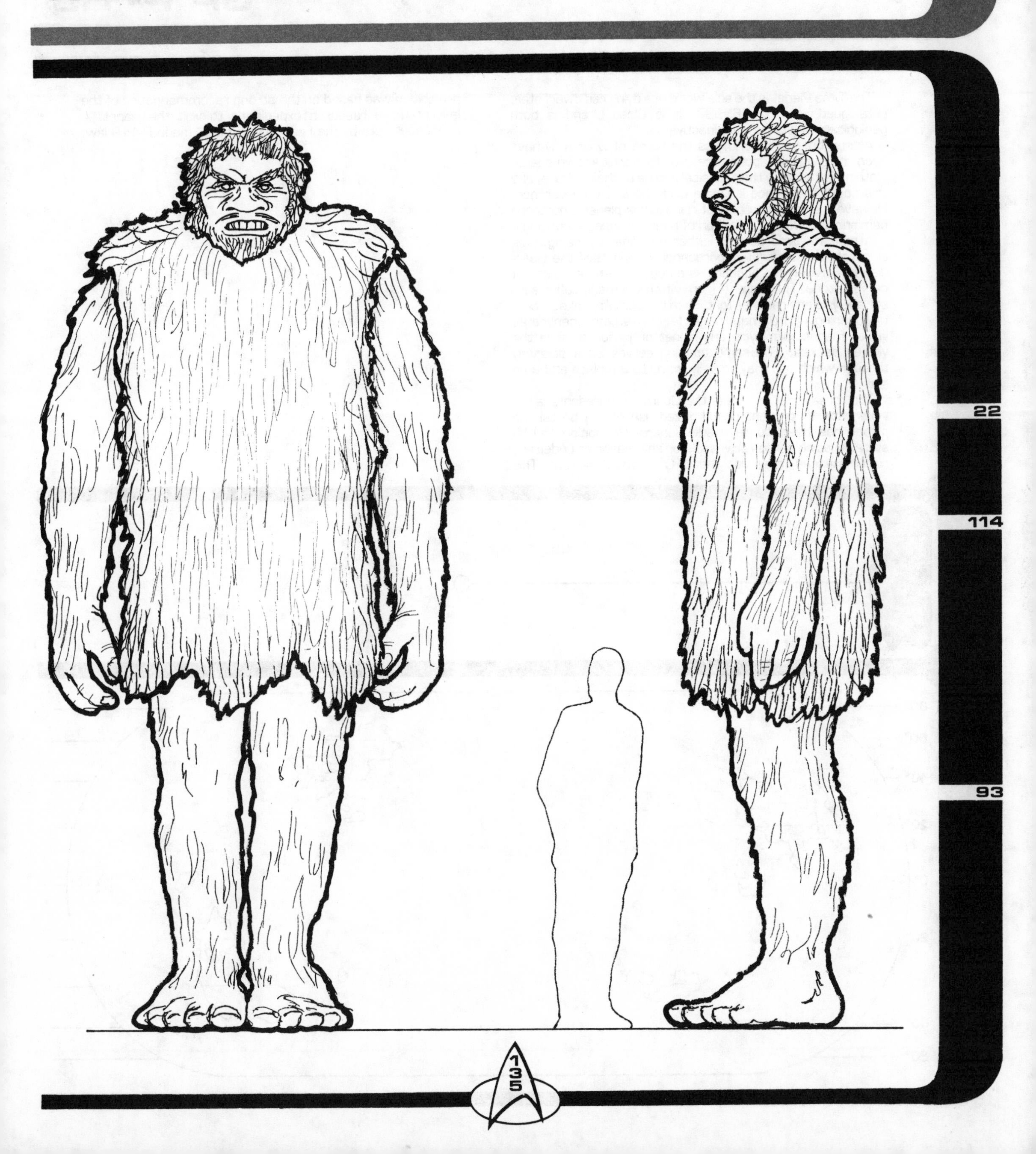

TIME PLANET (L)
INDIGENOUS NAME UNKNOWN
UFC 465537
[STELLAR LOCATION CLASSIFIED]

GP P-119

The Time Planet is the sole world of a dying red dwarf star, catalogued as UFC 465537. It is Class L and is both geologically and organically inactive.

At one time this world was the home of what may have been the most advanced race ever to inhabit known space. Nothing is known of their physical nature or their culture, and this now-extinct race left little evidence of their existence. However, a small grouping of ruins in the planet's northern hemisphere gives an indication of their advanced technology.

A sentient time portal, neither machine nor being, was discovered by Federation personnel. It calls itself the Guardian of Forever and appears as a doughnut-shaped piece of carved stone. The material from which it is made defies sensor analysis and radiates light when the portal speaks. A central opening, approximately eight feet in diameter, generates visual images, displaying any planet or period of time the viewer desires. The same opening serves as a doorway through which one may actually travel to the place and time shown.

The threat that misuse of the Guardian represents is obvious, and to prevent unauthorized use of the portal the planet has been quarantined. General Prohibition P-119 states that no person or vessel, for any reason or under any circumstances, may visit the UFC 465537 system. This prohibition was based on the strong recommendation of the last of three research expeditions to visit the planet. A unanimous vote by the Federation Council made P-119 law.

12

254

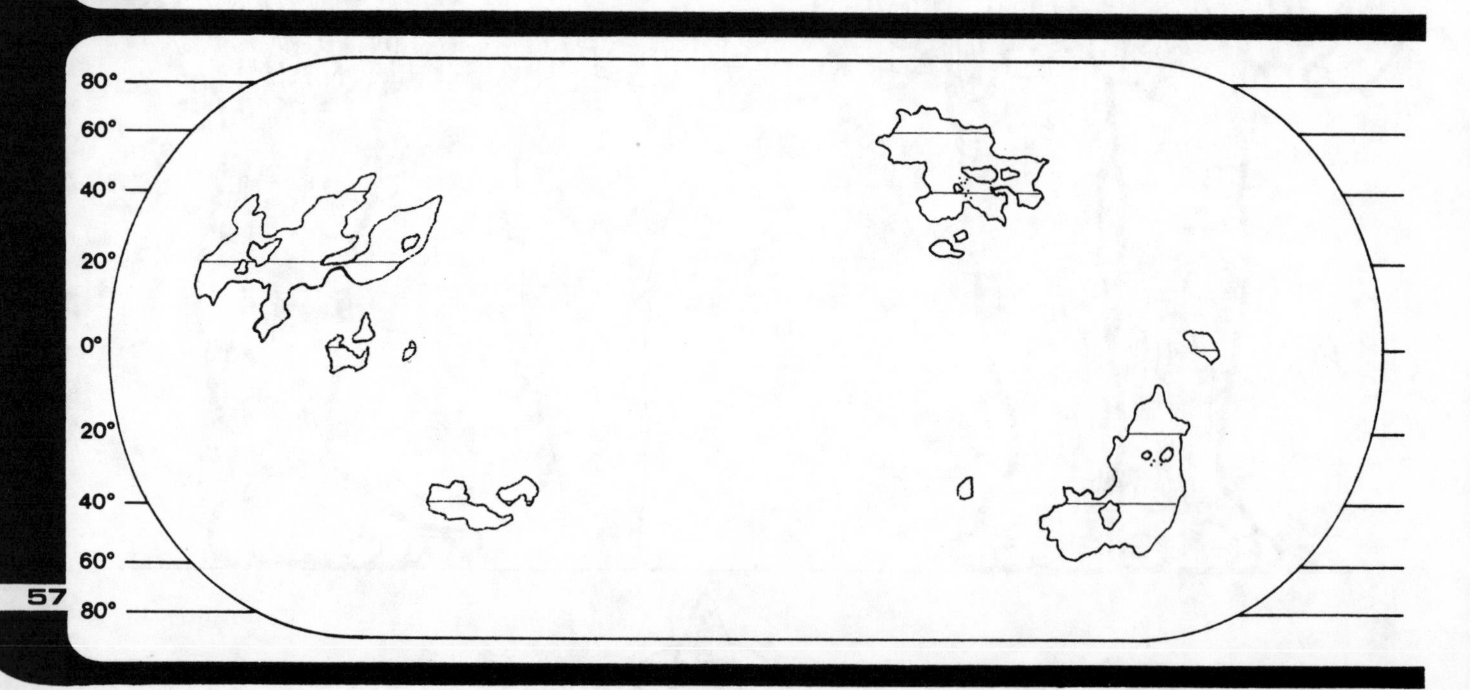

LIBRARY COMPUTER — USS ENTERPRISE (NCC-1701-D)
DATABANK EXTRACT (HARDCOPY)
SUBJECT: GUARDIAN OF FOREVER

432

08

56

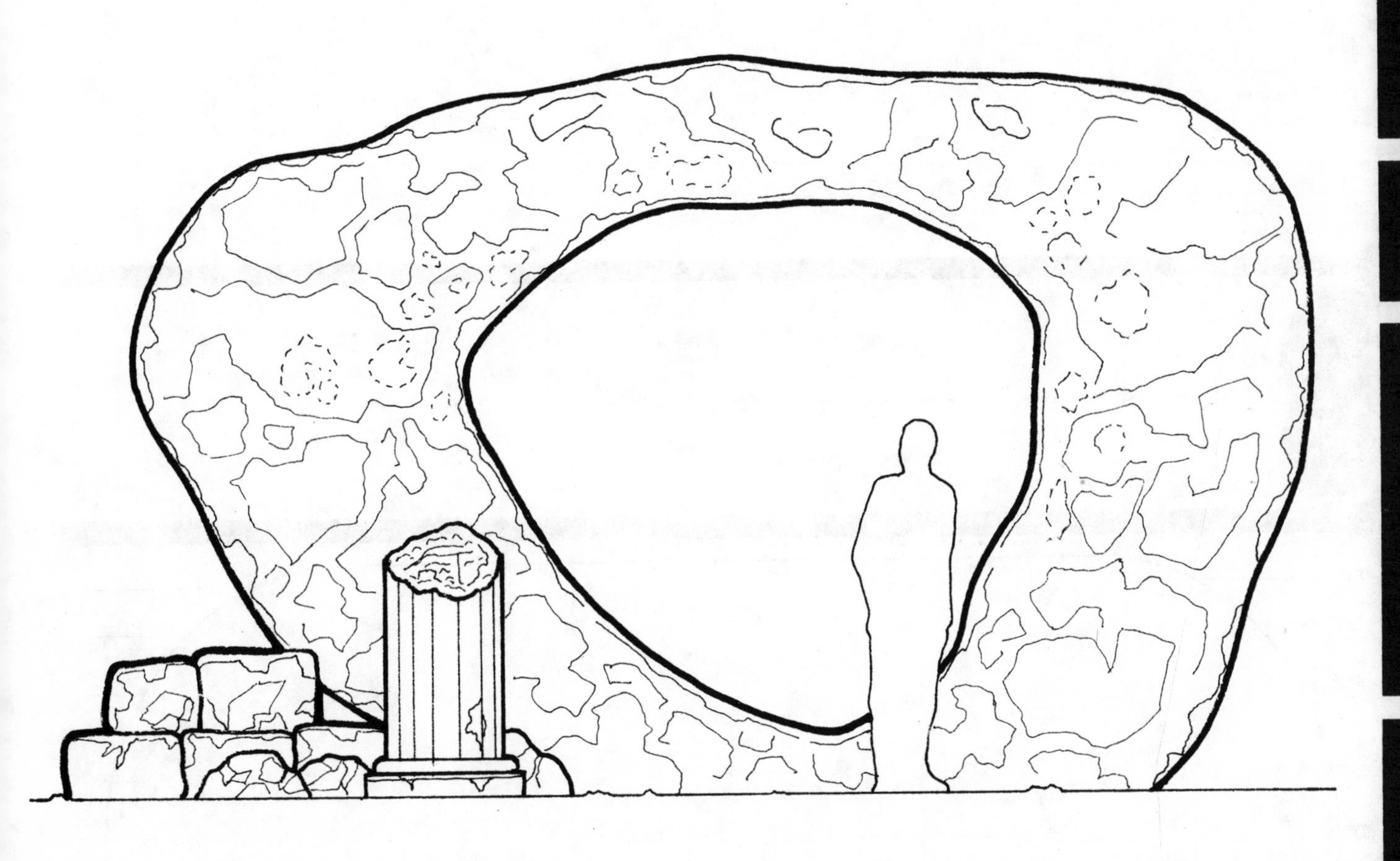

VELARA III (K)
INDIGENOUS NAME UNKNOWN
VELARA
[199.2, 18.4, 45.7]

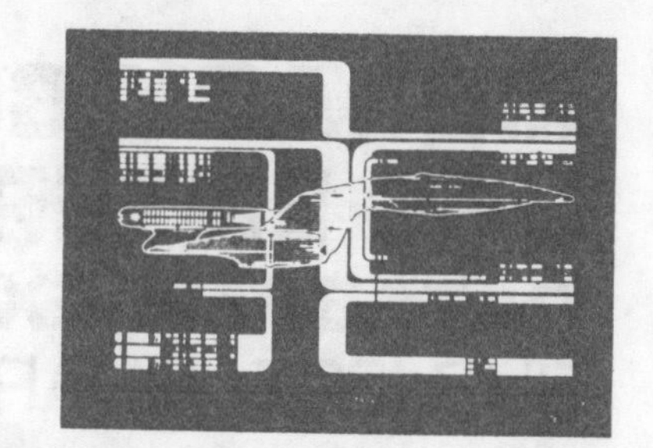

Velara is a small white dwarf near the Pleiades Cluster that supports a system of four planets. The first, second, and fourth worlds are all Class I barren rock bodies. Velara III is Class K and devoid of organic life. However, a startling discovery that has opened a new chapter in Federation science was made during an effort to terraform the planet.

Velara III harbors a planetwide habitation of a sophisticated crystalline life form. Millions of individual crystals make up a collective intelligence, much as individual chips, when combined through a communication medium, make up a computer. In the case of the Velara crystals, the connective medium is a thin layer of subsurface saline that covers much of the planet's surface and lies just beneath the sandy topsoil. These "microbrains" are also photoelectric and rely upon the light of Velara for life. The cadmium salts within the crystals may indicate that it is infrared light that feeds the creatures.

The terraforming colony on the planet has been withdrawn, and Velara III is now off limits to Federation personnel. However, the Federation hopes that the Velaran crystals will eventually seek contact.

88

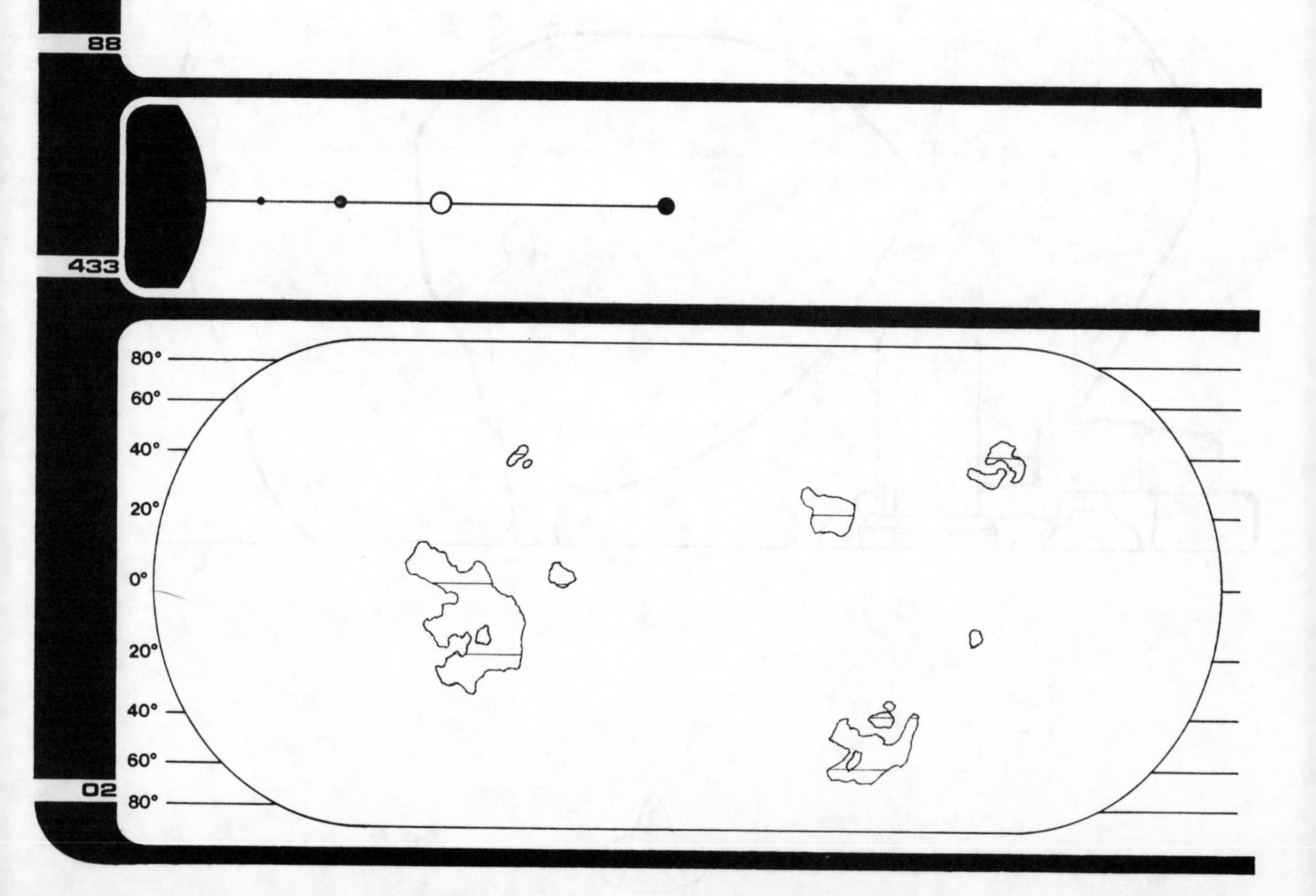

LIBRARY COMPUTER — USS ENTERPRISE (NCC-1701-D)
DATABANK EXTRACT (HARDCOPY)
SUBJECT: VELARAN TERRAFORMING STATION

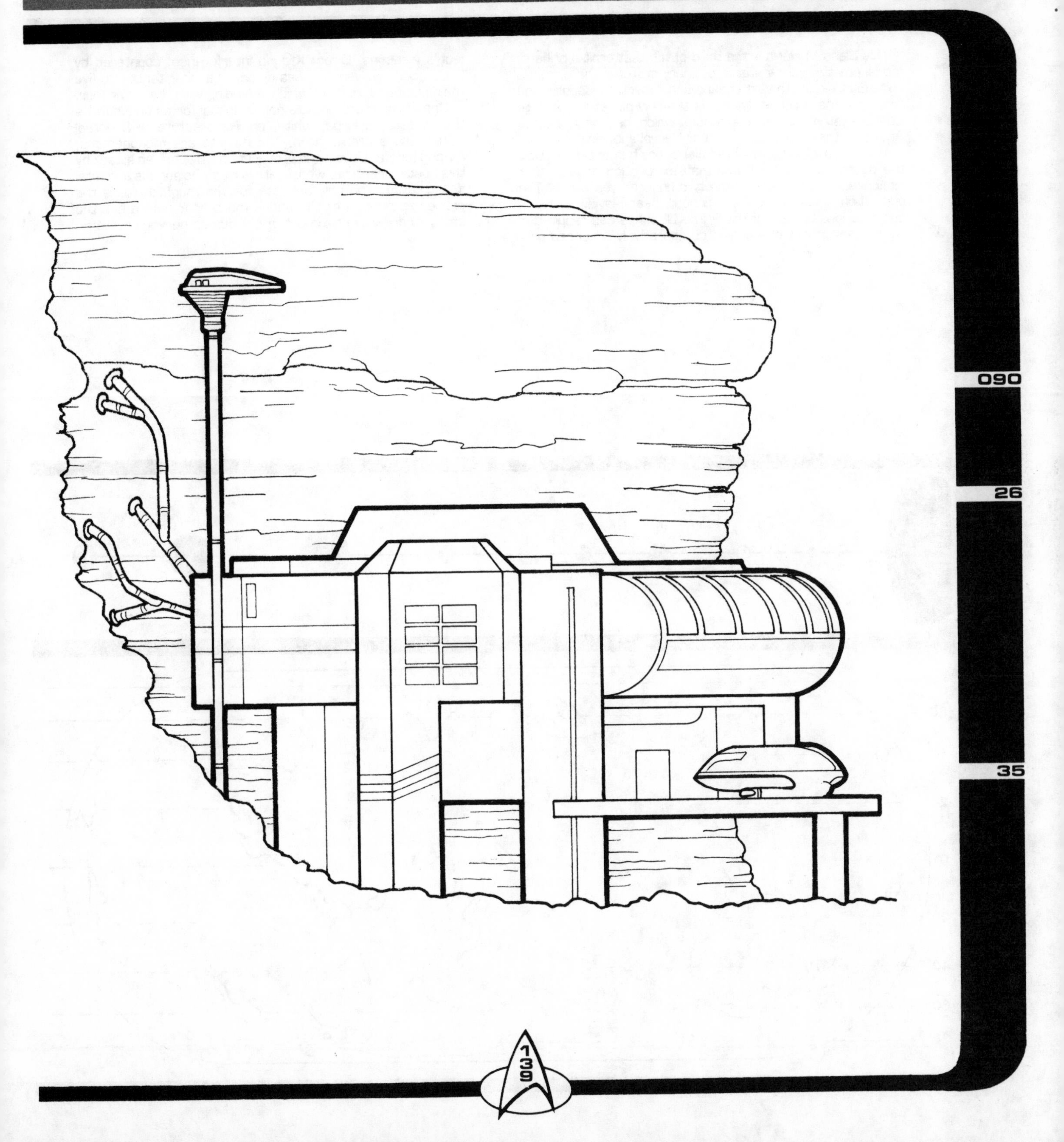

ZETA BOOTIS III (M)
NEURAL
ZETA BOOTIS

[57.8, 114.1, 33.1]

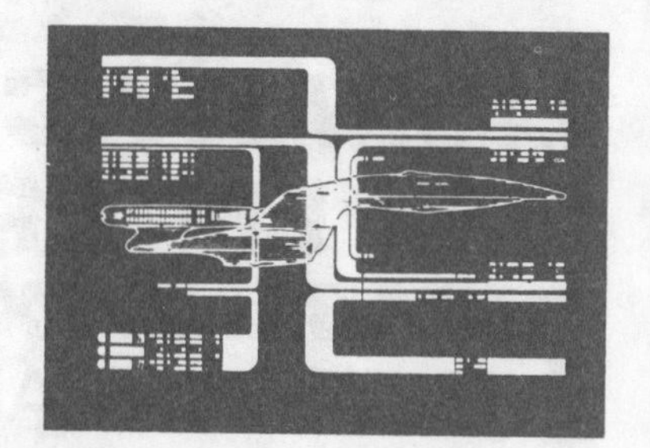

This Class M world is the third of ten that orbit a brilliant, moderate-size yellow star in a binary system. The planet is quite Earthlike, with vast oceans and desert, moderate, and tropical climate zones. Neural is the only planet in the Zeta Bootis system to have a moon, which has been named Asetia by the native population of Neural's lower desert.

The native inhabitants of the planet are humanoid, possibly the descendants of a Centaurian exploration mission that disappeared in the area some two hundred years ago. The population was once one of tranquil, peace-loving hunters, but a serious breach of the Prime Directive has resulted in their development of war and comparatively advanced projectile weapons. Direct Klingon interference, countered by Federation involvement, has divided the inhabitants into five major factions, each of which is feuding with the other four.

One of the more notable native animal forms on Neural is the mugato, a large, white, apelike creature with dorsal spines and a cranial horn. The mugato are monogamous, mating for life. Little or no provocation will spark an attack by this hostile creature, whose bite is highly poisonous and fatal if untreated. The only antidote for the mugato bite is the proper application of the native mako root, which has the ability to draw the toxin out of the human nervous system.

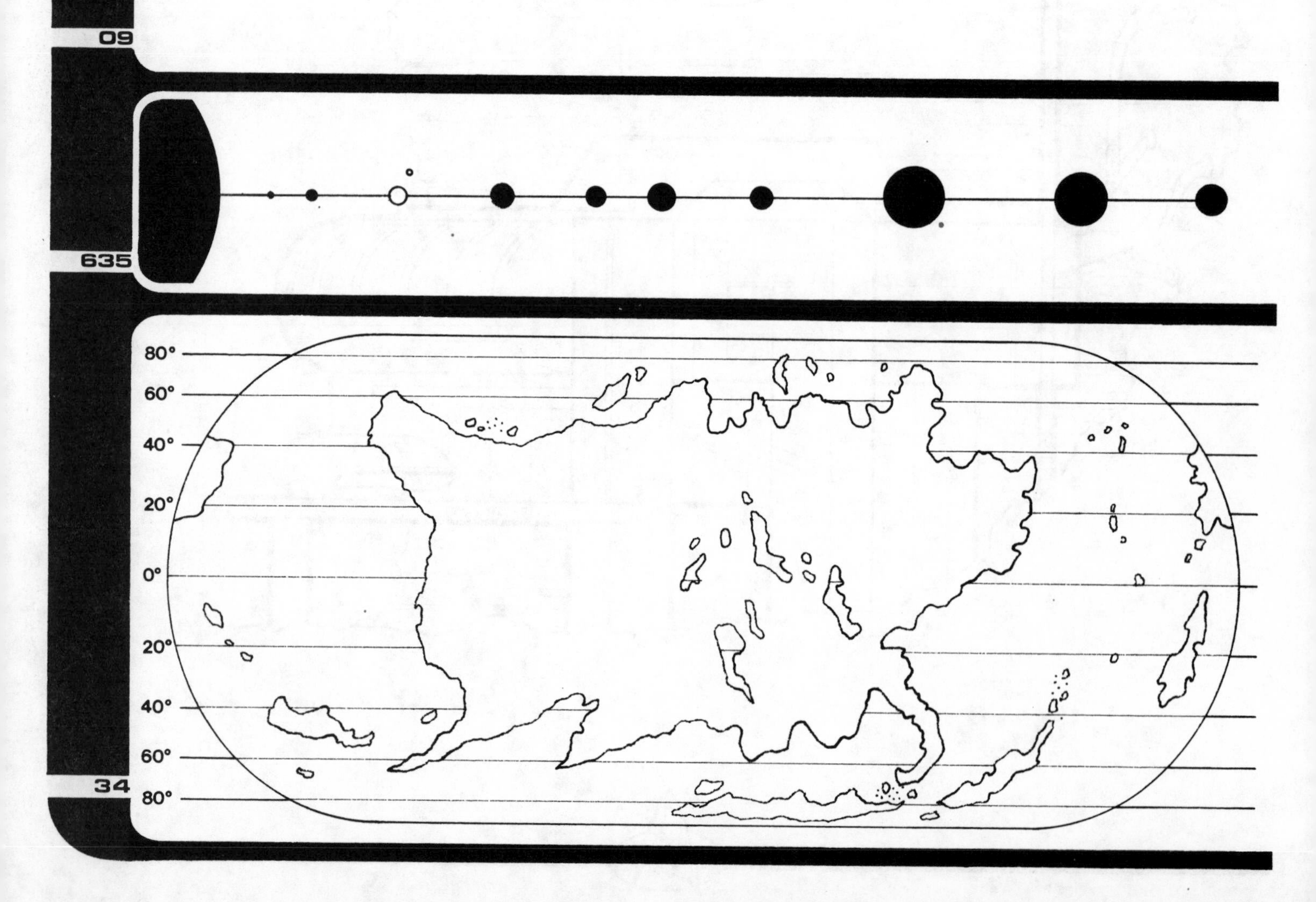

LIBRARY COMPUTER — USS ENTERPRISE (NCC-1701-D)
DATABANK EXTRACT (HARDCOPY)
SUBJECT: NEURALIAN MUGATO

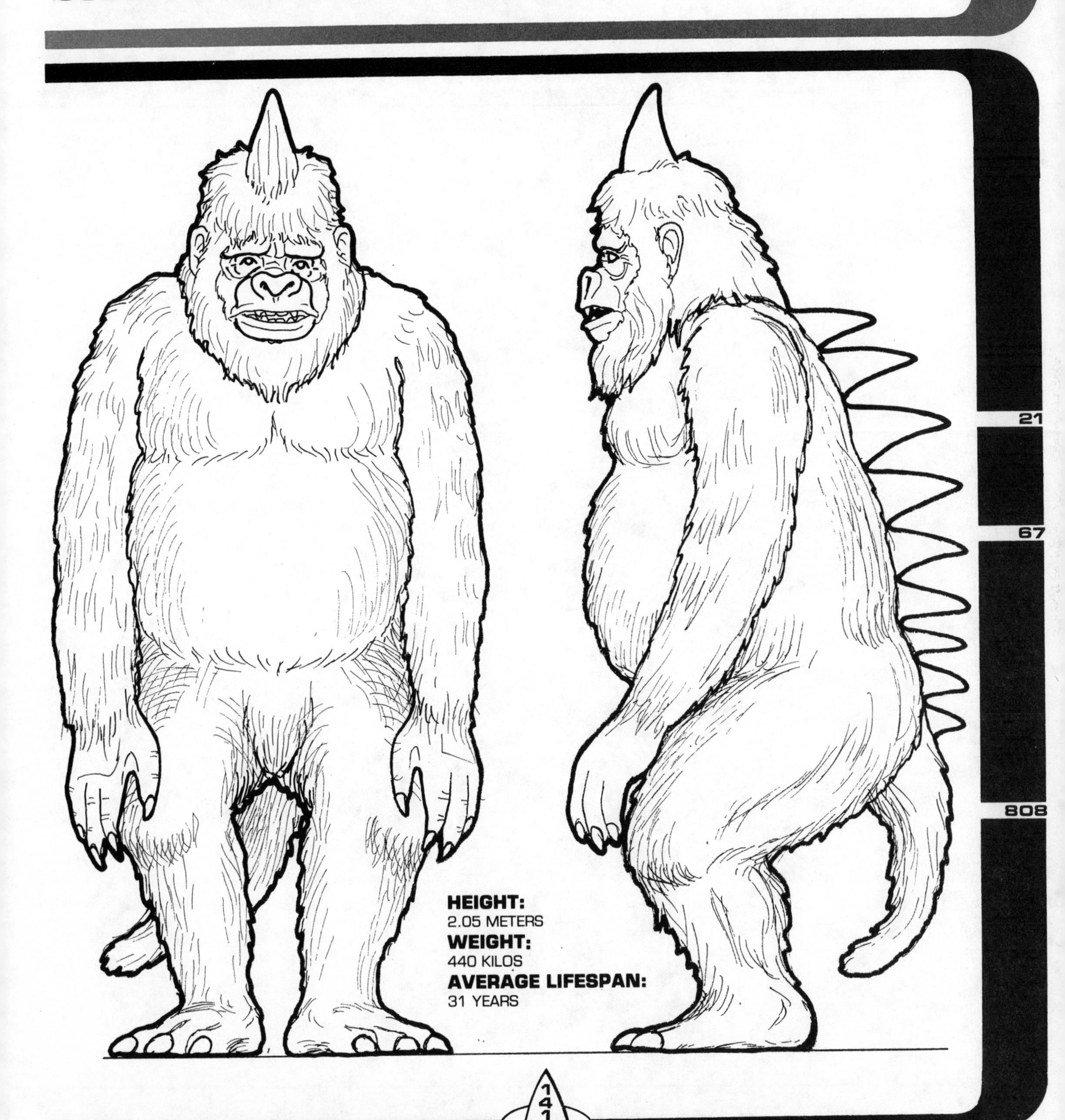

HOSTILE WORLDS

FERENGAL (M)
FERENGAL
PRIMARY UNKNOWN
[COORDINATES NOT ESTABLISHED]

Virtually nothing is known about the Ferengi, a humanoid race that originates beyond the southern boundaries of Federation space. Until fairly recently their very existence was dismissed as unfounded rumor.

Several years ago, the USS **Carver** detected motion at the extreme limit of sensor range. Pinpoint sensors followed the moving object for twelve seconds before it disappeared. Computer enhancement revealed a vessel of unknown configuration; however, analysis by Starfleet showed conclusively that the vessel was Ferengi.

Almost simultaneously, in the distant Maxia Zeta star system, a vessel later identified as Ferengi attacked the Federation starship **Stargazer** without provocation. Captain Jean-Luc Picard used a strategy now known as the Picard Maneuver to destroy the Ferengi ship. However, the **Stargazer** was so badly damaged that she had to be abandoned.

Since then, the Ferengi have shown themselves an extremely greedy, capitalistic people who are motivated purely by a desire for profit. They have shown warp drive capability and a technology on roughly the same level as the Federation.

Ferengi culture is extremely patriarchal. Females are bought and sold and kept unclothed. Social and military rank is determined by personal finances. Wealth and power are interchangeable.

The Ferengi have referred to their home world as Ferengal. Though nothing else is known about the planet, it is almost certainly Class M. The size of Ferengi ears seems to indicate that the atmosphere is thinner than that of Earth.

322

STAR SYSTEM UNKNOWN

34

FERENGI BATTLE CRUISER (UNDERSIDE VIEW)

NOTE: NEW ATTACK FIGHTER IN DOCKING BAY

56

LIBRARY COMPUTER — USS ENTERPRISE (NCC-1701-D)
DATABANK EXTRACT (HARDCOPY)
SUBJECT: FERENGI

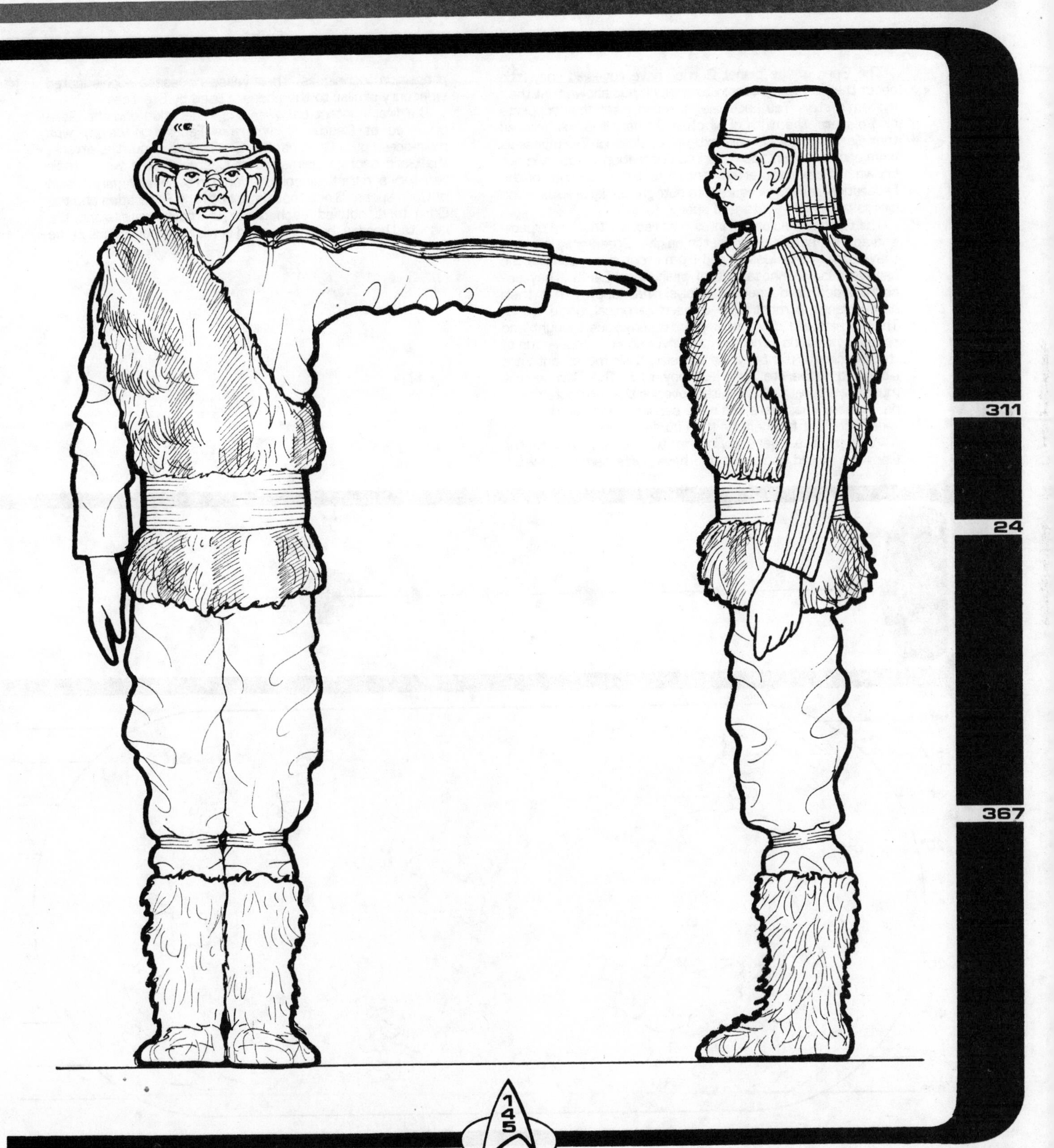

TAU LACERTAE IX
GORNAR
TAU LACERTAE
[−421.3, −166.7, 67.7]

89

The Gorn of the planet Gornar have revealed very little about themselves. Distant observation has shown that their system's star, Tau Lacertae, is a red giant that supports nine planets, the ninth of which is Gornar. It is not believed that Gorn territory is very extensive, although Gorn vessels have occasionally made raids into Federation space. It is not known if these raids are meant to test the strength of the Federation or if they result from outright denial of Federation claims to certain sectors of space.

The Gorn are a race of intelligent reptiles that are bipedal and approximately seven feet in height. Green-gray in color, they appear to be descended from creatures much like the carnivorous tyrannosaurids of prehistoric Earth. They are cold-blooded, and spectral analysis has shown that their home planet is most likely a warm, tropical jungle world. Their brains are devoted largely to conscious thought and speech, with little cerebral mass involved in the operation of the muscles of the body. As a result, their movements are slow and deliberate, yet very powerful. The Gorn eye is multifaceted, with a hard outer covering that protects the inner lenses. Their ears are quite sensitive and can detect a wider range of frequencies than humanoid ears.

While physically generally inferior to humanoid species, the Gorn are skilled engineers and have perfected space-warp propulsion techniques. Their vessels possess sophisticated weaponry similar to the phasers used by Starfleet.

The first contact between the Federation and the Gorn occurred at Cestus III, where a Federation colony was massacred by a Gorn vessel. Confronted about the attack, the Gorn captain claimed that Cestus III was within their territory and that the colonization had been an illegal invasion of Gorn space. Since that time, both the Federation and the Gorn have notified each other of movements along the disputed border, hoping to avoid similar confrontations in the future.

670

435

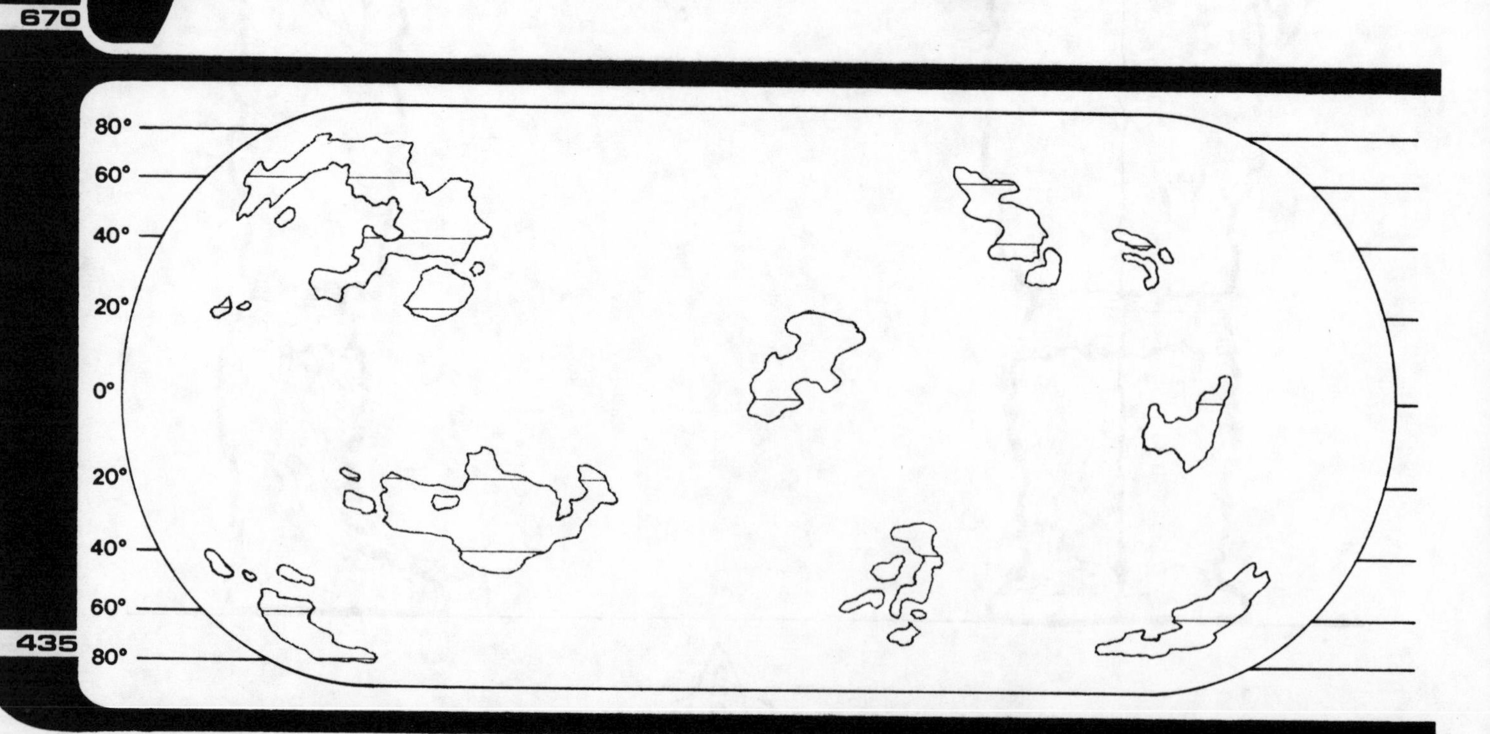

LIBRARY COMPUTER — USS ENTERPRISE (NCC-1701-D)
DATABANK EXTRACT (HARDCOPY)
SUBJECT: GORNARAN ARCHOSAUR (GORN)

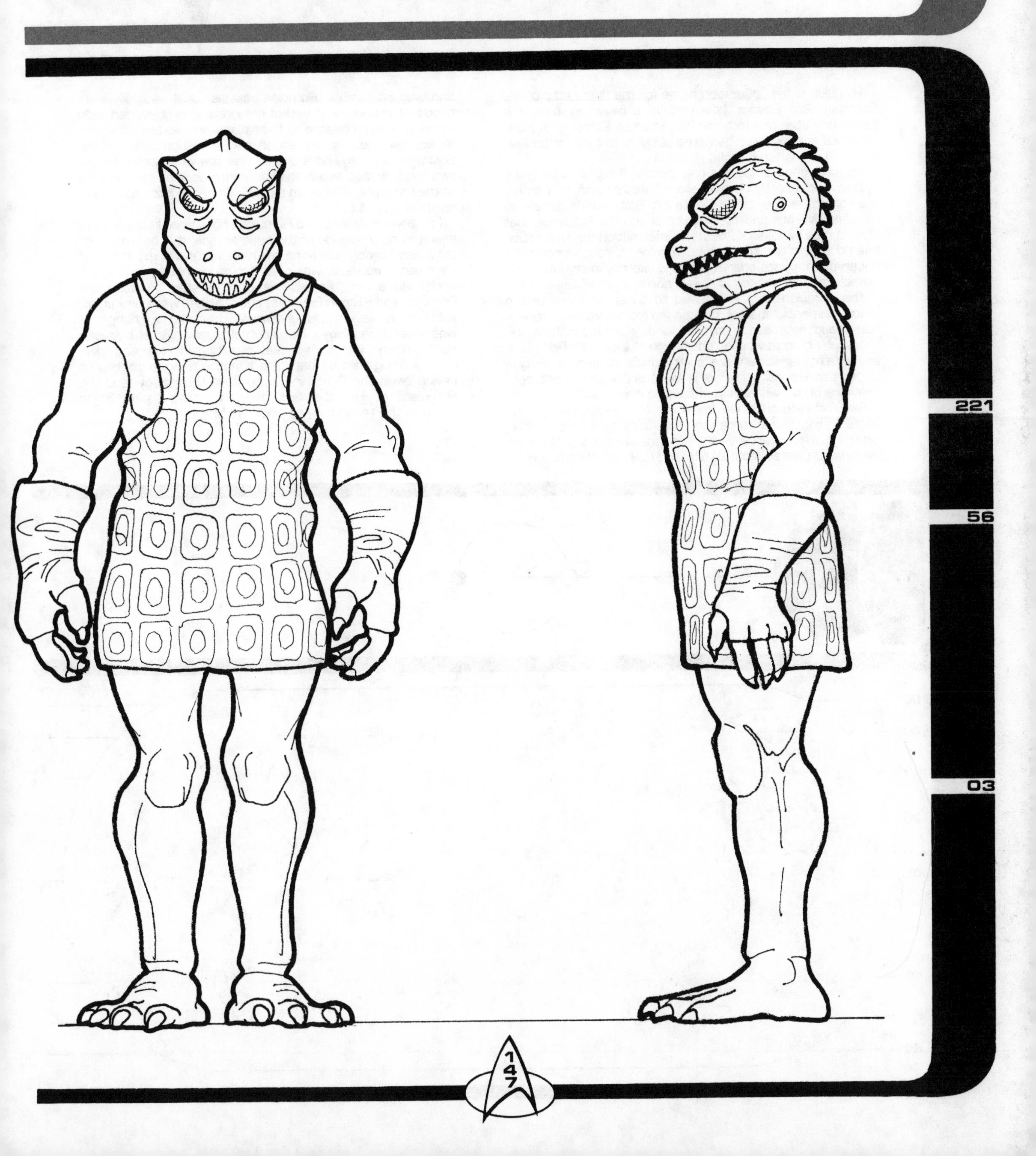

ROMULUS (M)
INDIGENOUS NAME UNKNOWN
ROMULUS
[−176.3, −158.5, −1.8]

Romulus is the Federation name for the home star of the Romulan Star Empire. It is part of a binary system, the secondary star of which has been named Romulus B. Little data has actually been gathered about these stellar bodies, but both are white dwarfs.

Romulus and Remus, the only planets thought to be in the system, apparently revolve around each other in a trojan relationship as they circle their suns. Both worlds appear to be Class M, but uncertain spectral analysis indicates that Remus may be Class K. All of the information the Federation has about this territory has been gained through long-range observation, pirate charts, and the sketchy information the Romulans have chosen to reveal about themselves.

The Romulan race is believed to be an offshoot of the Vulcan humanoid species, descended from a Vulcan colonization group established on the planet Romulus before the philosophy of logic was introduced on Vulcan. The Romulans are quite militaristic and make very efficient warriors. Duty is placed above personal safety in all instances and at all times. They are brutal warriors and take no captives.

Federation authorities knew of the existence of the Romulan culture for more than a century before Federation personnel had ever seen a Romulan. During the Romulan War, which lasted from 2106 to 2109, visual communication was impossible. Romulan vessels could be easily identified by the enormous bird-of-prey insignia emblazoned upon them, a custom related to their planetary worship of a condorlike war god. The war ended in a Federation victory at the Battle of Cheron, and a treaty was drawn up between the two factions that established an immense, oval neutral zone at the Federation/Romulan border. Entrance into this area of space is an act of war.

For several decades no Romulans have been in the area of space along their side of the neutral zone. It is believed that they may be concentrating their efforts in the expansion of their other borders, which, as far as is known, lie in open, unclaimed space. An alliance once existed between the Romulan and Klingon Empires, but relations were broken off following a severe disagreement over the exchange of weapons technology. No neutral zone exists between Romulan and Klingon spaces, resulting in repeated skirmishes along that border. The Klingons now deeply regret having given the Romulans warp drive technology, and the Romulans deplore the fact that they gave their Klingon enemies the technology to cloak warships.

78

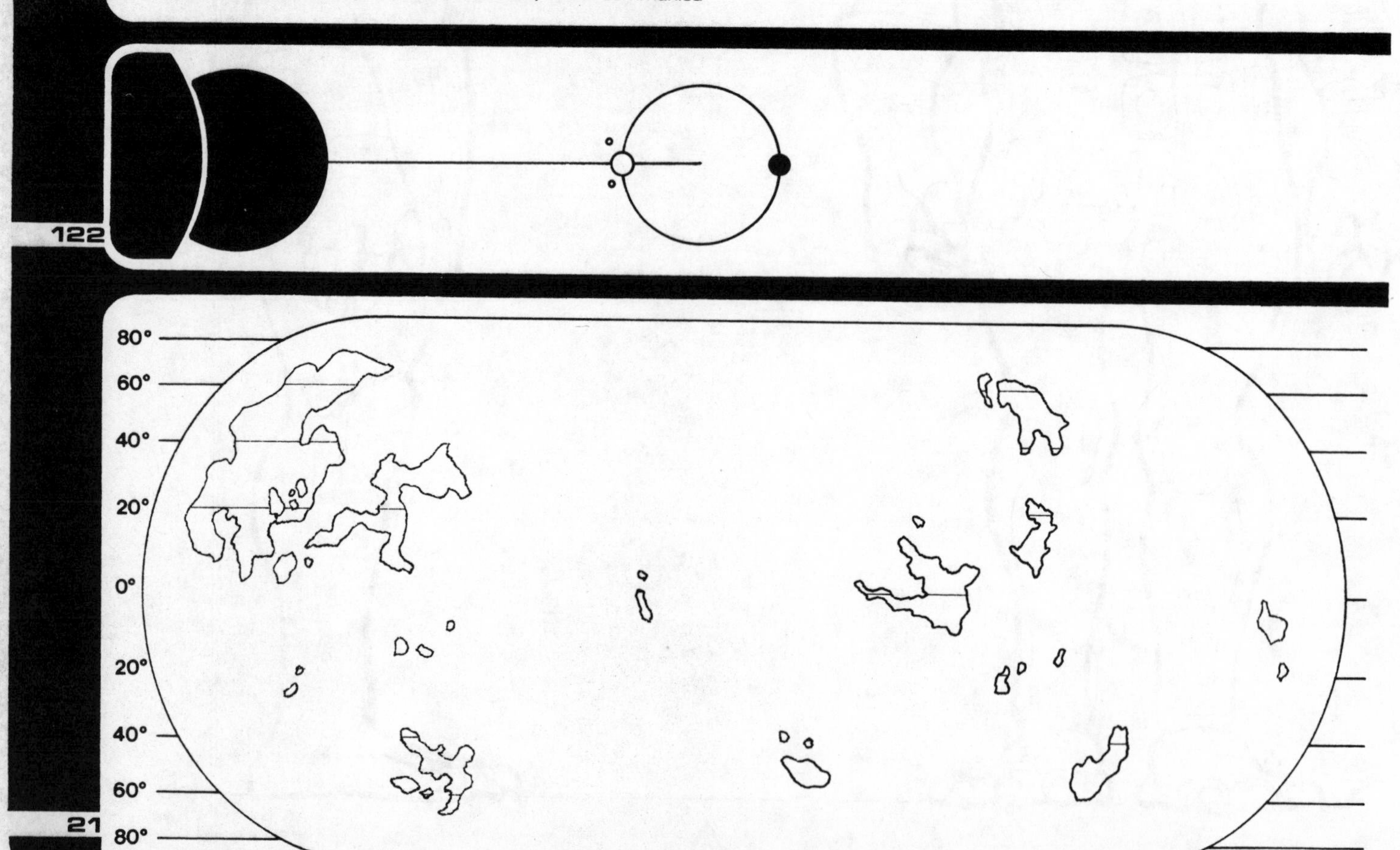

LIBRARY COMPUTER — USS ENTERPRISE (NCC-1701-D)
DATABANK EXTRACT (HARDCOPY)
SUBJECT: ROMULAN

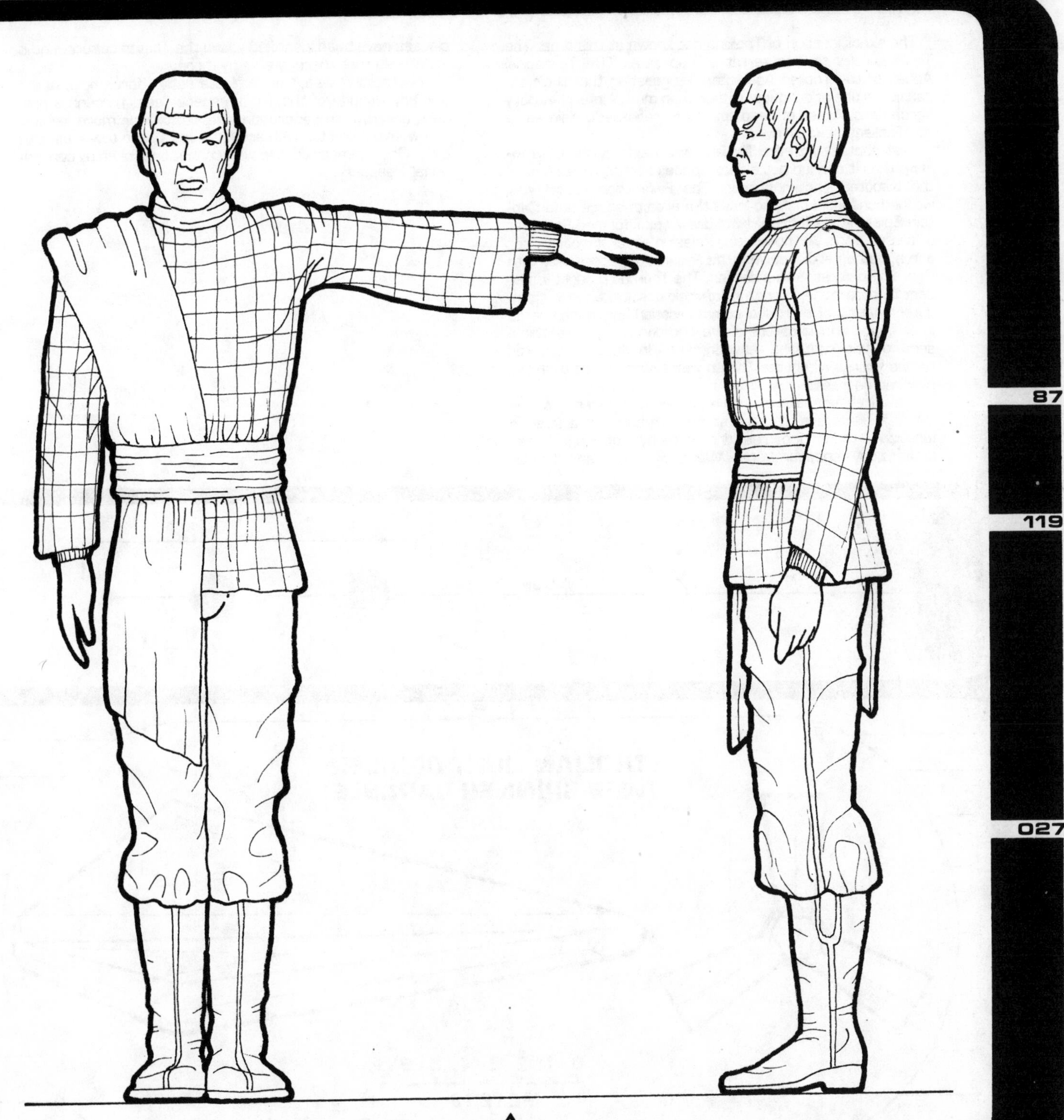

87

119

027

THOLIA II (C)
THOLIA
PRIMARY UNKNOWN
[COORDINATES NOT ESTABLISHED]

The exact location of Tholia is not known at this time. The Tholians refer to their territory in space as "The Territorial Annex of the Tholian Assembly," suggesting that their expansion is one of conquest rather than mutual interplanetary agreement. Areas of deep space are repeatedly claimed by the Tholians as their own.

First contact with the Tholians was made by the USS **Intrepid** as it carried out a deep space charting mission near the disputed Tholian border. The Federation vessel was warned unconditionally to leave the area of space, and Captain Spiak of the **Intrepid** withdrew and informed Starfleet of the contact. A Tholian transmission several weeks later demanded an audience with the Federation, specifically with Captain Spiak, at the border line. The Tholians thought it prudent to determine the nature of their possible enemy. Computer analysis of the visual communication has yielded some information on the nature of the Tholians. They live within a searing hot methane environment. In fact, estimated temperatures within the Tholian vessel were more than five hundred degrees.

They are members of a hive culture and possess a hive mind. Tholians are modified at birth to perform a specific function in adulthood, resulting in many highly specialized outer body configurations. Warrior, ruler, and builder classes have been identified within the Tholian culture, and it is believed that there are many more.

The Tholian "web," an intricate netlike force field, is the primary weapon of the Tholian space fleet. Through a process unknown to Federation science, two or more vessels can weave a tractor web around a vessel and tow it back to port. Once completed, the web cannot be broken by conventional weaponry.

23

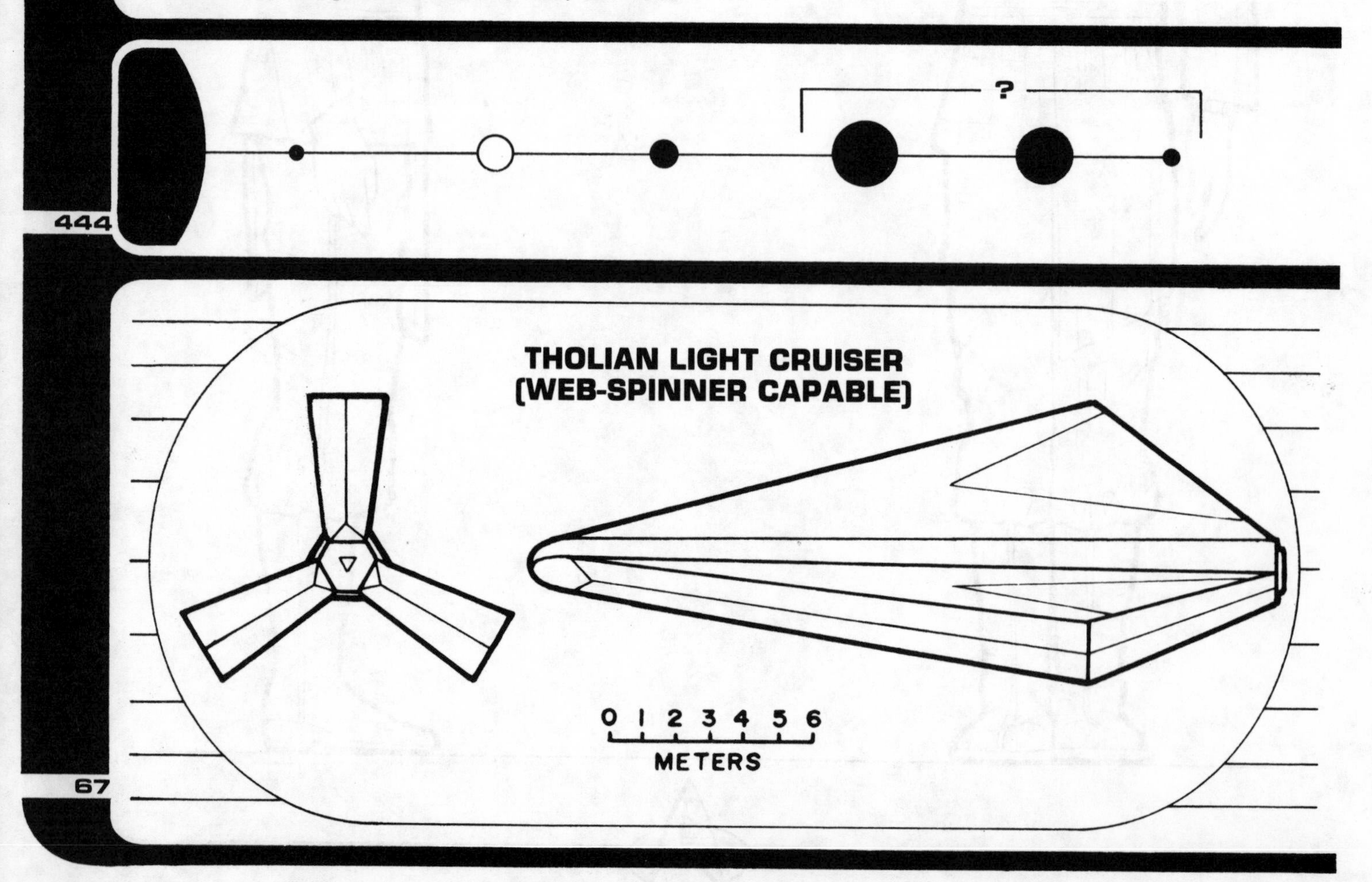

SUBJECT: THOLIAN

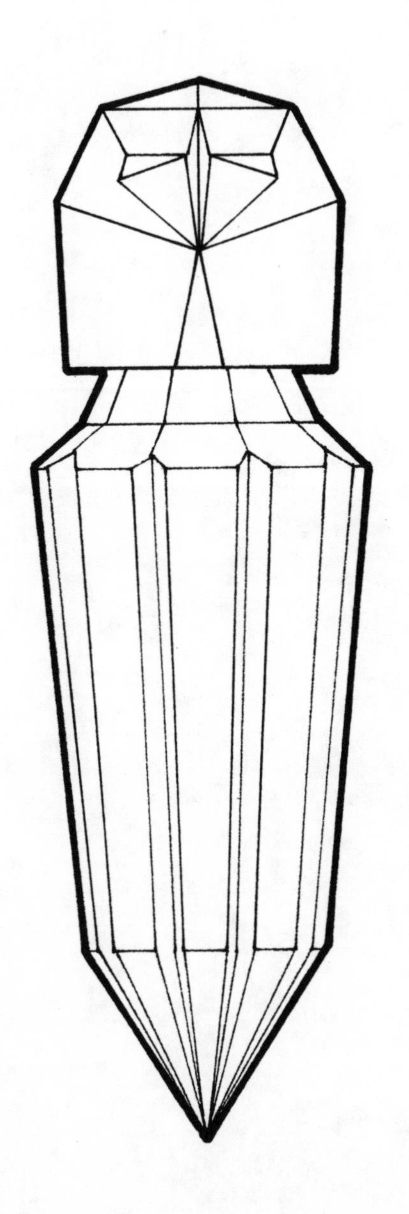

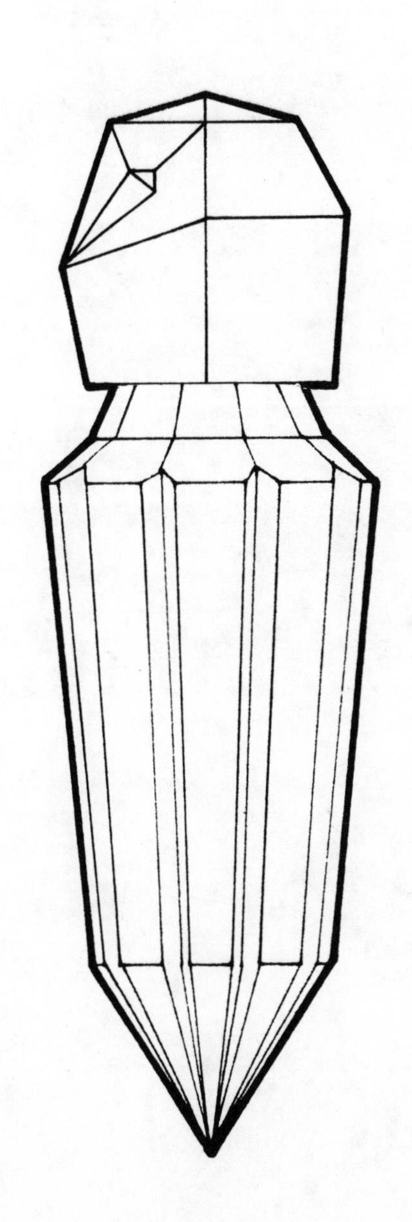

APPENDIX

MEMORY ALPHA HISTORICAL ARCHIVE
DATABANK EXTRACT (HARDCOPY)

SUBJECT: **THE WORLDS OF THE FEDERATION**

FEATURED PLANETS
AND THEIR PRIMARIES

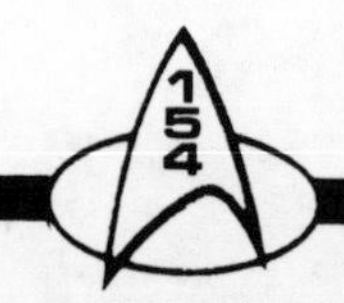

PLANETARY AMBASSADORS

UFP MEMBER	AMBASSADOR	PAGE
Aldebaran	Farrell Tensen	48
Alpha III	James Kara	26
Alpha Centauri VII	Zella Rancine	24
Andor	Shrall K'Tik	22
Antos IV	Llire Ner Naba	40
Argelius II	Vantir Plassen	52
Aurelia	Aleek-Aur	56
Benzar	Meldir	76
Betazed	Perateca Kif	72
Bynaus	10011011	74
Cait	M'Roaa	38
Catulla	Tongo Sil	42
Coridan III	Deo Dica Mataal	62
Daran V	Misan Phoalla	54
Delta	Iloran	64
Deneb II	H'T' Jera	30
Deneb IV	Ferguson Smith	
Deneb V	Will Perkins	
Earth	Benjamin Adams	16
Izar	Harold Taft	34
Mantilles	Samuel Griffith	58
Marcos	Seril	32
Medusa	Kollos	60
Merak II	Andrew Leigh	46
Mu Leonis II	Tresus	50
Phylos II	Agmar	78
Rigel II	Robert Klymyshyn	36
Rigel IV	Kenneth Brice	
Rigel V	T'Sedd	
Rigel VII	Daniel Cheney	
Rigel VIII	Kin Passa	
Sauria	Ket'k Loka L'T'S	66
Tellar	Gartiv	20
Terra	Benjamin Adams	16
Theta Kiokis II	Arshosha	70
Tiburon	Cino Desdin	44
Vega IX	Chris Bara	28
Vulcan	Sarek	18
Yonada	Natira	68

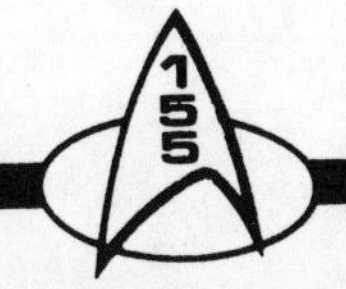

UNITED FEDERATION OF PLANETS

"... to boldly go where no man has gone before."

– from the Starfleet charter